WICKED WEBS

CORALEE JUNE
RAVEN KENNEDY

Copyright © 2019 by CoraLee June & Raven Kennedy

All rights reserved.

No part of this book may be reproduced in any form or by any electronic or mechanical means, including information storage and retrieval systems, without written permission from the authors, except for the use of brief quotations in a book review.

Cover by Nichole Witholder

Edits by Helayna Trask

❦ Created with Vellum

For Helayna, the best editor out there. Thank you for sticking with us through this monster of a book—pun intended. We love your jokes and your expertise. Our books wouldn't be the same without you.

Chapter 1

YOU'D THINK that a graduation ceremony at a prestigious academy for hundreds of supernaturals would have less nudity, but for some damn reason, every time one of the shifters was called to walk the stage, another graduation gown was ripped off, howls erupted, and then dicks and boobs were swinging like pendulums before they made their shift and pranced off the stage. Shifters were so damn obnoxious sometimes.

The camaraderie was infectious, though. Friends and supernatural-sanctioned cliques giggled excitedly, and proud parents cheered in the auditorium. You could taste the sense of nostalgia in the air. Everyone was sad to leave Thibault Academy behind.

Everyone but me.

Luckily, I didn't have to wait too long for my own name to be announced. There seemed to be a quiet sense of boredom when "Motley Coven" was called out, with just a few polite claps. I didn't let it bother me, though. I sashayed my vampiric ass across the stage and scooped up my diploma with pride.

Headmaster Torne barely spared me a glance before he turned to greet the student after me. Of course, *they* got a smile and a congratulatory pat on the back. Some might be bitter at the dismissive way this school treated me, but I'd learned not to expect much from my five years of attending Thibault as a scholarship student.

I was pretty much the scum of the school. I was put down for my weaknesses as a vamp and lack of a good family name, but I didn't give a fire-hell fuck. I got to attend one of the best supernatural academies in the world. Because of that and this diploma now clutched in my sweaty hand, I was going to make something of myself.

As I descended the stage, I looked down at Aunt Marie, who was standing off by herself in the corner. Her bony hands shook as she clapped for me, and I could see the pride on her face. It had been a long road to get to this point. Everything I did was for her.

I might not have had the roaring applause that the populars or the paragons got, but I had a cheering section of one, and that was all I needed.

I walked out of the room through the door behind the stage and headed into the reception area in Thibault's ostentatious ballroom, where the rest of the graduates were already milling around. Naturally, all four of the breeds had segregated themselves in a corner of the room—vampires, necromancers, shifters, and elementals tended to stick to their own kind. And then there was the lowly scholarship charity case like me, and I just kept to myself.

I made my way over to the vampire's area, my mouth already watering from the smell of bloody cocktails being served. I snatched up a champagne flute brimming with O negative from a passing server and downed the drink in one go. With slightly shaking hands, I leaned against the wood panelled wall and studied the thick roll of parchment in my hand.

This was it. Whatever slip of paper was inside my diploma would determine the rest of my long, immortal life. Because today wasn't just about graduating from Thibault. Today, we also received our placements into internships, higher education, or jobs in the supernatural community. In short, it was a big fucking deal, especially for me.

I didn't have pure blood or a big, important family name. I didn't have an overabundance of power or friends in high places. I was smart, and I was driven. That was it. Which was why I busted my ass at this school for five years—so that I could get a good position in society and work my way up from there. I was done being the poor, parentless Motley Coven charity case. I was going to be *more*.

"You weren't going to open that without me, were you?" a kind, motherly voice said to my left.

I smiled and turned to see the red-haired woman who'd approached. "Aunt Marie," I greeted her warmly.

My sweeping gaze assessed every nuance of her expression. The corners of her eyes were wrinkled, and her lips, although coated with pale pink lipstick, seemed dry. Her shoulders were stiff, lifted so high they nearly touched her fashionable silver hoop earrings. She was tense—beautiful, but tense.

I'd learned to look out for signs of bloodlust since her first episode when I was seven. I still remembered that day. The gentle woman who sewed me dresses with pockets and baked bloody cookies had turned into a frenzied, ravenous animal. She tore our living room apart and screamed for blood, her manic need forcing me to hide in the cupboard under the kitchen sink.

When it was all over, I found her in the bathroom, with dozens of empty blood bags littering the floor. She'd eaten everything we owned—every carefully rationed ounce of it. We lived off a very strict allowance, so that loss had taken weeks to recoup. But just when we caught up, Aunt Marie had another episode and decimated our stash again. So we faced facts that it wasn't a one-off, that her bloodlust would only get worse, and we prepared for it.

It was our secret. Vampires with bloodlust were either taken away to be imprisoned or put to death. Our council simply eliminated the problem instead of researching the disease. But I wouldn't let that happen to her.

So ever since I was a kid, I helped to hide her condition from the world. We kept to ourselves. We made sure to have hundreds of blood bags in the house for when a frenzy hit. It was the cheap stuff, since we couldn't afford anything else. She'd stay locked in our shared bedroom with chains and bars, while I prayed to the gods that my aunt's mind would return and the frenzy would subside.

My greatest fear was that this would be it—this would be the time when she wouldn't come out of it. But she did. She always fought it. For me.

The dynamic in our relationship switched drastically because I had to take on a lot of the responsibilities, but there was loving give and take. She was my biggest supporter, and I was her advocate. It didn't matter to me that I had to catch wild animals and toss them at my aunt when the frenzy was particularly bad. It didn't matter that she couldn't leave the house sometimes because of her fear of an episode coming on. All that mattered was that she was my family, and I took care of my family.

We'd had plenty of close calls over the years, but we were careful. We had to be. And though it was hard and scary at times, I wouldn't have had it any other way, because that woman was my rock.

Aunt Marie took me in when I was just two days old. I

was the bastard of an apathetic woman and a proud man who didn't want me tainting his family line or revealing his transgressions outside of his public marriage.

Aunt Marie didn't have much, just a one bedroom apartment in the vampire community. But she had love, and a lot of it. She gave up most of her life to raise me and battled the bloodlust to stay sane during my childhood. It wasn't always easy, but it was worth it, and I couldn't imagine sharing this moment with anyone else.

"I couldn't open it without you, Aunt Marie. Hell, I wouldn't even be here without you," I told her with a smile.

She came forward and held her arms out to me, blood-red tears filling her eyes as she enveloped me in a big hug. When she pulled away, I laughed at the dress she was wearing—I hadn't noticed it before.

She was in a knee-length black cotton dress with clowns printed all over it. Leave it to Aunt Marie to not bother with traditional garb on a prestigious day. I loved how, despite it all, she clung to her quirky personality. One of her hobbies included going to local thrift shops, finding the most ridiculous fabrics she could, and then turning them into something she loved.

"I like the dress," I said with a wink while noting that one of the clowns was sucking a phallic looking banana.

"You know I hate stuffy clothes. Everyone here is dressed for a funeral," she said in a disgusted tone while looking around the room. She wasn't wrong. It was like looking out into a sea of mourning wear.

Aunt Marie was fun despite her grim diagnosis. Even though most of my life was spent worrying about when the bloodlust would become too much—when she would finally snap—she never made it feel like a hardship. She just made the most of everything we had.

"You should have worn your cantaloupe boob dress. That would've really livened things up," I teased.

Aunt Marie laughed, but her joy suddenly cut off. She sniffed the air and squeezed her eyes shut, every muscle in her body going stiff. She was hungry. I'd gotten to the point where I could predict when another episode would come. Bloodlust was like a boomerang, every time we thought we had gotten through the worst of it, her illness would circle back to haunt us.

I noted her shaky hands and the dull, glassy look in her eyes. She looked happy, but there was an underlying desperation creeping to the surface.

"Let's open this, yeah?" I asked, feigning nonchalance while squeezing her hand.

We didn't have much time, and she needed to go home soon. Her episodes were sporadic, but they could be triggered when she was around too many people. Aunt Marie had a thin thread of control when it came to fending off the bloodlust, and I couldn't let it snap today. Not here, where there were hundreds of vampires around, including political leaders of our community. If they saw her fall into a mindless frenzy, they'd take her away quicker than I could blink, and there would be nothing I could do to stop them.

"Yes! I'm on pins and needles," she said, her smile shaky.

Distraction. She needed a distraction.

I tore off the ribbon tying the rolled parchment together and unfurled it, revealing my diploma.

Just my diploma.

No invitation to work at the council. No slip of paper stating I was offered an internship. No acceptance letter to attend a university abroad. Just...nothing.

"What the fuck?" I whispered under my breath before looking up at my aunt.

She was waiting with bated breath, a proud grin on her face. Luckily, she seemed clueless that something was wrong.

Aunt Marie never got the opportunity to attend Thibault. She dreamed of attending and one day working for the council. She loved everything about this school, but she hadn't been strong enough or rich enough to get in. In many ways, she lived vicariously through me, and I didn't want to let her down.

I opened and closed my mouth, at a loss. I wasn't sure what to tell her. I didn't know how to explain that the weak, nobody vamp, the one who'd busted her ass to be top of her class, didn't get an assignment *at all*.

"So? What did you get?" she pressed.

I coughed a bit to cover the emotions bubbling up in my chest, trying my best not to cry in front of her. Aunt Marie had sacrificed so much to raise me. I wanted to take care of her. How the fuck was I going to do that if I didn't have a job?

"Secretary! A-at the council headquarters!" I blurted out with a stutter. It was the first thing I could think of.

Shit.

She squealed in excitement and wrapped me up in a bone-crushing hug, her tears of joy drenching my black graduation gown. Aunt Marie's happiness almost made the guilt I felt disappear. "This is amazing, Motley! A secretary now and maybe a vampire representative one day! I'm so proud of you."

Shame like nothing I'd ever felt before filled me from my toes up, but I didn't falter. I wanted to give her this joy. Just once. I could figure out what I was actually going to do later.

When she pulled away, I noticed how her skin had started to turn gray. She began to tremble, and her fangs descended, dripping with venom. Bloodlust was coming.

My lips thinned into a grim line. I hated how quickly it took over her.

"I—I think I need to go home," she whispered in a low, strained voice.

"Want me to take you?" I offered, but she thrust her hands up in protest at my offer. She hated feeling like a burden.

"No, no. I want you to celebrate. Mingle with your peers," she insisted.

I had to suppress a snort. If only she knew that I had no peers to mingle with. I hadn't made any friends while at Thibault. I was a loner. My closest friend was the librarian, Mr. Kinley.

This place wasn't prestigious for no reason. Only the offspring of the most powerful and successful families attended here, or the few scholarship students like me. And those of us here who got in for our brains or impressive abilities had to stay highly competitive. It wasn't exactly a place that fostered friendships. Not that I would've told my aunt that.

"Stay here. I'll catch a portal home."

"Are you sure?" I asked. If I were being honest, all I wanted to do was curl up in a ball and cry about my dim future, but I wanted to be there for her.

"I'm positive. Go. Have fun. I'll be fine. I can hold it off for another hour at least. That's plenty of time for me to get home." She grabbed me for one last hug, and I squeezed her tight, though I couldn't ignore how every muscle in her body was coiled with tension.

As I watched her walk away, the only thing I could think of was *how the fuck am I supposed to take care of us now?*

I WAS DROWNING my sorrows with spiked blood, lingering at the bar top while I listened to everyone excitedly discuss their placements. Enforcer training. Paralegal to the Judge. Internship for Blood Regulations. Shifter military. Department of the Dead.

Everyone but me seemed to have been offered prestigious placements with promising futures. Part of me wanted to knock on Headmaster Torne's door and demand an explanation, but I knew it was no use. I arrived here as nobody, and I'd leave here as nobody.

"Heard you got an empty diploma."

I stiffened at the voice and looked over to find none other than Stiles Trant.

The rich, handsome, powerful, prodigious son of the well-connected Trant family. He was the Vampire Paragon, the someday council ruler of our kind, and the guy that all the girls swooned over.

But to me? He was just my secret half-brother.

I hated the fucker.

The man who dumped me off at Aunt Marie's house when I was two days old? Yeah, that was our father. The only difference was he kept Stiles and tossed me away. I'd come out of the wrong cunt, I guess.

"How did you find out?" I asked, hating that he knew.

Stiles had been pissed when I was accepted into Thibault on the scholarship program—he'd felt like I was encroaching on his territory. He *always* liked to remind me this was his place and not mine. He was more territorial than the fucking shifters. Stiles had inherited his sense of entitlement from our father. Me? The only thing I inherited was the Trant blue eyes. Stiles and our father had blond hair and strong jaws, while my hair was a cherry red ombré, and my features were far more delicate.

"Everyone knows," Stiles said with a mocking smirk as he

sat down beside me. He looked handsome and affluent like always, his expensive black suit setting off his shiny hair. I looked around, noticing for the first time that people were definitely talking about me. They weren't exactly being subtle, staring at me as they whispered, tossing me knowing smirks throughout the room.

Thibault had set up this little after graduation party, but most of the parents and professors had left hours ago, and the once dignified celebration was now just a bunch of graduated students grinding on each other to the dance music and getting drunk off the spiked drinks.

"Great," I muttered into my cup, turning away from the gossipers.

"You're really surprised?" he asked, sounding like the pretentious dick he was.

"Fuck you, Stiles," I snapped, swiveling in his direction. "I worked my ass off here for five godsdamned years. I deserved to be the highest ranking student, and everyone knows it. But Headmaster Torne couldn't let me win that, could he? And now they won't even give me a placement," I seethed. "They're punishing me for being fucking poor with a bastard last name, and it's pathetic."

Stiles simply shrugged, as if my outrage didn't matter, and signalled to the bartender, who immediately brought him a glass of fresh blood. He took a long swallow before deigning to respond. "This is Thibault. Did you really expect anything else? They have a reputation to uphold. You think these polished wood floors and marble statues pay for themselves?" he asked, waving a hand around the room. "Thibault is one of the most prestigious supernatural academies in the world, because they cater to the rich and powerful. You don't fit into that demographic. I've been telling you that you don't belong here for years."

I wanted to rage at him. "Why are you even over here

talking to me?" I asked, wanting him gone. In our five years of attending this academy together, he'd only ever either ignored me completely or bullied me alongside some of the other entitled assholes here.

"Can't I come over here for a chat with my half-sister?"

I cocked a dark brow. "Careful. You wouldn't want for people to overhear. The Trant family name would be tainted," I said bitterly.

Stiles took another drink from his glass. "I never said you tainted the Trant family name," he said, making me wary. "I just said you didn't belong here, and I stand by that. I think my point has been proven hundreds of times by now, don't you?" he asked rhetorically. "Every time you were ridiculed. Every time you were looked down on —not just from our peers, but even the professors. Tonight should prove it to you once and for all. I was meant to come to Thibault. You weren't. But you never accepted your place, so you suffered through this needlessly."

Needlessly.

He called my suffering *needless*. As if it was my fault. As if I deserved to be treated this way simply because I was a poor bastard.

Stiles fucking Trant was handed everything on a silver platter, and I hated him for it.

I suddenly felt utterly exhausted. I was so tired. So tired of always keeping my head up despite how everyone looked down on me. Tired of pushing myself to be the best and never getting any recognition for it. I was tired of being the Trant's dirty secret.

All that work. All that...enduring. The fucking juvenile bullying. Being passed over. Being known as Thibault's charity case. I handled it all with my chin up and a chip on my shoulder—all because I knew graduating from Thibault and getting a placement was my only shot at digging myself out of the proverbial slums.

And none of it mattered.

"Just go away, Stiles," I said defeatedly, turning away from him.

I didn't have it in me to fight for myself right now. I felt the hot prickles of tears behind my eyes, which was crazy, because I never cried. I kept my emotions in boxes and shoved those impassioned bitches deep, deep down in the cellar of my soul.

I heard Stiles sigh, and then he was slipping another drink in my direction and leaving cash on the bartop to pay for his and mine. "For what it's worth, Motley, at least you can leave now. Find some place where you fit in. Life will be easier for you that way."

He got up and sauntered away, immediately being welcomed into the vampire cliques and having a great fucking time shooting the shit with them.

I left the drink he'd bought me untouched on the bartop.

As soon as I was on my feet, I flashed away using my vampiric speed, even though I probably shouldn't have since I was a bit unsteady on my feet from all the spiked blood I'd ingested.

Everyone was a blur as I passed by, their smiling faces full of excitement, which was taunting to the despair I felt. It wasn't until I was back in my dorm room with the door slammed shut behind me that I finally let free the ragged breath stuck in my chest.

Gods, my life sucked.

I ran a hand down my face, not caring that I was definitely smudging my makeup. At least Stiles had been right about the one thing I could look forward to. After tomorrow night, I could finally be done with Thibault, and I could leave all of these people behind.

I'd worry about how I was going to live and take care of Aunt Marie later. For now, I just wanted to sleep and forget.

I tucked the loose strands of my red hair behind my ears and kicked off my shoes, letting them slam against the wall. It was a good thing my roommate wasn't around, or she'd have plenty to say about the noise it made. I slumped on the bed and let my head hang down.

It just wasn't fair. None of it. I'd been busting my ass all my life, working twice as hard as everyone else to make up for my unimpressive circumstances. I'd done everything in my power to claw my way out of poverty. I kept to myself. I'd endured the bullying from entitled rich kids. Buried my head in textbooks and played the studious, unflappable role, and for what?

"Fucking assholes. All of them," I murmured while standing up and stripping out of my graduation gown. I let the smooth fabric pool on the ground, but I stopped before removing my uniform skirt when I noticed an envelope on my pillow.

It was perfectly placed, with my name typed on the front. I glanced around the room, noting that there was an identical envelope on my roommate's bed, too. That was odd.

Tentatively, I walked over and picked mine up, flipping it over and noting the unique seal with the letter *S* on the back in hardened gold wax.

I ripped it open and tore out the thick parchment.

DEAR MISS MOTLEY COVEN,

You have been selected for an internship position at Spector Incorporated. This is a very selective and classified program, intended for only the most qualified. We invite you to attend a banquet tomorrow evening at eight o'clock, where you will be inducted into the program and start your training immediately. Formal attire is required, and food and drinks will be served. An escort will be sent to bring you to the banquet should you choose to accept this offer.

Please be advised: For purposes of sensitive information not to be compromised, you are not permitted to discuss this invitation or Spector Incorporated.

Sincerely,
Lorenzo Belvini
President, Spector Inc.

I READ the words over and over again, trying to make sense of the cryptic invitation. After a third read-through of the invite, I had the thing memorized, right down to the president's suave name. I'd never heard of Spector Inc. before, so I didn't know a damn thing about them.

For the first time since opening my empty diploma, my hopes had lifted. I had a placement.

I had a fucking placement!

A smile spread across my face, and I let out a relieved half-laugh, half-sigh. This position sounded not only incredibly exclusive, but secretive too.

I went to bed that night thanking the Spector gods. And while I might know fuck-all about them, I did know one thing—I was going to take this internship and pave my way to a better life for Aunt Marie and myself once and for all.

Chapter 2

"YOU'RE NOT WEARING THAT, are you?" My roommate's nasally voice sounded from the corner of our small dorm room as she looked me up and down. "You look kinda...homely."

My teeth clenched at her words. She was about as bitchy as she was predictable. But above all else, Cheryl was talkative. I had to brace myself for yet another one of her monologues.

"You know, my second cousin's ex-girlfriend is a stylist in Milan. She has so many dresses just lying around. But they're all size four, and I'm a size two. Like what, am I supposed to just gain twenty pounds to fit in some Gucci? No, thank you."

I stood in front of our ornate full length mirror, doing my best to ignore her. I pulled at the soft, satin material of my blood-red dress I was wearing. It wasn't anything fancy, but I felt sexy despite whatever the fuck Cheryl said.

The dress was long with a subtle slit up the thigh that showed off enough of my porcelain vampire skin to be sensual while still maintaining some elegance. The front dipped between my cleavage and curved in the shape of a heart. My Aunt Marie had sewed it for me last year, using discount fabric that probably cost her a few precious blood bags.

It wasn't a designer dress, but it was made with love and matched my red ombré hair and lipstick perfectly. I had spoken to my aunt on the phone earlier, but since I wasn't allowed to talk about Spector, I kept up my original lie to her and told her I was attending an orientation for the council job tonight. The pride in her tone made the lie worth it. I just hoped this secretive internship worked out.

"I've never really liked Gucci," I replied with a bored sigh while clasping a cheap bracelet around my wrist. I'd never even seen a designer gown up close, let alone had enough money to purchase such a thing. But I'd learned over the years that it was easier to go along with Cheryl's monologues than point out how vastly different our socioeconomic situations were.

In the reflection, I could see my roommate sipping on her bloody cocktail, her feet dangling in some sky high stilettos that no doubt cost more than a year's tuition. She hadn't bothered to get dressed yet and was lounging around in her black lace lingerie, probably hoping to entice our escort for the evening.

It drove me insane that she'd received an invitation too. Five years of sharing a room with her should have been torture enough, but no. It seemed that fate wanted me to spend even more of my life listening to her nasally, never-ending voice.

To be honest, Spector lost a bit of its prestige in my eyes since they'd invited her. Cheryl was...well, Cheryl. Annoying as fuck and dumb to boot. The only reason she was in Thibault was because her family apparently had good blood and an even better bank balance.

Our escort was supposed to be here any minute, and I had no doubt that Cheryl would make it a point to answer the door still in her underwear. She was always trying to entice prominent members of our society, no matter how inappropriate. She liked to be desired.

"I still don't understand why they invited you too," Cheryl whined, not for the first time. She'd been making subtle digs at me ever since she saw me with my letter. "I mean, if it was a blood thing, you wouldn't have been invited," she mused. "Your last name is totally unimportant. Who did you say your father was again?"

I shrugged. "Just some weak vamp vagabond douche," I lied. One major stipulation for attending Thibault and receiving our annual allowance was to never reveal who my father was. It was a secret I was happy to keep. Aunt Marie couldn't work because of her bloodlust, and if we ever lost the tiny stipend the Trants secretly sent us, there was no way we could survive.

"Hmm. Well, Spector can't have made their selections for being well connected or having money. Because you don't have those either," she pointed out.

"Right, and I guess it can't be intelligence, because that would rule out your attendance," I shot back.

"Oh, please. No one cares about that," she huffed.

"Yes, they do," I argued, but some of the usual fire behind my words had tempered. I'd always believed that being smart mattered. That I could change my circumstances if I worked hard enough.

I got accepted to Thibault Academy's scholarship program because I was smart. I stayed at the top of my class because I was driven. But Thibault had taught me that intelligence and drive really *didn't* matter, and that was just fucking depressing.

But dammit, I didn't care what Cheryl thought. I deserved this opportunity.

And tonight? I had every intention of standing up and claiming it. No amount of insecure bullshit or outside hate was going to keep me from the future I wanted.

I would do whatever it took until I had a job that would protect and provide for Aunt Marie and me.

"I saw you talking to Stiles Trant last night," Cheryl said as she continued lying on her bed, her blood martini glass balanced in her hand like she was posing for a photo shoot in *Vogue Vampires*. "I tasted him last month, you know. And not just his blood, if you know what I mean," she said, wagging her brows. "His cock was impressive too. Not the biggest I've seen—shifters are traditionally bigger—but it was big enough to make waves."

I made a disgusted face at the mention of his...parts. She might not know that he was my brother, but I did, and this was the last thing I ever wanted to hear about. Fucking gross.

"Cool. Are you gonna get dressed or what?" I asked, trying to steer the conversation away.

Cheryl sat up, letting her short blonde hair bob around her jaw. She'd hated it when I'd become her roommate five years ago. She always bragged that she was some baroness in her homeland of Germany, but her family had split off to come live in the states so that she could attend Thibault, since this program was the best for vampires. *Baronesses shouldn't have to share a room with bastards*, she'd said. I'd traded out all of her uniforms so they were three sizes too big for her for that.

"He was delicious," she prattled on, ignoring my attempts at changing the subject. "You could practically taste the superior breeding in him. He was like a fine glass of Pinot Noir from the vineyards of Italy. Have you ever been to Italy? My family owns a chateau there overlooking a cliff..." she went on and on and on, drawing out each word and running her tongue over her fangs like the sound of her own annoying prissy voice was getting her off. "I should invite Stiles there. My family would *love* him."

"Do you blow everyone you want to drink, or is that just a paragon thing?" I asked.

Her brown eyes flashed over at me. "*Ohmygods*, you're, like, totally jealous, aren't you?" she asked, drawing out her valley girl accent before giving me a pitying look. "You have to understand, you're just not really in Stiles Trant's league, you know? Don't take it personally. You can't help that you're not as pure blooded or pretty as me."

Oh for shifter shit's sake.

I sighed and tossed my mascara on the desk behind me. "What did I do in a past life to deserve you as a roommate?" I mumbled under my breath while smoothing my hair.

"What?"

I turned around to face her. "I don't care about Stiles Trant or your little suck and fuck session. I care about this internship opportunity from Spector."

Cheryl rolled her eyes and placed her glass down on the bedside table before standing up and walking over to me. "For how smart you claim to be, you sure are ignorant sometimes," she said, looking me up and down with a clear dismissal. "You were obviously invited tonight for political reasons."

I tensed, though I tried not to show that her words made my insides stutter. After five years, I should've known better than to engage with her or let her bother me. But fuck, she was a bitch, and it was hard to always keep my guard up. "How do you mean?"

"It's obvious, isn't it?" she asked with a blasé laugh. She reached forward to tug on one of my wavy red locks like she was a critical mother fixing her daughter's hair. "It'd look very good for Spector to hire on a charity case as an intern, wouldn't it? You know how it goes," she said with a bored shrug. "They need diversity. Less powerful supes to make them appear inclusive. But no one actually wants you there."

My gut twisted.

I didn't know anything about Spector, so I couldn't know if she was lying or not, but honestly...it was something that happened regularly. Maybe she was right. Maybe I *was* just offered a charity case position to make Spector Inc. look better. Hell, Thibault had done it.

A knock suddenly sounded on the door, but before I could turn toward it, Cheryl grabbed my arm, holding me in place. She leaned in and grazed her lips against my ear. "It's better you realize that they're not actually interested now, rather than embarrass yourself later. I'm doing you a favor," she said before placing a kiss on my jaw and spinning away to the door.

My fists clenched at my sides.

I suddenly felt very stupid.

But then again...so what if Spector wanted a poster child for underprivileged supes?

Fuck it.

I'd be the best damn poster child vamp they'd ever seen. They wanted to use me? Well, I'd use them right back. There was nothing wrong with mutual benefits.

I fixed a perfect smile on my face, pushing down the disarming disappointment swirling around in my gut. I watched Cheryl adjust her boobs in her bra before she swung open the door. She thrust her hip out and leaned against the frame, eyeing whoever was on the other side.

My eyes widened when I noticed it was my damn brother.

What the fuck was he doing here?

"Oh! Stiles! I didn't know it would be you escorting us tonight," she said with excitement.

He gave her a terse nod, sweeping that cobalt blue gaze up and down her slender body. "I've been interning for Spector for six months," he told her before his gaze flicked over her shoulder to look at me.

At seeing me standing there, his entire body tensed. His blue eyes widened for a fraction of a second before flicking over to the door that Cheryl was still holding, as if double checking he'd gotten the right room number.

"Motley," he said slowly. "Shouldn't you have moved out of Thibault today?"

"I would've...If I hadn't gotten an invitation from Spector," I said, holding up the envelope with my name clearly typed on it.

"That's...that's not possible," he said, storming in past Cheryl.

He snatched up the envelope and opened it, probably double checking to make sure my name was there. When he read the letter clearly addressed to me, he tossed it down on my desk and ran a hand through his blond hair. "There must have been a mistake. You can't have been selected for this."

My teeth snapped together in annoyance. It was always the same fucking thing with him. He was pissed about me getting into Thibault, and now he was pissed about me getting into Spector, too.

"It's not like I knew you were in this program," I said, defensive anger lacing my words. "I hadn't even heard about it before last night.

"You're not going to accept," he actually had the audacity to say.

A humorless laugh burst out of my chest. I saw red. I wanted to punch him in his godsdamned face and take a photo for our dear ol' dad. "You don't have the authority to dictate what I do or don't do."

His hands fisted at his sides. Our blue eyes locked, fury brimming in both pairs.

"Wow, this is tense," Cheryl chirped.

Both of us slowly turned our heads to look over at her.

She had her hands on her hips, watching us with a curious look on her face.

"The invitation said *formal wear*," Stiles snapped at her. "You obviously shouldn't accept either. Spector doesn't want people who can't read simple instructions."

Cheryl's nose wrinkled. "Oh my gods, Stiles, I can read," she huffed in annoyance. "I just didn't want to get makeup on it. My mother always says to wait until the last minute to slip into your dress. It keeps it in pristine condition. Just wait like three freaking seconds while I get dressed."

Stiles's frown deepened, but he didn't say anything else as she sashayed into the closet. I arched a brow at him. "Now you're trying to get her not to go either? Gods, what is it with you and Spector?"

He levelled me with a look. "I just know what sort of supes can handle Spector, and you two can't."

I reared back, his words offending me so much that my fangs started to come down. "Fuck you. I can handle anything."

"I can handle Spector, too," Chery called, her voice slightly muffled. "I even have the perfect dress for tonight," she said as she pulled something from a hanger. "My best friend got it for me while on vacation in Paris. She had to bribe the boutique to give it to her because they were reserving it for the lead singer of *Bite Me*. Do you know her? Charlie Rogue? I met her at a party once, and she was lovely. You know she told me I had a pretty voice? We sang on stage together and—"

"Can you just finish getting dressed?" Stiles interrupted. "We're on a tight schedule."

Cheryl just waved at him dismissively while tapping her lips in thought at which heels she would wear. "Shoes are like, *really* important, Stiles. You can't rush these decisions. One time, my cousin was in New Orleans, and she wore shoes *totally* wrong for the occasion. I told her not to wear platform boots to a Sunday soiree, but did she listen to me? Nope. Oh, and then she—"

"For fuck's sake," Stiles growled. "I am going to leave without you."

With an exasperated sigh, Cheryl flashed around, her figure just a blur, and then she was standing there, perfectly poised. "Ready," she said cheerfully, beaming up at Stiles.

"*Great*," he said sarcastically.

I looked her up and down. "*That's* what you're wearing?" I asked.

I looked at her ridiculous violet dress. It was so short one stiff breeze would show her vagina off to the masses. And I knew this with certainty, because there were zero lines indicating any usage of panties going on under there.

She jetted out her hip and inspected her nails with practiced coolness. "This is *couture*, Motley," she told me. "Gods, I just can't even with you." She looked at Stiles. "We going or what?" she asked, as if he and I were the ones holding us up.

Stiles's jaw tightened. "We're going."

"Super. And where exactly are we going? I have a fur coat for cooler climates, but it goes better with the black Valentino. And will there be dancing? I have a higher pair of heels—"

"No. Just...no," he cut her off. "No more changing clothes, no more questions. We're already late."

"Fine, sheesh."

Stiles reached up and grasped both of our arms, and then he flashed us away. Since he was in charge of the movement, it was slightly dizzying and felt like I was being pulled through the air at warp speed. He stopped right outside an unused classroom, and I had to straighten my dress from where the rushing air had tangled it around my legs.

I followed behind Stiles and Cheryl as they walked inside the classroom, where there was a portal waiting. There was an instructor sitting boredly beside it—an elemental teacher, I think—who barely gave us a second glance once he saw that it was Stiles leading us.

I braced myself before entering it, not knowing what would be on the other side. Cheryl latched onto Stiles, wrapping her willowy arm around his and digging her sharply pointed nails into the thick fabric of his tux jacket. He led Cheryl through, and I took a deep breath before heading in after them.

Magic coated my skin in gentle waves, pulsing through my body as we traveled through the sickly sweet energy. It was only about ten seconds of walking through nothingness, but while in the haze, Stiles turned to look back at me, displeasure clear on his face, while determination was on mine.

I can handle anything, I'd told him. I just hoped I was right.

I WASN'T EXACTLY sure where in the world the portal had brought us, except that the huge room was decorated elaborately and the lighting was dim. There were banners hanging from the fifty-foot ceiling that draped between the chandeliers, all of them with an S symbol for Spector Inc. It was a snake in the shape of an S, but at the bottom curve, the snake was clearly wrapping around to devour itself in a neverending loop.

Well, that was a cheerful logo.

Cheryl sucked in a gasp. "Oh my gods, is that George Loom?" A tiny squeal of distress escaped her. "I should have worn the Valentino dress," she cursed before looking over at me. Her eyes took on a tragic look as she eyed my dress. "I should have let you try to squeeze into one of mine. You probably would've had to take out a few inches of zipper because I'm *much* slimmer than you, but that would've been better than what you have on now." I had to stop myself from rolling my eyes. She was just secretly jealous that I had bigger boobs than she did. "Well, it can't be helped now. Sorry, but I can't be seen with you."

"Bummer," I drawled.

She shook her head, her eyes continuing to scan the room. "Is that Vang Lewis?" she asked, stretching her neck to better see a group of men across the room, speaking with Headmaster Torne.

I followed her gaze and saw that she was right. I recognized him from the articles I'd read. "It is...but I'm surprised *you* know who he is," I told her honestly. "I didn't think you'd be interested in the shifter with one of the largest peaceful packs in the continental United States."

She smoothed down her blonde bob. "He's super hot, Motley," she said in irritation, as if that should've been obvious. "Though I'd never date a shifter. Coital bliss between the species is such a social faux pas. Nothing wrong with a little flirting, though." She winked.

"Oh. Right. How silly of me," I deadpanned.

Cheryl scampered off in her heels, a flurried trail of excitement lifting each of her steps as she went up to Vang and started flirting with him. Huh. I guess she wasn't a stickler about sticking to her own kind like most everyone else.

"She sure is something," Stiles mused.

"That's one way to describe her."

The further we walked into the room, the more others turned to look at us. The gathering was an odd mix of students and professionals in the supernatural community. Necromancers, elementals, shifters, and vampires were all milling around the lavish room, drinking cocktails and eating finger foods that passing servers offered them.

I saw a couple dozen Thibault students aside from Stiles and myself. Some of them I knew, some of them I didn't, but all of them looked surprised to see that I'd been invited. I could see it in their raised brows and pointed looks, and then came the whispers.

What's she doing here?
I thought this invite was exclusive. What's with the charity case?
Why is Stiles Trant with her?

And on and on it went. My peers were so friendly.

I fixed my expression into a mix between oblivious professionalism and resting bitch face. Basically, the same face I'd worn my entire academic career.

Stiles kept at my side, tense but seemingly oblivious of the numerous eyes on us. "Can't you go away and ignore me like you always do?" I hissed, while smiling over at a creepy necromancer in a glittering tux.

Stiles glanced over at me with irritation. "It's not like you don't ignore me too."

"Of course I ignore you," I said with exasperation, careful to keep my voice at a low murmur. Never underestimate the power of supernatural hearing. "You made it clear from the start that you're not interested in being my brother or even my friend. So just scurry off and leave me alone to fend for myself against the wolves like you always do. You're good at that, just like your father."

The skin around his eyes tightened at the words *your father*, but for once, he didn't argue. Deciding to ignore him, I turned away, watching everyone and trying to gain a sense of what this corporation was all about. I'd rather gnaw on my own foot than try to get answers out of Stiles. He'd just hold it over me like a bone to a dog.

Maybe if I mingled a bit, I could pick up some clues? I was well informed when it came to the supernatural community, especially powerful organizations. I had to be because I intended to work for one. So the fact that I'd heard nothing about Spector Inc. had my interest piqued.

"I'm gonna go get a drink," Stiles said. "How do you take your blood?"

I turned to glance over my shoulder to see who he was talking to, but there was no one there. I raised my brows. "You're offering to get *me* a drink?" I asked suspiciously. "Why? You gonna spit in it?"

He sighed and yanked on his tie. "Do you always have to be so fucking difficult?"

"I think it's a family trait," I retorted.

He muttered something under his breath that I didn't catch. "Can you just tell me what kind of blood you like?"

I snorted. That was such a rich thing to say. "Uhh, just red and warm."

He blinked in surprise. "You don't have a preference? Supernatural breed? Blood type?"

"Stiles, I'm a scholarship student. Aunt Marie and I barely scrape by. You actually think I get to pick from exotic blood flavors like you? Come on, you're smarter than that," I said, patting him on the shoulder patronizingly. "And don't bother. I can get my own blood."

He made a sound that was half-sigh, half-muttered curse, before he turned and stalked away from me. I watched his retreating back, filled with a mix of relief and disappointment. Being siblings, even if it was only half, always made things complicated between us.

A rush of air at my back was the only warning I got that told me vampires had just flashed over.

"I'm surprised you got an invite tonight, Motley," the first unwelcome voice said behind me.

"She probably sucked the Spector president's cock," another voice chuckled.

Oh, goody. My classmates had decided to come chat.

They'd always been eager to remind me I didn't belong, and I guess tonight would be no exception. I tilted my chin up, pointedly ignoring them as I pulled some red lipstick from the clutch I was carrying and applied it to my lips. Fuck them. It was always such a predictable cliché—tormenting the poor scholarship girl for not having a rich daddy or a connected mother. Yawn.

"Of course she did. I heard that's how she got into Thibault, too. She fucked every supe on the school board," a third voice added.

Irritated, I spun around to face the three jackasses talking shit. I frowned when I found a familiar black-haired vampire in the middle. I'd once had the displeasure of wasting twenty minutes of my life on him. Terrible decision on my part, but I'd been horny and hungry. It was a bad combo for a vamp, and it tended to make me a bit skanky.

"Oh. Byron. I didn't notice you there," I said, pasting a thoughtful look on my face. "Wait a minute, didn't I say the same thing to you when you were fucking me?" I asked with a smirk.

The other two vamps let out surprised laughs, while Byron's face mottled with anger. The funniest part? I wasn't even joking. For all his cockiness, this dude was a terrible fuck with a tiny dick, and his blood tasted like chalk. Probably too much in-breeding with other high-up vampires trying to hold on to their purer bloodline bullshit.

He straightened his spine so he could better look down

his nose at me. "Yeah? I'm not surprised you couldn't feel anything. You're just a bitch with a loose pussy," he shot back at me, making the vamps who'd laughed at him, turn around and laugh harder at *me*. No fucking loyalty.

I pressed my lips so hard together that some of the clay-like lipstick I'd just applied matted and fell in powdered crumbles down my chin, leaving a streaky line down the front of my dress. Godsdamned you, cheap fucking makeup. This shit didn't happen with name brands.

I dismissed him with a shake of my head and pushed away from the trio. Maybe I could find a bathroom and take a minute to myself before I had to face anyone again. I didn't want to be in a bad headspace before Spector did their presentation. Before I could make my escape though, Stiles intercepted me.

He stepped in front of me and held up two champagne flutes full of fresh blood. By the looks of it, he'd grabbed the clotted cheap shit for both of us. My eyes flickered up to his in surprise. Had he done it to make me feel more comfortable? That was...weird.

His eyes zeroed in on the line of makeup on my dress. "Something wrong?"

I knew full well he probably heard what happened from across the room, but he was testing to see if I would complain about it. But I wouldn't. Not to him. Talking about those dumbasses gave them power, and I preferred to keep my power to myself. I wasn't ashamed of the fact that I liked to fuck and did it whenever it pleased me. Vampires were sexual creatures, and yet they always liked to be judgmental about it. I didn't understand the point.

When I wasn't keeping to myself or studying, I was indulging. Zero strings. Zero attachments. I was a loner through and through—but with a healthy appetite for sins of the flesh. And despite the way those three vampire assholes had acted just now, I knew without a doubt, that if I turned around and invited them for a little suck and fuck, they'd jump at the chance. They were bullies, yeah, but they were still males with dicks. But talking about any of this to my half-brother who could barely stand me? Yeah, hard pass.

"Nope. Nothing's wrong at all." I shook my head in answer and tilted my glass back, drinking the blood with a hearty gulp. The buzzing power of cheap, regular human blood hummed appreciatively in my chest. Stiles watched me with a contemplative look on his face, but I didn't want him to look at me like that. I wanted him to keep on ignoring me with disdain from a distance, probably brooding over having to share DNA with me. That, I was used to.

"You have thicker skin than this, Motley. I know you do."

I turned to look at him, setting my glass down and crossing my arms in front of me. "You don't know me, so don't pretend like you do. We've been enemies for our entire academic career. Don't try to give me advice. I'm *fine*. I'm not some fucking weak damsel crying in a corner. I've been dealing with bullshit like that my whole life, so I don't need a fucking pep talk from you. I just needed a drink, a second to regain my chill, and then I'll have my head high again. I always do."

When a look that resembled pity crossed his features, it made my blood boil.

I was about to open my mouth to ream him some more, but Headmaster Torne had spotted Stiles, and he walked over with a group of supes and stopped at our side.

"Ah, Stiles."

Stiles looked over, one hand casually in his pocket and one holding his glass. "Good evening, Headmaster," he greeted smoothly.

Headmaster Torne beamed at him. It was no secret that

he had a fiscal hard-on for the Trants, so my brother was somewhat of a golden child in his eyes.

"I wanted to introduce you," Headmaster Torne said. "We were just discussing your potential on the council."

"*Good* potential, I hope," Stiles joked, making the other men chuckle.

"Stiles, I hear you did very well on the last council meeting. When Torne here told me you were present tonight, I knew I needed to meet the Vampire Paragon," the tall vampire to our left greeted. He had dark skin and black eyes, and even without the telltale scar across his neck, I would've recognized him anywhere.

"Oh! You're Edmund Pike," I said as I took a step forward, feeling a surge of excitement.

His dark eyes swept over to me. "I am."

I couldn't contain the smile that broke out across my face. I never dreamed I'd ever be in the same room with this man, let alone get to talk to him. "Can I just say, I *loved* your speech at the council's symposium last year. Your ideas about splicing necro genes to counteract the effects of bloodlust in vampires was revolutionary."

I'd pored over that speech for days, picking apart every fragment of his research. It was work like his that could help vamps like my aunt.

Surprise flitted over his features, and he turned to face me more. "What is your name?"

"Motley Coven, sir," I answered.

"Hmm. One of yours, Torne?" he asked, looking over at my headmaster.

Headmaster Torne had his gray hair slicked back, and his dark eyes bore into me. He was a strong elemental with equally strong bloodlines, and he looked at me like a bug stuck to his shoe.

"Yes," he answered coolly, as if my mere presence was a

bother. "She's one of Thibault's financial fellowship recipients. She received her scholarship for all five years of her attendance."

"Ah," Mr. Pike said, his eyes already dimming from their earlier interest in me. "Anyway, as I was saying, the council…"

And just like that, I was dismissed. My fingers curled into my palms, two fists at my side my only defense against the discrimination in the world.

Stiles shot me a sideways look, but I pulled away from the group. I stalked over to the bar and snatched up another flute of blood, downing it all in one unladylike gulp. I snatched up some dainty finger foods from a passing waiter, shoving three cucumber sandwiches with blood cream into my mouth.

Some of the pain and disappointment leaked through my expression before I could lock the cage around my feelings again. I slammed it into place and straightened my spine, licking the remnant of food off my fingers.

Just one more night. I just needed to get through one more night, and then I could leave Thibault and all of this behind. Spector Inc. was my chance, and I wasn't going to let anyone ruin it for me.

Chapter 3

THINGS GOT...WEIRD.

One moment, the banquet was in full effect, with dressy people drinking and eating and mingling, and the next, we were ushered into a new room. This one was just as large as the one before, but there were no decorations in the sparse space. It was just wood panelled walls and black marble tile, an expanse of windows lined up along one side of the room.

The only embellishment was a huge black rug laid out in the center of the room. The lights were just as dim as in the other room, and as soon as I made my way inside, I noted that there were a dozen men and women in Spector Inc. uniforms standing sentry along the walls.

My steps slowed, a feeling of unease spreading through me. When I saw Stiles, I snagged his jacket sleeve. "What's going on?" I hissed in his ear.

"Don't fight it," he replied back.

My grip tightened. "What the fuck does that mean?"

He shrugged me off as if I were a nuisance. "Spector obviously chose you for a reason. They can make you better,

Motley. Stronger. Just don't fight it, okay? It's bad if you fight it."

I blinked at him, and the foreboding feeling in my gut spread throughout my entire body. My fangs dropped down at my rising fear.

"All Spector intern invitees, please step into the middle of the room, and then we will begin."

I turned to look behind us, just as the door to the room closed with a click. I saw a searing bright light coming through the other side, letting me know that a portal had been opened.

Searching around the room, I saw that all the high society members hadn't come into this room. There were about two dozen Thibault students, including myself, Headmaster Torne, another man I hadn't met, and the Spector Inc. guards. That was it.

A slick sheen of sweat broke out on my skin. The other students looked curious, but wary, while the Spector members and Headmaster Torne looked...eager.

"Welcome," the man standing beside Headmaster Torne said, flashing a charming smile as he looked around the room. My eyes slipped down to the X mark on his pale neck. So he was a necromancer, then.

"My name is Cue Hafferty, and on behalf of Spector President Lorenzo Belvini, I'd like to welcome you all here tonight," he said warmly. "This is an extremely exclusive internship. Thibault Academy and Spector Incorporated have teamed up for this amazing opportunity, and you've been selected to participate in this program that will propel your careers. Each and every one of you fits into the very specialized attributes required, so you should feel very proud." Hafferty boasted his speech with pride, walking around with his chest puffed out and a grin on his face. "Now, if you accept the internship, please come forward and sign your name at the table behind me, then return to stand in the middle of the room, and we'll get started inducting you."

My eyes slid around at the others, noting the various expressions on their faces once more.

"What's the program?" a necro student asked. "What's required of us?"

"Unfortunately, all information is classified until you join," Hafferty answered, looking apologetic. "But I can tell you that you'll be working with Spector very closely. You'll be groomed to propel their vision and have opportunities to be placed in leading positions throughout the supernatural communities."

At that answer, several people moved forward to sign the contract.

"And what exactly is their vision?" I asked.

Hafferty faced me, his friendly smile still in place. "Again, I'm not at liberty to say very much. Spector Inc. is classified for good reason since our process is both foresighted and delicate. If this information became public knowledge, we wouldn't be able to protect the supernatural community the way we aim to. Just know that by enlisting with Spector, you'll be joining an organization that is striving to protect our kind and propel us to new heights that we never thought possible."

I considered his words, and several more people moved forward, lining up to sign their names one by one.

My gaze went over to Stiles and then to Headmaster Torne.

I had a decision to make, and I could feel the importance of it all the way down to my bones. I could walk out of here right now. I could leave this place, leave Thibault, and go back home to Aunt Marie. I could tell her the truth about not getting a placement in the council. I could try to get some low level vamp job befitting of my societal classification.

I could see my entire life playing out if I did that. Being stressed to the max, trying to juggle taking care of Aunt Marie—who's condition would only get worse—and working at a sucky, unfulfilling job that didn't challenge my intellect or my drive. That road was safe, but it was a dreaded road I'd been trying to run away from my entire life.

So when my feet carried me forward, I wasn't all that surprised. When my hand skittered across the paper to sign my name, I didn't even try to talk myself out of it. I had to make my life and Aunt Marie's life better than that dismal future. Despite the unease I felt, I had to do this.

Every single student signed the paper. I'm sure they all had their reasons, probably not all that different from mine. We were immortal. Positions of power were everything to us.

As soon as the last student had signed and taken their place in the center of the room, two of the guards moved forward and started rolling up the black rug beneath our feet. We had to shift around each other awkwardly as the carpet was moved away, and I nearly fell against Cheryl before straightening up again.

By the time I saw it, it was too late.

With the rug now gone, we saw what was painted at our feet. A circular design on the hardwood floor that had harsh, chalk-white lines with dozens of pentagons interconnected and an empty space in the middle where we stood.

It was a fucking ritual circle. For *demons*.

I'd seen them in plenty of textbooks to know what they looked like, and sometimes even in newspapers of rituals gone wrong. Supes would sometimes get cocky and think they could mess with the underworld, but it was ridiculously tricky and rarely worked the way they wanted it to.

Demons were different than the rest of us. We were immortal, sure...but high level demons were nearly impossible to kill, and their abilities were unrivaled. Supes were not supposed to fuck with demons. Hell, even low level creature demons were said to be fucking viciously powerful.

The four supernatural breeds may run this world, but that was because demons *let* us. I didn't need to be a genius to know that this was incredibly dangerous and not something we should mess with.

I guess I wasn't the only one who felt that way, because a female shifter at the edge of the circle shook her head. "Oh, fuck that. No one ever said anything about messing with a demon ritual. Did you hear about that lady that ended up with three dicks when she tried to summon a lust demon?" she asked, looking around at the rest of us. "Not one. *Three*. Three fucking gigantic dicks that hung down to her fucking knees. Nope. No way. Not happening," she rambled while throwing her hands up. She looked scared shitless at the sight of the ritual circle. Thick brown fur gathered on her knuckles, warning of an impending shift.

"That was because the people performing that ritual were uninformed. I can assure you that we've perfected this ritual, and your safety has been taken into consideration. We wouldn't risk your lives needlessly," Hafferty said with a placating look on his face.

"No, I'm not doing it," the shifter said, her voice becoming muddled with a panicked growl.

Hafferty cringed, as if he were about to tell her a terrible inconvenience. "Unfortunately, you've already signed the contract. You are no longer permitted to back out."

Her eyes widened, and more fur bloomed across her skin. "What? No. I want out!" she shouted before trying to run. As soon as she tried to leap over the lines of the circle, her body slammed into an invisible force. She stumbled back, shaking her head in a daze from hitting it so hard, and looked over at movement from four of the guards. They were surrounding our circle, holding their hands up and holding an invisible barrier around us. Air elementals.

The shifter girl growled, and then her skin tore away and her body grew, and a fully shifted grizzly bear stood in her place. The bear slammed against the barrier over and over again, making a few of the elementals wince.

A water elemental stepped forward, forming a sphere of water, and shot it toward her, engulfing her head. The grizzly roared, but it was drowned out by the water flooding her mouth and nose. The students beside her tried to help, but they were pushed away by another barrier, and even when one of the fire elemental students threatened to attack Spector personnel, he was overtaken immediately.

The grizzly thrashed around and choked until she crashed to the ground, blacking out from lack of oxygen. She hit the floor with a resounding thud, and the water splashed away from her head. In that second, every student in the room seemed to realize at once that this was not what they thought they signed up for. Panic ensued.

The necromancer started clawing at the barrier. A shifter crouched low and was about to shift. Even Cheryl's fangs were bared in defense as she looked around wildly. But we were trapped inside the barrier, unable to get out.

Stiles watched us alongside Headmaster Torne, his face impassive and his body still. My fangs grew, and I tried to flash away, but the air barrier was too strong, and I went flying backwards, falling into students behind me. Everyone was shouting to be let out, powers were flinging around the room, and just when total destructive pandemonium was about to break out, a voice halted us.

"Students, stop!"

I felt my body jerk to a stop, my muscles stiffening against my will. Everything about me was frozen, forced into a statue-like state that made me rage in panic.

What the fuck kind of magic was this?

A Spector guard waltzed forward and circled the room, his eyes blood red. He was tall and imposing, with a deadly energy about him that made me want to run—but I couldn't. Every Thibault student in the room was on pause, not a single one of us was even able to blink.

The man sighed and shook his head at us. "I don't know why you bother with the song and dance, Hafferty. It's so much easier doing things my way," he said while rolling his neck like he was bored.

"President Belvini prefers a sense of civility, Jones," Hafferty replied with a sigh.

"Yes, but it's better when they're willing. The success rate nearly doubles," the red-eyed man with the halting words replied. "But they're hardly ever willing, unless I *make* them be."

"Indeed."

"Well? *Make* them be willing, then," Headmaster Torne put in. "I don't want my most prominent graduates killed tonight. That wouldn't do well for my re-election as headmaster."

Rage festered inside of me. These people were talking about taking away our free will as nothing more than an annoying hurdle to jump over so that they could perform whatever fucked up demon ritual they had planned. I always knew the headmaster was a jackass, but this was some next level bullshit.

With a curt nod from Hafferty, the red-eyed man—Jones—walked in front of us. His creepy gaze slid over our frozen forms. "When I release you, you all will remain calm. You will perform the ritual as instructed, and you will not fight it."

His words dug into my brain like a maggot digging

through rotted waste. I felt it niggling into my consciousness, spreading through me like a virus.

"You are released," he said, his low voice like a murmur that travelled from my toes to my spine.

Instantly, my body let go, like a car suddenly kicking from neutral into drive. I faltered on my feet, my heel catching on the hardwood as I settled into a decisive stop.

Before I could decide to try to escape again, it was like my brain split in half. Part of me knew that I needed to run, to get the fuck out of there. But the other half of my brain refused to let me. Even my panicked heart had stuttered to a slow, calm beat.

This man's power, however he was able to do this...it was like a vice around my entire being, controlling my every reaction and movement. It scared the fuck out of me.

I bared my fangs at him—or at least, I would've if the compulsion power had let me.

I tried to fight it. I tried so, so hard, but it didn't work.

My body and my mind weren't under my own control. A shifter settled beside me and was heaving in and out, likely trying to fight against this power like I was. A necromancer stood at my back and closed his eyes as if meditating.

Cheryl was shoved into me, her willowy body pressed at my side as she shook with fear and rage. I felt bad for her. We hated one another, but I didn't want this for any of us. I still wasn't exactly sure what *this* was.

My entire body tensed, my mind screaming at my body to flee so violently that I started shaking. Part of me wanted to run far, far away, but the other half soothed me, like everything was sunshine and daisies. Every bone in my body felt strangled with warring tension.

I met Stiles's eyes from across the room. "Don't fight it," he mouthed.

My eyes blazed with fury, but he just burrowed his icy

gaze straight into my soul as his expression slipped into resigned indifference.

Don't fight it? Fuck him.

This was breaking every natural law we had. Supes weren't allowed to mess with demon magic. It wasn't our place. Demons were different from us. Powerful. Dark. And these students weren't even willing. This was so wrong on so many levels. No wonder Spector was so fucking secretive. When the council found out about this, they'd all be executed.

Against my will, I felt my entire body relax. It felt unnatural, but my lips parted on a sigh. The tension around my eyes went away. My muscles stilled until they were unclenched, and I stood there with all defiance leaked out of me, just like the rest of my peers.

"That's better," Jones said with a smirk. His rustic voice grated against my skin.

The Spector elementals finally dropped their hands, eliminating the barrier since there was no need for it now. Then one by one, the rest of the Spector guards closed in around the ritual circle, stopping right outside of it. They clasped hands and then immediately started to chant. The words were foreign, spoken in a haunting, monotonous tone that made the hairs on the back of my neck raise up to attention.

Sarathess rythirite lamentous orelustimenum...and on it went.

My heart raced with each uttered syllable of their raised voices. I could feel the anxiety in the room from my classmates as they looked on in bland fear, like the expression couldn't fully reach the surface thanks to our compulsion.

The voices grew louder and louder, and wind that seemed to come from nowhere started whipping at my cheeks. It started as a soft breeze but picked up in intensity, tossing around my hair and dress as it raged around me.

Cheryl's blonde strands stuck to the gloss on her lips as

her body went limp. She fell against me, and I instinctively shot my arms out to catch her, trying to keep her from face planting. The other students had to squint as they endured the harsh breeze, holding their hands up in front of their faces as they tried to ward it off while we were stuck in the center of its cyclone.

The room began to shake, the wind tore through us, and still, the Spector guards kept on chanting.

"Don't let go! Keep going!"

I looked over, tears ripping away from my windblown eyes, and I saw one Spector man's face twisted up in pain. The other two on either side of him were struggling to keep hold of his hands, their muscles bunched and their eyes squeezed shut as they continued to speak in the demonic language that wasn't meant for their tongues.

The lights began to surge in and out. The ground began to shake. The smell of smoke permeated the air and filled my nose. In an instant, I felt a tugging sensation somewhere deep in my gut. The feeling was just a light nuisance at first, but then it grew more and more insistent until it felt like my entire body was being ripped in half. Students all around me started screaming.

It was fire and pure, burning pain.

Every cell, bone, tendon, and organ burned with a hellfire of excruciating pain that made my mouth crack open on my own blistering cry.

It ignited my veins and drowned me with punishing smoke that filled my lungs. Whatever ritual they'd done...they hadn't just brought demons here; it felt like they'd brought hell itself and shoved it down my throat. I was covered in smoldering suffering.

All at once, the floor opened up and flashes of black light shot up inside the pentagrams. It surrounded us, engulfing our bodies with dizzying darkness. Cheryl stared at me, struggling to stand, her eyes wide with fear. She backed away out of my hold, and when she opened her mouth to scream again, the blackness shoved itself down her throat, swallowing all sound.

And then I was suddenly surrounded by my own swathe of darkness, and everything else was blocked off until all I could see was him. Her. *It*.

A huge, sleek black body. Legs. A bloody hourglass. Frightening reflective eyes that stared back at me like they could burrow into my soul. A spider demon. A black widow here to kill me. It towered over me, its body made of that unnatural black light and billowing smoke.

There were other demon shapes crowded around the room, facing off with the others, but I only had eyes for mine. It crawled closer and closer, moving stealthily. It seemed frozen with graceful decision, and then without warning, became a blur of legs rushing toward me. It leaped, and I opened my mouth to scream, but it entered me before I could let out a single sound.

Its shadowy presence slammed through my chest, soaking into my body like water to a sponge. I felt it under every inch of my skin. I heard its legs creeping over my soul. It scurried across the recesses of my existence, and every syllable of the continued chant had the creature burrowing in deeper and deeper until there was no way to discern where I ended and it began.

I could feel the moment I wasn't myself anymore. There was an intense shock of endless pain and then nothing but hunger.

My body lifted up off the floor, and I felt my limbs flail around as the creature assimilated to me. I could feel the stretching of its presence filling me up from the tips of my fingers all the way to my toes.

A sharp jab of pain seared into the skin of my throat, and

then my body was tossed to the floor, making me land in a pitiful heap of heavy limbs and shock.

I dragged in a ragged breath and desperately blinked away the darkness from my vision. The chanting had stopped, though I had no idea when.

I sat up with a wince, my whole body trembling with the echoes of pain. I brought a hand to my tender throat and hissed in pain when I brushed against the skin there. It felt like I'd been marked with a searing-hot brand.

"Check them," I heard Hafferty say. "If a demon successfully possessed them, take them through the portal. Burn the others."

I tried to get to my feet, but I fell to my knees. I desperately looked around. Everyone was on the ground like me, but some of the students were struggling to get up, some were unmoving, and others...their bodies were convulsing. Black smoke was stuck around their skin, demons hovering over them like they'd been unable to sink inside.

A Spector woman stopped in front of me. Gripping my chin, she looked me over with a nod. "How do you feel?"

Even with the echoes of pain and my drained energy, one feeling was pushed to the forefront of my mind. "Hungry," I croaked. "So hungry."

But she wasn't even listening. She was already moving on to someone else. Students were being picked up and dragged away to a portal, while the others were left inside the circle to writhe on the floor.

I wanted to get up. To run, to fight, to do *something*, but I was so damn weak, and my head was so hazy that I felt like I was in a dream. All while this unfamiliar hunger was clawing up my throat like thorny vines, a deadly rose garden spreading from my chest. I ached to feed—but it didn't just feel like my thirst for blood. This felt different.

Gritting my teeth, I shoved the strange sensation away

just as Jones came forward and crouched in front of me, cocking his head to the side. His red eyes were zeroed in on my neck, and he smirked before reaching forward to lift me up. "Let's get you into the portal."

Before I could even attempt to shove him away, the windows suddenly shattered. Sound exploded around us as splinters of glass rained down.

What the fuck was happening now?

I was too weak to lift my arms to protect my face, and Jones jolted up, shouting. I felt the sharp shards of glass cut into my skin, heard screams and running footsteps all around me, but all I could do was stay huddled on the floor, trying to catch my breath.

Before the glass could finish falling, the violent wind was back, but with it was the sound of angry birds shrieking, their caws piercing my eardrums.

Lifting my head, I looked up and saw shadows streaking into the room, flying in from the windows. The black tendrils converged into hundreds—or maybe even thousands—of crows, their cries echoing off the walls.

The elementals started trying to fight them back with air barriers, but there were too many birds, and they hadn't stopped them in time. Even when they managed to push back half a dozen through the window, a hundred more were there to take their place.

So many crows flew inside that soon, I couldn't see past them. I felt them everywhere, every flap of a wing added to the hurricane of wind as their beaks and feathers and claws scraped against me. I was going to be suffocated by birds. I was choking on rising panic and feathers, trying to make sense of what the fuck was going on.

I turned my attention to Stiles, but he was fighting off birds, batting them away with his hands. The moment he swatted them away, they flinched and squawked then dropped dead on the floor.

What the fuck?

At the sound of an agonized scream, I turned to see one of the Spector men being completely overridden with crows. Every inch of his body was covered with them as they dug their claws into his skin and pecked at him with their beaks. His infested body flailed around until his cries turned to gurgles, and he was left twitching on the ground, the crows merciless as they continued to attack him.

A shot of fire suddenly cut off my view of the dying Spector man, and a blaze of heat licked across my face as a huge fireball landed three feet away from me. I crawled backwards, scrambling away from the flames, only to realize that it *wasn't* a fireball from an elemental. It was the necromancer student, and his entire body was ablaze.

He struggled to get to his feet from where he'd landed in front of me, his skin curling up with burned edges before growing back again as the destroyed flesh dripped off his slender body. The crows flapped their wings around him, but they weren't attacking him like they did the Spector man. If anything, it looked as if they were trying to put the flames out.

That sight, along with the realization that the crows weren't attacking me either, spurred me into action. I was going to use this interruption to get the fuck out of here.

"Motley!"

Stiles was at my side, pulling me to my feet in an instant, his suit ruined with bloodied holes and tears all over the fabric, and his face covered in nicks and scratches.

"Stiles—"

"We're under attack," he said, cutting me off.

I shook my head. "No, the crows are trying to *help* us. I need to get out of here."

Stiles looked at me like I was insane. "You're not leaving," he said.

I ripped my arms from his hold, staggering back. "You're delusional," I shouted at him. "They forced us to be possessed by *demons*! How can you be okay with this?"

He opened his mouth to argue, but a shrill scream cut him off. I used the distraction to turn and sprint away, only to smack into the red-eyed Jones. Crows were dive-bombing him, their black bodies hooked into his clothes as he kicked and swung at them to get away.

As soon as he saw it was me who'd run into him, he clamped a hand around my arm and started tugging me forward. "Get the rest through the portal now!" he shouted, though I had no idea if any of the Spector people heard him over the wind and birds.

I struggled to pull away from him, but he was strong. Much stronger than I in my current weakened state. He pushed us through the room, using me as a shield so that the crows wouldn't attack. I tried everything to get him to let go of me. I kicked, I punched—I even sunk my fangs into his hand where he was holding me. But nothing I did had him letting me go.

As we inched closer to the wall, I noticed the doorway had been turned into a portal, and there was a Spector man already tossing one of the other students through it.

Panic seized me. I couldn't let them take me. I knew that in the fiber of my bones. I may not know who sent these crows, but it was better than the people who had forced a demon possession on me.

Before he could drag me to the portal, I suddenly caught my heels on the floor and then made my entire body a dead weight. The move caught him off-guard, and it was just enough of a surprise for me to slam my foot on his toes and elbow him in the gut. A puff of air left his chest as he flinched and bent over. I wrenched my arm out of his grasp and started sprinting away.

"Catch her!" Jones's voice bellowed behind me.

The crows seemed to act with one mind, because they immediately converged around my body, blocking me from his view. Then, dozens of crows descended upon Jones, burrowing inside of his open mouth and traveling down his throat. They clawed and stuffed with a flurry of feathers until his stomach started to inflame like a balloon. I couldn't stop staring. Not when Jones's eyes rolled back. Not when crows started pecking out of his stomach, carrying his intestines and bits of flesh.

But then Stiles was in front of me, blocking my path. "Motley, you need to come with me."

I screeched to a stop, shaking my head wildly. "No."

"You really don't want to fight this," Stiles said, not reaching forward to grab me.

I just needed to get away. To flee. To hide. It was like the walls were closing in on me, and Stiles's pinning stare felt like chains.

The room was suddenly too hot, my racing breath too labored. The crows were shrieking too loudly, and there were too many moving parts. The demon thing inside of me was rising up, pushing against my skin, the feeling terrifyingly foreign and too powerful to contain. I looked down at my shaking hands and saw strings stuck to my palms.

"What?" I muttered to myself.

I tried to wipe them off, but more came back. Confused, I lifted a hand up in front of my face, zeroing in on a single silky strand at my index finger that looked like a splinter imbedded into my skin. I tugged at it, and my eyes widened when the string lengthened, feeding out from my fingertip in a never-ending spool. They weren't strings. They were...webs. And I was making them.

"What's happening to me?" I whispered.

I was too caught up in the fact that webs were falling from my fingers to notice the Spector guards rushing forward. Two of them came up behind me, lifting me away from Stiles's grasp. "No!" I screamed, flailing and kicking as I was held in the air and led toward the portal. "No, you can't take me! Don't let them take me, Stiles!" I cried, but he just watched them drag me away.

I opened my mouth to scream some more, my fangs descending all the way down, but a hand suddenly slammed over my mouth, and then a voice was in my ear.

"Go to sleep, bitch."

The world went black.

Chapter 4

HUNGER.

That was my new reality.

I was something...else now. Something I didn't fully understand. All I knew was the consuming hunger taking over my soul.

Aunt Marie once told me that the frenzy she felt during a bloodlust episode wasn't true hunger. It was an uncontrollable craving, and that craving was driven by the fear of starving—the fear of never feeling satisfied.

Fear. That's what spurred her uncontrollable bloodlust episodes. That's what made her slip away from reality and fall into an animalistic frenzy.

And for once in my life, I understood.

This craving and fear were new emotions for me, but they crept up my spine with every passing moment. Every step closer I got to death, the more my fear muddled my morals, and the more the craving took over.

When I'd first gotten to Spector, I cried. I wasn't a crier. I didn't ever drown in my own salty misery. But I couldn't stop the tears that came. I was drowsy and confused. Weak and utterly unlike myself. Trapped. Scared. And then the paranoia kicked in. I had no way out. No way of knowing what they'd do to me. No way of knowing what the *demon* would do.

I'd never felt so lonely in my life. I cried for help, for my aunt, Stiles, the devil—didn't matter. I just wanted someone to come.

And somewhere between the lonely silence of fear and craving, I lost myself.

I didn't know who I was.

I wasn't just Motley Coven anymore. No longer was I a simple Thibault student. I had two beings warring inside of me—my own soul and that of the demon.

I felt the spider burrowed down in the pit of my spirit. It moved and watched—a foreign sensation that was so strange the hairs on the back of my neck would stand straight up whenever she made her presence known.

I always thought of myself as astute and resourceful before, but now, I could barely form coherent thoughts. I was overridden with the spider's occupancy, and we were both overridden with insatiable hunger.

The dozens of blood bags at my feet were completely drained. My stomach sloshed from all the attempts at nourishment, reminding me that I'd had more than enough, making me question why the hell I was still starving.

And I *was* starving. It was a slow progression, hollowing me from the inside out with the idea of food while filling me with empty solutions because *nothing* worked.

Not food, not blood, not water, or pills. I was dying from starvation, and I had no idea what my body needed to stop it. And from the looks of things, neither did Spector, because they kept throwing blood and food at me, but none of it was what I needed.

I rolled around on the floor, pressing my sweaty face against the grooves in the cold concrete while willing my webs to appear at my fingertips. The strange ability had stopped days ago—or maybe it was weeks. I wasn't sure. Time was just a passing concept that left me behind.

I knew the demon inside of me was dying. My lack of webs was proof enough of that, and her devious presence had burrowed down deeper inside of me. I also knew with complete certainty that I was dying right alongside her. If this hunger wasn't satisfied soon, we'd shrivel up and cease to exist. Twin corpses held in one tomb.

The trap door to my small cell slid open, and another platter of blood and food was shoved at me with a single command:

Eat.

I opened my mouth to tell them that wasn't what I needed, but I stopped myself. They wouldn't listen, and I didn't know what I *did* need, so what was the point?

The worst thing about all of this was that a part of me welcomed death. If I was going down, at least Spector couldn't use the evil within me. But that felt...horrible. To give up, roll over, to lose the fight in your own spirit. It was so unlike myself, but I couldn't escape the weighted blanket of depression that covered me.

Hours and days and minutes and weeks passed by. Or maybe it was just seconds.

At some point, I started vomiting up blood. It was all over my clothes, staining my white hospital gown with bright red rejection. My body was failing, and I was helpless to stop it. So I just closed my crusty eyes and slept.

When I woke up next, I was in new clothes and my cell was clean. Spector liked to subtly remind me that they had complete control—that they were always watching. They changed my clothes while I slept. They decided when I ate and how much. They even pumped the vents with heady fumes, forcing me to sleep.

I wished they would just let me sleep forever.

"Get up," a gruff voice suddenly said, startling me.

I struggled to open my eyes and push myself up off the floor. My heavy head looked over as a tall man in a Spector uniform with a smattering of black hair falling down his back stepped inside my small room that felt more like a cage.

Well, this was new. No one had come into my cell the entire time I'd been here—at least not while I was awake. And despite the fact that I was sure I hadn't moved in days, his proximity did something to me. My fangs suddenly ached and dropped down. A single thread of silk fell from my pinky finger. The hunger hit me like a baseball bat to the gut as I pulled myself up to a sitting position.

Whoa.

Hunger slammed through me at his presence, but something else started to boil up right alongside it. Something alien. Something…sensual.

The guard's nostrils flared, and his eyes snapped over to me. He frowned as he scented me, a look of desire and wariness battling over his features.

My spider pushed out more of the strange power, as if trying to hook him. I was weak, and sharing a body felt clumsy, but the spider still managed. I could feel it coming out of my pores in soft waves of whispering breath. It felt carnal. When I saw the guard falter, his pupils dilating, I realized what she was doing. She was luring him.

The guard cleared his throat, visibly trying to stop himself from reacting to the pull. "Get up and follow me," he said, his foot shoving at my thigh.

"Where are you taking me?" I croaked, wondering when I'd last spoken.

"Get the fuck up," he demanded angrily, using his meaty hand to pick me up by my hair.

A yelp escaped me, fiery pain exploding in my scalp as he used his brutal hold to lift me up until I was standing on shaking legs.

I cried out, but my back arched as sudden arousal flooded me from his touch.

What the fuck?

My body's response to this strange man's cruelty horrified me, and I tamped it down. It was part of whatever lure power my spider was using. It had to be.

He shoved me out of the cell, and flickering lights in the hallway assaulted my vision. Doors lined each side, and screams could be heard echoing down the long, dreary corridor.

I tried to remember each turn and twist as we navigated the many cells. My exhausted feet could barely keep up, but the man's thick fingers stayed on my arm as he stomped down the hall. My panties were drenched, my skin was on fire, and my legs shook as my clit pulled at my attention, pulsing with need. I didn't understand what was happening to me, but my silent demon was aching to take control, aching to be filled, and more power pumped from my skin in waves of dark desire. I fought it so hard I started retching again.

Why was the demon doing this? Why lure him? And why was my body reacting this way?

The man gave me a withering glare as I gagged. "If you vomit blood on my boots, I'll make you clean it with your tongue. Now stand up straighter."

Holding a hand against my mouth, I did as he said, and he guided me to a set of double doors. After using his free hand to push them open, he yanked me forward and shoved me inside, closing them after me. I fell to my knees, the hard ground greeting me.

"Get off the floor," a demand called from across the vast room.

I blinked. Once. Twice. My tired blue eyes adjusted to the dark terror of the bright room. It was like the fluorescent lights overhead were my first glimpse of the sun after months of rain, but I wasn't disillusioned by the brightness. I knew the storm wasn't over.

I stood and rolled my shoulders back, like a soldier preparing for battle. I was so fucking weak I could barely keep my feet from collapsing beneath me, but pride was an old friend of mine. She helped me survive the life as a bastard vampire, hated by society, and I knew she'd help me survive whatever Spector had planned too.

The room was stark and cold, with equipment lined against the walls and the tall ceilings that made me feel small. It was also separated by what looked like bullet-proof glass, and behind it, a group of six men sat at a long table, observing me like fish in a tank.

I recognized one of them.

Blond hair. Handsome, stern features. Polished suit and downturned lips. Blue eyes that matched my own.

My father.

He looked at me like I wasn't even worth the glance.

"Come forward, Miss Coven," one of the other men ordered. He was older, sporting a lab coat. Salt and pepper hair filled his head, and a pair of thick spectacles were perched low on his nose as he read from a stack of papers on the desk.

I reluctantly obeyed. My feet dragged with each step, but I moved closer to the men responsible for everything that had happened.

"Get on with it," my father said.

The man nodded. "Case six-two-seven has been eating

regularly and ingesting blood. We've upped her feeding by three hundred percent, but our nightly analysis shows that she is getting weaker. Our research and development team have even tried supplying her with our new trial of synthetic blood. It doesn't appear to be making any difference. Her vampire side is nourished, but her demon side is…"

"She's dying?" someone else asked.

My father stared pointedly at me. "Indeed. Look at her, she's withering away. Starving."

"Yes," the scientist replied. "We hypothesize that at the current rate she's going, she'll be dead within a week, possibly sooner."

My father wrinkled his nose, as if the news of my demise was distasteful. "Such a shame. Not that I'm surprised. She's a bastard vampire from a weak mother, is she not?"

Fury shook in my hands. How fucking dare he?

I was about to open my mouth and spill the truth about exactly whose blood ran through my veins, but before I could, he stood up and grabbed his coat, placing it over his arm with dignified indignation before addressing his colleagues. "I have a meeting to attend. Let me know if she dies."

And then he was gone. Flashed away, just like that.

No care or worry. No concern over his own flesh and blood. I was just as easily tossed away now as I'd been when I was an infant. Every time our lives intersected, it was always the same.

If I weren't so exhausted and drained, a glimmer of pain at his words would have bounced within my chest. But the hunger I so desperately despised was my savior.

Fuck him. I didn't want to give him the satisfaction of being hurt or disabused. I wanted him to be nothing to me, as much as I was nothing to him.

So I took up all the shattered pieces of my pride and molded it together by focusing on my ravenous need.

But now I knew a startling truth. My father, the great Rylon Stiles, was involved with Spector. He was now responsible for ruining my life *twice*.

There was a time when I thought I needed to forgive my father for abandoning me and leaving me without a name or a purpose. Sometimes, the only way to move forward was to let go of the things that broke you down. I used to think that the only path to peace would involve forgetting the things my father had done. But I saw now, I would never matter to him, so why bother? I just got a tangible reminder of how deep his apathy for me went. Forgiveness and forgetfulness were for fools. Now, there was only revenge. Now, there was only my spider.

"So what do you suggest?" the other man boredly asked, as if my survival was inconsequential to him.

My spider hissed within me, breaking past my lips with venomous hatred. I brought my fingers up to my lips, surprised at the outburst when for so long she'd been silent.

"We know that she's a black widow demon based on the hourglass mark on her throat and the webs she's made. We're hypothesizing that her demonic nature may need to feed through living entities, rather than through blood bags."

"That's the theory, anyway," the man in the lab coat said.

My hand flew up to my throat, and I tried to feel for the mark they claimed I had. I did remember feeling intense burning pain at the ritual, but I had brushed it off as being burned from some of the fire that was lobbed around the room. Taking advantage of the expensive metal machines in the room, I padded toward them, ignoring the men who droned on. I stopped in front of the shiny stainless steel and leaned in, catching my reflection.

And...wow, okay. I didn't look so hot.

My usually vibrant red hair hung in dull, tangled knots. My skin was so pale I looked sickly, and I had dark circles under my eyes, and my cheeks looked hollowed. But right there, in the dead center of the front of my neck, was a small red mark of a perfectly shaped hourglass.

So it was true. I really had become a black widow.

I was brushing my finger against the spot when the doors behind me suddenly opened. I turned to see a human male being shoved inside. He was handsome, with short dark hair and crisp brown eyes, probably in his late twenties, and there were steel cuffs wrapped around his wrists. His body writhed as he fought and searched the room for an escape, shivering as beads of sweat dripped down his face. He lunged for the doorway, but he was too slow. The door clicked shut, locking him inside with me.

My fangs dripped with venom at the sight of him while his fingers scrabbled along the cracks in the door, as if he could pry it back open. My spider rose to the surface, and I was helpless to stop the crashing vulturine appetite making every muscle in my body flex.

"We think she is a higher level demon that requires a different approach to feeding. She has predator-like tendencies, according to our tests. Let's observe if a live feed is what she requires," I heard the scientist say, but his droning words seemed like whispers against the roaring of my soul. More lure power was growing out of me like nectar for the bees.

The man finally turned to look, and when he saw that it was just me in the room with him, his panic faltered—but just for a moment. He may have seen a weak, small girl, but his intuition knew better. That was why, even as he stopped trying to get the door to open, his eyes were looking around wildly for another means to escape.

My body moved toward him like I was sleepwalking. Each step closer, I could smell the fear rolling off of him in delicious waves of ecstasy. My spider was controlling my movements, her hunger roaring to the surface and pushing all other coherent thoughts out of my head.

Need. Hungry. Must feed. Weak.

I positioned my body in front of the man, my head tilting to the side in an animalistic move. My fangs gnawed on my lips, my blood coating my chapped lips.

Whatever expression he saw on my face, it told him that he was right. He should fear me.

"Don't hurt me," he begged.

I lifted my hand to stroke his cheek, and he flinched but didn't otherwise move. My webs came out, stringing across his jaw and lips as I trailed my fingers along.

"Little fly, why do you cry?" a haunting voice asked from my chest, caressing his ears with the dark declaration of evil in my soul.

"What's wrong with you?" he asked, while looking over my shoulder to stare at our audience behind the glass. I didn't like his attention on someone else, I wanted him wholly consumed with me.

My hand gripped his scratchy cheeks, forcing his head forward. Mmm, very handsome for a human. "Look at me. *See me.* I'd like to drink from your lips."

He blinked, his brown eyes confused. "What? I—"

The sensual power that my demon wielded suddenly burst from my body in an explosion of need. Pheromones pumped in the air, releasing a deadly lure that was too strong to resist. The man's pupils suddenly dilated. His breath caught on a groan. His dick hardened in his pants.

And just like that, I caught him.

He relaxed at my touch as my power flooded his system. I reached for his shirt and slowly ripped it from his body before sinking to my knees to unbuckle his pants.

Harsh breaths could be heard around the room, as well as

the observing men murmuring about what I was doing. My humanity screamed that this was wrong. So, so, terribly, inconceivably wrong. But I couldn't stop.

"Wh-what are you—"

"Stop talking," I demanded before pulling out his hard length. I stroked it, licking my lips at the sight of precum coating his cock.

His mouth slammed shut as he rolled his head back in ecstasy. My touch was lazy and lacked enthusiasm, but he behaved as if it was the best damn touch he'd ever felt.

When his moan echoed off the walls of the large room, I stood up and shoved at his chest, knocking him down to the ground with a playful grin. It felt like I was toying with him, teasing him for our audience to rev them up for the real show. My skin was on fire, burning for a single touch as I slipped out of my hospital gown, leaving nothing but my bare body to the room.

Everything was a mass of confusion and demonic hunger. It was clear that my spider was in total control.

"Whoa," he croaked, hands automatically coming up to knead my breasts. I positioned myself on top of his cock, sliding my slick folds along his hardness as I bent over to suck on his ear, earning another groan from him.

That dark voice from my mouth returned with a vengeance. "You're going to die, my prey. But it's going to be such a sweet death."

With that serving as my warning, I sunk onto his length and simultaneously lashed out to sink my fangs deep into his neck. I fed like the dying woman I was—without shame, without remorse. I claimed my need to survive with a vengeance, while he moaned at the lusty vampiric venom flooding his system and lure power stunning his senses.

"Yes," my demon's voice breathed.

This. This was what we needed. This was what we'd been hungry for.

I felt it as soon as he penetrated me—a sliver of a tether flaring from his soul. His thread shimmered with vitality, and I knew instinctively that it was his life's essence. My spider lashed out, grabbing onto it, and then she tugged. And just like that, we began to feed.

She pulled and pulled on that thread, sucking it like a straw as we drank from his soul. She consumed violently and without pause, demolishing the scrap of light in his eyes as she continued to ride him.

My demon tugged on his existence, even while our audience watched, even while my humanity screamed against how wrong this was. Even as my heart broke into the realization of what I already knew.

I was a monster. A deadly, carnal, wicked monster.

While my demon fed from his essence, I fed from his neck. I drank until there was nothing left in his body, and I was just slurping on thinned veins and an empty heart. He didn't even fight. The lure and venom I'd pumped into him was too strong.

I knew the exact moment I'd drained him dry—both of blood and his essence. A new vivacity filled me up as she pulled out the last of his essence, and then the deadly spider sighed in pleasure.

I pulled off his body, ruby blood coating my breasts as I hummed in satisfaction. My spider was still in control, because if it were me holding the reins to this train wreck, I would have been sobbing on the floor.

When she looked up at the row of men watching behind the glass, she smiled, revealing her massive, sharp fangs.

"Of course," one of the men whispered in awe, like my display of raw, sexual power excited him. "She's a black widow. Sexual cannibalism."

The other men watched me with new wariness blotting their features. "So what does she need?" another asked.

I picked up the metal chains still wrapped around my prey's wrists and crushed them in my fist, displaying a level of strength I'd never had before.

"More," my spider replied darkly. "I need *more*."

Chapter 5

EVERY TIME I FED, I lost a little bit more of myself.

My spider was ravenous. She claimed without remorse or shame.

It was terrifying.

Sex used to be an empowering act that I felt in control over. It didn't matter who I was or where I'd come from, we were just fighting bodies looking to get off.

But now it felt clinical. Crowds of Spector employees watched while delivering humans to me on a silver platter. There was nothing romantic or exciting about it. Data was collected and skewed. My body's responses were noted. Each soul I fed from left me wanting more. My nature led to nonconsent. It was either me or them, and the darker side of my spider made me choose myself. I was helpless to stop her. I was helpless to stop Spector.

I grew to hate the sound of their clapping at the subtle displays of strength my spider exhibited under their watchful eye. I could feel my body slowly grow more toned, more vibrant with life that didn't belong to me. I felt invincible but destructive.

As a female vampire, I'd always loved sex. When my dark thoughts drifted, I couldn't help but wonder if I'd been possessed by the black widow demon because of that fact. Did she inhabit me because we both shared a propensity for carnal ecstasy? I didn't know, but I hated it. I hated that sex couldn't simply be fun anymore. It was a necessity to survive, and I'd been turned into a sexual cannibal who lured partners in so that I could drain them dry.

"Get up," my guard demanded as he opened the door to my cell.

I was lazily lying on the concrete floor, fading in and out of control. It was a constant tug of war, the battle of our wills. I knew what she needed, and the taste of her sin was too delicious to resist. It filled me with shame.

"I've already fed today," I argued.

Their demands were getting more brutal. The last several days, I'd been forced to feed from six humans. Their faces were a blur of necessity. I became accustomed to the act of carnal destruction, and it terrified me.

Not one of the humans had survived.

"Get up," he ordered again, this time with more force.

Webs spilled from my hands in angry tendrils as I stood. It was still a strange sensation, like water dripping from inside my fingertips. They extended in gossamer threads, the strands tugging from my skin and spooling out of me in directions I had total control of. Though they seemed soft and fragile, they were actually strong and easily manipulated. They felt like an extension of me, ready to do whatever I wanted them to.

The guard grabbed my arm, like he did every time he came to collect me, but this time I jerked free, my new strength aiding in my efforts. His eyes widened in a flash of shock before twisting into anger.

"Listen, bitch—" he growled, but I cut him off.

"Unless you want me to feed from you the way I feed from those humans, then don't touch me," I threatened.

It was immensely satisfying to see the pulse in his neck jump.

"You'll be punished if you step out of line," he replied, his expression stormy. "You don't get to make threats here."

I ignored his words. "Keep your fucking hands to yourself before I break them."

In response, he shoved me hard, making me fall to the floor on my hands and knees. Pain shot through me at the impact.

"That's where you belong," he spat, looking down at me with disdain. "You're just a Spector pet. A dog learning new tricks. You need to be trained how to behave."

Motherfucker.

My anger snapped. I flashed back to my feet faster than he could track. He blinked in surprise at seeing me standing right in front of him again, but before he could move, I shoved him against the wall and shot webs from my fingers, covering his torso and sticking him into place.

"What the—?"

He tried to jerk away, but my strings were too strong, the sticky threads trapping him against the wall.

My lips spread with a smirk. "Look. I learned a new trick."

My spider was taunting him, while I was begging from the sidelines for her to behave. I wasn't sure what Spector was willing to do for obedience, but I didn't want to find out.

Despite how hard he tried to get away, the webs cemented him to the wall, holding him there. I smiled in amusement until flames erupted from his skin. An elemental? I rolled my eyes. It was almost too easy.

My webs moved to wrap around his neck, squeezing until the veins in his head popped. I could see his fear as I tried to direct his flames to the trap snaring him and cutting off his oxygen supply. He didn't attack me directly, though, which told me he wasn't allowed to.

I leaned in closer until my lips were at his ears. "I think you realize who's stronger now, don't you?" I asked as his face began to grow purple. "And it's obvious that the only obedient Spector dog here is *you*. So keep your hands to yourself."

He nodded slowly, as if submitting was hurting his male ego. I immediately retracted my webs in a single flourish. They snapped back toward my palms like a rubber band being released. The guard fell on his knees to the floor, coughing and taking in rugged breaths.

"Good boy," I said with a shit-eating smirk.

I chuckled darkly and turned, making my way down the hallway without waiting. I'd been shoved through this maze of a building so many times that I knew how to get to the rooms they brought me to, I just didn't know which way led out.

I heard him scramble to his feet and rush forward to catch up to me, but when I stopped at the doors leading to the lab room, he cut me off. When he automatically moved to grab me, he blanched before dropping his hand again. Smart man.

"Not today," he said with a shake of his head. "You get to interact with the other hybrids. You're permitted to eat in the cafeteria today," he said, while leading me down the corridor.

He took a couple turns, and then I was being led through a set of sliding glass doors I'd never been to before.

"Eating what?" I asked warily.

"Just blood and food. You're not allowed to fuck anyone outside of the lab," he clarified. "Especially not the demon-hybrids. They're far too valuable."

The fact that they saw humans as invaluable left a bitter taste in my mouth. They were so callous. They didn't give a shit that every time I fucked and fed, I was ending someone's life.

"Noted," I replied stiffly before walking into the room.

The moment I walked through the doors and looked around, a nasally voice stopped me. "Motley! Oh my gods, you look just positively *awful!*"

I blinked with a heavy sigh. I'd forgotten just how grating that annoying voice could be.

I'd also forgotten that Cheryl was even here. I'd been stuck in my own little prison, most of my time spent in pain and starvation, so I'd forgotten about the others. It almost scared me how I hadn't thought of the other students once since arriving here. I was a loner through and through.

"How do you have real clothes? They just keep dressing me in hospital gowns," I said as she strutted up to me in skinny jeans and a flowy top.

Cheryl was practically glowing. Her eyes were bright, and her hair seemed shinier than usual. It was like she'd spent the last month at the spa. "You like? It's not my usual, but Stiles got it for me. I was getting really tired of those gowns. The color really washed me out."

I stiffened at the mention of Stiles, but she didn't notice.

"I guess the hospital gown thing doesn't really matter for you," she went on, looking me up and down. "You never did care about how you looked. But for goodness sakes, Motley, would it kill you to run a brush through your hair?"

"Oh, I'm sorry that I'm not glamorous enough for you. I've been kind of busy being held prisoner by Spector and forced to do fucked up things while they took away my free will," I deadpanned.

Cheryl nodded, smoothing down her blonde bob. "It's alright. I'll go ask one of the guards to get you something. They're always *very* helpful for me," she beamed mischievously.

"Eww." I gagged at the implication.

She turned and flitted away, leaving me to look around the sparse space of the depressing cafeteria.

I saw a few Thibault supes sitting around, eating from plastic trays, but most of the people inside I didn't know. There were only a couple dozen or so, but the thought that all of us here were probably possessed by demons wasn't a comforting feeling.

"Here."

I flinched in surprise as a woman with a hairnet and a white uniform shoved a tray of food into my arms. I was barely able to catch it before it could tumble onto the floor. I looked down, finding blood stew with floating pieces of meat and potatoes in it, and some kind of pudding. I think.

"Uhh. Thanks?"

The woman was already walking away, disappearing into the back room that had to be the kitchen.

There were plenty of empty tables to choose from, so I picked the one closest to the exit. It didn't escape my notice that there were Spector guards stationed around the walls, watching all of us carefully. It also didn't escape my notice that some of the other Thibault vamps were eyeing me, obviously surprised to see I'd survived.

Ignoring them, I lifted the spoon to my mouth, taking a bite. The bloody stew wasn't the best I'd had, but it wasn't the worst either. I sipped it slowly, my shoulders tense as I tried to gain my footing. I guess everyone just...hung around here? While I'd been dying in starving misery, they'd been getting clean clothes and eating food in here and talking to each other. They'd been going on as if this was just another extension of Thibault Academy.

"So you *did* survive, Motley," a voice said, just as the three douche vamps plopped their asses on the benches beside me. Byron took the seat directly across from me.

For fuck's sake. First Cheryl and now them? Couldn't I catch a break?

"Yep," I said, slurping more stew and praying he'd go away.

"Damn. I lost two hundred bucks," Byron said with a chuckle. He exchanged a look with his friends. "I thought for sure that low blooded vamps would be culled through this shit."

Offended anger tensed my spine. I felt my spider curl up within me, like it was crouching and ready to pounce. But I didn't need my new demon bodyguard to handle these pricks.

"I may be low blooded, but Spector kept me locked up for longer because I was too dangerous. Too *powerful*," I stressed. "They seem to think I can handle it now, but…" I allowed my voice to drift off, letting the implications of my statement hang in the air long enough for his eyes to widen.

Byron really was a dumbass. He got off on making people feel inferior, but when push came to shove, he was a gigantic pussy.

"You're lying," he argued. "They just didn't want someone like you mingling with us. I have a higher level demon, you know."

Within me, I could feel my spider bristle with amusement, like she knew there was no merit to his words.

"Oh, they didn't want me mingling, alright," I replied with a smirk. "They were too afraid I'd kill you all. Maybe I should prove them right?" I asked before leaning closer, letting webs form in my hands.

His charcoal eyes zeroed in on the ropes of silk that danced from my fingertips and started slithering toward him across the table like a snake. He reared back, his gaze fearful when he felt them start to wrap around his legs. A flash of him suffocating danced across my mind, and I knew exactly what my spider had in mind.

But of course, the other two asshats had to intervene.

One second, I was creating a cocoon around Byron's body, planning to constrict the fuck out of him, and the next, there was a shove at my back, and my face was being slammed down onto the table. My tray went skittering across the slippery surface, bloody broth sloshing as my cheek was pressed hard against the table.

"Stop doing that, you fucking crazy bitch!" Byron's buddy hissed in my ear. He and his friend were holding me down hard, but they were trying to be quiet so that the guards wouldn't intervene.

I was about to move my hands to shoot webs around *their* fucking necks, when I heard a familiar sound.

The noise of shrieking crows exploded around us, and then I felt a new presence at my back.

"Get your fucking hands off her."

The voice was low. Deadly. Totally unfamiliar. And yet, my spider exulted.

One second, I was being held down, and the next, the sharp claws and unyielding limbs were torn away from my body. I sat up, panting, and when I looked over, I saw a man covered in shadows and crows.

As soon as my eyes locked onto his piercing violet eyes, my breath caught in my chest. But not in a way like I was startled or overcome. It was like something inside of me—inside of my spider—erupted.

He had vibrant blue hair. A dark five o'clock shadow over his strong jaw stood out against his smooth pale skin. Crows dissolved and reformed from shadows to feathers right before my eyes as he stood there staring down at me.

"*You*," I breathed, unable to look away.

He was the one who'd brought the crows to Spector's ritual. I knew that with certainty.

Byron was furiously ripping webs off his body, while his friends were behind me, batting away crows.

In seconds, six guards were there, breaking it up. The guy that came to my rescue didn't look fussed that the guards were threatening to lock us up in solitary for a month. He just smiled at me with a secret promise I didn't understand. And my spider? She fucking *sighed*, like seeing this dude was the best damn thing to happen to her since the first time we'd fed.

I didn't get it.

"You know the rules, Crow," one of the guards told him, taking a step forward with a thick black baton like he was ready to thump my rescuer over the head.

"Yeah, yeah. No powers in the common areas. Maybe if you were doing your job, I wouldn't have had to intervene," he said with a roll of his eyes. "They were hurting her."

The guards glanced at me, but I bristled. "I was handling it," I argued.

Crow's lips twitched in amusement. "Sorry for interrupting, then."

The head guard was typing on his tablet, likely alerting the Spector leaders that there had been a fight.

"No powers," he said with a resounding warning. "You use your powers again, and it'll be solitary and no food as punishment."

I cringed at the idea of starving. I never wanted to feel that empty, desolate nothingness again. It was a slow sort of torture, to waste away, and I had every intention of doing whatever necessary to avoid that.

The guards walked off, leading Byron and the others away until it was just the two of us.

"Well, you know my name is Crow. What's yours?" the hot blue-haired man asked as he held out his hand.

"Motley," I replied as our skin touched. A slight shiver

traveled up my spine, and I watched in awe as his eyes flashed red for a brief moment.

"Don't use your powers, remember?" he said, his gaze slipping down to our joined hands. To my surprise, tender, intricate lace had spread from my fingertips and wound around his wrist.

Embarrassed, I yanked my hand back before my spider could make any more. "Sorry," I mumbled.

Something about him had my fangs aching. I noted the scar on his upper lip and the way he looked like he hadn't slept in weeks. He was wearing simple black sweatpants and a black shirt, both with the Spector logo on them like everyone else seemed to be wearing. Well, everyone except Cheryl and me. For some reason, when I looked in Crow's violet eyes, there was a sense of familiarity in his stare. I found myself leaning forward, wanting to take his hand again and press my head against his chest, which was just fucking weird.

"Motley! I got you this!"

Cheryl suddenly appeared, slightly breathless, and shoved Crow out of the way to force a pile of clothing into my arms. I looked down and picked up the pieces with pinching fingers. "Uhh…"

Bubblegum pink lingerie, something that I was pretty sure was a cape, and bell-bottom jeans is what I had to choose from. "Seriously?"

She shrugged. "Well, I may have picked through the pile first," she admitted. "But I'm sure that cape thing could be used for a nice wraparound dress."

Crow reached over her and plucked up the pink lace. "This needs a try-on at least," he said with a smirk.

Blushing, I snatched it back from him, bundling the fabric up in my hands.

"Well?" Cheryl pressed, staring at me.

"Well what?"

She sighed. "A thank you would suffice."

Was she serious? She kept looking at me expectantly. *Oh, yep. She was serious.*

"Thank you *sooooooo* much," I replied in an overly exaggerated voice.

"You're welcome," she said primly, before flashing away again.

I shoved the clothing onto the bench before turning back to Crow. "It was you and your birds who broke into the ritual," I said, looking around to make sure we weren't being overheard.

He nodded, brushing off a crow that had landed on his shoulder. "It was."

"Why? I mean, why did you do that?"

"Because I want Spector to burn to the fucking ground," he said evenly, not even trying to be quiet about it.

My eyes darted around to the guards nervously, but if they heard him, they didn't seem to care. Huh. I guess Crow was often vocal about his distaste of Spector.

"So you're a...crow demon?"

A grin stretched across his face. "Something like that."

I watched him carefully, and for some reason, I felt desire start to rise from my gut. I shouldn't need to feed again. Not after the constant stream of humans they'd been bringing me. But for some reason, Crow was making my spider hungry.

I mean, *really* fucking hungry. I needed to shut that shit down.

"So," I began with a cough while taking a step backward. I was starting to think that being here with the others was dangerous. Something was seriously wrong with my spider. Would she ever be satisfied? Or would I always crave *more*? "Does everyone meet up here every day to eat?

They've been keeping me in my glorified dog crate this entire time."

"People have been slowly joining the group. Once they think you have a good hold on your demon, they let you play with the others," Crow explained while looking me up and down. "Sometimes it takes others longer, depending on how dangerous they are."

"How many are left?" I asked, while looking around the room.

"Some didn't survive. Some I suspect are still in their own glorified dog crates," Crow answered. "But don't be disillusioned by this mandated group time. This entire building is still a cage. Just bigger."

He leaned even closer to me, and I breathed him in as his haunting words fluttered over me. He was absolutely right. This *was* a cage. We were stuck answering to Spector's whims. The number of dead bodies in the training room because of me was proof enough of that. But I was in survival mode. I didn't trust myself out in the world right now. It was easy to blame Spector for the terrible things I'd done, but when it came time to feed on my own terms, I wasn't sure the last strands of my morality could handle the decisions I had to make if I were out there on my own.

That harsh realization made me bristle. Why the fuck was I flirting with this guy? He was hot, yeah, but with my new demon involved, there was no way I could ever act on my interests. I would never be able to fuck for fun again. I'd never be able to find someone I liked and share intimacy with them. I'd have a lifetime of partners and a full belly, but I'd never have love.

"I should go back to my room. I'm not really hungry," I muttered.

I started to walk away, only to feel him following me. "What are you doing?" I asked, turning around.

He skidded to a stop, frowning like he hadn't even realized he'd been trailing me. "Er, nothing," he said, scratching at the back of his scruffy blue hair.

"You were following me."

"I..." His frown deepened when he noticed one of his crows suddenly flap over and land on my shoulder.

I stiffened, my blue eyes going wide. I was not a fan of birds. Outside, fluttering around all singsong and shit was fine. But any time people kept birds for pets, it kind of freaked me out. Plus, now the crows were sort of tied to the ritual, and I was pretty sure I had PTSD from that.

"Get it off!" I hissed, too afraid to move.

Crow ignored my panic, cocking his head at his bird. "Interesting."

"What's interesting? Did it shit on me or something?" I turned my head to look, but the thing pecked lightly at my ear—not hard, but like it was giving me a playful nip. An embarrassing little squeal escaped me, and I snapped my head back to face front. "Crow..."

The bird hopped closer along my shoulder, and then the damn thing thrust its beak against my hair. "Is it...*nuzzling* me?"

Crow's eyes crinkled at the side, and he let out a laugh. "Shit, I think it is."

"Tell it to stop!"

"You don't understand," he said, shaking his head. "My crows don't like other people. Ever. They tolerate those who are around me that pose no threat. But I've never seen them act like this."

Before he'd even finished his sentence, I suddenly had three more birds landing on me. One by one, they hopped over my shoulders, their beaks nipping at my hair, cawing playfully as they ruffled their smoky feathers. And all the while, Crow was just watching it all, with a mix of fascination and amusement.

Obviously, I'd get no help from him.

Reaching up, I grabbed a bird in each hand and dropped them on his shoulders. The other two, I brushed off me in a shooing motion, and they cawed at me and landed on the ground with something that sounded like disappointment.

"Stay," I ordered, pointing at them where they were gathering at my feet. There were more of them gathering around, and they were looking at me like I was a shiny new birdfeeder they wanted to nest on.

Before they could decide to take up permanent residence in my red hair, I slowly backed away to the doorway. I had a feeling that if I showed them my back, they'd pounce.

"Oomph."

My back hit a body, and I turned to see the same guard who'd escorted me here. "Done already?"

"I think that's enough mingling for me today," I said with a nod.

He grunted and gestured for me to walk ahead, and then he led me down the hall toward my room.

I looked back once, seeing a dozen or so birds watching me as I went. A flock of crows was called a murder, so the fact that I seemed to have them as a fan club did not seem like a good omen.

As we rounded a corner, my steps skidded to a stop when a booming noise ripped in the air in front of me, followed by a gravelly, inhuman shout.

I screamed and ducked as a door three feet away from me was suddenly exploding open in metal splinters, a body made of black stone careening out of it and landing hard against the wall on the other side. The plaster cracked where his body fell against it, but before the black-stoned man could get to his feet, Spector guards were on him. Vines appeared from nowhere and wrapped around his unyielding body as earth elementals trapped his limbs and pinning him to the floor.

With another shout, the man punched his fist into the ground, making the entire floor shake with his fury. I scrambled for purchase, throwing my arms out to catch myself as I fell to my knees. The movement made his head snap over to look at me, and then a surge of power and hunger rose up inside of me as our eyes locked.

Out of my control, webs shot from my fingertips and wrapped around the guards.

And this wasn't the usual few strands that slowly worked their magic. This was like five thousand strands immediately hooking onto the guards and swathing them in the silky ropes. They were thicker than usual—and from the way the guards were struggling to break them free—they were stronger too. *Much* stronger.

"Oh shit," I breathed, as power lashed out of me, sending more and more webs to his attackers, watching the guards drop like...well, flies in a web.

When the guard behind me made a choking sound, I noticed that some of my webs had come for him, too. They were wrapping around his neck like a noose, ready to hang him from the ceiling.

Well, that escalated quickly.

A screeching sound made me drop to my knees, its high pitched shriek making pain lance through my system like thick knives. My webs immediately receded as my head sliced with pain.

"Enough, Cheryl. Thank you for your assistance," a bored voice called at my back as the sound was cut off. I turned my body with excruciating steadiness as I faced the source of my pain. Cheryl was standing with blushing cheeks and downcast eyes, and one of the scientists stood there beside her, removing noise-blocking headphones.

"Tomb, it's as if you *want* to be locked up," he said with a roll of his eyes while walking up.

His black shoes clicked on the ruined marble tile, stepping over webs and pieces of plaster as he approached. I looked up at him with tear-stained eyes when he stopped in front of me.

"Oh, Miss Coven. I see you were involved in this little hissy fit too," he said, tsking under his breath at all the webs the guards were still tearing away from their bodies. "You and Mr. Tomb here seem to have a problem with cooperating, so you both can spend a few days without food in the tank."

"But...you and I both know what happens..." my voice trailed off as I glanced at the guards and the stone man at the end of the hall. "When I get hungry."

The scientist smiled even more broadly, showing me that he didn't give two fucks about my ravenous spider and her needs. "I've seen firsthand what happens when you're hungry, Miss Coven. I always enjoy the show."

I felt wave after wave of disgust hit me like a punch to the gut.

This entire experience was so incredibly violating. I could try to convince myself that it was just feeding, that it was just a necessary transaction where others paid with their life so I could live. But there was something sinister and foul in the scientist's hungry gaze that made me feel sick to my stomach. It was me on full display, and they were getting off on it. And now, they were willing to risk another hybrid like me to study me even more. To punish us for defending ourselves.

Guards swarmed in on me, but I didn't put up a fight. If I was going to have a chance at not feeding off the strange stone man's life essence, I needed to preserve all the energy I had left.

Chapter 6

THE TANK WAS NAMED APPROPRIATELY. It was probably a bit larger than my cell room, but it felt even more isolating. The shape of a capsule, it was buried deep under the winding halls of Spector, and took thirty minutes to get to. The human side of me hated it.

But my spider? She felt right at home, enjoying the seclusion *and* the company.

Tomb was brooding in the corner, looking at me like I was a rock in his boot. I couldn't help but stare, though. He was completely naked, nothing but chiseled stone muscles for as far as the eye could see.

And a cock, of course. I know I should've been mostly concerned about the protruding, hard, scary-big cock staring me in the face, but I was trying to be mature in this weird situation and not put all of my attention on his rather impressive appendage. I found myself way too curious about it. Like...did he jack off while he was in his solid stone form? *Could* he jack off? Did his cum come out like sand?

See? Way too curious.

"You might as well sit and get comfortable," he said in a

gruff voice. I hadn't even realized I was pacing the floors until he'd said that.

"How long do they usually keep people in here?" I asked before placing my back against the wall and slinking down it until I was a pile of frustrations on the floor.

He shrugged a shoulder, the harsh light glinting off his body. "However long they like."

I studied him, wondering why the hell my spider had this urge for me to slide closer. "So you've been put in here before? They must *really* like you," I said sarcastically.

Tomb grinned, which was a somewhat odd look coming from a walking, talking statue. "They're gonna *really* like you too now. You probably shouldn't have shot webs at them. Best you choose more carefully next time before fighting alongside me."

"I don't care who it is. If they're fighting against Spector, I'll fight with them," I said vehemently. "Besides, my spider kind of acted for me. I wasn't in total control."

My admission made him twist his head in contemplation. "The webs kind of gave you away for being a spider hybrid, but I'm curious. What kind of spider are you?"

I hesitated, not knowing what I should tell him. I should probably warn the guy who he was trapped in a room with, but I also didn't want to have him hate me. It was nice having someone to talk to. So unlike my lonely time at the academy.

Besides, he really did look like a chiseled statue of masculine perfection. Every line of him was purposeful and handsome, all hard angles and smooth features. I wanted to enjoy his company for a little while at least, without him looking at me like the monster I was.

"What kind of demon did they put in you?" I asked, turning the subject around on him.

For a moment, I thought he wasn't going to answer me,

but then he shrugged. "I was an earth elemental. The gargoyle demon latched onto me right away. I suppose it was a congenial attachment, since we both have power over soil and stones."

My eyes swept over his body. "A gargoyle, huh? That makes sense. So can you turn back, or are you always..." I trailed off, not knowing if that sounded rude.

"Am I always solid stone?" he asked with a smirk.

I nodded my head, and then his body rippled with change. His once solid onyx mass changed to smooth, dark skin. His cock was still hard, heavy and full against his hip, and I had to snap my eyes away from him before I humiliated myself.

"Neat trick," I said.

"Hmm. It has its perks."

I ignored the obvious one jumping against his leg. "You mean like smashing out of your cell and tossing around the guards like they're rag dolls?"

"Yes. But I'm sure they'll make me pay for it during *training*," he said with obvious disgust.

"What sort of training?" I asked.

"They like to see how impenetrable my skin is. It started with knives. Needles. Poison. Then guns. Rockets."

My mouth dropped open in shock. "Does it hurt?" I asked.

"What do you think?" he gruffly replied. "Just because my skin is stone, doesn't mean I don't feel."

They were torturing him. Fucking *torturing* him.

"I'm so sorry."

"Why? Is it you doing all those things to me?"

I looked at him, horrified. "No, of course not."

"Then you have nothing to apologize for, beautiful."

I blinked in surprise at him calling me *beautiful*. No one had ever called me that before, and I was almost pissed that it was wasted on such a dour moment. I was in a white hospital gown stained with bloody broth from the cafeteria, my hair was knotted, and I had chapped lips and webs stuck all over me. I did not, in any way, look *beautiful*.

But still. It was nice to hear.

"We have to get out of here," I mumbled, but there was no power in my words. Our situation felt dismal at best, and I didn't think there was a way out of it.

"Yeah, that's not going to happen," he said, echoing my thoughts. "The best you can hope for is a few days in the tank. At least down here, they won't bother us. Try to think of it as a vacation from their tests and trainings."

I looked around the concrete cylinder we were in. Nope. My imagination was not good enough to pretend that this was any form of vacation.

"How'd you end up with Spector anyway? You didn't go to Thibault." I didn't recognize him from any of the students, and he also looked slightly older than me.

"Is that where you new lot came from?" he asked, scrubbing a hand over his jaw. "I wondered. So what are you, eighteen?"

"Nineteen. Just graduated the night before Spector came, actually."

He made a disgusted grunt. "Those fuckers are taking students now?"

"I guess. I don't know how long it's been going on. I'd never even heard of Spector before I got an invitation to join their secretive *internship*."

He chuckled humorlessly. "Gods, they're getting arrogant and bold."

"So how did they get you?"

"I worked as a janitor at the elemental city's headquarters. There was an opportunity presented to us, probably similar to what they invited you to. A new program, they called it," Tomb said, his glossy lips turning downward. "I thought I was signing up for a security position. It would've been a hell of a promotion from scrubbing toilets. But they did the ritual on me. Apparently, I fit their credentials. No family, no prominent position in society. Someone no one would really miss."

I had someone that would miss me though, someone that relied heavily on me. Aunt Marie was probably worried sick, but I had no way of communicating with her.

"That doesn't fit the narrative of Thibault students, though," I replied thoughtfully. "All of them are high-society supes with powerful families."

"All of *them*?" he questioned.

"Yeah, them. I'm just a bastard scholarship student. But I still have family. My Aunt Marie is probably freaking out, not knowing where I am."

"Hmm, then that just shows how arrogant and bold they really are getting. They must be done with testing it out on low-class nobody supes like me. They're going for the young and powerful so they can mold their new little army."

I stiffened. "Is that what they're doing? Building an army?"

Tomb shrugged. "What else could they want from a small force of supes with unmatchable powers?"

I shook my head, his words swarming my mind. "That's insane. If the public knew about this, there would be a war."

"Which is why it's a secret still. They need to make more of us."

A frown drew my brows together. My father was involved in all of this. *Stiles* was involved in this. It made me sick.

"I feel like I don't even know what happened to me. I don't understand how they're even doing it."

He looked steadily back at me. "There was *a lot* of trial and error. When they did it to me a couple of years ago, I was one of the only ones who survived. Their survival rate is higher now, but it's still not very high."

"But *how* are they doing it?" I asked again, needing to understand.

"I don't know where they learned how to do it, but the ritual rips demons from the underworld. It happens against their will, as much as it was against yours. Most of the demons that come out are lesser demons. They're always creatures of some sort, and they'd never survive topside on their own. Spector somehow found a way to call them up and force supes to be possessed by them. It enables them to survive up here, while making us stronger."

The memory of the spider sinking into my body left me feeling cold. The idea of Spector having control over so many of us made the whole thing feel hopeless.

"So, now that I told you all of that, are you going to tell me what kind of spider you are?" he asked while giving me an assessing look, like he was trying to figure me out. "I've been here long enough to learn a few things. Maybe I can help with whatever struggles you have with your demon."

I knew I couldn't help my nature—that I didn't decide this life for myself, but I was still embarrassed. I cleared my throat awkwardly. "I'm a black widow."

His eyes widened in shock, but he quickly schooled his expression. "Interesting."

"What is?"

Tomb looked me up and down, as if trying to figure out the right words to say. "Possessions are forced, yes, but you only join with the demon most compatible with you. Think of it as merging with a similar kin already there."

My frown deepened. "That's *not* true. I'm not a fucking psychotic sex cannibal who likes to steal people's life essence!" I blurted out. As soon as the words were out of my mouth, I felt humiliated.

Still, I didn't like what he was implying—that the spider had chosen me as a host because I had that same dark nature already inside of me.

Tomb shook his head. "I didn't mean to imply that," he told me, his gravelly voice low. "The black widow could have seen your independence, your strength, your..."—he coughed uncomfortably—"sensual nature. Those could've been the things she felt a kinship to."

I blushed at his words. He wasn't wrong. I was all of those things, and sex had always made me feel powerful in ways I'd never been able to articulate.

"For example," he continued. "My earth ability as an elemental means I could already control things like rocks and stones. But even more, I've always been a natural protector. I raised my younger half-brother until he died. Gargoyles are ancient demon soldiers created to defend," he explained. "I sometimes wonder what humans would think if they knew they've been posting sculptures of demons at their church doors."

I snorted at the thought, temporarily placated with the knowledge that I wasn't chosen by the black widow because of some serial killer tendencies I knew nothing about.

"You should rest," Tomb said, resting his head against the wall. "Sleep makes the time go by faster."

I watched him for a few moments before I curled up on the floor, propping my head up on my arm and closing my eyes. Time in the tank wasn't so bad with Tomb here with me. He knew what I was, and he didn't look at me with fear or repulsion. That knowledge made a soft smile spread across my face as I closed my eyes. I could get through this. I just needed to make sure I didn't get hungry.

DAYS PASSED.

It was fucking boring.

No one ever brought us food to eat, but twice a day, someone would come by and shove water bottles through a slot in the door. The toilet in our confinement was true prison style, but I'd erected webbed walls to give us both some privacy. Tomb had smirked at that, but I wasn't about to just do my business in front of the hot gargoyle. I did have some dignity left despite my rough appearance.

We mostly talked or slept, coming up with stupid games to play and pass the time. His favorite was tossing the ball of web I'd made him back and forth. Mine was asking him twenty questions.

Still, every day that they left us in here was another day that the hunger inside of me grew. My vampiric body needed blood, my human parts needed food, and my demon self needed life.

I was feeling the hunger riding me harder and harder, which was why every time I awoke, I was careful to keep myself busy. That was how I'd ended up making socks out of webs. They were surprisingly soft and comfortable too. I even made Tomb a pair of boxers, which he had just laughed about.

When I realized I could make those things, I started making other things too. My favorite was the hanging hammocks I'd constructed. The thick ropes of webs stretched from wall to wall so we could sleep more comfortably in them. It sure beat the hard floor. All in all, I was learning that this ability as a spider was actually really awesome.

But today, I woke up twitchy. My demon was agitated. She needed essence. I needed blood and food. I was a trio of hangry.

Tomb seemed unflappable though, like having no food didn't bother him at all.

"Sit down, Motley," he said from his hammock. "Pacing will only drain your energy faster."

"How can you be so calm?" I snapped. I knew it wasn't his fault, but I needed to get out of here soon. Fear was tormenting me almost as much as hunger was.

"I've been through this a few times," he answered.

"Yeah, well, this is my first, and it sucks ass," I said, licking the tips of my fangs that wouldn't stop throbbing.

"Come here."

His order had me stopping to look over at him. "What?"

"I forgot. It's been a while since I've been around a vampire, so you'll have to forgive me for being a dense idiot. Here," he said, holding out his arm.

He was in his skin form right now, and saliva instantly rushed my mouth at the offering of blood, but I shook my head. "I can't take your blood when you're weak from no nourishment."

"I'm okay. Really. Take what you need."

The throbbing in my fangs intensified, and I felt venom drip down the sides and land on my lip. His dark eyes followed when my tongue darted out to lick the venom away.

"Give me a kiss, and I'll give you a drink."

I stared at him, horrified. "What? No."

He chuckled. "One kiss. One sip. That seems fair."

Gods, I was thirsty. I was aching to find out if he tasted as good as he smelled. Even my spider wanted me to taste his blood.

"No."

He tilted his head in that thoughtful way of his. "What have they forced you to do?"

"What?"

"You're scared to drink from me. And it's more than you simply worrying about me being too food-deprived to give blood," he decided. "So is your blood thirst tied together with how your demon feeds?"

All the humans I'd fucked and killed flashed before my eyes, and I felt the blood drain from my face.

"The Spector man who ordered us in here mentioned watching you feed. What do they make you do?"

The tips of my ears went red hot. I didn't want to tell him, but he persisted.

"I've heard talk," he said carefully.

My eyes flashed to his. "So you know?" I asked, both angry and embarrassed. "You know how they make me feed?"

"I'm asking."

"Fine. I feed off of energy. Someone's life. But I can only get it once I've been..."

"Been what?" he persisted.

"Penetrated," I said with shame, dropping my eyes. Admitting it out loud made me sick. It sounded so fucking wrong.

"So that's what they make you do? They bring you humans to fuck and then you feed off them and kill them?"

I nodded miserably. "Yeah, happy now?" I asked bitterly. "You're stuck in isolation with a fucking monster."

He cocked his head to the other side. "Is that what you think? That you're a monster?"

"Aren't I?" I challenged. "Aren't all of us?"

"If that's the way you choose to see it. But I personally would have to disagree."

I stared at him incredulously. "How? How can you deny it?"

"Power doesn't make a monster. A monster makes himself."

I shook my head, feeling irrationally angry. "You haven't seen what I do. What my spider *makes* me do. As soon as someone...well, as soon as they enter me, I latch onto their essence and drain them dry. It's vicious."

"You have to feed," he answered with an annoyingly calm tone. "Just because it's a different way than you're used to, doesn't mean it's wrong."

I couldn't believe what I was hearing. "I'm fucking killing people," I snapped. "Of course it's wrong. And you're delusional if you think otherwise."

"I'm not talking about the end result. Obviously, that's something you need to learn how to control if you can. But if you *can* control it, then simply feeding off of one's essence wouldn't make you a monster. It's no different than feeding off of someone's vein, right?"

I opened my mouth before closing it again like a gaping fish. Could I learn to control it? Could I learn to feed without killing them completely? The thought never crossed my mind. My spider was always in total control, draining until there was nothing left. But maybe he was right. Maybe I could cut it off.

"Let me give you some advice, from one *monster* to another," he put in.

"Fine. What advice?"

"Stop fighting her," he said simply.

I tensed at his words. "I can't do that. She's a *demon*. Wrong. Unnatural."

"She's a part of you," he interrupted. "Whether you like it or not, you and your spider are joined together now. The sooner you stop fighting her, the sooner you can learn to work with her and control your new abilities."

I looked down at my lap and picked at my dry, cracking cuticles.

"If you want to fight against Spector, you're going to fail. *Unless* you embrace what you are and use it to your advantage," he said firmly. "Stop treating your demon like a tumor you want to pluck out. Let her thrive inside of you, and you'll thrive right along with her. She'll make you stronger if you let her."

I let his words sink in for a moment before letting out a long sigh. "Let's see if you still feel that way in a couple more days. My spider is already hungry, and you're the only person here," I replied.

I expected fear or unease to cross his features, but instead I was greeted with a smile.

"I look forward to it, Widow."

Chapter 7

I WAS FUCKING HUNGRY. Starving. Ravenous. Dying. Again.

Just like when I first arrived at Spector, I couldn't tell time in the tank. I wasn't sure how many days had passed, but I knew I'd gone long enough between feedings that I felt hollowed from the inside out.

Tomb didn't seem scared of me, despite the growing manic frenzy building in my chest. We spoke some, but the hunger was beginning to be too much. It took most of my concentration just to hold it and my spider at bay. Every once in a while, I'd realize that she'd come out, watching Tomb in her predatory way. She was fascinated by him. And just like with Crow, there was something else too. A deeper craving that went beyond the need to feed. It scared me.

"You don't look so good," Tomb said from his corner of the room.

He'd been doing push-ups for the past half hour, tempting me with his chiseled, sweaty body.

Every slick of sweat that dripped down his muscles made my tongue dart out to lick my lips. Every masculine grunt made me hold in a whimper. My spider wanted him. *I* wanted him. It was getting harder and harder to hold back.

"I'm fine," I gritted, though my voice had taken on a feral quality I didn't recognize.

It was difficult for me to associate nourishment with lust. I'd always craved orgasms and satisfaction, but I'd never needed them to survive. The desire I had for Tomb was a mixed up mess. I didn't know where simple attraction and lust ended and my need to feed began. Did I just want him because I was hungry? Or was I getting hungrier *because* I wanted him?

I busied myself again by wrapping webs in small circles. It seemed innocent enough, but I was ready to slip them over my wrists at the first sign of my spider taking over. I'd sooner chain myself up than hurt him, although I wasn't sure what good it would really do, since my webs seemed to follow my every whim. Still, it was worth a shot, and it gave me some semblance of hope. Knowing that I would snap and have zero control was a daunting thought.

Was this how my aunt felt during a frenzy? I was so fucking worried about her, and being in this tank left me to nothing but my thoughts. Thoughts about how she was doing. About the thundering hunger in my chest.

About Tomb...who was now doing sit-ups, showing off his abs.

I groaned and rubbed my hands down my face. "Can you please stop?" I asked him as he huffed out an exhale. His eyes flicked over to me, and he paused for a brief moment, but then he resumed.

Another drip of sweat trailed down his six pack. My mouth watered. "Fuck," I cursed before turning to face the metal door locking us in.

"What's wrong, Wid?" he asked, and I didn't miss the teasing lilt in his rough voice.

"I need to get out of here," I said, working faster to create thicker rope, praying that it would be strong enough to hold me.

"We aren't getting out of here until they want us to," he said before I heard him walk over and grab one of the water bottles. I couldn't help but look over at him, watching as his throat bobbed with every gulp. His Adam's apple, his dark stubble, his slick skin...it was erotic.

"Can't you go all gargoyle and smash us the fuck out of here?" I demanded.

He shook his head. "Why do you think they put us in here? We're buried under hundreds of feet of solid concrete and steel. If I bust through that door, it'll collapse, and even if I could survive it, *you* couldn't."

I let out a frustrated growl and pulled at my hair. "What do they fucking want from us?" I yelled, my shrill voice echoing against the walls.

I was going to snap. I could feel my time running out.

It wasn't until I felt his cold, marble-like skin against my back that I released the breath I was holding. "You're starving, aren't you?" he asked quietly, brushing my hair over my shoulder.

"I'm not," I lied, hating myself a bit.

"You are," he argued. "You need to feed. So feed from me."

"No!" I said, shaking my head and closing my eyes against his tempting words. Why was he doing this to me?

"I want you to. Don't overthink it," Tomb whispered against the ridge of my ear.

I whirled around to face him, an incredulous expression on my face. "Don't overthink it?" I asked, totally baffled by his attitude. "It's all I can think about, and if you were smart, you'd be thinking about it too. Stay on your side of the tank, stop working out, and try to cover your cock for fuck's sake."

I gestured at the growing length between us, then shoved at his chest.

He didn't move an inch. "I don't fear you, Widow," he said in a husky voice.

"Why the fuck not? You should. You haven't seen what I'm capable of, but I've told you. You should be screaming at them to let you out of here."

Tomb tucked a strand of tangled red hair behind my ears. "How do you think it feels for them? When you drain their essence?"

His question caught me off guard. Images of all the men I'd killed flashed through my mind. "Why would you even ask that?" I asked in a shaky whisper. "I have no fucking idea. It's not like my spider took a time out so I could interview them on how it felt being murdered."

His cool hand cupped my jaw, and my spider preened beneath the surface. She wanted to surge forward. To claim his mouth and then the rest of his body. My shoulders shook, trying to hold her back.

"Stop fighting her. Stop fighting your hunger. I *want* you to feed on me."

I shook my head, suddenly terrified. I didn't want to do this. At least the men I'd fucked and killed had been strangers. Tomb and I were anything but.

When I tried to flinch away from him, his hold tightened around my face. Infuriated, I slapped his hand away. "Stop it," I snapped.

"Give in," he retorted, his dark eyes shining like glass.

I shoved my fingers into my hair, tugging at the strands. His proximity, his naked body, the lust coming off of him...I couldn't take it. "No. You don't know what you're asking, so just *stop it!*"

My spider was digging into me, burrowing deeper and deeper, pulling at the webbed strings of my control. She was like the puppeteer, and I was hanging by a single silken thread.

But Tomb wouldn't back off.

He crowded me again despite the fact that I was pacing, trying to get away, trying to put distance between the spider's domination and my shaky hold.

When I tried to turn around again, Tomb cut me off, forcing me to stop with him in front and the wall against my back. He leaned in closer until his lips were just inches away from mine. "I know exactly what I'm asking, Motley," he replied, his gaze seeping into me.

I whimpered when he wrapped his large hand around my wrist.

"Do you understand?"

No. I didn't understand a fucking thing. Not him, not myself, not how my life had changed so drastically.

But gods, he smelled good. Mouthwatering.

My spider hummed. My will wavered.

And then I was leaning in toward him against my better judgement.

"*Kiss me*," my voice suddenly demanded.

Tomb crashed his lips to mine. His kiss was a delicious blend of cold and hot, melting me into his touch, his lips a perfect contradiction of supple warmth and unyielding marble.

"Take your fucking clothes off, Motley," he said against my mouth.

I shook my head and closed my eyes, trying to regain my restraint. "I can't," I said, even as I continued to nip at his lips. Yet every kiss felt like a death sentence. Every touch reminded me of what I'd become. That every time I fed, my spider took over, and I snuffed out another life.

But I was so hungry, and Tomb smelled more delicious

than anything I'd ever encountered. Instead of me luring him, it was like his scent was luring *me*.

Terrified, I looked up at him with a wobbly lip. "Don't let me do this," I pleaded. "She wants you so badly. She'll fuck you and drain you dry if you don't help me stop this," I admitted, hoping my bluntness would help him see reason. "She thinks you belong to her."

But the gargoyle just smirked. "That doesn't sound so bad."

Pissed, I shoved at him again, but he still didn't budge. "Stop it! This is serious, Tomb. She's strong. Stronger than you. You're just a fly in her web. You're nothing to her. Just another weak meal."

Lightning quick, he reached forward and gripped my ass in his strong hands, tugging me against him. My breath caught in surprise, and I held my breath, trying not to take in any more of his scent. His erection pressed against the juncture of my thighs, and I wanted to part them. It took everything in me to stay still and to keep my hands pressed against the wall.

"You know what I think?" he asked, his tone low and gravelly as he gave my ass another possessive squeeze. "I think my gargoyle likes your spider. And I think your spider has fucked enough weak flies."

His hand moved up, slipping past my hem so that his bare hand was touching my skin. All I could think of was all the places I wanted his hands to rove.

His face slid closer to mine, and I took in a gasping breath, nearly moaning at the influx of his earthy musk. "And you know what else I think?"

My eyes fluttered closed, and my head turned up, like a flower trying to reach for the sun. "What?" I whispered.

His lips skimmed against my brow. "I think you *and* your spider need to be reminded that sex isn't just a meal. And I think you'd like it if someone fucked *you* for a change, and fucked you hard."

Holy shit.

My fangs dripped, my back arched, and my body quaked with arousal. Tomb's hand wrapped around my throat, squeezing just enough to make my pulse race.

"You don't want to do this," I said, making one more half-assed attempt to get him to stop. But if I was honest with myself, I didn't know if I *could* stop anymore.

"There are worse things than death, Black Widow," he replied ominously.

My eyes popped open, and I raked over his hard skin, noting every scar, every hard line that defined his time here at Spector.

"You need to feed. Take what I'm offering."

And then it finally clicked. He wasn't simply being reckless. He truly did want me to feed from him. "You want to die, don't you?" I whispered.

The idea that this strong man had been beaten down so hard that he sought the final escape of death...it made me sick.

"I want to get out of Spector." His unwavering tone held no room for arguing. "And feeding you? It would be the best way to go. So stop thinking. We can both give each other something here. You want to survive; I want a way out," he murmured before lifting up the hem of my hospital gown.

I didn't even try to stop him. I was losing my restraint. My spider was taking over, and I was letting her, because it wasn't just her who craved him—it was me, too.

"What do you want, Motley?" he asked before he pulled the gown up and over my head, letting it fall to the ground. With his eyes locked on mine, he sunk to his knees, and I looked up at the ceiling, squeezing my eyes shut as he exhaled over my sensitive skin. I was slick with desire.

"To get out of here and have my life back."

But he shook his head in reprobation. "Let me rephrase. I'm not speaking to Motley right now. What do you want, *Black Widow*?"

"I want to feed, and I want to come, motherfucker," I growled, my voice dark.

"Good to know," he smirked. "But not quite the answer I was looking for. Tell me what you *really* want."

I shook my head and clamped my mouth shut, stopping her from being able to speak.

Tomb pinched me lightly on the ass. "I want to hear what she wants. I want you to face it. You'll never survive Spector unless you accept yourself. So say it."

Shame filled me up. I *couldn't* say it. I couldn't admit it aloud.

"Say it, and I'll reward you," he promised before using his teeth to drag my cotton panties down my thighs.

My legs trembled, and a sigh shook out from my lips. "I don't want to be hungry anymore," I admitted.

He hummed in approval, and then his mouth descended on the point where my thighs met, and I felt a hot, smooth tongue sneak out and tease me. More breath whooshed out of me, and I had to lean against the wall for support.

"And how do you want to satisfy that hunger?" he asked, his voice slightly muffled as his lips started caressing their way up my leg.

I had to seriously concentrate in order to hear his words, since he was filling me with a strong haze of lust. All of my attention was focused on the direction of his mouth and how desperately I wanted him to lick over the place where I'd started to pulse.

"Umm…"

His hands trailed up my thighs, pulling my legs apart, his fingers clasping me firmly. "Answer me."

Godsdamn, that authoritative tone almost made me whimper.

"By feeding," I breathed out.

His mouth hovered *right* over my clit. I could feel his breath over it like it was a gentle touch. I had to resist the urge to grab him and shove him against me. If he had hair on his head, I would've had my fingers buried in the strands.

"And how do you feed, Black Widow?"

My attention and desire stuttered at the name. My eyes snapped down to his where he was looking up at me with challenge. "Stop calling me that."

"That's who you are."

I swallowed hard, clenching my teeth. "I know what you're doing."

He smirked. "Is that so?" he asked before lazily dragging a finger across my folds and making me bite down on my lip.

Anger seemed to latch onto my desire, fueling me with even more heat than before. "You want me to come to terms with it. To admit that I'm this…this thing."

"Mmm. Tell me what you are," he demanded.

"I'm a monster."

I propelled off the wall and Tomb got to his feet and circled around me. He moved closer and closer until his chest was pressing against my back. He swept my red hair over my shoulder and grabbed the curve of my waist. "You're *not* a monster. You're the Black Widow. Your demon is not something to be feared or hated. Your demon makes you stronger. Now admit to me what it wants. What *you* want, and what you're too afraid to say."

"I want to fucking kill, okay?" I snapped, my voice piercing the tiny room. "All this damn spider wants right now is for you to fuck me hard and deep so that we can latch onto your essence and drain you dry while my fangs are buried so far in your throat all you can do is groan into my ear as you die."

I was panting with the admission. Shame burning my face, lust still boiling in my gut. Hunger throbbing with my arousal.

"Mmm, that's the sexiest thing I've ever heard," he growled in my ear, and my pulse jumped when his hand on my waist started to travel down until he finally connected with my clit. My body flinched against him at the sudden pleasure, and my arm swung up to curl around his neck behind me.

"Fucking psychopathic gargoyle," I said, but the words turned into more of a moan.

"At least I've accepted what I am," he countered.

My moan turned into a squeal when I was suddenly lifted in the air and my center was planted against his mouth. My hands flew to his shoulders to balance myself, and the continuous stream of rambling and doubt in my head disappeared with each skilled strike of his tongue.

He lapped me up, gliding his tongue up and down my slit while easing my thigh over his shoulder so he could get a better taste. And fuck if it didn't feel incredible.

My entire body shook, and I was barely aware of him setting me down onto the floor, careful to make sure my naked body was placed on top of the soft padding of my webs. Then he was right back to it, feasting on me like I was the best thing he'd ever tasted.

I'd never been savored like this. I wasn't thinking about my victims, my shame, or my new reality. I wasn't even consumed with my hunger anymore. All I could think about was him. Tomb moved with a calculated aggression that contradicted the safety and care I felt in his arms.

"Fuck, Tomb," I groaned when he hummed against my

clit. I vibrated with pleasure that was spiking up higher every time his tongue moved over me. "I need…"

"What do you need?" he asked, his hard body sliding up over mine.

Webs started to spin from my fingertips, but I curled them into fists, trying to stop it. I clenched my eyes shut, trying to hold her at bay, my entire body shaking with the effort.

"Come out to play, Black Widow."

Tomb's dark voice made my concentration slip. "No," I gritted, a tear escaping the corner of my closed eye.

"Yes," he replied, and then his fingers were splaying over my folds, parting me, while his cock slid up and down my clit with firm, measured strokes.

"I can't," I cried. I saw all those humans that I'd drained. Their unblinking eyes. The gaping wounds in their necks. The way I'd stolen their essences and left them nothing but husks.

"I want her. I want *you*," he said huskily, his strong body poised above me. "All of you, and she's a part of you now."

I shook my head and fisted my hands in the webs beneath me.

"Let go," he ordered.

"But—"

"Let go."

And I broke.

Like a tether pulled too tightly. Or a silky strand of a spiderweb suddenly snapping.

The spider inside of me rushed to the surface. My eyes flashed with hunger. My fangs elongated. My nails grew. More webs shot out, covering the room, and pungent pulses of luring pheromones seeped from my skin.

And instead of showing fear, instead of trying to get away, Tomb fucking *grinned*.

"There you are, Widdy."

"Fuck me," I heard my spider-demon demand in my voice.

With his grin still firmly in place, his hand came up and wrapped around my throat, right over my hourglass mark, his touch digging into my windpipe. I hissed, baring my fangs that dripped with venom.

"I'll fuck you, Widow. And I'll feed you, too."

The demon hummed in approval, and my hand trailed down his stomach until my fingers curled around the velvety skin of his cock. He was all dark skin and delicious length, heavy and hard and waiting. My hand pumped him once, but that was all he allowed.

He pushed my hand away, and then grabbed his length in his own grip and ran the head of his dick over my opening.

"Yes," my voice moaned out.

"I'll give you what you need," Tomb said, while pushing the head of his dick inside of me.

My legs came up to wrap around his waist, and my hips lifted up, trying to get more of him inside, but he teased me instead. He slipped back out and slid over my wet folds, before teasing inside with just the head again.

Pissed, I reached up and pinched the skin on his pecs as hard as I could. "Fuck me," I demanded, my voice guttural and foreign to my own ears.

He chuckled, the sound reverberating all the way down to where we were just barely connected, and then he thrust in so hard that my body slid up against the floor. A surprised gasp flew out of me, but before I could catch my breath, Tomb was yanking out and then shoving back in so hard and fast that I saw stars. Beautiful, flashing, endless stars.

I couldn't think.

I couldn't process anything other than the mix of stinging pain from his size, and the blooming pleasure that every scrape of his cock shaved from my insides.

"*Yessss*," my voice hissed, sounding like the rasp came from the fiery pits of hell that the demon ascended from.

With his blissful penetration came my spider's deadly thread, and it immediately latched onto Tomb's life core. The spider pulled and fed. Her ravenous appetite purred at the taste of his smooth, smoky essence. He tasted better than every human she'd fed on. He was delicious, and she wanted more. She wanted it *all*.

Tomb's dark eyes latched onto mine, and then I watched as he suddenly rippled with change. His body morphed until his skin was gone and stone was in its place, and his smirk let me know that his own demon had come out to play.

Fuck.

His cock hardened to stone inside of me, and my eyes rolled to the back of my head at the intense solidity of it. "Oh *fuck*."

"My Black Widow loves my rock hard cock, doesn't she?" he asked.

"Tomb!"

"Say it, Widdy. I need to hear you say it."

I panted against him. "Fuck. Yes! Yes, I love it!"

"That's my good Black Widow."

He thrusted in harder and harder, the noises from my dripping wet pussy sounding around us.

It should've felt odd. Wrong. Cold. Alien. But instead, it felt so fucking good, so different than anything I'd ever experienced before, that all I could do was moan and whimper and writhe. And my spider? She felt like she was *home*. Like being with Tomb was exactly where she belonged.

Tomb didn't falter. Despite his impossibly hard, smooth length now drilling into me, he didn't once slow. And I *loved* it. Not just the demon inside of me, but *me*. Somewhere between when my demon emerged and Tomb started fucking the hell out of me, I'd turned from just a bystander to a partner taking up equal participation. Unlike the times before, the demon and I were equal. Merged. Excitement and adrenaline surged through me.

"More," I demanded.

In reply, Tomb gripped my body and flipped me over before yanking up my hips so that my ass was pointed high into the air. And then he buried himself in my pussy so hard that a screaming orgasm tore out of me in a violent burst of shock.

My back arched up, and he immediately wrapped an arm around my front to help hold me against his chest as he continued fucking me.

I grabbed onto his arm, my fangs throbbing, but that part of him was stone too, so my sharp teeth couldn't pierce him. My spider hissed at that, and my fangs slammed into his arm anyway, but of course, it was like biting into granite, with no give whatsoever.

"Oh gods!" I cried, the jarring sensation sending an uncomfortable pain through my skull as my fangs clanged with the force of resistance.

But I was vibrating with challenge. With being denied and having to fight for it. Unlike all of the terrorized humans, Tomb wasn't afraid of me. He was meeting me thrust for thrust, need for need. It made everything so much more carnally exciting.

Tomb dragged his dick out of me before ramming in again, his hold on my body the only reason I didn't go flying forward. He dropped his hand down and started pressing and pinching my clit, the move both possessive and harsh—and fucking blissful.

My angry hiss turned into a heady moan, but my spider started to tug harder on Tomb's thread of life. I spun in his arms, somehow still keeping him inside of me, my eyes searching for any part of him that was still skin. Shoving him to the ground, I rode his cock while noting the spot at the curve of his shoulder. Licking my aching fangs, I attacked.

The tips of my fangs scraped against hot skin, but just as I was about to pierce him and get rewarded with his blood that I so badly craved, that part of him turned to stone too.

"You son of a rockcocking bitch," I snapped, my eyes flashing with anger. I wasn't sure if it was me or my spider talking, but I was so greedy for blood that my fangs were dripping.

Tomb's gargoyle grinned at my spider's insult.

A flash of fear suddenly spurred through me when his big hands grabbed me roughly by the ass, and he shoved his hips up into me, making my head fall back in pleasure. For the first time, I realized that maybe I wasn't the only one I should fear. Tomb's demon was strong too.

"You just remembered that I'm not a weak fly trapped in your web, didn't you, Widdy?" he asked with dark amusement. "You remembered that you're not the only predator here."

In reply, my spider tugged on more of his essence, determined to satisfy that hunger faster since his gargoyle wasn't giving us his blood.

"I think you like that I'm not making this easy for you," he went on. "You like riding my thick, hard cock and being fucking *owned*."

I was going to come just from his filthy mouth. I rocked my hips back and forth as he continued to fuck me, my hands splayed down on his chest. I was being impaled on top of him, hitting a spot so deep inside of me that I hadn't even known was there. And as he continued to deny me his blood that called to me, my spider was both infuriated at the challenge he was flexing, and thrilled by it.

She lashed out again, this time trying to sink into the skin visible on his wrist, but faster than a blink, he changed that too. Pretty soon, his entire body was solid stone.

I came again, by the sheer ferocity of his thrusts, but it wasn't enough. I needed his blood. I needed every part of his life flooding into me. I bared my teeth at him, probably looking as demented as the hell my demon came from. "Let me drink," my spider and I demanded.

Tomb pinched my clit hard. So fucking hard. And I came in the most violent, ecstatic orgasm I'd ever had in my whole godsdamned life.

And then, just as Tomb's balls tightened and he started to shoot hot ropes of cum inside of me, my bitch of a spider *yanked*. She pulled on his thread of life so hard that his breath was stolen from his chest.

One second, he was pumping his release, and the next, his string snapped away from the center of his soul, and he was drained of all life.

Tomb's hard, glorious body collapsed against mine while he was still buried deep inside of me.

And just like that, the gargoyle was dead.

And I was still thirsty.

Chapter 8

I WAS SURROUNDED BY WEBS.

They dangled from the ceiling, stretched from wall to wall, some pulled taut, and some hanging listlessly down. There were intricate designs in each woven thread, and every inch of the room had been covered in them.

Every inch...except where Tomb's cold, lifeless body lay.

I stared at it, my knees tucked against my chest. I was naked still, and the remnants of our fucking were dry and crusted against the insides of my thighs. But my eyes wouldn't stop watering.

Tomb was dead. I'd killed him. Me.

I couldn't blame his death solely on my spider, because I'd participated too. Unlike every other time, I'd fucked him right along with her, and I'd enjoyed every second.

My eyes travelled over his body, which had returned to skin not long after he'd died. There were so many scars on him that I couldn't keep count—I knew this because I kept trying to count them all anyway, but then I'd lose track and have to start over again.

He'd wanted this. I kept trying to remind myself of that fact, but it didn't help. Not at all.

I'd only spent the last several days in the tank with him, but I wasn't wishy-washy, and I wasn't one who felt the need to be constricted by time. If I liked someone, I liked them. If I was attracted to them, I didn't fight it. If I wanted to fuck, well, I fucked. It didn't matter how long I'd known them. I followed my gut.

So I wasn't surprised that I'd grown so attached to him so quickly, especially given the fact that we'd spent every waking second together in our confinement. Maybe it was because we shared a mutual hopelessness about our situation, or maybe it was because he didn't look at me like I was a deadly monster. Whatever it was, there was something comforting about him. But I was surprised at the intensity of my spider's attachment. She'd never shown anyone attention like she had with Tomb. With Tomb...and Crow.

My heart ached, and I drew in a shaky breath. My limbs had gone numb from the awkward crouched position I stayed cramped in, but I didn't care enough to move. The webs offered some comfort at least. It was like I'd created a warm, silky nest for Tomb's...tomb.

"Why?" I asked, as if the spider within me could answer. She had been noticeably absent, calm and sated, and it made me sick to think that she enjoyed what she'd done to him. I felt at war with myself. Half a woman grieving, while the other half felt nothing but content.

Was this what my life would always be? My body was a gory shrine to Spector's whims and my spider's hunger. Sex would forever come at a price I couldn't afford.

Maybe Tomb was smart to want to leave all of this. He'd been enduring it for a lot longer than I had, and I'd even had my weak moments where I wanted to give up. Did I really want this to be my life forever? Part of me was numb to the parade of tests and corpses. But Tomb had urged me to become one with my spider. To accept her. But how could I when this was the result?

I closed my eyes as silent tears streamed down my face. I imagined the sort of loneliness and solitude I would spend the rest of my life simmering in. For so long, I'd voluntarily isolated myself from my community to protect my pride. But now that the choice had been taken from me, I craved companionship more than ever.

A low sound reverberated around the room, and I winced, assuming that it was Spector men coming to take me away. I'd killed one of their precious hybrids. Would they punish me? Or had they expected this?

Another sound echoed around me, and I opened my eyes, preparing for the metal doors of our cell to slam open and for Spector guards to rush in.

When the door didn't open, I frowned at it, shoving aside webs to get a better look. But nope, not even water bottles were being dropped through the slot.

When I heard the noise again, my head whipped around to Tomb's body. Except instead of lying there lifeless and cold, his head had turned over, and he was looking *right* at me. Those piercing, glassy dark eyes of his forced goosebumps to erupt all over my body.

Did eyelids just reflexively open like that on dead bodies?

But then his mouth parted. "Wid?" he croaked out.

The blood drained from my face, and I flinched back. "Holy shit."

My hand flew to my chest as my heart galloped and tried to run away, because this couldn't be happening. There was no way this was happening. I pinched the shit out of my arm to make sure I wasn't dreaming, but nope, I was very much awake.

Tomb sat up and looked around dazedly. "What

happened?" His voice sounded all rustic and husky, like he'd just woken up from sleep.

"Y-you're alive? How is that even possible?" Part of me wanted to run to him and wrap my arms around him, the other part was terrified.

Tomb frowned and looked down at his body, as if he'd just remembered what we'd done. His gaze darted back up to me. "You fed?"

I nodded numbly. "I fed. She...*we* killed you," I confessed.

"But I'm still alive." Tomb ran his hands over himself as if brushing off the residual death.

"Nothing *still* about it. You were dead. One hundred percent corpse," I insisted. "But...you came back."

Tomb's touch went up from his arms, and then ran along his neck. He winced slightly, and my eyes zeroed in on the spot. A gasp flew out of my mouth because there, against the glossy black of his skin, was a stark red mark. *My* mark.

"Your throat," I whispered in horror. What had my spider done to him?

He rubbed at the tender skin of his neck and got to his feet. "You...what happened? How is this possible?" he asked, looking over at me.

I shook my head, still staring at him like he was some weird apparition who would disappear any second. "I don't know. You're dead, Tomb. This isn't real," I said, closing my eyes against the panic burning against my lids.

"Hey," he said gently, and suddenly he was right in front of me, his big hands cupping my face. In gentle strokes, he wiped away the tears from my cheeks using the pads of his thumbs, holding my face like I was precious. "It's okay, Wid. I'm here. I'm right here."

"You were dead," I said again, my voice shaky. "I'm dreaming, aren't I?"

In reply, one of Tomb's hands reached around, and he

started stroking his long, capable fingers through my hair and massaging my scalp. I hadn't even realized I'd been holding any tension there until a sigh escaped me, and I melted into his touch. "Feel that?" he murmured. "I'm here. I'm not dead, and you aren't dreaming. Stop crying, beautiful. It's making my gargoyle go fucking crazy."

Fluttering my eyelids opened, I took in his handsome face. "How is this possible? I felt my spider suck out the last of your essence. I heard your heart stop. You were dead, Tomb. So how did you come back?"

"I don't know, but I suddenly realize that I want to live," he confessed, his tone holding both awe and vulnerable honesty. "Very badly." He peppered kisses along my jaw, leaving a molten trail of affection on my skin with each touch. "It's you. What is it about you?"

I shook my head before pulling out of his grasp. My mind was spinning. What if my spider was making him affectionate? What if she was luring him in? What if he died again and didn't come back next time?

"How do you feel?" I asked.

"I feel—" His words were cut off as the metal doors to the tank suddenly slammed open, and a team of guards stormed inside. In a flash, I was shoved against the wall by three guards, and Tomb went wild with rage. He shifted into his stone form in an instant and then started tossing aside guards left and right. An air elemental tried to hold him back with a barrier, but Tomb simply crushed his rock-hard fist into the side of the man's face, sending him flying against the wall. Two more tried to shoot some sort of steel net at him, but he evaded it, and then he started to pummel them to the ground.

I struggled against the guards that were holding me against the wall. With a flick of my wrist, I shot webs out to wrap around them, successfully getting one of them lifted to the ceiling and held there without hope of getting out.

Within seconds, Tomb was there, ripping the other two guards away from me. Then he stood at my side, heaving with rage as he glared at the intruders, as if daring them to take him on.

One of the remaining guards was stupid enough to try him. Tomb's hand flashed out, and he grabbed the man by the neck, squeezing so hard that all I could hear was the snapping of bone as the man's head lopped to the side, dead. Tomb dropped his body to the ground as if it were nothing.

The next guard tried to lunge for Tomb, but the man was far too slow. Didn't they realize that the gargoyle was in full demon mode? He would kill each and every one of them if they gave him the chance.

"Enough," a voice echoed out. "Release the chemicals. Someone call a janitor to clean up all the webs and blood in here. Oh, and we need a ladder to get Gerald off the ceiling."

All of us looked up at the same moment to see the guard —Gerald—completely mummified and hanging upside down from where I'd trapped him in my webs.

My spider grinned pretty smugly.

But that victory was short-lived because all at once, the room started to fill with smoke, and guards were yanking on some sort of gas masks.

With new panic, I tried to clamp my mouth shut and hold my breath, but the smoke moved too fast. It was like I could feel it sinking in through my pores.

"Wid," the gargoyle demon groaned before dropping to his knees.

My own head felt dizzy at the toxins flooding my system, and it was already too hard to see through the smoke.

I fell to the floor a second later, but to my surprise, my body didn't crash to the hard tile or even against sticky webs.

Instead, Tomb had somehow gotten to me in time to catch my fall. He held me cradled to his body, tucking me against him as if he could keep the world from hurting me. And for some reason, even though I knew it wasn't true, I felt safe.

The last thing I heard before blacking out was the scientist's mumbled words. "Hmm. Subject three-four-two seems to be very territorial of the black widow hybrid now."

He was right. Tomb's steely arms wrapping around my body were evidence enough. But what the scientist failed to notice was that my spider had started to wrap webs around Tomb, as if she were trying to hold him right back.

Territorial, indeed. But I had no idea what it meant.

Chapter 9

"AGAIN," the bitter voice of my trainer boomed before another knife came careening toward my skull.

I'd been at this for hours. Sweat poured down my face as I wrenched my arm up and shot out a cage of webs to try and stop the sharp weapon from slicing my cheek. I learned the hard way that they wouldn't wait for me to be ready. The dried blood on my ear was evidence enough of that.

I lifted up my black Spector t-shirt and used the bottom hem to wipe the sweat from my forehead. Besides the *S* logo on the front, the shirt and sweatpants were a step up from the hospital gown I was used to wearing.

After what happened with Tomb, they decided to start training me. Strength, endurance, offensive, and defensive moves, they made me do it all until I collapsed in my cell every night in a puddle of sweat and exhaustion. My days all blended into each other, starting with breakfast served in my cell, then training for hours on end, a quick cold shower, and a chemical induced sleep.

I hadn't seen Tomb in a week. I learned to keep time based on my routine, and I was thankful for the small pleasure of knowing how long had passed, but it was a bittersweet gift. Each day that went by, I grew more and more worried that Tomb had been punished for protecting me. Or that they'd been doing tests on him for coming back to life. I wasn't naive enough to think that they hadn't monitored us in the tank. I knew better than that.

I'd begged for answers, but I got none. I kept my eyes peeled in the training room, but he never showed up. I searched for his familiar face in the halls, praying that whatever I did to him didn't hurt him, but I never spotted him.

I worried. I missed him. It was like there was a hollow disconnect in my chest, as if a part of me was missing.

I craved more of Tomb. Not just physically—though the sex was amazing—I missed his easy smile and determination to accept me. I liked that, with him, I wasn't the villain.

"Why do we have to do this?" I asked Oz—the stingy man responsible for my training. He was dressed in black fatigues, with a mop of brown hair and a scowl.

I wasn't expecting an answer from him. I'd grown accustomed to Spector's secretive ways. They refused to tell me where Tomb was or what their plans for me were after what had happened in the tank. Tomb was dead—I'd seen it. And then he woke up with my spider's mark on his neck, leaving me with unanswered questions and an intense longing for him.

The strangest thing about feeding from Tomb was that he sustained me for much longer. When I'd fed from the humans, it had felt like I was on a crash diet, trying to fill myself with empty meals that didn't fully nourish me. But Tomb had been a five course meal, leaving me fully satisfied despite the fact that I hadn't even had any of his blood.

At first, when the hunger didn't return, I wondered if I'd been cured. I briefly allowed myself to hope that feeding from him had somehow eradicated it for good. But I soon learned that I wasn't cured. Just full.

But the more Spector made me train, the more my reserves ran dry. I wanted to go as long as I possibly could because I wasn't ready to kill again, and the thought of having sex with anyone but Tomb made me sick. But at the current rate I was going, I would need more food—and soon.

"The researchers need to see how quick your reflexes are. Apparently, they were up four hundred percent after your last feeding, but based on how horrible you've done today, you've steadily declined," Oz answered.

His answer surprised me because I hadn't expected him to actually respond at all. In my week of training, the only words spoken to me were demands.

"I see."

Oz just confirmed what I already knew. Spector wanted to push me, monitor me, see how I'd changed in response to feeding off of Tomb. Tomb had resurrected, while I'd become stronger. And Spector was going to use that. My particular skills were so unique that it terrified me to think of exactly *what* they'd use me for. I didn't want a lifetime of seducing men and killing them for Spector's agenda.

My eyes drifted across the space, noting the several others also currently training in the large room. Everyone was doing different things based on what kind of demon hybrid they were, and all of us were kept away from the others.

But despite the fact that we were separated, my eyes drifted over to where a particular shaggy blue-haired hybrid was standing. Crow was leaning against the gray padded wall, commanding his birds with barely a twitch of his fingers.

I knew I shouldn't stare, but I couldn't help but watch him. There was just *something* about him. I was attracted to him, sure, but it was more than that. My spider was definitely interested too, which had me a bit freaked out since that's how she felt about Tomb, and she'd killed the poor stone dude. Even though he'd come back to life, I still hadn't forgiven her for that one.

I watched as Crow lifted up his arm to let one of his birds land on him, and it made his bicep bulge. My tongue darted out to lick my lips. I couldn't help but imagine how his arms would look if his body were poised over mine, or how it would be to sink my teeth into that muscled part of his body. Gods, I bet he'd taste *amazing*.

I wanted to taste him—him and Tomb both. That dark desire of mine was rising up like water from a hot spring, bubbling beneath the surface and getting hotter and hotter every minute.

My carnal musings were cut short when sharp pain suddenly pierced my left thigh. "Ouch!" I looked down, just as the knife Oz had thrown at me fell to the floor from where it had hit my leg. My angry eyes lifted to him. "That *hurt*."

"Pay attention," my trainer snapped in response.

"I need a break," I said, still panting from exertion.

"That *was* your break. Now get your spider ass in gear, or you're gonna catch more knives in you."

"Careful," my spider warned, unfurling from the core of my being. Her voice was quiet, but deadly. Oz blanched before he could catch himself. "You know what I am. So you know that if I wanted to, I could trap you in so many webs that it would give me *plenty* of time to lure your cock out and consume your life before any of the guards could get to you."

Oz's face paled, and his hands automatically went in front of his dick, as if he could keep himself in his pants. My spider grinned, and he grew notably embarrassed at his vulnerability, his face mottling red.

"Water break," he bit out. "Sixty seconds."

I patted him on the shoulder. "Isn't it nice to work together?" I said in false politeness before walking away.

I noticed the frowns on the faces of the guards and the observing scientist—Lowell—in the room as their eyes followed me, but I ignored them as I walked up to the water table and downed a cup. I was probably going to pay for that one, but fuck them.

Once again, my eyes found Crow. Aside for yesterday, he'd been in every training session with me this week. We weren't allowed to speak to one another while we worked with our individual trainers, but a quiet longing still simmered between us. Sometimes, I'd catch him staring at me as he argued with Spector. He fought them at every turn, and I loved that about him. Based on that display I'd just done, I think Crow's rebellion was wearing off on me a little.

Crow's trainer, Freddie, was currently screaming at him to organize the flight pattern of his crows, but it didn't seem to be going so well. Every time he gave Crow a pattern to replicate, the birds would peck at the man's head or dive for his feet instead.

Based on the sly smirk on Crow's face, he was causing the chaos on purpose. I had an inkling that Crow could control them right down to the minutest flap of their wings, but he wanted to fuck with Spector...or simply not reveal just how in control he really was.

"Enough!" Freddie shouted, ducking and dodging the feathered menaces. "Let's try something else." He looked around amid the other hybrids training, and when he saw me standing at the water table watching, his trailing eyes stopped. "Hey, Oz! How about a face-off with our trainees?" he called over to my trainer.

Oz stuffed his remaining throwing knives in the holster in his belt and walked over to me. "Sounds good." He got to my side and tipped his chin up. "Break's over. Get over there with them. You can fight the hybrid."

I frowned. "What? No. I can't fight Crow."

Oz sneered at me. "It wasn't a fucking question, spider bitch. Get your ass over there. Now."

A knife was in his hand again, and my eyes flicked down to it. My interactions with Spector employees had always been rough, but they'd grown increasingly violent. I didn't need my vampiric sense of smell to know why. They feared me. And this fear caused them to use more and more force to keep me in line. But that line was going to snap if they weren't careful.

Crow looked steadily back at me from his spot in the training room as I turned to look at him. There were mats on the floors and a mix of mats and mirrors on the walls, and despite the fact that the entire place spilled with light, there weren't actually any windows.

I didn't want to move closer. I barely knew the man, but my spider liked him, and obviously, that attraction was dangerous. Tomb's death and subsequent resurrection were still very fresh in my mind, haunting me at every moment. I refused to let that happen again.

When my feet didn't immediately move, I felt the sinister press of Oz's knife at my back, the sharp edge puncturing my skin. "Move, spider bitch."

Clenching my teeth, I followed his orders and crossed the training area. As I drew closer to Crow, my spider seemed to flex within me. The closer I got, the more my spider went crazy in my chest. She could sense his nearness and enjoyed it. *A lot*.

Once I was in front of him, I finally looked up at Crow, only to be shocked at the anger in his violet eyes. Within seconds, three of his birds were attacking Oz, diving at his face with their razor-sharp claws and beaks.

"What the fuck!" Oz screamed while swatting at the assailants, dropping the knife in the process.

The moment I was free from its sharp edge, Crow

wrapped his arm around my middle and pulled me over to his side. My breath hitched at the contact, and his hand warmed me through the fabric of my shirt.

"Sorry about that. I guess I need more training," Crow said to Oz with an impish smile. "They're just impossible to control."

I had to place a hand over my mouth to stop the snort in my throat.

"Fucking pests," Oz cursed while wiping his bloodied lip.

"I think more training is definitely in order," Freddie replied stonily, making dread gather in my gut. I didn't like the predatory way he was staring at Crow and me.

"You're going to fight. Your birds can fucking peck at the spider bitch for a change," he said, sweeping his eyes up and down my body. Freddie had attended a few of my feeding sessions, so his presence here was unnerving.

"And what if I don't want to?" Crow asked. His birds flocked around him on high alert, staring down at the Spector men with irritation as they cawed and clawed at the air.

At Crow's question, Freddie smiled meanly. I could feel the malice rolling off of his expression. "Then you'll be punished. You remember what happened yesterday, don't you, Crow?" he asked, while cocking his head to the side. "I can always put in a request for the researchers to do more *tests*, since I know how much you enjoyed it last time."

Crow's face turned pale at whatever insinuation was hidden behind the man's dark words. Crow wasn't in training yesterday, but I hadn't thought anything of it. I was simply thankful for a break from the strange allure between us. Now, I wanted to know what they'd done to him.

My spider wanted to make them pay.

A low growl rumbled in my chest, surprising me. The sound must have pulled Crow out of his shock, because he cleared his voice. "Sure thing, asshole," he said in forced nonchalance before turning to face me.

The apology in his eyes made me worried for what was to come. His birds—although freaky as hell—seemed to like me. Just like that day in the cafeteria, some of them were hopping around at my feet, looking up at me expectantly.

They still freaked me out a bit, to be honest, but mostly because they made me think of the night of the ritual. I couldn't help remembering how the birds had pecked Spector guards to death, carrying bits of flesh in their sharp beaks. The memory made me shiver.

"Alright, you two are to fight head-to-head until one of you takes the other down or we call for you to stop. We'll be observing on the sidelines," Freddie said as they both made their way off the mats.

We had plenty of space away from the other trainees, and our section was separated by a thick wall of glass.

"What did they do to you yesterday?" I asked in a soft voice, not wanting the trainers to hear. I was disproportionately concerned for Crow. Realistically, we all were suffering here. It was every man for himself on Spector's turf. But I cared for Crow and Tomb. The idea of them suffering was unsettling for my spider and me.

"Oh, so now you want to talk? I thought you were avoiding me like the plague, Little Spider," Crow teased while crossing his arms over his chest, as if he wasn't in a hurry to do what the trainers said.

"It's not like I've had much of a chance. These training sessions are intense," I deflected.

"So intense that all you can do now is throw quick glances at me when I'm not looking and then turn away when I meet your eyes? I thought we hit it off in the cafeteria. What changed?"

My eyes flickered to the glass wall separating us from Oz

and Freddie. I wasn't sure how much they could hear or if everyone knew what I'd done yet.

"It's complicated. My demon…" my voice trailed off. I wasn't sure how to explain myself. I felt too vulnerable in that moment, strung between my odd desire for Crow and the fear of what I'd done to Tomb.

"I know about Tomb," Crow whispered while glancing at the glass, as if expecting them to intervene at any moment. It was like he could read my mind. Luckily, Oz and Freddie seemed to be in deep discussion with one of the researchers, so we had a little more time. Crow and I pretended to be stretching, like we were preparing for a run rather than getting ready to try and attack each other with our demon powers.

"You've seen Tomb? How is he?" I rushed out. "Is he okay?" A million questions and concerns poured out of me.

Crow swung his arms around, more and more birds materializing out of the shadowy vapor that came off of him in black wisps. "That's a tricky question," Crow said thoughtfully. "What exactly happened while you were in the tank, Motley? It's like he's…invincible now."

Invincible? "What do you mean?" I asked, my mouth dropped open in shock.

"He can't die, Motley. No matter how hard they try…"

It was my worst dreams come true. I'd changed Tomb. He wanted to escape this place, but I gave Spector more of a reason to keep him.

A chill skittered over my pulse points. "What do you mean how hard they try?" I asked warily.

Crow looked somber. "They've tried to kill him over and over again. They've been bringing in other hybrids. They even forced me to do it—or my crows, rather. But no matter what I did, he wouldn't stay dead."

Horror crawled down my throat and pinched in my stomach.

"They're testing how far they can push him. Poison, draining his blood, suffocation. Hell, even decapitation. He dies, but every time, his body renews or rejoins...and he just comes back. It's fucking awful," he said, looking noticeably disturbed.

His words made me crumble. The thought of Tomb being subjected to something so horrible because of me was devastating. But even more than sorrow, I felt an anger like nothing I'd ever experienced in my life. I wanted to burn this place to the ground for hurting what was *mine*.

Mine? *Oh fuck*.

Inwardly, I gaped at my spider, and my fingers brushed over the red hourglass on my throat—the same one Tomb now had on him. Is *that* why we'd marked him? Had my spider demon...chosen him as a mate?

This just became a whole lot more complicated. And my spider was *really* pissed.

I could feel her vengeance burning me up like hellfire. She was livid to hear what Spector was doing to him. She wanted to make them pay. *We* wanted to make them pay. I just didn't know how. This place was incredibly guarded, and I was fairly certain we were underground. They pumped us with chemicals and threatened us constantly. We were in a guarded maze with no way out.

But I'd find a fucking way.

When I glanced back at the trainers, I noticed they were finishing up their discussion with the scientist. We didn't have much longer to stall. My energy was slowly depleting, but I had faith that I could take care of myself. Within me, my spider seemed to preen at the possibility of a challenge. I was starting to realize that she was a prideful, cocky motherfucker who was always up for a fight. Always looking to show someone up. We were similar in that aspect, I suppose: determined to prove ourselves and ambitious to a fault.

"Do you know what demon I am?" Crow asked softly, and the tenderness in his voice made me pause.

"Some kind of crow whisperer?" I quipped lamely.

"I have a malphas demon," he replied ominously. "I attended Thibault too, you know. You probably don't even remember me, but I graduated two years ago, a scholarship student."

I peered up at him, trying to place the bright blue hair and mischievous smile. I didn't recognize him, but then again I was always so stuck in my own world that I didn't pay much attention to anyone else.

"The exact same thing happened. They offered me an exclusive opportunity I couldn't refuse. Brought me to the ritual room. And then bam, I became *this*. Tomb was my first friend in this place."

I wanted to ask him how he went from being one of Spector's playthings to attempting to rescue us from a ritual, but refrained. I wasn't sure if he would actually answer me or if we could be heard from the other side of that glass.

"Look, they think they can control us—our powers—through fear and anger. So they make us fight, test us, make us hurt one another. It's par for the course in this place," he said bitterly. "I used to never feel in control of my crows. They weren't an extension of me. They were just this wild, angry entity pecking everything in their path."

I shook my head while glancing around at the crows where they were hopping around the floor or flying around in lazy swoops above our heads. It was strange to see them so...docile. Especially when I'd seen firsthand what they were capable of. They were so in sync with Crow's movements, too.

"So what changed?"

He brushed his long blue hair out of his face. "I came to accept that my birds were a part of me. And that they wanted one thing."

"And what's that?"

"To protect me. That's what all of our demons are doing," he said, holding my gaze. "So I want you to think about that, okay?"

It was a simple explanation, but he was right. My demon had always protected us, from the very beginning, even though she was forced to possess me. That realization, along with Tomb's advice about accepting her as a part of me, clicked into place. She wasn't my enemy. This was done to her as much as it was done to me, but now we had each other, and together, we could either be at odds or accept one another. Then, we might actually have a chance of surviving this and taking the fuckers down.

Holding Crow's eyes, I nodded, my inward epiphany shining in my eyes. "You're right."

As I uttered the words, it was like the turmoil of fighting my spider finally subsided. Like a tumultuous sea, the storm passed over and we were finally in calmer waters.

"Get fucking started right now," Oz shouted over at us, shocking us both out of the intense conversation we were having.

Crow's jaw tightened, but he nodded over at my trainer before he began to walk backwards, giving us both some room to fight. "I'm going to order my birds to attack—even though they *really* don't like the idea of attacking you. But I know you and your spider can handle yourself. Protect. Okay?" he said quietly as before grabbing my hands.

I nodded. "Protect."

Closing my eyes, I drew out that instinct—the need to protect me, her, *us*. As soon as I did that, I felt her shadows coalesce inside of me. Her head dipped, her legs unfurled, and her presence came forward in my head like I'd woken her up.

"It's working," I murmured, a small smile spreading across my face. I couldn't believe how *easy* it was. Now that I wasn't at odds with her, her powers were right at my fingertips to use without the need to first feel threatened. Not just the webs, but her core strength seemed to bolster me. My vampiric senses were even sharper, my energy boosted. It was like we were finally mixing ourselves together rather than holding them in separate containers within a shared body. It felt *right*.

"Good," he said quietly, still holding my hands. "Do you feel that need to protect? Feel how in control you are?" he asked. "How you merge into one?"

My fingertips began to tingle. "Yes," I replied.

"Good. That's how I feel, too. I'm going to attack, and I want you to remember that I'm in control of my birds. Not Spector, not my anger or fear, *me*. I would never hurt you, okay? And your spider won't hurt me."

"Why are you saying this?" I asked, opening my eyes.

"Because I don't want you to fear me, Little Spider," he replied in a playful yet meaningful tone. "Or yourself. Just think of this as a little play time for our demons," he said with a smirk.

"If I have to tell you *one* more time, you won't like what happens," Oz's voice boomed.

"No need to get your Spector sweats in a shit twist," Crow called back. "We were just mentally preparing and all that."

He looked to me with a nod, a smirk ghosting over his lips. "Ready?"

I let my anxiety go and did exactly what he said—viewed this as nothing but playful sparring between our demons. We weren't going to let Spector pit us against one another. If anything, we'd show them how well we could band together. "My spider is gonna kick your feathered ass."

Crow laughed, the sound warming me up. "You wish, Little Spider."

With a clap of his hands, the entire outline of his body vibrated with moving shadows that misted off his body and then materialized into more birds.

While he built his feathered army, I didn't waste any time. Holding my hands up, I started building a webbed wall between Crow and me, hoping to block them off. I forced webs to move with decisive energy. I flung my left arm out, and webs shot from my fingers and attached to the glass wall. I did the same thing with my right hand and then moved my hands in sync, adding more and more strands until there was a wall of a thin yet intricate web that separated us.

Crow smiled at me from the other side. "Well done, Little Spider," he praised. "But let's see how you do when they get past your little web."

Dozens of crows animated on the spot, their bodies flying toward my web. They cawed and circled, looking for weaknesses in my wall, searching for an opening. One part near the glass had a small gap, and birds dive bombed through it with excited flaps of their wings. My heart rate picked up as I shot web after web at them, trying to catch them, but they zoomed out of the way.

"Have to do better than that!" Crow hollered at me with a laugh in his voice.

"Fucking cocky ass bird boy," I grumbled to myself.

One of his birds shot through the web and came at me, nipping at my shoulder. Another whirled around my hair, cawing as it tangled its body inside the red strands. Another one got through before I could get the gap filled in, diving for my hands and curling its claws around my fingers, trying to get me to stop throwing out webs.

A crow landed on my shoulder and nipped at my ear, and I realized I needed to change tactics.

I shot my webs out, wrapping them around the birds one by one in little nets, where I set them on the floor. I smirked at Crow triumphantly. "Ha! I won!"

Crow's violet eyes narrowed. "You really think that was it?" he asked.

Then shadows exploded out of his hands. Like a missile, it careened toward the center of my webbed wall, and then hundreds of birds were moving in a single intent, their beaks breaking through the barrier like a rocket. I screamed and dove for the floor, barely able to throw up enough webs to keep the birds from attacking me. I squealed and covered my head with my arms, knowing it was just a matter of time before they'd break through and cover me. I wasn't afraid of Crow's birds anymore, and I admittedly *was* having fun, but the birds still kind of made me anxious.

"Okay, okay! I surrender!"

"I win!" Crow called cockily, swaggering over. His birds immediately calmed and started hopping around, their weight bearing down on my little web cave. I could barely see him through the tiny igloo-shaped barrier I was crouched under. Hundreds of birds were all over the place.

"You cheated," I huffed.

Crow laughed. "Did not."

"Can you send your little murder away now before they start crapping on me?" I asked, my voice slightly muffled.

Crow scoffed. "My demonic feathered friends would never poop on you," he said. "Unless I ordered them to."

My eyes widened. "Don't you dare!"

He laughed, and then all at once, the birds evaporated back into shadows and sunk into his body. With a relieved sigh, I flicked my wrist, and the webs parted for me, letting me crawl back out. Crow took my hand and helped me stand up. He smiled down at me, but it wasn't a friendly smile. It was a roving, hungry one as his eyes took in my flushed face and heaving chest. Gently, he reached forward and plucked some webs from my hair.

"This is a good look on you," he said, his voice low and genuine.

"What is? A sweaty loser?" I joked.

He shook his head, and then suddenly his mouth was pressing against the edge of my cheek, his lips skimming my ear. "No. You at one with your spider. Smiling. Playing. Using your powers." His lips grazed up, and when his tongue darted out to lick the shell of my ear, my stomach flipped over. "You looked fucking sexy as hell, Little Spider."

Before my heart could even stutter out a beat, Crow had pulled away, walking off, and I was left gaping after him with heat in my core and a black feather behind my ear.

Chapter 10

"YOU HAVE thirty minutes to clean up, then go back to your cell," Oz said gruffly while escorting me to the locker rooms. He lingered for a moment, and I thought he was going to follow me inside and watch me strip out of my sweaty clothes. I nearly gagged. I didn't want his predatory eyes on my body.

"Okay," I gritted in response while walking through the double doors.

Thankfully, he didn't follow after me, and I breathed a sigh of relief when I saw the small tiled room with lines of showers along the walls. There were no dividers between the streams of water, but no one was in here with me, so at least I had some privacy.

It was blissful, turning on the hot water and standing under the stream. It was the first time since arriving that I didn't feel the intrusive stare of my captors as I took hurried showers in the training locker room. My body ached and stung with wild abandon from the intense training session. Each beaded droplet of water slipped down my sweaty skin, washing away the feel of Spector embedded in the grime. It was a private mercy, and I relished in it.

As I was dipping my head back under the water, the door suddenly opened, revealing a sweaty, shirtless Crow. His blue hair was clumped with moisture, and his muscles were gleaming. He stopped in his tracks when he saw me. I stood frozen beneath the stream, not knowing if I should cover my nakedness, too caught off guard to react. But when I saw him trail those dynamic eyes of his up and down my slick body, I drowned in his gaze, my body flushing at the attention.

"Sorry. They told me to get cleaned up," he said roughly, though his tone lacked any signs of remorse.

I sure as shit wasn't sorry. A shirtless Crow was sexy as hell. My spider was thrilled. She wanted to explore the intrinsic connection between us and sink her fangs into his veins. Hungry saliva rushed into my mouth at the thought.

We didn't say anything for a long moment. We simply exchanged hooded stares and silent pleading, both of us drinking in the sight of one another as awkward tension made my throat close. His body was beautiful. Rolling abs that rippled in their defined glory flexed with each inhale of his heaving breaths. There was a delicious *V* that led my hungry eyes down to the waistband of his training sweats, where his hand was poised and ready, like he was asking my permission to undress.

"Y-you better hurry. Oz said we only have thirty minutes. You don't want to miss out on a hot shower," I said, feigning innocence when all I really wanted to do was beg him to strip and show me what was causing the impressive bulge in his pants.

Watching me, he slowly flicked his button open, then slid down his zipper with excruciatingly sensual confidence. He took his time easing his tight clothes over his muscular thighs before dropping them to the wet floor.

"Oz is taking a nap outside. We have plenty of time," he replied suggestively before running a hot palm over the front of his black boxers, making his cock bob behind the strained material.

My mouth filled with wanton venom, coating my lips and tongue with a flooding need. My breathing was rapid. There wasn't enough air in the small shower room. All I could breathe in was steam coated with his lusty scent.

"You alright, Little Spider? I didn't go too *hard* on you today in training, did I?" he asked while stepping closer to me.

His bare feet scuffled across the tiled floor as I put soap in my palm and started rubbing it along my body. I was pinned under his stare and desperate for friction against my sensitive skin. What would he think if I touched myself?

I couldn't risk sex with Crow. I didn't understand what happened with Tomb or if I could recreate it. And I wasn't *too* hungry, so I didn't have the excuse of demanding and feverish need directing my every move, though I could feel desire swiftly sweeping through me with each passing second.

Right now, my craving and hunger had nothing to do with the spider in my soul and everything to do with my own selfish need to fuck and feel normal for a moment.

"I thought I handled myself pretty well," I teased. "A little more practice and I'll be kicking your ass, Crow."

I turned and faced the stream of water, letting the steady downpour hit my face as I trembled in anticipation, knowing his gaze was hot on my ass. It wasn't until a hard body pressed against my back that I moved.

"What are you doing?" I asked breathlessly.

"Touching you," he murmured, his fingers coming up to trail lightly over the curve of my hips.

I shivered at the touch and spun back around to face him,

my hands colliding with his chest. I licked a droplet of water that had collected on the top of my lip, wishing I was licking water off his skin instead. My eyes flicked down to his black boxers which were drenched and slipping, the heavy material sliding down in the most torturous strip tease of my life.

"You're soaked. Why don't you take your boxers off?" I asked.

"Take them off for me, Motley," Crow demanded in a low timber. Sparks of tension bounced between us, the electricity so tangible, so lifelike, that I wondered if we'd electrocute ourselves with the palpable power.

"No. You saw what happened to Tomb," I argued while taking a step back. My body collided with cool tile, making a shiver travel up and down my spine. "Do you want to be tortured? Do you want to die, Crow?" I asked. My hands were braced against his pecs, shoving him away while still refusing to break the contact. Despite the turmoil racing through me, I appreciated the hot comfort pulsing where my fingers connected with his skin.

"Take off my boxers, Motley. I want to see you lick your lips when you see my cock. I want to feel your soft hands wrap around it," he rasped while pressing into me. Our bodies molded together, water the only thing between us.

I didn't want just another fuck driven by my need to feed or the demanding lure in my bones. I wanted to take my time. My fingers trailed, slipped, dipped. I sunk them down his abs and toward the sagging fabric. I pet the soft hair just above the band of his underwear with sacred appreciation.

I stopped.

"Why did you try to save us that day? How did you even get out?"

"I don't know," Crow replied softly before reaching up to palm my breasts. His fingers gripped hard, plunging into the pillowy skin and kneading my flesh. I gasped and moaned, hating the distraction of his touch when I so desperately wanted to understand him.

"What do you mean?" I asked the moment he pinched my nipple between his thumb and index finger. My back arched off the tile, crashing us even closer, sending his hard cock pressing against my stomach.

"I escaped. I nearly died. Went into hiding and made plans to never return here," Crow began before leaning in to lick a trail up my neck. Slow, slow, slow, like he was savoring the taste. The low growl of approval that tumbled around in his chest made me whimper. It was too hot. Too much. "And then one day, something felt wrong. My crows were restless. It was a pull like nothing I'd ever felt before. At that point, I'd learned to trust their instincts. They were why I'd escaped Spector in the first place."

He bit my earlobe and sucked on the skin right below it. Pulling with his mouth between gasped words and revealed intuitions.

"What did your demon want?"

Crow chuckled against my skin before pulling back. He grabbed my wrists and positioned my hands on his hips, using his thumb to stroke my skin. "I didn't know, at first. When he led me to that building and I saw that there was another ritual going on, I laughed from the irony. When he urged me to break through the windows, I wanted to cry." He leaned forward and kissed my lips then, a tender, slow, sensual, taunting, invigorating, stroking, tugging, enrapturing kiss. Our lips moved in tandem, our tongues tangling with desire.

When he pulled away, he stole my breath. I was nothing but gasping need.

"But when I saw you, Little Spider, I felt nothing but understanding."

I didn't understand, but I didn't need thoughts. I needed

to *feel*. I felt the connection between us, something timeless and precious and so unpredictable. I knew what we were. My spider knew. We'd met somewhere in the middle of our existence and accepted this undeniable pull.

Despite how new it was, despite Spector breathing down our necks, we found a tether connecting us. It started as fine silk but was fortified over time, becoming something stronger. Sometimes connections were bred from tragedy. People were scuffed, torn, and branded with pain. This connection I had with Tomb and Crow was like fine polish, making me new again. We found each other in the clutches of evil.

I grabbed the waistband of his boxers and slowly slipped them down. His cock sprung free and brushed against my trembling hands as the soaking wet material fell to the tile with a sloshing sound, scattering water like fireworks over my shins. He stepped out of them with a smile, our eyes still locked on one another in a delicate dance of boundaries. If we crossed this, there would be no coming back. If I fed from him, I could kill him.

"Your demon came for me," I said in awe.

"And I stayed for you," he added.

I dropped to my knees and winced at the hard tile that met my achy bones. There were no webs spilling from my fingers. There was no impulsive, famished spider pulling haunted, tantric words from my lips. She wasn't directing my yearning body or my dripping pussy. She had slipped into the back of my mind, as if letting me feel like *me* again. For this.

For Crow.

"You going to put me in your mouth, Little Spider?" he asked.

My eyes were met with his hard cock and the silver piercing poised directly on the head. I wanted to feel the metallic taste on my tongue. I wanted it inside of me. "Yes," I whispered before dragging my lips along his shaft, whispering prayers and salacious little nothings in my mind as he twitched from my delicate touch.

"Taste me," he pleaded. "I want to see that fierce mouth consuming me, Motley."

Thrill spurred me forward. I wrapped the lips he seemed to love so much around the head, sinking and sinking, inch by delightful inch, until his thick dick was poking the back of my throat—until I was gagging on cock. Until I was drowning in his smell and moaning at the way he twitched.

"*Fuck*," he rasped. "You were made for my cock, baby."

I'd felt power before. My sex life had become an exchange of control since Spector possessed me. I'd come to expect my deadly prowess, but right now, I was able to appreciate the power I had of simply being responsible for his pleasure.

I loved pumping his cock with my mouth. I loved feeling him slide all the way down my throat. I loved taunting him with my tongue and watching the way his muscles rippled with tension which each command of my body.

I didn't need my spider to be in control. This was all me.

I thrust against him with broken whimpers, hollowing my cheeks and tightening around him as I did. He tasted good—salty and sweet. He tasted like divine magic meant only for me.

"I want to feel that tight little pussy clenching around my cock, Motley," he urged while pulling my hair and guiding me off of him. His hardness slipped out of my mouth with a pop, and I licked my swollen lips for the remaining taste of him while looking up at his hooded eyes from under my lashes.

"Are you sure about that?" I asked. The darkness of my spider was easing her way back to the surface. She'd given me my time. She'd allowed me to take back my power for myself.

But she was the ultimate conductor. She'd taken my body as her own, and now it was time for her to take Crow.

He yanked me up and slammed me against the tile again. That cock—that perfect, hard, thick erection poked at my most sensitive point. Each press, each angry demand of his body, made me writhe.

"Come out to play, Little Spider," he moaned before wrapping his hand around my neck and squeezing.

My pulse roared against his grip as he devoured my mouth. I felt utterly consumed. Treasured. Wanted.

His teeth nipped at my lips, and I parted for him, lapping up his tongue and taste with decadent strokes.

"I need you," I said against his mouth.

"Then you'll have me."

He hiked up my leg even higher and then placed the head of his cock at my entrance, before slipping back down, coating the length of him in the wetness gathered at my slit. I rocked my hips against him, as if my body was demanding his entry, making him smirk.

"You like that, Little Spider?" he asked with a grin, bringing the head of his cock back up.

"I want you inside of me."

Crow groaned, reaching up to run a hand through his wet blue hair. "Hearing you say that is the sexiest fucking thing in the world."

In true Crow style, he started pushing into me, just the head, before slipping back out and doing it again. And again. And again. Never giving me more than an inch or two, never rushing.

I was panting, writhing, trying to gyrate my hips to get more of him, but he continued to tease and take his time.

"Crow!" I finally demanded, hearing the desperate whine of my voice.

"If I could, I'd tease you like this for *hours*," he said,

bracing a hand on the wall beside my face, his arm muscles bunched and dripping with water.

I whimpered, picturing in my mind all the things he'd do to me. I needed to come *so* badly. I needed to feel him deep in the recesses of my body, coaxing out the pleasure I so desperately wanted.

Taking pity on me, he finally started to push more of himself inside. It was slow. Torturous. Reveling. I felt every miniscule movement as his thick cock grazed against my sensitive walls. His piercing stroked my insides in a stimulating caress, the metal grinding into my pleasure points and making me groan. Until finally, *finally*, he was all the way inside.

"*Yes.*"

"Fuck, Motley, you feel godsdamned amazing."

"Move," I demanded, needing that erotic friction to take me higher.

In reply, Crow reached down and gripped me by the ass, suddenly lifting me up completely. Both of my legs curled around his hips, and then he began to move.

He slicked in and out of me, continuing his slow tempo, and yet his movements were hard, his cock thrusting in and out of me in his rhythmic movement that sung to my soul and harmonized with my pleasure.

His mouth latched onto mine, his tongue fucking me in the same sensual strokes that he was using with his cock. I watched as shadows scattered off his skin, rising around him right along with the steam. I could feel the energy of his demon as my spider latched on and began to feed, could hear the softest call of his crows like they were a whisper in the vapor around us.

I was filling up, not just of his essence, but of *him*. Every thrust of his cock, every swipe of his tongue, every press of his hands was like sustenance to my spirit. My hips rocked with every movement, my moans swallowed down by his mouth. I touched him everywhere I could reach, swiping both water and soap suds across his skin.

"You feel that, baby?" he asked. "You feel how perfect I fit inside of you? You feel how good I pound that dripping cunt of yours? Take it all." Each dirty word that spilled from his lips was accentuated by his deep invading thrusts. I could feel it, how perfect this was, the complete rightness of it all.

It felt so good that I didn't think of the monster in my chest when I threw my head back and came with a hiss. I didn't think about my deadly body sucking from his deep pool of life. His grunts and moans were a pleasant cadence to my roaring orgasm, and his pleasure followed after mine. The fullness within me twitched and jerked as hot cum spilled into me from his cock.

"Fuck," he growled.

For the first time since joining my demon, I truly felt in control enough to stop, but I didn't want to. Something within me wanted to see this to the very end. I wanted to snap his essence and drink every last drop until my mark was branded on his neck. It was a territorial necessity. I couldn't end this until he was *mine*.

My spider yanked on the last of his offering, shadows and feathers erupting out of Crow's body like lava spitting from a volcano.

Only with my vampiric strength and reflexes was I able to catch him before he fell to the tile. Only with my supernatural hearing was I able to hear his heartbeat stop over the spray of the shower.

My spider was satisfied, my body still sang in the remnants of our love making, and I'd killed another man I cared about. All because that relentless drive to finish what I'd started had forced my hand and taken the rest of his life essence.

And yet, as I sat naked with his head in my lap, his blue hair tangled over my thighs, and my skin pebbling under the cold spray of water, I didn't panic. I didn't mourn.

Because there, beneath the shadow of his jaw, was a blood-red hourglass mark on his skin.

Chapter 11

I WAS SITTING in the common room, sipping on blood and trying to ignore Cheryl's constant talking. It was proving to be difficult because on a good day, Cheryl's voice was annoying. On a hangry day? It was making me downright murderous.

My reserves were running low. It had been a week since my time with Crow, and though feeding from him had been as satisfying as Tomb, my spider was anxiously waiting for another meal. I would've been able to preserve my energy better if I weren't being constantly forced to train. I was dreading the moment Spector realized I was hungry again, so I did everything I could to keep my face fixed in a pleasant smile and not reveal the roaring hunger barreling through me.

But I wasn't just hungry. I missed Crow and Tomb. I wanted to see them so badly it hurt. After Oz had found Crow dead in my lap, Spector had put two and two together and monitored him, watching as he came back to life. Meanwhile, they'd forced me to keep going through rigorous trainings, plus strict eating and sleeping regiments that left me exhausted.

"I'm not saying you're a bad friend, I'm just saying that not *once* have you checked on me since we got here," Cheryl went on.

She'd been talking for a good twenty minutes. The moment I entered the common area, she swarmed to me like shifters on shit. I wasn't really paying attention, though. I was too busy worrying about Tomb and remembering Crow's lips on my skin to really focus on her shrill voice and self-importance, but her last statement caught my attention.

"Wait, what?" I asked, looking over at her. "Are you seriously mad at me for not checking on you while I was locked up in the tank?" My voice was incredulous. Cheryl had always been selfish, but this was getting ridiculous. It wasn't my fault I couldn't hold her hand.

Cheryl let out an exasperated sigh. "Well, yeah! I mean, I get that you've been busy with training and whatever, but I thought we were friends. You came in here and just sat down. You didn't even say hello to me."

I frowned and studied her. She was wearing a sequined shirt, and her blonde hair was sleek and smooth, like she wasn't a miserable mess in here like me. She had an overstated pout on her perfect face, but there was a sense of authenticity to her words. I didn't get it. Our entire cohabitation consisted of her telling me that I wasn't good enough to be in her friend circle. I kept to myself, and she kept up the pretense that she was being forced to live with me. We didn't really like one another. So why was she upset?

If I were being honest, I was too busy worrying what other test Spector was going to do to me to really concern myself with her. Not to mention, Crow had been noticeably absent since our time in the shower. I'd barely gotten a few glimpses of him since, like Spector was purposely keeping us apart, and I still hadn't seen Tomb either. I was distracted and worried, but I didn't expect Cheryl to care about me being distant.

"Is that so?" I asked, prodding her more.

"Yeah. I mean, we lived together for five years, Motley. I thought I meant something to you," she huffed while toying with a bracelet on her wrist. The vulnerable slump of her shoulders made me pause. Maybe I'd misunderstood our relationship.

I cleared my throat and put down my drink on the cafeteria table. "I'm not trying to be an ass, but I didn't think we were friends, Cheryl. When we first were placed in our dorm room together, you told me I wasn't good enough," I replied while giving her a pointed stare. "You never went out of your way to hang out with me and were always reminding me that we didn't run in the same circles. Forgive me for not wanting to check on someone that claimed to not care."

There was an added bite to my words, but I stuck to them. I didn't appreciate the double standard, and since I no longer had to share a room with her insufferable ass, I didn't mind being transparent about my feelings.

Cheryl's eyes turned bloody with unshed tears, and she blinked them away as her lip trembled. "I know I haven't really been nice to you. I don't make friends easily. But you didn't make it easy, either. You think I don't notice your underhanded comments, but I do. Plus, you're so stuck in your own world, I didn't even bother."

"Fair enough," I began. "I've always kept to myself. It was easier that way." I never really socialized, outside of the random one night stands. I didn't see the point, no one would have accepted me anyways.

"I get it. You're the loner, and I'm the amazing socialite you're jealous of," Cheryl replied with a sniff. I opened my mouth to tell her to take a hike, but she cut me off before I could. "But I'm really freaked out. You've always been so smart and tough. I couldn't handle half the shit people have said to you, and I know if anyone could get us out of this"—she paused to look around as she leaned closer, dropping her voice so only I could hear—"it's going to be you. So I'm here. I'm sorry for what happened in the past, and I'll do whatever it takes to get the hell out of this place. They...they're making me hurt people, Motley. Have you ever tried getting blood out of cashmere? It's, like, *impossible*. They're so primitive."

I pursed my lips so I wouldn't smile. "So, what are you, anyway?" I asked while taking another sip of my drink. I was definitely hungry and was certain the blood sloshing around my stomach was no longer enough to sustain me. "You stopped Tomb and me from attacking the guards before they took us to the tank. I'm not blaming you," I quickly added when I saw her gear up defensively. "I know they forced you. I just want to know what you are."

Cheryl sat up straight. "I'm a Siren! Well, kind of. I just sing and everyone kind of passes out from the pain. Sometimes they die if they make me sing for longer than a minute."

My brow shot up in surprise. Her voice killed people? How...appropriate.

"Oh?" I asked, trying not to laugh at the irony of her demon. I'd been saying for years that her voice would be the death of me, and now it could actually come to fruition.

"Yeah. They make me sing. *A lot*. They just cart humans in, then wheel them away. It's awful, Motley. A lot of them d-die."

My mouth dropped open in shock. I'd been so caught up in the evil, violating things Spector did to me and the guys, that I didn't stop to think about what everyone else was going through. I looked around and observed my peers. When we first got here, there was a sense of pride and excitement. But slowly, the numbers thinned, and people had clearly lost their enthusiasm. I hadn't even noticed the silence of the room or the dull way people stared at their food.

I reached across the table and grabbed Cheryl's hand, giving it a friendly squeeze. "I'm really sorry they made you do that. Are you okay?" I asked.

She swallowed before looking at where our hands connected before shaking her head. For once, Cheryl was speechless. She had nothing to say, but the regret and sadness was written on her perfect face. She pulled her hand back and wiped her eyes, somehow strategically smoothing her blurred makeup in the process.

"Anyway. What do they do to you?" she asked, changing the subject and making a pit of shame fill me up.

I debated on telling her a lie, but ultimately settled on the truth. After all, she'd told me about her demon, so it only seemed fair. "It's complicated. Basically I fuck people to death," I replied, though it felt like a hollow explanation. What I did was far more gruesome than I could ever really articulate.

Cheryl's eyes widened, and she let out a puff of air, as if debating on how to respond. "So let me get this straight. Your vagina kills people, and my voice makes their ears bleed. We'd make one hell of a porno, spider girl," she teased before taking another sip of her own bloody drink.

I let out a short chuckle, relieved that she was making light of our conversation. I had expected her to gasp and tell me how terrible I was. Maybe Spector had matured her some.

"So you're not scared of me?" I asked. For some reason, I needed her acceptance. I'd been so worked up over my demon that I was clinging to anyone that didn't run away screaming. It was nice not to be feared.

"Why would I be scared? It's not like I have a desire to

fuck you. I mean, maybe if you made an effort with your appearance." She looked me up and down with a frown. "But even then, it would take some *serious* alcohol before I could even consider it. I still think you should give bangs another shot. I really liked that look on you. It was so chic. You should let me give you another makeover," she said decisively.

"A makeover? You cut my hair in my sleep, Cheryl," I deadpanned, cringing at the memory of that terrible haircut I had my first year at Thibault.

"And it looked fabulous," she replied with a smile.

I rolled my eyes, but a small smile graced my lips too. "I looked ridiculous," I replied.

We laughed for a bit, then settled in awkward silence, like we weren't sure what to do with this newfound truce. Cheryl finally spoke, though. She never was good with silence. "The thing is, I don't think my parents are going to come for me, Motley. Hell, they couldn't even be bothered to attend my graduation." Cheryl looked off in the distance, and surprisingly, I felt bad for her. I hadn't realized that her parents didn't show up. In fact, for all her talk of her parents, I hadn't seen them once during our five years at Thibault. "We need each other if we're going to survive this place. I mean, this is worse than Jeremy Lovit's bar mitzvah. And my dress *ripped*, Motley."

I shook my head with a quirk of my lips. Cheryl might be annoying as hell, but she had a point. If I wanted to get out of here, I'd have to build alliances. Besides, she'd already befriended some of the guards. This truce would be good.

"Stiles has been training with me. I made his ears bleed," she said with a hint of pride.

At the mention of my half-brother, a sour taste filled my mouth, and I completely lost my appetite. Although, hearing that he was stuck with Cheryl's deadly screams made me feel a little bit better.

"Where is Stiles, anyway?" I asked. "I haven't seen him since we got here."

A dark look crossed Cheryl's face, and she crossed her arms over her chest. I knew that look. She gave it to Mary Catherine our second year at Thibault when she tried to date Brandon Cooper, a senior vamp with more money than he knew what to do with. Cheryl had been pissed since she'd claimed him for herself.

"Why do you want to know?" she asked with irritation. "We've been getting *very* close lately. He's been totally kind, bringing me clothes and helping me understand my powers. I really hope you don't have a crush on him, Motley, because it's obvious he likes me."

I wasn't completely sure anything about Stiles was *obvious*—especially when it came to caring about someone other than himself. But I wouldn't be the one to burst her bubble.

"I promise you, Cheryl, I'm far from interested," I replied with a frown.

She didn't look convinced. "We've bonded, Motley. I don't think he really supports his father in all of this. He doesn't like how Spector is treating all of us, you know. I think his dad is pressuring him somehow."

This bit of information was intriguing. I briefly mulled over the moments leading up to the ritual. Stiles didn't want either of us to attend the banquet. He was uncharacteristically kind to me that night—or at least his version of kind..

I wasn't completely sold on the idea that Stiles was innocent in all of this, but I wanted to learn more. I decided right then it was time to let Cheryl in on the Trant's dirtiest secret.

"Cheryl, can I tell you something in confidence?" I asked, and her eyes lit up with glee.

"Ooh, a secret? I love secrets. When Marlene Vatterby

told me she got pregnant with a shifter hybrid while engaged to her vamp fiancé, I didn't tell a single soul," she replied excitedly while practically jumping in her seat.

I scrubbed my hand down my face. "No, this is different. You really can't tell anyone, Cheryl. Okay? I'm serious."

She nodded, her grin growing broader. I was probably going to regret this, but we both leaned in closer over the table so I could whisper.

"Stiles is my half-brother. His father slept around on his wife and had me. They gave me up a few days after I was born," I rushed out, then watched in apprehension as Cheryl's green eyes widened in part shock, part horror.

"You have a crush on your half-brother?" she hissed. "That's fucked up, Motley!" She gagged a bit and shook her head in disgust.

Gods give me patience. This woman was going to be the death of me.

"I do not have a crush on my brother, you psycho!" I said a little too loudly. The tables around us turned to stare, and my spider shot a web out, warning them to mind their own damn business.

"Look," I began while Cheryl processed my words. "Mr. Trant is my father. I want to know what he's up to and figure out Stiles's role in all of this. We can work together, okay? Figure out what he has over Stiles. If my brother is being forced to help Spector, I want to know. And if he's not?" I paused for dramatic effect, giving Cheryl a sympathetic frown in the process. "It's probably better we both know. You think you can do that?"

Cheryl stared back at me, eyeing me up and down with newfound understanding. I didn't like the pity in her stare.

"So you've been a Trant all this time?" she asked. "I mean, you're a *scholarship* student. You were a social pariah; why didn't you say anything?"

Thoughts of Aunt Marie coursed through me, and tears filled my eyes. Maybe if people knew, I would have had more opportunities in life. But then again, we depended on the Trant's monthly allowance to keep us going. My aunt couldn't work, and neither could I until I graduated, so we needed that income. Besides, I didn't want to gain anything off the back of my absentee father's name. He would've denied the claim anyway, and then I would've been viewed as a liar as well as a pariah.

"It was a stipulation of my monthly living stipend that they sent to my aunt. She can't work... So anyway, I really didn't have a choice," I said in a low voice, feeling dejected.

Cheryl puffed out her chest before reaching across the table to squeeze my hand, mimicking my earlier gesture. "I'll see what I can find out, okay? We're going to get out of this," she promised.

I was shocked by the vehemence in her voice and the determination in her eyes. Cheryl didn't make fun of me for being an unwanted bastard, nor did she judge me for keeping this secret for money. She accepted me fully and offered her help. Maybe I'd misjudged her all these years.

Who was this girl?

"Besides, I once got Jolene Mathington to admit she was stealing history tests from Professor Lox. I even convinced her to share them with me in exchange for backstage passes to an Alpha Pack concert. That chick is a frigid bitch, and she sang like a canary! I think I can handle the Trants."

Ah, there she was.

Chapter 12

"YOUR FEEDING WILL BE different today, Motley," Lowell, the observing scientist, said while checking his tablet.

I tried to keep my roaring famishment under control as I followed behind him, but after two more days had passed, Spector noticed that it was time to feed again.

I was dreading it. I didn't want to be forced to feed on humans that I would inevitably kill. I didn't want to fuck a stranger and watch the light fade from his eyes.

But my spider was hungry. She needed to feed, and that drive dragged my feet down the hallway, keeping my eyes trained on the floor and my teeth clenched in apprehension.

When we got to my usual room where they brought me humans to drain, I was surprised to find that the room was filled with people. Not just the scientists who sat behind the observation glass, or the guards by the door, but the other hybrids too.

What the fuck?

My eyes scanned the crowded room, and I froze when I saw Tomb standing off to the side. He looked okay on the surface, brimming with life and light. But there was a sense of pain in his expression that made my heart clench.

When our eyes met, his chest puffed out, and he took a step toward me, only to be stopped when the guard behind him pulled him back. My eyes watered. I wanted to run to him and burrow my head in his neck. That invisible tether between us strengthened tenfold, and I had to lock down my demon to keep her from getting us killed by fighting our way over to him.

Beside him, Crow was staring at me with a look of pity. He was breathing heavily, as if in anger, and watched me with a hard stare while one of his crows was perched on his shoulder, pecking and cawing in distress.

"Differently?" I asked while turning my attention to Lowell.

Were they going to make me feed in front of *everyone*?

The thought made my anxiety spike.

"When you fed from participant three-four-two, you made him immortal. We've tested extensively and concluded that he cannot die thus far, through every means we've tested. He continuously regenerates."

I already knew this because of Crow, but hearing it still shocked me. As a supe, we lived long lives, perpetually young and strong, but we could still get hurt. We could still die if our attacker was dedicated enough.

I clasped my chest, staring at Tomb with apology in my expression. I hated the idea of him suffering to test more of Spector's theories, all because of me and what I'd done to him. This beautiful, strong man had wanted to be done with life, and instead, I'd made him unable to die.

"So? What does that have to do with my feeding today?" I snapped, though I had a sinking suspicion I already knew.

"We are going to prove that this deathless phenomenon

you've infused into the gargoyle can occur in other hybrids when you feed off them."

My stomach dropped.

Lowell motioned behind him to the gathered hybrids. "Byron Wills has volunteered to go first. He mentioned that you were partners in the past. Perhaps having an emotional connection will help with the indestructible connection."

Byron stepped forward, drawing my eye to him. He wore a smug grin and had his arms crossed over his chest. My fists curled at my sides. I had an emotional connection, alright. I wanted to murder him in his sleep.

"I don't think it works that way," I argued as Byron was led forward and hooked up with some various wires at his neck, heart, and temple.

"We're going to test it regardless, Motley," Lowell replied, like my inhibitions were irrelevant.

I didn't want to sleep with Byron, especially since he was so cruel to me, and I definitely didn't want to do this in front of all my peers. But I was hungry. I could feel my spider within me unfurl with an intense desire to feed.

"His dick isn't going anywhere near me," I protested.

"Oh come on, Motley, you weren't saying that last time," Byron joked, making all of his friends laugh.

I could feel my spider hissing, demanding retribution. Protective energy was like a vice wrapped around my neck. She *wanted* to give this guy what he deserved. She wanted to end his life and feed.

"I'm not fucking him," I croaked once more to Lowell, who was writing on his notepad, nodding his head but not really listening to me.

"So long as you're feeding off his essence, the means don't matter," he said distractedly.

The means don't matter. This motherfucker.

I looked around warily. "I don't want to do this with an audience."

"You don't have a choice."

I bristled. I never had a fucking choice when it came to Spector. It was one thing to feed with an audience of Spector scientists and guards. That felt clinical and controlled, but at least they were strangers. Doing this in front of Tomb and Crow...it felt like a betrayal somehow, and both shame and anxiousness filled me.

"I can't do this," I argued desperately. "*Please* don't make me do this." Begging anyone from Spector left a bitter taste in my mouth, but I'd rather lose my pride than be touched by Byron in front of the guys and the others.

"The other hybrids are here for you to feed on as well, if all goes well with Byron."

Realization clicked into place, and my mouth dropped open. "You want to see if I can make *all* the hybrids resurrected and indestructible?"

He didn't answer, but I could see the truth in his pursed lips. That was *exactly* what they wanted. Nausea somersaulted through my gut. I shook my head, backing up a step, only to collide with a guard right behind me. The man's hand came down hard on my shoulder, holding me in place. My fingers twitched to send webs flying. I could have him hanging by his neck in a second, but I held back.

"You can't make me fuck and feed off of everyone!" I yelled to the scientist, ignoring the guard's tightening grip.

The man finally looked up from his tablet and gave me a patronizing smile. "On the contrary, Miss Coven. We can do whatever we want. You belong to us. The moment you signed your name to Spector, you lost your rights of choice. We *made* you, and we'll use you as we see fit," he said, his tone emotionless. "Now approach the subject and begin your feeding process."

"Or *what?*" I challenged. "You'll stick me back in the tank? I think I'd rather go there."

He laughed at me. "No, of course not." Turning to look at one of the guards across the room, he said, "Let's give her an example of what will happen should she refuse to follow instructions."

Lowell produced a gold token from his pocket and tossed it in the air. I watched as the light shimmered off of it, and my spider recoiled within me. "What is that?" I asked, sensing a change in the demeanor of the room. Behind Lowell, a few of the demon hybrids flinched in fear.

"This is an ancient relic," he said casually before rubbing his thumb along it. "It was created centuries ago, intended to ward off demons. The wealthy would purchase them from saints and keep them in their pockets. We learned how to produce more of them."

Lowell started making his way toward a smaller girl I recognized from school. She was a necromancer paragon, top of her class. She seemed to cower under his gaze, her tiny frame shaking with fear. What the fuck was he doing?

"It's lost some of its power over the years, but it still gets the job done. Spector is working to mass produce it now. I particularly like the ones we've powdered down and installed into firearms."

As he spoke, two guards flanked the necromancer and held her shoulders. I wanted her to fight back. To use her demon to get them away, but she was terrified. In the next breath, Lowell slammed the gold coin against her eye.

She screamed.

It was a blistering sort of sound, reverberating around the training room as the smell of burning flesh invaded my nose. She writhed and scrambled at his hand, trying to get him away, blood coating her face and Lowell's fingers. But he continued to jam the small, seemingly harmless coin against her eye. It seared past her eyelid and burrowed into her socket, melting her gaze with just a simple touch and leaving nothing but an empty hole in its place.

She fought against them, shaking her body and kicking her legs, but the guards held her down. You could see the way their meaty fingers dug into her pale skin.

Nobody moved. The rest of the guards held their guns up in an obvious threat, successfully subduing the rest of the hybrids whose terrorized faces watched.

I cried for her, begging them to stop, but my words fell on deaf ears. Spector wanted to make an example of my insubordination, and they were doing it happily.

"Please stop!" I screamed.

It wasn't until the girl fell to her knees and blacked out that Lowell stopped pressing. The entire room went deadly silent, and my eyes flickered to Tomb, who was rippling with change.

With a roll of his eyes, Lowell bent over and fished the coin out of her eye, then used the hem of her hospital gown to clean the blood off of it.

"As you can see, it's quite effective. Just a graze of it against a demon's skin causes intense burning and pain," he said, making my horror stricken face turn toward him as he slipped the coin into his pocket. "So, as I was saying, you will follow instructions, or more of your peers will suffer for your insubordination. Understood?"

I saw black. Not red. But pure, endlessly wicked black. My fangs punched all the way out, and my nails elongated. My spider was there, sharing my consciousness as we stared back at him.

We were going to kill him. I couldn't say for sure when or how, but that was a promise seared into my own being, just as much as that coin had been seared into the girl.

He smiled at me, like seeing the death threat flashing in

my eyes got him off. He turned to the other scientists watching behind the glass. "Subject six-two-seven, the black widow hybrid, will now feed from subject six-one-eight," he droned on in his analytical tone.

My blue eyes flicked over to Tomb and Crow. They stood next to each other, staring back at me with tense bodies and furious eyes. But I knew that fury wasn't at me. It was *for* me.

I meant what I said. I wasn't going to fuck Byron. I knew that my demon's magic required my body to be penetrated in order for her to latch onto his essence, but I was going to control this, and I sure as shit wasn't letting his dick anywhere near me.

I moved forward, and then I stood in front of Byron while the rest of the hybrids stayed on the other side of the room with the guards, watching warily.

Byron gave me a shit-eating smirk. "Remember when you turned me down that one time, when I wanted to fuck you in the hall? I guess we're going to get an audience anyway," he said, his tone full of amusement. "Get on your knees and suck my cock, and then if you do a good enough job, I'll stick my dick in you."

Faster than he could fathom, webs shot from my right hand and planted against his mouth, wrapping around his head until he was totally gagged.

"That's better," my husky voice said, my spider and I feeling utterly smug.

His hands came up, trying to rip the webs away from his mouth, but my smile widened when they were too strong for him. He let out a muffled string of curses at the guards, but everyone ignored him. Lowell sighed behind me. "What?" I asked innocently. "No one said I had to let him talk. Just that I had to feed."

"Continue on, Miss Coven," he said in a warning tone.

I turned back to Byron and shoved my fingers through his

hair, wrenching his head back at an uncomfortable angle. "The only thing I'll be sucking is your blood, and your dick stays in your pants, or my webs will wrap around it so tightly it'll fall off from blood loss. Understand?"

His face went utterly pale, and he swallowed hard. He must've seen the truth in my eyes, because he nodded slowly.

"That's a good little fly," I said with a fanged grin, releasing him.

As soon as I let him go, Byron's eyes fluttered, and then he started to shake.

But it wasn't a normal shaking. It wasn't trembling or the way your body shivers when you have a chill. It wasn't even like he was shaking from anger. It was almost like he was...flashing, except he was staying in one place. His body thrummed in hyper speeds, making him appear blurred. In a creepy display, his head began jolting left and right, and then different faces started to flash across his own.

I gaped at him, caught between uneasiness and rising fear. "What's wrong with him?"

"Seems you provoked his demon to come out," Lowell answered, seemingly nonplussed.

Oh shit.

"What kind of demon is he?"

"Nothing for you to worry about. He's a nightmare demon. He shows you your greatest fears when he feels threatened. Kind of a pointless demon, if you ask me," he said, mumbling that last part.

I turned back to Byron, realization hitting me like a slap when I took a moment to observe the faces appearing over his own features.

They weren't random people. They were my victims. Every single one of the nameless humans that Spector forced me to feed on.

One by one, they zoomed before me, each of them gagged

by my webs, their eyes lifeless and haunted. Some of them were crying out from when my fangs pierced their skin, others had dazed looks of lust in their expressions, their lips already blue.

I felt sick to my stomach.

"Continue, Miss Coven. He won't stop until his demon calms down. Use your pheromones if you must."

Dropping my eyes down to the floor, I took a deep breath and let my spider know I needed her. If I kept stalling, I had no doubt Spector would punish another hybrid. I couldn't let anyone else get hurt because of me.

Slowly, I was able to get a hold on my emotions enough to tamp them down and breathe. My spider sidled up beside me as if to bolster me, and along with her help, I forced my lust to rise to the surface.

When I looked back up at Byron, the flashes of faces were still rotating, as if shuffling the deck of my greatest fear. I almost expected Byron's demon to show me a mirrored reflection of myself. After all, my greatest fear was what I was capable of.

But finally, he stopped flashing and settled on a face that I'd grown to know very well.

Tomb.

"Interesting," I heard Lowell say at my back, making my stomach clench, my heartrate kicking up a notch as sweat slicked my palms.

Byron's entire body morphed to look like Tomb, all the way down to his rounded fingernails. And yet, it was off. What made Tomb...*Tomb* wasn't quite there. The kind openness wasn't in his gaze. The steady comfort of home I felt when he was near was absent. I felt no attachment to the scarred, beautiful man standing in front of me, and my spider certainly wasn't interested. But my heart panged all the same.

I pumped out more lust, subduing Byron's demon and changing his emotions from anger to desire. He took a step closer to me, cocking his head to the side in order to study me. His hand came up, and bright joy filled his eyes when I let him stroke my cheek.

Then my spider lashed out faster than a blink, wrapping a web around his wrist. She did *not* like that he was impersonating Tomb.

Steady, girl.

As much as I wanted to let her claw our nails down Byron's face and force him to stop mimicking Tomb's body, I couldn't. Spector was just waiting to mete out punishments to us, and I couldn't give them a reason to.

I turned my back to find the *real* Tomb, and our eyes locked across the room. My spider instantly calmed. I stared at the angry gargoyle as Byron breathed down the back of my neck and wrapped his arm around my waist.

My spider hissed at the touch, and that nausea inside of me flipped like pancakes in my stomach, landing with a heavy splat.

We just need to feed, I told my spider. Just feed on the fucker, and then this can be done.

She didn't like it.

Neither did I, but I knew we had to do this if we were going to leave this room. So with my eyes still locked on our real Tomb, I forced myself to hold still as Byron's hand snaked over my stomach.

We can do this, I chanted to myself.

Byron's hand moved lower, and I felt his erection press against my back. It was almost laughably puny. When I glanced down, the hand was Tomb's. Dark skin, smatters of scars, rough hands that had held me before. But the touch wasn't the same.

Tears filled my eyes, and I squeezed them shut. Saliva

rushed into my mouth—not in thirst, but revulsion. Oh gods, I couldn't do this. I *hated* his touch. I was going to puke. I was going to—

"Eyes on me, Wid."

My eyes flared open, landing on my gargoyle.

He nodded at me across the room, helping me, trying to get me through this. Because Tomb knew the truth. He could fight, just as I could, and we might get a few good licks in. Maybe some of the others would even be brave enough to join in.

But we weren't stupid. We were newly made hybrids only weeks after our rebirth. This place was guarded by hundreds, maybe thousands of highly trained Spector employees, some of them probably hybrids themselves. We weren't getting out of this room even if we fought. And if we *did* fight, it would be at the expense of the others. Which is exactly why Spector threatened them. Because they knew I wouldn't willingly get anyone hurt.

So instead, I forced myself to pretend like it was my Tomb holding me close, that it was him caressing my body. His hand snaked lower down my stomach, leaving hot trails of menacing heat in its wake. Hungry need filled me up.

Skin brushed against my cheek, and I turned to face Byron's demon, still expecting to see him impersonating Tomb, but I found violet eyes and shocking blue hair. He'd changed into Crow.

Byron's nightmare demon kept flashing between Crow's and Tomb's faces, showing me my greatest fear. Maybe to the others, it didn't make sense, but I knew the truth. I wasn't afraid *of* them. I was afraid to fall for these men that I could never have. I was afraid to hurt them. I was afraid that we'd never make it out of here.

I snatched up Byron's hand, my spider and I taking

control. Then I shoved it down my pants and slipped the barest inch of his pinky inside of me.

That was all it took.

Yanking his hand away and pushing him back, I whirled around and yanked on his life's tether that I now had access to. I'd expected it to feel more potent, but Byron's essence was bland compared to how Tomb had been.

I turned my head and sunk my teeth in his neck, sating my thirst at the same time. Byron's demon caroused in the heady lust I was pumping into him. I devoured his life and his blood, not bothering to save a single drop.

I could feel everyone's eyes on me. The room was utterly quiet except for the sounds of Byron's moans and my gulps.

And then Byron started to struggle. Through the disorienting fervor of his desire, he probably realized that I was draining him of his most essential piece. But my spider wasn't going to let him go. Not when she'd caught her prey so easily.

We pulled and pulled, straining that tether of life as he moaned against the gag I'd created for him. My spider loved it. She loved the terror he was feeling as he began to unravel. She loved watching him realize that he was going to die, and the feeling of empowerment that kindled that. She loved that there was nothing he could do to stop her.

She was a vengeful beast.

And so was I.

With one last vicious pull, we snapped the cord connecting us, smiling in satisfaction as we guzzled down the last of his essence. He dropped to the floor, his arm bent at an awkward angle, and I wiped his blood off my mouth with a swipe of my hand. As Byron lay at my feet lifelessly, it wasn't Tomb's or Crow's face looking vacantly back at me, but his own.

"Start the timer. I want to see how long the resurrection takes," Lowell instructed, breaking the spell of the room.

I wasn't ready to gain control yet or return to reality. I wasn't ready to deal with the embarrassment or indignity of looking at my classmates and seeing the shock on their faces. I kept back, letting my demon celebrate her kill.

"Black Widow, can you explain why the nightmare demon showed the hybrids Crow and Tomb? Why are you afraid of them?" Lowell asked me.

She moved my legs, and we slowly walked over to Lowell. Before he could stop her, she plucked the coin from his pocket, brushing a predatory finger over his cock in the process. Lowell's mouth parted in shock, and guards started stalking toward us, ready to defend the Spector scientist.

The coin burned through the skin on my fingers. It was a searing discomfort, but it was nothing compared to the determination my spider felt. She held the coin up, showing him how unaffected she was, then pushed the coin to her cheek at the place where Byron's demon skin had brushed against mine, as if to burn the feel of him away.

"I fear nothing, little fly. I *am* fear," my dark voice croaked.

I dropped the coin, and it landed on the tiled floor and rolled away, the sound echoing through the room. Everyone's eyes seemed to follow it. All except for three.

My eyes locked on Tomb and Crow, and my spider grinned.

Mates.

The thought was so clear that I gasped. With that, she burrowed back inside of me, curling up in satisfaction, while I was left to stare at them wide-eyed as the realization of her word thrummed through me.

It was then that I knew with certainty that Byron Wills would never wake up.

Chapter 13

THE TRAINING ROOM WAS TENSE.

I could feel everyone's eyes on me as I struggled to do the moves that Oz was putting me through. His new favorite thing was to make me run until I puked up red-hot blood and then force me to shoot webs straight up to the ceiling and climb my way up the silken rope. I fell. *A lot.*

I couldn't ignore the fact that my body buzzed, though. Byron's essence had sated me and my spider. Not as well as Tomb had, and he hadn't tasted nearly as good, but drinking from him was still leaps and bounds better than drinking from humans.

My fellow hybrids kept stealing looks at me, but unlike the way their stares had felt hostile or mocking while we'd been at Thibault, now it felt wary. They feared me.

Maybe if I were different, I would take advantage of that. Use this opportunity to turn the tables and bully and torment *them*. But that wasn't me, and I still wanted what I'd *always* wanted—to be accepted.

My arms shook as hard as an earthquake while I struggled to heave myself up another few inches of the web rope. I hadn't managed to make it to the top even once. Every time I fell onto the floor, Oz was there in my face, telling me to do it again.

My whole body hurt, and sweat was pouring down my face, my red hair in a messy topknot at the crown of my head. The Spector shorts and tank top I wore were damp as well, and they did nothing to protect me from the rope—or web—burn I now had on my palms, arms, and legs.

Just as I gripped the web to climb, using its stickiness to keep me suspended, my hands slipped, and I went falling down. Again.

Right before I hit the mats, I threw my hands out and caught myself in a quick web that sent me bouncing on my back as I stared up and tried to catch my breath. *That landing was way better than the mats.*

I barely stopped bouncing against my soft web before Oz was hovering over my face, scowling down at me. "No webs to catch yourself," he reprimanded. "Now get up and do it again."

I shook my head. "I-I can't," I panted.

My palms were bleeding, and my arms felt so weak I couldn't even lift them up to wipe the sweat off my brow.

But Oz was an unfeeling prick, so he looked down at me with utter derision. "I said get the fuck up, spider bitch."

My spider wanted to hand him his ass, but after hours of this, even she was feeling tired.

It was all so ridiculous. Sometimes I wondered if Spector was really trying to build an army or if they just got off on feeling powerful. The guards were too aggressive. The conditions were unbearable, and I still hadn't quite come to terms with what they made us do. I didn't think I ever would.

"Back off of her."

The voice defending me sounded like steel and home. I pushed myself up with wobbly hands and twisted my body to look at Tomb. He was covered in dust, like he'd spent hours chiseling rock.

"Get back to your station," Oz growled at Tomb before turning his attention back to me.

I didn't have time to prepare myself. One second, I was shaking with exhaustion and looking up at Oz, and the next, he was landing a swift kick to my gut.

Searing pain shot through me as a surprised grunt of pain flew from my mouth. His steel-toed boot was hard and fast, making me coil in on myself and clutch my stomach. My spider rattled against my rib cage.

"Get the fuck up!" he yelled once more at me, while placing his meaty hand on his holster.

Everyone in the training room seemed to stop at once. They all stared unabashedly at us, waiting to see what would happen next.

Tomb acted fast. He grabbed Oz by the neck, pulling him up. I tried scrambling to my feet, but I tripped over the side of the web and stumbled to the floor.

"Don't fucking touch her," Tomb growled in Oz's face. His skin rolled with change. Hard rock fought for dominance over flesh.

"Excuse me? Get back to your fucking station, or it'll be the tank for a month," my trainer threatened, furious spit flying from his mouth. "You think that just because you're immortal you have clout around here?"

I was finally able to pull myself up, and I gravitated closer to Tomb, keeping my eyes on the brutal trainer clutched in the gargoyle's grasp.

"You're no one. You're just a toy. Disposable. So get back to your trainer, or you *and* your little spider bitch are going to regret it," Oz sneered, but there was obvious fear alongside the rage in his eyes.

At Oz's words, Tomb lost control of his gargoyle and

completely shifted. His smooth, glossy skin was replaced with hard rock. Within me, I could feel my spider beaming with pride and appreciation. But this was dangerous. Fighting Spector had consequences.

Tomb dropped him on the floor and cracked his knuckles, but Oz didn't stay on the ground for long. He took Tomb's sudden shift for the threat it was, and pulled out his relic coin, prepared to burn Tomb. It was almost humorous to watch. It was clear on Tomb's blasé expression that the threat of pain didn't bother him. He'd been conditioned to endure torture.

"Back off," Tomb growled again when Oz switched his attention to me.

Although I was thankful that Tomb intervened, things were going south fast, and the other guards around us observed with charged anger, ready to put us hybrids under their boots and assert their dominance.

I reached within myself, pushing past the exhaustion and pain. I accessed that protective vitality within me, and my spider welcomed me with open arms, like she'd been waiting on me to ask for help.

And then I exhaled.

My meditative sigh was heavy with power. During feedings, my spider would lace the air with lust to calm her prey. And Oz? He was our prey.

"What are you doing?" Oz asked cautiously as I walked toward him.

He was already hard by the time I made it in front of him. It was like sex appeal dripped from my skin. I felt sensual and confident. Each move, each breath was like delicate foreplay.

Once I was toe-to-toe with Oz, I brushed my knuckles along his cheek. There was something satisfying about the way he shivered with lust. On the surface, it seemed sensual, but the core of my lure wasn't hardened cocks or slick panties—though those were added benefits. The core of my spider's abilities revolved around control.

Every ragged inhale forced our chests to clash. In the background, I could hear footsteps heading toward me. I could feel Tomb's heavy stare.

"Little fly," I rasped before lifting up on my toes and dragging the tip of my fang across the ridge of his ear. "Stop fighting me. I want you to dismiss us for the day."

I felt the conflicting emotions war inside him. He wanted me, that much was obvious. All the signs were there. His hard cock, the sweat on his brow, the shudder in his breath.

Oz's body responded exactly as my spider intended—and he hated me for it. His teeth were clenched as I scented him. The adrenaline-filled arousal tinged my nose, and there was nothing he could do about it. He was a slave to desire. His body betrayed him with the basic need to fuck, and I was the master of his lust.

"You have more training to do," Oz rasped, trying to fight it.

I studied the effects of my lure through a scientist's eye. I made mental notes of the battle on his face, realizing that my pull could only reach so far. It couldn't control his actions, just dull his inhibitions. My spider's lure might not fully control him, but I could make him so uncomfortable and drawn to me that he did whatever I asked.

"I don't want to train anymore," I said again while backing away.

I sauntered backward until my back collided with a stone chest. Arms wrapped around me, steadying me.

Oz ran his hand down his torso and grabbed his cock through his pants with a quiet groan. A longing ache traveled up his spine. "*Fuck*," he croaked.

None of this was arousing for me. Nothing about Oz attracted my spider, and it wasn't until Tomb's rumbling chuckle vibrated against my skin that a true longing settled within me.

"Dismiss us for the day, and I'll stop," I told him with a shrug. "At this current rate, you're going to have a very public, very unsatisfying orgasm," I said. I kept this odd balance between my demon's sinister desires and my own humor. "I don't think any of us want to witness that."

Oz looked around the room in rock-hard embarrassment.

I looked around the room too, only to notice that all of the trainers were headed my way, coins in hand.

Shit.

"Get on the ground, spider bitch," one of them said. "Hands flat on the floor."

My spider turned, watching as the trainers converged around us.

Beside me, Tomb's gargoyle tensed, his cool, hard arm touching mine. "If you touch her, I will kill you," he said, his voice a growl of gravel and threat.

"Your skin is indestructible, but hers sure as shit isn't," the other trainer replied. "How many relics burning into her skin at one time before she passes out from the pain, do you think?"

It was such bullshit. We were some of the strongest supes in the world, but the sight of those glimmering, glorified quarters had me trembling.

The other hybrids shifted on their feet, watching nervously, probably wondering if I was about to get everyone punished. Crow stepped forward, slipping next to me, as if he was ready to intervene. I heard some of his birds flying over my head, ready to protect me at all costs.

When the trainers formed a circle around us, the tension in the room spiked, and my palms twitched, ready to send out webs to snatch up every damn coin and trainer in this room.

Shit was about to go down.

"Trainers, stand down."

The sudden voice took everyone by surprise. I whipped my head over to see heavily armed guards marching toward us, and one man wearing a suit. Tomb and I exchanged a look. This was bad. Really bad.

The suited official had an earpiece in his ear, and the guards flanked him while he spoke to someone. "Yes, sir. Of course, sir. I'll bring her up immediately, sir."

The guards formed a row in front of us. Crow placed his fingers on my lower back in silent reassurance, and Tomb placed himself in front of me, ready to fight.

Once the Suit was done appeasing whoever was speaking to him over his earpiece, he turned his attention to Oz. "President Belvini wants to speak with the Black Widow immediately. He says no one is to harm her, or there will be consequences."

My mouth dropped open in shock. President Belvini wanted to see me? What could he possibly want?

Oz blanched. "Victor, you can't be serious. She used her powers against me! You know the rules; she needs to be punished. I deserve to be the one to do it," he said through clenched teeth.

The suited man looked unamused. He was a thin man with cold eyes and thinning hair. I sniffed the air. Was he...*human*?

"President Belvini makes the rules around here. The only thing you deserve is a demotion for not knowing how to handle your trainee."

Oz's cheeks mottled a furious red, and he looked like he wanted to argue more, but it was a bit hard to take him seriously with the raging boner still poking through his slacks.

Luckily, Lowell came forward from where he'd been observing the entire thing. "Of course, Victor. Miss Coven can be taken there immediately. And please let President Belvini know that we will have the reports he requested on his desk in three hours," the brown-nosing scientist said.

"Better make it one hour, Lowell." Victor slid his eyes to me before continuing. "Due to recent developments, we are pushing up the timeline for our plans. I suggest you have your team ready."

Lowell turned pale but nodded his head. "Of course."

"Come along, Miss Coven."

I hesitated, watching Victor warily from around Tomb's body. "What does he want with me?"

The man sighed and looked up at the ceiling, either to appreciate my roped web or out of impatience. "You are in no place to be asking questions."

Crow's hand was still at my back, and he gave me a little brush of his fingers to comfort me, but Tomb was still a statue standing sentry in front of me. I stepped around him, reaching down and squeezing his hand once in reassurance. He looked down at me, worry and disagreement warring over his features. "It's okay," I told him.

Afraid that he might try to haul me up over his shoulder and carry me out of here, I quickly slipped out of his grip and stepped toward the guards. "Lead the way," I said, sounding way more relaxed about it than I really was.

I was quickly shuffled out, walking in the middle of guards boxing me in from every side. We went out of the training room and into an elevator, where we went up at least a few floors. The guards were straight-faced, silent, and tense, while Victor was talking on his earpiece the whole time, bossing people around.

"No, no, no. Get the *Howell* files for the noon meeting, and the *Howl* files for the soonest meeting! Honestly, it's like I'm talking to an imbecile."

The short elevator ride brought us up to a floor I'd never

been to before. I couldn't see much between the guards' bodies, but unlike the thick concrete walls and white tiled floors, this part looked more like an executive building in a high rise than a military bunker. There were even paintings hung on the wall, as if an interior designer came in to spruce the place up.

The guards led me all the way down to the end of another hallway, where there was a prim looking secretary typing away, while two armed guards stood by a pair of frosted glass doors.

As soon as the secretary saw us coming, she jumped to her feet. "Finally! He's been waiting for a full four minutes!" she hissed, looking distressed. "Hurry up and get her in there before he blows a gasket."

My nerves shot up. From her reaction alone, I already knew what kind of man President Belvini was, and I wanted to meet him even less than I did before.

A stern hand at my back pushed me through the doors, and my feet stumbled as I tried to straighten myself. The last thing I heard from Victor was a hissed *behave* before the door was shut, locking me inside.

The room was modern and sleek. A cleared desk with a single file folder on top of it sat near large, expansive windows. I nearly gasped at the sight of the bright sun and lush greenery. I hadn't seen the outside in what felt like months. I had to physically stop myself from walking over to it and placing my fingers against the glass.

"Beautiful, isn't it?" a masculine voice in a clipped accent said to my left. I turned my attention toward him and felt my spider revolt.

I'd been in some fucked up situations since signing my life over to Spector, and my spider had reacted accordingly. But I'd never felt such an intense scattering within myself as I did right now. I took in his pressed suit and tall stature.

Lorenzo Belvini's face was smoldering handsomeness made up of sharp angles. You could have cut stone with his jaw and pointed chin. His cheekbones were high and defined, accenting the way the rest of his face seemed hollow and sunken in.

I took a deep breath, trying to scent him and pick up on what sort of supe he was, but the only thing I inhaled was sulfur. No woodsy shifter scent. No cool vampiric blood. No deadly musk of a necro or the sickly sweet magic of an elemental.

This man was one hundred percent demon.

"Are you done scenting me?" he asked with an arched brow as he stood up from behind the desk. "I'm guessing by the look of terror on your face, you've figured it out. I'm impressed. Most take longer to determine what I am."

He took a step toward me, and I felt wave after wave of his dark energy course through me. Even my spider was uneasy. "Why am I here?" I asked while fixing my face in a stern, unconcerned expression.

He chuckled, a dark sound that made my stomach clench. "Brave little thing. I wonder...is it you that's so hardened, or is it your demon? It's such a beautiful phenomenon, the blending of powers. I do like to see what mixture comes out of it."

He sauntered over to me with an outstretched hand. I looked down at it with trepidation, not sure what sort of demon he was or what a simple touch could do.

He smirked and instead gestured to the chair. "Please, have a seat."

He walked back around his desk to sit behind it, and I took a moment to look around his office as I sunk into the chair. Minimalistic shelves hung on the wall to my left, and on top of them were gems and strange metals spaced perfectly apart.

"I'm a collector of sorts," he said smoothly, as he unbuttoned the front of his suit jacket, like it would help him seem more casual.

I swept my eyes up and down his body. "I noticed. The dozens of hybrids downstairs sort of tipped me off."

At my words, he tipped back his head and laughed. It was better than him killing me on the spot for mouthing off, but I still flinched at the sound, while he revealed his dazzling white teeth and sinister grin. "You're a delight, Miss Coven," he said, his laughter tapering off. "It will be such a shame to have to destroy your spirit."

I tensed, my fingernails digging into the black leather of the armrests.

"Let's get down to business, shall we?" he asked, flipping open the file in front of him.

My eyes flicked down, and I saw my school picture and basic information on the first page. The page on the other side had pictures of me in my cell here at Spector, as well as surveillance photos of me feeding off various humans.

"I was intrigued by your demonic rebirth," Belvini said, flipping through the pages. "I'll admit, some of my hybrids are favored more than others. But yours has a certain allure to it."

"If sexual cannibalism is your thing, then I guess you can say it has tons of allure," I deadpanned.

Another smirk broke across his face. "Indeed," he agreed. "As it were, I think you can do great things here at Spector, but unfortunately, you do not seem to be acclimating. Instead, you are headstrong and belligerent, fighting my employees at every turn."

I swallowed, but it was becoming harder and harder to remain stoic in his presence.

"You have a choice, Miss Coven. Fall in line and take your new role as a Spector employee. Follow orders. Be what our supernaturals need us to be—guardians to propel us into the future."

"And if I don't?" I asked, my hands shaking so badly that webs were spreading across my thighs.

He tsked at me. "If you don't see reason and follow your new role as Spector's employee, we will have to use other means to ensure you do what is required of you."

He grabbed something from the file and flung it on the desk in front of me. I stared down at the photograph of Aunt Marie, and I forgot how to breathe. My ears started to ring, and my fangs punched down, puncturing my bottom lip as I raised glassy eyes back up to the demon.

"What did you do to her?" I couldn't even recognize my own voice. There was shock, hurt, and dark menace lacing my words.

"Nothing. Yet," he answered, watching me with his cold, fathomless eyes.

Stuck in terrified fury, I glanced back down at the photograph. My aunt's red hair was blowing around her face as she walked from the mailbox back to the front door of our home. She looked gaunt and fragile, like she'd just come out of a bloodlust haze and it had taken its toll on her.

"So if I don't follow orders and be a good little hybrid, you'll hurt my aunt?" I asked boldly, crossing my arms in front of me like I was putting on a breastplate of armor.

He had the audacity to chuckle. "Of course not," he said, surprising me. "I'll simply have one of my employees tip off the council about a possible vampiress living near the city who's gone mad with bloodlust."

Horror made me jump to my feet. "No. You can't."

President Belvini looked at me coolly. "I assure you, Miss Coven, I *can*. And I will," he promised. "Tell me, what do you think they'll do to her once they see how far gone she is in the disease? Do you think she'll be executed by the council immediately? Or do you think they'll imprison her?"

The thought of either of those scenarios happening to my aunt made bile rush up my throat. "P-Please," I stammered. "Please don't do that. I'll do what you want," I blurted, the promise both giving me hope for my aunt's life while damning my own.

President Belvini's eyes flashed with victory before he got to his feet and came around the desk. When he got closer, I noticed a silver chain hanging from his neck, with an amber amulet hanging from it. It glowed slightly as he came nearer, and my spider shied away from it. This male had a serious obsession with strange gems. Bringing my eyes back to his face, I was forced to lift my chin since he was at least a foot taller than me.

"Let's see how reformed you are, shall we?" he asked rhetorically. "Use your lure on me."

I blinked at him, thinking I'd heard him wrong. "What?"

"I don't like to repeat myself, Miss Coven," he said, his expression leaving no room for patience.

Swallowing, I prodded my spider, though she didn't want to come out. I'd never seen her so apprehensive before, but it was clear that President Belvini frightened her. That knowledge in itself was disconcerting. My spider was never afraid of anything. Which meant that this male was far more dangerous than he looked.

After a bit of coaxing, I was finally able to get my spider to emerge, and I squeezed my eyes shut in concentration. Lure was the very last thing I wanted to put out. Every instinct was screaming at me to get him *away* from me, not lure him in closer. But he'd found the perfect carrot to dangle over my head, and I had no doubt that he would do exactly what he threatened to Aunt Marie.

Which is the only reason I was able to push through and

force lure to seep from my skin and push toward the demon in front of me.

As soon as it was out, President Belvini breathed in deeply, letting out a long sigh. "Ah," he said, his voice dropping lower and his dark eyes flickering with newfound hunger. "So it does work on me," he mused. "How utterly perfect you are." He smiled down at me like a wolf baring its teeth to a sheep. "I have a job for you, Miss Coven."

My spider recoiled back into the center of our shared soul. I wanted to recoil right along with her.

Chapter 14

FOR THE FIRST time since being kidnapped and taken to Spector's headquarters, I was finally getting out of here—temporarily.

After my meeting with President Belvini, the high-strung Victor came to collect me, and then I was escorted to a new suite where there was a team of female supes waiting for my arrival. Two drop dead gorgeous blonde vamps, a dark-skinned water elemental, and a shifter with hair down to her knees were all talking animatedly as I was led through the sleek black doors.

The space was modern, decorated in reds and whites, with a wall of mirrors, clothing racks, and an entire wall dedicated to what looked like cosmetics and hair products.

As I stepped inside with Victor, all four of the supes stopped talking and looked over at me assessingly. Their sharp eyes ran over my Spector issued clothes and messy topknot, and one of the vamps shook her head like the sight was truly pitiful.

"Ladies, this is Miss Coven. You've already received your orders," Victor said, looking over at me and then visibly shuddering. "I don't envy your jobs. Just...do your best," he said, as if he had zero faith in the matter.

"Don't worry, Vick, we'll make her look at least passable," the elemental said.

"Good luck." He turned and fled the room, leaving me with the foursome of model lookalikes.

Immediately, the four of them swarmed around me like flies to shit. They started brushing their fingers along different parts of me, tugging lightly on my hair or tilting up my chin to get a better look as they all circled around me and offered notes.

"Her brows need more arch."

"She's got tangles for days."

"Exfoliation is a must."

"She'll need to be practically scrubbed raw."

"Her lips look like a rabid dog has been gnawing on them."

"She's a bit pasty."

Round and round they went until I felt a bit like Dorothy stuck in the middle of a tornado, except instead of gale-force winds, I was surrounded by feminine appraisers.

"Umm..."

"Alright." The vamp clapped. Actually, now that I was getting a better look at them, I realized that the gorgeous blondes were actually identical twins. "Let's get her into the bath. We can't work our magic until the layers of grime are washed off her anyway."

The other twin nodded in agreement. "Mm-hmm." She looked over at the elemental. "Jules?"

"Yeah, yeah," the woman said, flicking her wrist in the direction of the open door that I guessed led to the bathroom. "Already way ahead of you. The bath is ready." She said that last part to me. "Do you need assistance?" she asked.

"Uh, no. I can bathe myself."

"Excellent," she smiled. "We'll be pulling some looks together for you. Just holler if you need us."

I gave her a nod before turning and heading toward the bathroom and closing myself inside. As soon as I was alone, I rested my back against the door and closed my eyes. I felt like my mind was spinning, unable to catch up with all the changes in the last hour.

I've been around a lot of very powerful people. I've been around a lot of cruel assholes too. But none of them were anywhere near the level of dominant force like President Belvini. I wasn't even in his presence anymore, yet my skin still felt itchy with nerves.

I looked around the bathroom, noting a huge circular tub with steaming water rising out of it. There was a wraparound bamboo bench, with stairs built into it to easily climb into the tub, and all over the bench were various soaps, oils, razors, and towels.

I looked over, noting the huge window letting in light at the far end of the room. It would be all too easy to shatter the glass and attempt an escape. I wanted so badly to be out of Spector's grasp. But right now, someone on Belvini's payroll was probably watching my aunt's every move. One tip. That was all it would take, and then enforcers would overrun her and take her away forever.

Gritting my teeth, I turned away from the window and stripped off my clothes before settling into the tub. I immediately hissed at the heat, but that hiss turned into a sigh as my skin got used to the temperature. I dunked my head under and then relaxed back, letting out a sigh as the hot water soothed my exhausted muscles. I was already feeling better after the training, since both my vamp genes and my hybrid side made me heal super fast. But Oz had pushed me way over the limit today, and I was still sore.

As I washed, scrubbed, shaved, and oiled, I thought about the job that President Belvini was making me do.

I have a job for you, Miss Coven.

His words from earlier echoed in my head.

I knew it was going to be dangerous. As soon as he made me test my lure on him, I knew that whatever job he had planned wasn't going to be easy or innocent. Right before I was dismissed, he told me that I would receive the details for my mission after I met with his team of women to get *groomed*. Those were his words. As if I were a dog to be primped and showcased.

Belvini didn't need to spell it out for me. I had a pretty good idea of what he was going to make me do, and the thought had me freaking the fuck out.

I dunked my head under the water again, letting out a scream beneath the water. Crow's and Tomb's faces swirled in my mind. The way they'd tried to protect me earlier, the way they'd stood by my side, it made my heart swell. I wished that I had more time with them to explore this connection between us. I felt safety in their presence and an instinctual connection that couldn't be denied. But I wanted to know them. Their pasts, likes, dislikes. It was strange knowing my spider had picked them for mates when I truly didn't know much about them.

I just hoped that I'd have the chance to know them better before Spector ruined us all.

I emerged from the water and gnawed on my lip, anxious about everything that was going to happen.

"Psst. Motley?" a familiar voice called. I whipped my head to the side and stared wide-eyed at Stiles's back. *Where had he come from?*

"Cover up, will you?" he said, his tone rushed.

"Oh my gods. Why are you freaking in here?" I hissed, scrambling for a towel.

"Trust me, this is fucking awkward for me too," he snapped, his shoulders tense. He was practically kissing the wall, standing as far away from me as possible and keeping his face nearly smashed against the wallpaper. "This this is the only chance we have to talk alone."

"What do you want to talk about?" I asked before stepping out of the bathtub and wrapping myself in a fluffy robe.

He still didn't turn around, but answered me. "I heard you got put on a mission. I wanted to make sure you weren't planning on doing anything stupid, like trying to defect."

I walked over and tapped him on the shoulder, letting him know it was okay to turn around. He flinched at my touch but finally faced me, and I gasped at what I saw. He had two black eyes, what had to be a broken nose, still with blood caked to his swollen nostrils, and greasy hair. My brother always seemed so put together and refined, but right now he looked utterly beaten.

My heart gave the slightest twinge.

"What happened to you?" I asked.

"I don't have time to get into that. Let's just say I got an unimpressive demon and our father expects only the best," he said in a dead voice while shaking his head. "Look, we probably only have five minutes at best. I've tried coming to see you before, but they have you on lockdown, and Dad doesn't like it when I mingle too much with the other hybrids."

I assessed him with a frown, not sure why he was even bothering. I remembered what Cheryl said, about Stiles not liking some of the things Spector was doing. Maybe she was right. "Okay...So why are you here?"

"I'm here because I want to make sure you do whatever they ask you to do, Motley."

"Why?"

Stiles sighed and scrubbed his hands down his face. "I'm

working on something, okay? And I'm *so* fucking close to figuring out how to do it. I just need more time. Then you, me, and Cheryl can get the fuck out of here. Play the game, do what you need to do, and don't give them any more trouble. Please."

My mouth dropped open in shock at the pleading look on his face. Stiles had always seemed like he was a daddy's boy, following in his footsteps with a grin on his face and money in his pocket. "Why are you doing this? Why do you want out? I thought you were a part of this."

Feminine laughter came from the room next to us, and he flinched at the sound. Grabbing my hand, he led me toward the other side of the bathroom. "Because this place is fucked up," he said quietly. "Because what they're doing is fucked up. Because I did my best to keep you away from all of this, but you still got sucked in anyway."

"I'm surprised you even care. It's not like we've had a normal sibling relationship, Stiles. You've made it clear I don't belong."

His face fell. "I know. I *know*, okay? But I need you to trust me. I need you to keep your head down until I can figure this out. And once we're out of here, I'll explain everything. I promise."

I doubted his intentions, but there was no mistaking the genuine worry shining in his blue eyes. "Alright," I said with a nod. "But I'm not doing it for you. They threatened Aunt Marie."

Stiles grimaced. "I know how much she means to you."

"She's my family," I said, probably with too much bite behind my words. But Stiles didn't argue that he was my family too. He simply nodded.

"Be careful," Stiles warned before giving me an awkward pat on the shoulder.

"You too," I replied.

Stiles's head turned toward the door as if he were listening. "Time's up. Open the main door for me to flash through," he said in a whisper.

Before I could answer him, he flashed to other side of the room, and then hid himself inside the small bathroom closet where more robes were hanging up. The second after he clicked the door shut, the bathroom door swung open and the twin vampires came in.

"Finally," the twin on the left said to me. "You've taken *ages*. Come on, we need to get you primed and then try different looks on you."

I followed the pair of them back into the main room, stealing one last glance to the closet before facing forward again. I walked straight over to the main door and yanked it open.

"What are you doing?"

The shifter with the long hair strode over to me immediately, a frown marring her pretty face. Before she reached the door, I felt a rush of air breeze past me, and Stiles's blurred body raced past me and down the hall.

"Nothing," I said innocently, turning toward her. "Just wanted some fresh air."

The shifter's eyes narrowed. "From the hallway?"

I shrugged, and she slammed the door shut and rolled her eyes. "Come on."

With a tug on my arm, she brought me to a plush white ottoman and sat me down. From there, the four of them proceeded to shove different fabrics in my direction, holding them over my skin and hair in order to envision my "color palette." Once they narrowed the clothing options down, I was given midnight blue lingerie that consisted of a strapless bustier and matching panties.

I looked at the three of them, clutching the skimpy lace in

my hands and feeling more and more awkward by the second. "You want me to put this on right here?" I asked.

"Obviously," the elemental drawled. "You can't try on the dresses until you've got your knickers on."

At my distress, the shifter rolled her eyes. "Please, we've dressed hundreds of women for President Belvini. You don't have anything we haven't already seen."

Pursing my lips, I turned my back on them and de-robed, blushing at the fact that I had to get dressed with an audience. Honestly, I was surprised I had any modesty or embarrassment left, considering all the public feedings Spector was forcing me to do.

I tugged on the lingerie as quickly as possible, feeling incredibly stupid as I turned around. "Well?" I said, lifting my arms up before they landed against my sides again.

The twins came forward, and to my absolute horror, they reached inside my bustier and lifted up my boobs before tightening the lace straps at the sides. "There," Twin One said. "I had to plump up the goods."

My face was on fire. "Umm, thanks?"

After that, they forced dress after dress onto me, each one nitpicked and torn to verbal shreds for all the reasons it looked terrible on me. Until finally…

"This is the one!" the shifter beamed. The twins nodded, and the elemental gave a resigned shrug. From her, that was practically applause.

I looked down at the tight black cocktail dress I was now wearing. It had see-through lace on the arms and the back, ending just above my ass. The front had a sweetheart neckline that dipped down slightly and showed off the massive amounts of cleavage I was now sporting thanks to the bustier *plumping the goods*.

"Perfect. Now slip the robe back over it so nothing gets on it while we do your hair and makeup," Twin Two said.

After I did as told, the twins led me over to a makeup table and plopped me down in front of the lighted mirror. I winced at my pale, tired, disheveled reflection.

"Mm-hmm. Our thoughts exactly," Twin Two said.

"Gee, thanks," I drawled.

"Don't worry, we'll get you looking good in no time."

While the twins started tackling the cosmetics, the shifter began to rub my legs down with lotions and then began to paint my nails. Meanwhile, the elemental got to work on my hair, first sucking all the water out of it using her powers, and then tackling my horrid tangles and using a curling iron to form long loose curls in my tresses.

I don't know how long it took for my grooming. I was so thoroughly combed and tweezed and painted and primped that I lost track of time. I sort of just zoned out, not really seeing or feeling anything as the four women went to town, while I marinated in my worry.

Belvini needed to know if my lure worked on a demon. And now he'd ordered me to have a full makeover. It didn't take a genius to see what direction my *job* was heading. That fact, added with Stiles and Aunt Marie…it meant that anxiety was bubbling through me like acid.

"There. You look absolutely adequate," the elemental said with a nod as the four of them stood me up and placed me in front of the full-length mirror.

"She's better than adequate. She's gorgeous," Twin One said with a fanged smile.

I stared at myself in wide-eyed surprise, taking it all in: black heeled boots paired with the dress that hugged my curves and ended mid-thigh, lace that gave me a sexy but still covered look, and makeup that made my features pop. Perfect shimmery eyes and pouty lips, and my red ombré hair that was downright ready for a runway. I looked chic. Sexy. Like a godsdamned model. I barely recognized myself.

Victor swept into the room while I was still gaping at the mirror. "Thank gods," he said dramatically. "Come on, Miss Coven. You're already late."

He gave an air kiss to the girls, and I waved awkwardly at the four of them, not knowing what else to do. I wasn't sure what the correct protocol was. Were you supposed to thank the people who made you pretty so that you could lure someone against your will because a nefarious demon was forcing you to?

Luckily, I didn't have to decide, because Victor pulled me out of the room and escorted me down to the elevator. We were accompanied by a pair of guards, and I didn't miss the way their eyes slunk over my body.

Victor was tapping furiously over the tablet in his hand, completely ignoring me as I fidgeted beside him, watching the numbers go up as we ascended.

"So are you going to tell me what I'm supposed to do?" I asked, a little more bite to my tone than necessary. I really was going to listen to Stiles, but that didn't mean I had to like it.

Victor hummed under his breath. "Mmm, yes. There is a high level demon that President Belvini would like to collect. He'd be very valuable to Spector. A top asset, if you will. The success of this mission would open many doors for you, Miss Coven."

I grimaced. He made it sound like I should be excited about the opportunity. If I'd learned anything about this experience, it was that demons were volatile and deadly. Luring one didn't sound like an easy job.

"So how exactly would you like for me to *collect* him? Seduce the bastard and trap him with my magic hybrid cunt? My skills are pretty limited." My spider bristled. She didn't like the idea of me thinking her incapable. I knew that I'd grown substantially stronger since arriving here, but that didn't mean I wanted to test my skills out on a high level demon.

"You just need to get him alone," Victor began as the elevator doors opened. We both walked out, and he paused to fish something out of his pocket. He put his tablet under his arm and then grabbed my wrist. His ice-cold fingers dug into my skin as he lifted up a shimmering bracelet and clasped it on me.

"See this?" he asked while pointing at a charm. "Press it when he's alone, and we will take it from there. Use whatever methods necessary to get him alone," he said pointedly. "Understand?"

I looked down at the bracelet and ran a finger over the charm he indicated. "And why do you need me? What are his powers?"

Victor rolled his eyes, as if my questions annoyed him. "He is a risk demon. The second we get too close, he amplifies his powers, and it becomes a game of chance we can't win. We need him...disarmed. We have it on good authority that he has a weakness for pretty faces. Just amp up those powers and do your thing."

Do my thing? Do my fucking *thing*? The nonchalant way Victor spoke made me want to gouge his eyes out with my freshly painted nails.

"Fine."

Victor nodded, like my lack of enthusiasm was good enough, then led me toward a wood paneled door. "Your portal is here. Try to get this done quickly, yes? We're on a very tight schedule. You'll be going alone. He can...sense us. But don't even try to run. We'll be watching your every move."

I nodded and reached for the handle, but he stopped me with his next words. "You look the part of the Black Widow," he said, looking me straight in the eye. "But be sure to act like it tonight as well. You understand?" he asked carefully, and for the first time, I got the feeling that Victor might not like everything that went on in Spector.

Tapping a finger against the hem of my dress, I read between the lines. "Don't worry, Vick. I know how to own my sexuality and use my...assets to my advantage," I said with a smirk.

He nodded, and then his mask of busy obliviousness came back on his face. "Good. I'd hate to have to inform President Belvini that you acted like a silly blushing schoolgirl and failed the mission. That makeover would be such a waste," he tutted.

I snorted at his backhanded way of trying to prepare me for the job. "I won't disappoint you," I told him wryly. Then I realized I still didn't even know who exactly I was looking for. "Wait, how will I find him?"

Victor huffed before handing me a purse. I could see bright green cash stuffed inside of it. "Just make a bet, Miss Coven. We have faith he'll come to you," he explained before opening the door.

I stared at the money, not quite understanding what he meant. But before I could question him, Victor reached up and shoved me through the portal.

Fuck.

Chapter 15

AFTER JUST SEVERAL seconds of staggering through clammy magic that clung to my skin like sweat, I was pushed out through the other side, only to land on a toilet.

I was barely able to catch myself before falling ass-first into the water. "Fucking gross," I hissed before using the grab bar to my left to haul myself to my feet. At least no one had been using the damn thing before I landed on it.

I quickly opened the stall door and walked out, teetering on my heeled boots as I went. I froze immediately when heads turned in my direction. Just heads. Because their bodies were currently pointed at the wall, where there was a neat row of urinals.

Did they have to put me in a godsdamned male restroom? Fucking misogynistic pricks probably thought it was funny.

"Uhh, sorry," I stammered, quickly making my way to the exit. "Carry on."

A few of them chuckled, and I nearly ran into another man coming in when I wrenched open the door. He blinked down at me in surprise. "Well now, I didn't know these bathrooms had happy endings."

"They don't for you," I said with a pleasant smile before tapping him on the chest and slipping past him.

Once I was out of the male restroom, I took a deep breath and looked around to gather my bearings. I saw a smoky haze, blinking lights, and people everywhere.

"The *make a bet* thing makes more sense now," I mumbled to myself as I looked around the crowded casino. Still semi-hidden in the bathroom's alcove, I reached in my dress and re-plumped my goods just in case. Then I steeled my spine, arched my back, and strutted my ass like I wanted people to look. I needed to play the part.

Since signing my life away to Spector, I learned to compartmentalize what was happening to me. I was just a girl at a casino. I was meeting a man and luring him. Easy.

I could feel the amusement of my spider. She wasn't fussed about being out of Spector and luring a man. If anything, she was excited for the opportunity to prowl. I breathed in the smoky scent of the casino and stared at all the flashing lights. People cheered and clapped, while some of them cursed and sucked on cigarettes.

There was so much energy here. Sex, power, addiction, and greed. My spider felt right at home.

"Drink, miss?" a cocktail waitress asked while holding a tray toward me. She had bleached teeth and hazel eyes. Her long legs were accentuated with stilettos, and she looked totally bored, already scanning the crowd around me.

I grabbed a shot and downed it whole, wiping my mouth with the back of my hand before offering her a shaky, "Thanks."

I walked around the casino, staring at each of the machines and observing everyone. I knew Spector wanted me to hurry, but I was enjoying the freedom. It was tempting to walk out the doors and run for my life, but the threat of Aunt Marie hanging over my head made me stay. By the looks of it,

I was in Vegas, which was four hours from her home. Even if I managed to portal there somehow and whisk her away, Spector would probably find me before I got there. Then there was Tomb and Crow. My spider was absolutely repulsed by the idea of leaving them behind.

No, I wouldn't be running anywhere until I could bring them with me and ensure that Aunt Marie was safe. I couldn't forget about Cheryl, either. I'd spent so much of my life as a loner I didn't know what to do with all these people to worry about. Even Stiles.

Scanning the different slot machines, I made my way over, but before I could even sit down at one, I was intercepted by casino staff. "ID?"

I plastered on a smile, even though my insides churned. Shit. I was going to get kicked out before I was here for five minutes. Unless… I looked down at the purse Victor had given me and popped it open. Moving aside the bundle of crisp bills, I plucked the plastic card waiting inside. I glimpsed down at the fake ID with my smiling face on it before passing it over to the man. He studied it, scratching the back and looking like he was reading a novel as he scanned over every inch before passing it back. "Have a good night, Miss."

"Thanks," I said brightly, before stuffing the ID back in my purse.

Letting out a relieved sigh, I sat down at the slot machine and tossed in a few bills, feeling a little out of my depth. I'd never been to a casino before, and I had no idea what the demon looked like that I was supposed to lure, so for a few minutes, I simply pressed the buttons, my eyes constantly looking around.

After I'd lost a fair amount of Spector's money, I determined that this definitely wasn't working. What had Victor said? He was a *risk demon*.

Gods, I was being stupid. I'd never pique a risk demon's interest by sitting at a twenty dollar slot machine. I needed to go big.

My eyes skirted over to a poker table. Aunt Marie and I used to play for fun, but I'd never gambled before. There was a good chance I'd lose all the money Spector had given me, but what else could I do? I got the impression that they were shooting in the dark with this demon, and they couldn't expect me to lure him in if I couldn't even find the male.

I got up and straightened my dress, trailing my hands down the smooth fabric. Then I sauntered over to the table and found a seat. "Buy-in is five grand minimum, sweetheart. Go back to your penny slots and let the men play," a gruff player with scraggly hair and yellow teeth said.

A couple of college kids that looked like they had no idea what they were doing snickered. It was obvious that they were spending their daddy's money at the poker table.

My spider didn't like any of them one bit. Neither did I, if I were being honest. But maybe I could use their condescending attitude to my advantage. A lie was a risk, wasn't it?

"Well, I stole all this money from my cheating bastard of a husband, and I'd really like to lose it in a game. Kind of like he lost his wedding ring at the strip club last night. Ten grand should do the trick, right?" I said in a snarky tone while opening my purse for everyone to see.

The old man blanched and sat up straighter, suddenly very interested in what I had to offer.

"Well, darling. Why don't you have a seat? I'd be happy to win your husband's money," the man said with a raspy cackle. "And if you really want to get back at him, my dick would look great in that sassy mouth of yours."

I nearly gagged, though my spider was intrigued by this offer. Not because she was attracted to the scrawny sixty-year-old asking for a blow job, but because she wanted to make him *pay*.

Down, spidey. We need to find the risk demon, first.

An idea struck me. Risk. It was all about risk.

I needed to up the ante. Adrenaline spiked in my blood, pushing me to offer more than I wanted to bargain.

"How about this? If you manage to win all my money, I'll gladly give you a blow job," I replied with a sly smile.

He blanched, like that was the last thing he expected me to say. The sniggering college guys had eyes as big as saucers. "Holy shit, are you for real?" one of them asked, giving me a once-over.

"Yep," I said with a sultry smile.

The one to the right with shaggy blond hair held up a hand. "Wait a minute. You don't want your mouth anywhere near that ugly fucker," he said, tipping his head in the man's direction. The toothy sixty-year-old let out a string of insults that went ignored. "How about we make this deal a little steeper?" he challenged, his brown eyes flashing as he stared at my cleavage.

The beat of my heart kept going faster. "What are the terms, pretty boy?" I asked, not revealing the nerves I felt.

"You beat everyone at this table, and I'll match your winnings."

His friend cursed. "What the fuck, Gabe? Your dad will blow a fucking gasket."

"And if I lose?" I asked.

Blondie shared a look with his friend. "You lose, then you come back to our hotel room and show us a good time."

Fucking pig.

The odds of me winning were very, very bad. My pulse was going out of control. My palms were slick with nervousness, and I had the feeling I should run.

Which is why I knew I was finally hitting the mark. There

was no greater risk than putting myself in this situation. And no greater risk for these humans to be stuck in a room with me.

I smiled and snaked my hand across the table to seal it with a handshake just as the dealer called for buy-ins. "You boys have yourselves a deal."

I exchanged the entirety of my Spector cash for poker chips and rubbed my palms along my legs, eagerness pumping through my veins as the cards were dealt.

This was it. I was about to play for everything I had—both my money and my body. If I lost, I was losing more than those things, too. I was losing my shot at doing what Belvini wanted from me, and failure meant Aunt Marie's life was on the line. Everything depended on the cards being shuffled. Everything could go terribly wrong.

The dealer was just about to start passing out cards when a hard hand suddenly wrapped around my arm. Heat embraced the side of my face as deliciously rough stubble scraped against my ear.

"Black Widow, I have to say, this is a nice look for you," the haunting voice rasped.

My mouth parted as a shaky exhale left my lips, my body frozen. Everyone at the table looked over at the newcomer warily, but excitement flooded my veins. It was *him*. I wasn't sure how I knew, but I did.

Woodsy sulfuric air filled my nose, and I had to force my spider not to spill webs from my fingers. "Sorry, gentlemen," the smooth voice said as he straightened up behind me, though he kept his hand placed possessively over the nape of my neck. "Your game has one less player. This woman is a hustler and has been banned from the casino for a while now."

My heart skipped a step, and I noticed the dealer press a button, probably to call over security.

"Bullshit. She made a bet, and I want to cash in," the older man said, baring his yellow teeth.

Gross.

I still hadn't seen the demon's face, but his presence was palpable. My spine was straight as a rod and heavy with tension. Each raspy breath escaping my chest was erratic and harsh. Unease like anything I'd ever expected flooded my system, and suddenly, I wasn't sure I was up to the task.

The risk was too great. What if I failed? What if my lure didn't work? What if they hurt Aunt Marie because I couldn't do this? What if I never saw Crow and Tomb again?

Fucking risk demon. He was winning already, and I hadn't even seen his face.

When I finally willed myself to turn and meet his gaze, what I saw took my shaky breath away.

His eyes were dark and brimming with a raw, demanding power that had my spider salivating. He had a defined jaw and rough, dark facial hair casting shadows on his chiseled face. There was a timeless appeal about him, and he was utterly gorgeous in a tailored suit, swathed in dominating presence. He stood with the pride of someone that was self-assured, maybe even a bit cocky, but there was a mature aura in his presence that added to his mysterious allure. His style was understated but lavish, like he spent thousands of dollars to look good but blend in all the same.

It was like staring at the face of your sweetest nightmares and begging to never wake up.

"She's done," he repeated while moving his hand to pull me up from my seat.

My heel wobbled, and I pitched sideways, but he swiftly turned me to his chest, where my palms braced against him to catch my fall. My webs spread like cords of frost along his suit, and he arched a brow at the display.

Unlike how my spider had tucked tail and tried to hide

away from Belvini, right now, she was practically purring in this demon's presence. I had to force her back into the recesses of my mind to avoid more claiming silk from tumbling out across his chest. He didn't bother to wipe it away.

"She's *not* done. We made a deal," blondie frat boy said while pounding his chest in a purely caveman move that had me rolling my eyes and pitying him. Didn't he realize that he stood no chance against this man? Couldn't he feel the waves of dark power?

Ignoring him, the demon trailed his gaze slowly over my face. I could feel his attention like licking flames of fire. He was going to make me burn. I just didn't know if the fire was going to be punishment or pleasure.

"Shall I get rid of your competitors? They seem to be arguing with me," he said quietly, though his tone was clear with warning. "I dislike being argued with."

"No. I will," I answered quickly.

I knew that the three men at the table could be destroyed in a blink of this demon's eye if I didn't handle it—and quickly. They were skeevy, sure, but I *had* set them up after all. I couldn't leave their fates on my conscience.

I turned to the collegiate duo. "Sorry, boys. Seems my husband is here to re-claim me, and he's *deathly* jealous," I said with an ominous warning. Reaching across the table, I pushed my chips toward them. "Consider this my recompense."

Three burly security guards walked up just as I turned to leave. The demon cut them off. "No need for an escort," he told them before placing his hand on my lower back and leading me away.

It took everything in me to walk evenly at his side as he led me through the casino. As we passed people by, both men and women turned to look before quickly getting out of our way. My heart was slamming against my ribs, my fear bruising me from the inside out. Was Spector watching this right now? I had to get him alone—and fast. I knew my limits. I could only fake this for so long before my façade began to crumble.

"If you wanted to see me, Black Widow, all you had to do was call," the demon said at my side. The heat of his hand was practically burning through the lace of my dress. The heat felt amazing against my spine, but I didn't miss what he'd said. He recognized my spider. "Possession is beneath you, beautiful. Though this could be fun," he added, while trailing a thumb down my arm and making chills scatter over my skin.

I shook my head, trying to control my body's response to him. I couldn't decipher between my spider's fondness of this demon and my own attraction.

"Well, this possession wasn't consensual for either of us," I admitted, apparently forgetting that I was supposed to be a seductive machine luring him into Spector's clutches. For some reason, the fact that he knew my spider from...hell...made me feel this odd sense of hope. I wasn't prepared to do a trust fall off a building or anything, but a little prodding for information couldn't hurt.

"Is that so? Interesting," he replied.

We were getting closer to the exit, and I knew I was running out of time. Looking around, I noticed a hallway that led to the elevators for the hotel portion of the building. I quickly grabbed his arm and walked in that direction, gently leading him. To my surprise, he didn't try to redirect me. Slowly, I started to let some of my lure power seep from my skin. I knew I needed to be careful. It wasn't like I had the element of surprise or mystery. He already knew what and who I was.

I was spinning a proverbial web, straddling a thin strand

where I wanted to trap him, while also gain whatever answers I could. The strings were precarious, but I had no choice but to weave them.

The closer we got to the hallway, the more lure I put out. When we reached it, I pressed a shaky finger to the button, calling for an elevator. One dinged immediately, and when I walked in, the demon followed.

I backed up, pressing my body against the mirrored wall of the elevator, watching him silently as he stood in front of me, and the doors snicked shut behind him. I had him alone. And it was both thrilling and terrifying at the same time.

For a moment, we just stared at each other. The elevator didn't move at first, and neither did we. I pushed more lure out, hoping it would daze him enough for me to get my questions answered. "How did you know my demon?" I asked, my voice sultrier than I anticipated.

"We go way back," he replied dryly, like I was somehow supposed to know the answer. "Now, why don't you stop using your lure on me so we can have a conversation without the sexual tension, hmm?"

My mouth dropped open in surprise, and then embarrassing naivety filled me up with shame. *Of course* he would see through my seductive attempts. His cocky smile greeted me, so I pumped out even *more* pheromones. Maybe I hadn't used enough?

"*Fuck*," he croaked while shaking his head and sending me a dark, hungry look. "You're really putting this new body of yours to work. What would your mates think?"

At the mention of my mates, I froze, and all my lure evaporated. It was like all the humid tension was sucked from the air, leaving behind the dry reality that this man knew far too much, and he had the answers I desperately needed. I'd learned to accept my spider, but that didn't necessarily mean I understood her.

"My mates? What do you know about them? Who even *are* you?" I asked.

He cocked his head suspiciously, as if trying to understand my question. I knew it was the wrong thing to say the moment he hit a button on the elevator that stopped our ascent, causing our metal cage to slam to a screeching halt and shrill alarms to sound.

He shoved me against the wall. "You want introductions? Fine. I'm Risk. Who the fuck are you, and what are you doing here?" he growled with predatory intent, his body pressing against mine, his hips holding me in place.

I moaned. I fucking *moaned*. What the hell was wrong with me? Maybe I was hungry again? Shit, I thought Byron would've satisfied me longer than this. Embarrassment flooded my cheeks, but when I tried to push him off, he didn't budge an inch. The hand I'd used to shove at his chest lingered, and I had zero excuse for that other than the fact that I wanted to feel him.

"Spector sent me," I replied without hesitation, though my voice was thick with desire. "They want to bring you in."

Wow. I wasn't an expert at this, but I was fairly certain that telling your mark the truth meant you failed. Well, I guess I'd just royally fucked up this mission. I'd chosen a side, and it clearly wasn't Spector's. It was like my spider's trust in him was bleeding into how I responded.

"Why?" he growled.

"Hell if I know," I snapped, trying very hard to keep my hands from wandering over his chest. "They forced a fucking possession on me, tortured me, and now they're threatening my family if I fail this mission."

His eyes zeroed in on the mark on my throat, like he was trying to gauge if I really was the Black Widow. I still didn't understand how he'd recognized me.

As if being summoned to prove herself, my spider fought

through the haze of my consciousness and broke through, bringing her deadly, demonic power to full control. "Hello, Risk," her dark voice whispered. "Aren't you going to help an old friend?"

His eyes flashed in recognition, and he stared at my lips as if he could see the haunting words that had escaped them. Lure was pooling out of me without control. I couldn't even rein in the desire if I wanted to. I was working on my spider's instincts, allowing her lust to fill the cramped elevator. My panties were soaked. The hunger within me roared with defining determination as webs fell like trailing ribbons from my fingertips. My hands began to graze up his chest of their own volition until they circled around the hot skin of his neck, and I was toying with the black hair at his nape. I wanted to touch him. The need was so pure and intense that I couldn't stop myself. I didn't want to, either.

"How much time do we have?" he finally answered, pinning me with his dark stare.

I lifted a shoulder. "I don't know. I'm supposed to press my bracelet once I've lured you on our own. But they have eyes everywhere," I whispered while glancing around the cramped elevator, as if expecting to see shadowed faces in the glass.

Those plush serpent lips of his, spilling with cursed chances and risky behaviors, greeted the ridge of my ear. "Then I suppose we should give them something to watch." He shoved his thigh between my legs, and I gasped when my core settled on top of his hard muscles. His hands moved to grasp my waist, searing into my skin, and I nearly moaned aloud again.

I breathed in, brushing the pebbled peaks of my breasts against his chest, praying for a break in the thick tension. My lure was heady and hot, taking our chance encounter and elevating it to a need I couldn't grasp. I was thudding. Pulsing. Slipping with slick desire.

I was drawn to Crow and Tomb. I craved them. They were both objects of desire for my spider and me, and they helped me compartmentalize the things that Spector made me do—helped me accept my demon and who I was now. But even more than that, they were mine. My spider had a claim on them before I ever understood what that meant.

But this desire with Risk was different. It felt different, yet familiar. It felt hot and reckless, needy and tempting. Like he was the forbidden fruit I'd always wanted to ensnare. Just being in his presence was sexy. Dangerous. Thrilling. I loved it.

"How do you feel about taking risks, Black Widow?" he asked seductively. The low timber of his voice made my skin tingle.

"It has a certain appeal," I replied, wanting to stretch onto my tiptoes and skim my lips over his.

"I'm glad you think so," he murmured. "Because what I'm about to do is incredibly risky." He grabbed both my wrists and squeezed tightly, the padding of his thumb lining up with my thudding vein. "Hold your breath," he demanded before a strange popping sensation started to erupt within every fiber of my being.

Every cell. Every muscle. It was like I was being squeezed in a vacuum. Reality blistered with a deafening snap. One second, we were entwined against the wall of the elevator, and the next, I was sucked through the straw of existence. It felt like an eternity, but it could only have lasted a matter of seconds.

Folding, unfolding, burrowing, burning. My body shaped and molded, bent and broke. And then I was spit back out into a stark white room.

I stumbled, but his hands were there to catch me. "What

the fuck was that?" I gasped while convulsing in his arms. His steady grip kept me still as the molecules of my being realigned themselves and settled back into their places.

"I needed more time away from prying eyes," he explained. He was still *so* fucking close. He didn't create any distance between us, he simply peered into my eyes like he could see the fabrication of my warring souls. "I'm glad you survived. Not many do."

That statement made my eyes widen. Fucking risk demon.

Chapter 16

"SO THEY'RE FORCING POSSESSIONS? I'll fucking *end them*," Risk gritted out while pacing the...room. It was hard to describe this place as anything, really. It just felt like white space that went on forever and ever. It was giving me vertigo.

After we'd landed through his impossible transportation, Risk explained where we were: The Between. Apparently, he'd found it during a drunken night in the thirteen hundreds. It was a place between worlds. A timeless gap of nothingness. Endless space and endless realties all bending to meet at a single point—here.

I nodded as I watched him walk back and forth. "It's pretty fucked up. From what I've heard, they only focus on getting low level creature demons, but I guess they want you now," I replied while shifting on my heels.

My muscles were so fucking sore, and my feet were killing me, but there wasn't a single chair in sight. I bent over to rub at the place where my shoes were digging into my ankles, and I heard Risk immediately stop pacing. At his abrupt stop, I glanced behind me, still bent over, my hair hanging down and my ass probably looking like an invitation. I couldn't even say the move was innocent. He made me feel like I was a body of needy desire. At least I'd managed to turn off my spider's lure, but the sexual tension was still thick. So was the bulging shape in his black slacks, I noticed.

He cleared his throat when I straightened back up, and he snapped his fingers, making a leather wingback chair appear. "Have a seat," he offered before continuing to pace.

Once my body was settled and sinking into the plush comfort, he continued, "Not all creature demons are low level," he said, surprising me. "*You're* a higher level demon. In fact, it doesn't make sense. Black Widow could have easily outpowered a simple possession spell."

I frowned. "What do you mean?"

"Exactly what I said. Your demon *allowed* herself to be possessed by you."

I pressed a hand to my throat, tracing over the red hourglass mark. "Why? Why would she do that?"

He didn't answer me for a moment, and I was left to chew on my spider's motivations and spit them back out. Why would she *want* to be here? Why would she possess me if she didn't have to? During vulnerable moments, I'd even felt bad for the demon. I thought we were both forced into a cohabitation against our control.

"Can you think of no reason why your demon would willingly merge with you?" he asked, watching me carefully.

My mind swirled, but I was at a loss. Until… My eyes widened. "Oh my gods."

Risk nodded slowly, placing his hands in the pockets of his slacks and leaning against…well, nothing. Nothing that I could see, anyway, but his body was leaning against that nothingness regardless, and he looked sexy as hell doing it.

"Tomb and Crow."

He nodded again, a hint of a smile over his lips like he was proud I'd put the pieces together.

"They were mates in hell?" I guessed. "My spider, the gargoyle, and Crow's malphas demon?"

"Indeed. If her mates were summoned here against their will, then it makes sense that she'd willingly come."

Visions of a spider, gargoyle, and crow having an orgy assaulted my imagination, and I snorted at the visual. I didn't even know how that worked.

Risk's lips quirked up in amusement, like he knew what I was thinking. "Mates in the underworld aren't as physical as they are here—though it does happen when beasts are compatible. It's more like a divine partnership. A unique connection that can't be severed. It transcends sex, though I have a feeling you will enjoy having compatible bodies now," he said slyly.

Enjoy, indeed. I could still practically feel Tomb's body rocking into mine—pun intended. Not to mention how Crow's heady gaze made shivers travel up and down my spine.

"So how did she feed when she was below?" I asked, playing with the lace sleeves of my dress while averting my eyes. The question was embarrassing, but I was curious. "Here, she has to have sex to survive. She has to kill…" my voice trailed off.

"Coming topside comes with a cost. She was still the Black Widow, but she didn't have to feed in the underworld because it wasn't necessary, she was already dead."

"I don't understand," I replied with furrowed brow.

I could tell Risk didn't know how to explain. It was evident in the way his mouth thinned in concentration. I got the feeling that the demon realm was an abstract concept hard for supes to fathom. "Take me, for example. I'm a risk demon. When I come topside, I feed off the risky behaviors of others. But I don't need to do that below. Hell sustains us."

"She must really hate this then," I replied. "Feeling hungry. Having to feed."

Risk shrugged. "Not necessarily. When a demon comes topside, it's like awakening to your higher purpose. It's instinctual. We don't have the same fear or objections to death as you do. We don't have the same moral compass, either. She's probably enjoying her new purpose. It's natural for her."

I nodded, reveling in all of this new understanding. Stealing a look at Risk, I chewed on my lip. "Did we...uhh, I mean, did we ever...?" I let a hand motion between us before it dropped lamely in my lap, my cheeks burning. What the fuck was I thinking asking him something like that?

A slow, sensual smile spread across Risk's gorgeous face. "Did we ever *what*?"

"I-I mean...we aren't mates too...are we?"

He watched me for an uncomfortably long time, making me fidget in my seat. "Why do you ask?" he finally replied. His grin let me know how much he was enjoying this.

"Never mind," I mumbled, burying my gaze in my lap.

He was in front of me in an instant, using the crook of his finger to lift up my chin. I stared up at him, unable to blink. "Tell me."

"Because we're drawn to you," I admitted, my face feeling like it was on fire.

"You mean you want to fuck," he corrected.

"No!" I denied hastily, getting to my feet so I could put some distance between us.

I heard him chuckle behind me. "You're a terrible liar."

"I'm just saying—"

Hands wrapped around my waist, and then I was suddenly spun around until we were chest-to-chest, hips to hips. Webs rained down from my fingers as I stared up at him, the heat of his body soaking into me. *"You're just saying* that ever since we met, all you can think about is me touching you," he said, his voice husky, igniting sparks in the pit of my stomach. "*Teasing* you. Hiking up your leg," he said, moving to do just that. He yanked my thigh up, my knee automatically hooking around his hip, and then he trailed his hand from my thigh to my ass, squeezing the plush skin. "And then letting you grind your slick, sweet-smelling pussy against my cock."

I shook my head, trying to deny it. "N-No. I wasn't."

"That's the second lie," he replied, shaking his head. "Every time you lie, you're going to owe me a gamble."

I swallowed hard, feeling my fangs pulse in my mouth. I was suddenly dying of thirst. "What kind of gamble?"

He smiled darkly. "A wager. I bet you right now that you're fucking soaked through your lace panties. That you're so wet, your juices would coat my tongue."

A whimper escaped me, but I couldn't deny it.

He smirked. "That's what I thought. Don't take a chance on lies with a risk demon. You'll lose every time."

My core was throbbing. My hips jutted forward, unable to be stopped. I was grinding against him shamelessly, like a wanton woman out of her mind with lust. "Why do I feel like this? Are you making me feel this way?" I asked breathlessly. I'd gotten used to my constant *hunger*, but this was something else entirely. I wasn't driven by the need to feed or claim, I was driven by a wanting so crystal clear that it left me shaking.

He shook his head slowly. "That would be a lust demon's abilities. Not mine. This is...something else," he murmured. "I feel the pull too. And I believe it's coming from you."

"I don't understand. I'm not using my lure," I admitted, sounding needy and gasping. I would've been embarrassed if I wasn't so godsdamned horny. My body's responses were spinning out of control. I was boiling with newfound hunger.

Drumming with need. I needed to feed. I needed to fuck. I just *needed*.

"I've always been drawn to Black Widow's sensual aura. But topside...the fact that you kill all those you fuck unless they're your mates—that mortal risk is intoxicating to me," he admitted. "Plus, you're sinfully sexy."

So was he. I wanted to strip off his jacket and pop open his fly. I wanted to feel his skin against mine and rake my nails across his back. I wanted to feel him *everywhere*.

"But it's more than that," he went on. "I believe your demon is...trying to make me a mate."

My eyes widened. "What?"

"Demons mate with those that they desire. With those they are compatible with, and who will also sustain them."

"Oh my gods, I'm so sorry." I tried to push away from him, but he continued to hold me against him.

"I think I'm going to let you," he murmured, shocking the fuck out of me.

"*What?*" I exclaimed, shaking my head. This was moving so fast, and yet, it felt like I was taking too damn long. Like this was exactly what was supposed to happen. "You don't even know me. We just met. I was sent here to fucking trap you."

Solid black smoke rose from his palms, rising around us like we were an inferno. "I've decided that I want you," he said definitively, as if that was all he needed to know. "And I like to take risks."

"This is crazy," I stuttered.

"This is delicious," he countered.

"But I have other mates," I said, suddenly feeling guilty, though my entire body still ached.

"Mmm, indeed. Would you like them here too, my Wicked Love?"

A sudden vision of having all of them here, worshipping

me carnally, feeding me with their blood and their essence, the thought made me combust. I moaned when his fingers brushed against my breasts, zipping sensation spreading through my peaked nipple. My dress was riding up higher and higher, my hips rocking against him.

"Would you like all three of us here to lick you? To touch you, to *devour* you? To fuck you and feed you until you're sated and spent?" he asked, every word like a vibrating pulse landing directly onto my clit. "Answer me."

"Y-Yes," I admitted. "I want that."

"Then you'll have it. Next time," he added. "Because right now? Right now you're mine."

Then he took my mouth.

And I mean he *took* it. He owned me completely. The kiss was hard, crushing, and utterly possessive. Risk's tongue didn't just dip into my mouth or caress my lips. He took me like he was demanding my mouth and dominating my body. I moaned into him, unable to even breathe as my back bent with the weight of his body.

"We have to go back," I turned my head away from his lips, panting with breath. "Spector is waiting," I said, even as I leaned forward, starting to trail my lips over his neck like I couldn't help myself. I sucked on the skin where his pulse thrummed, my fangs aching to pierce it—just as my core ached for him to pierce me.

"Time works differently here," he said, grabbing my ass and rocking his hips into me, letting me feel the hard press of his erection. "It doesn't pass unless I let it."

I met his eye. "Then don't let it."

With a slow nod, he raised his hand and snapped his fingers, and then my dress was just...gone.

I gasped, looking down at my lingerie clad body, the deep blue color setting off my long red hair. I was about to snap at him for removing my clothes, but the look on his face stopped me. He stared down at me with such all-consuming desire that the words died in my throat.

He stood back, taking me in with a slow swoop of his eyes before landing back on my face. "You are wicked exquisiteness, and I'm going to devour you," he said with dark promise.

My throat bobbed. "I'm going to let you."

I jumped. He caught. We clashed.

The Between clanged with the echo of our collision.

Webs hung suspended from thin air. Smoke rose around us like a blistering promise. Power rippled into the nothingness.

His hands gripped my ass and tore the scrap of lace from my body. My fingers popped the button of his slacks, shoving them down to free him. "Take me," I demanded, fisting him in my hand.

"You were mine the moment you sat down at that card table."

Without warning, he surged his hips, entering me in one brutal thrust.

I cried out, my head thrown back so that my hair tickled the globes of my ass where he held me. I was so wet that his cock slipped fully inside of me, and when he began to lift my body up and down over his cock, my slick desire coated him completely.

"Fuck, you feel godsdamned divine."

I braced my hands on his shoulders and started to move up and down, helping him so that I could bounce over his cock. He walked us forward, and then he was lowering me down where he'd conjured a massive bed on the spot. My back hit silky sheets and plush pillows as Risk braced himself over my body.

"I want to feel your skin," I demanded, both my spider and I needing more.

He smirked down at me, but he allowed me to yank off his suit jacket and tear his dress shirt right down the middle, sending buttons flying. He tsked. "Feeling needy?"

I was. My chest felt too constricted. My fingers ached to touch him everywhere. I let them graze down his strong, muscled chest, my fingers hooking on the lines of his abs. "You do a lot of bench presses and sit ups in hell?" I quipped.

His grin widened. "I've been topside for centuries, love. And I prefer a good hellfire fight."

"Of course you d—"

My words were cut off as he suddenly took my bustier and ripped it away from my body, without me feeling even a pinch. His eyes lingered on the rise and fall of my breasts. "These looked fucking fantastic in that dress and lingerie, but they're even better bare."

He lowered his head and took a nipple into his mouth, sucking gently. I nearly bucked off the bed, but he thrust his cock into me again, pressing me against the mattress.

"I'm going to fuck you hard now, Wicked Love," he said with a wicked gleam in his eye. "And you and your demon are going to feed from me. I want to feel you sucking on my vein like it's my cock, drinking your fill of my essence until you're burning with my power and you're full of me *everywhere*."

With inhuman speed, he gripped my hips and started pounding into me. Again and again and *again*. Webs flew from my hands, attaching to the footboards, and I gripped them hard so I wouldn't go flying up the bed from the vigor of his pistoning length.

Licks of flame seemed to dance over my clit, teased from the smoke that was dancing over his skin. My eyes rolled to the back of my head, and I came with such ferocious depth that I blacked out, caught in a starless night of pleasure and heat.

"Hellfire, your cunt feels amazing clenching my cock like

that," Risk growled into my ear. His hand reached down between us, and he began pressing my clit.

"Too sensitive," I breathed, still coming down from my peak.

But he wouldn't be deterred. "I'm going to make you come again and again, until my cock explodes so deeply inside of you that you feel my cum dripping down your legs for days to come."

Holy hell.

"Now bite me."

I didn't need another invitation. With fangs bared, my body lifted, and I struck the crook of his neck, venom shooting into his body as his blood filled my mouth. He tasted like smoked sugar. Bitter, yet decadently sweet at the same time.

In perfect synchronization, my spider began to gulp down his essence with every pull I drew from his vein. We fed in tandem, and Risk erased all memory of Byron from my body and mind.

"That's it," he growled into my ear. "Take more."

I unlatched from his neck, licking the trail of blood falling from my lips. "The only sounds I want to hear from you is your cock slamming into my pussy."

A deep, rumbling laugh came from his chest, but I was already fang-deep in him again, drinking my fill.

I fed and fed and fed. My spider and I took everything he was offering. Every little bit we could get.

But feeding from a high level demon was different than humans or hybrids. No matter how much I took, there was still more.

My head sagged against his chest, unable to drink another drop. My spider, too, relented her grip on his thread, a glutton of total gratification.

Risk looked down at me, his expression full of male smugness. "Too much for you to take, hmm?"

My hands shot forward, wrapping around his neck, and I flipped us so that I was on top. "I take what I want," my spider and I answered.

"So do I." He rolled his hips, tipping up into me at this new angle and hitting a spot so deep inside of me that I groaned.

Bracing my hands on his chest, I rode him fast and hard, my breasts bouncing until he caught them in his hands and plucked the tips.

"Come again. I want to feel you like this, gulping on my cock while I fill you with my cum."

It was like he trained my body to do exactly what he said. The words had barely left his mouth before I was screaming his name, seeing stars all over again as an orgasm ripped through me. Risk shoved his hips up, burying himself inside of me with a guttural groan, and then I felt searing cum burn through me with satisfaction.

I collapsed on top of him, unable to move, barely able to breathe. With my head nuzzled against the crook of his neck, I watched as a deep red hourglass appeared on his throat.

Holy shit.

I just made a high level risk demon my mate.

Chapter 17

I WAS LYING on a pillow of clouds, literal clouds that my new...*mate*...had conjured in this mysterious between world for me to rest on. "Are you going to keep pretending to sleep, Wicked Love?" he asked, while stroking my cheek. I wasn't ready to admit that I'd *mated* him.

Mates.

Fucking *mates*.

I kept rolling that word around in my head, trying to piece together what this meant for my future—our future. I didn't know this man. I didn't know if he had skeletons in his closet or crazy habits, or if he was a serial fuck 'em and feed 'em sort of guy. I knew nothing about him, and now a part of my demonic side was tethered to him...forever.

"I can sense you freaking out. There's always this high after a big risk and then the inevitable crash. You're burning with turmoil, and I can practically taste it. What's going on in that pretty head of yours? Regretting this already?"

That was one thing I definitely knew about him: The man was blunt.

I swallowed, trying to think of what to say without

offending the only person that could transport me out of this place.

"I'm just processing," I cautiously replied. "That was very impulsive, you know? I don't even know you, not really." I winced when his brow furrowed, but continued. "Isn't becoming mates a bit...permanent?"

I was about to start hyperventilating. When this was all said and done, I was going to have a stern group meeting with my spider and my vagina. They can't just go all sex crazed and leave my brain behind.

"I'm not the demon of thinking through and responsibility," he said wryly. "I told you before. I love the risk," he purred. "I *live* for it. In fact, I haven't felt this good in years. What if we hate each other? What if you clip your toes at the dinner table, or worse...what if you turn out to be a *vegetarian?*" he shuddered with a chuckle. "The possibilities are endless."

His blasé, pleased face confused the hell out of me. I stared as he folded his hands behind his head and looked up at the expansive blank sky overhead, not a care in the world. I glanced at the bright red mark on his neck, and my spider preened.

"Is it reversible?" I asked.

"Nope. Isn't that fun?"

"You're insane," I deadpanned.

"And you're overthinking this. You wanted me as a mate. I wanted the risk. You need to feed, and I need to fuck you again and again. This arrangement can be mutually beneficial. Besides, we have much bigger problems."

At the mention of said *problems*, I closed my eyes and forced all thoughts of Spector away. I wasn't ready to leave, even though I was uncertain about this whole mate business. I knew that the moment we went back, Spector would bring us in and we'd be trapped once more.

"We have to go back, Wicked Love," he whispered before turning on his side to face me. I let out a shaky exhale.

"I know. My aunt is in trouble, and I can't leave Tomb and Crow there. My spider came here to rescue her mates, and I want to help her."

"It's so odd how you consider yourself separate entities. They're *your* mates, too. This is *your* mission as much as it is hers," Risk observed before trailing a finger up my thigh. I shivered with lust.

I knew what he was saying was true. The line between her needs and mine had become so blurred that I couldn't make sense of where I ended and she began. "So what are we going to do? You can't just turn yourself in to Spector," I said, changing the subject. I didn't like the way Risk knew what I was feeling.

"Why not?"

I shot up from my seat in the clouds and twisted my body to stare at him. Naturally, his eyes completely avoided my incredulous expression and zeroed in on my bare breasts. "Did you not hear what I was saying? Spector is a powerhouse of crazy, and they want you. You need to stay far away."

"Sounds like a fun risk to me," he replied while reaching out to cup my neck. His palm was hot and needy, and in an instant, he was pulling me on top of him. More tension filled the air as I straddled his hard, powerful body.

"You're crazy," I said, shaking my head at him.

"You're *delicious*," he replied, leaning up to suck and nip at the curve of my breast.

I smiled and threaded my fingers through his hair. "You know, Tomb is going to want to beat your ass when he finds out you're my mate too."

Risk chuckled. "He can try."

"He's a gargoyle."

"I'm a full demon," he countered. "It'll be an entertaining fight. What about Crow? Will he be angry? Two against one sounds like fun odds."

I chuckled. "Crow isn't as possessive as Tomb."

"Shame. I was looking forward to kicking both of their asses."

The humor seeped from my expression, and I yanked on his hair to make him look me in the eye. "You won't actually hurt each other, will you?"

He leaned forward and sucked my lower lip into his mouth before answering. "Demons are alphas. It's in our nature to battle. But...it's also in our nature to fuck our mate, and that one usually wins out."

"*Usually?*" I stressed.

That infuriatingly sexy smirk of his came back. "You're going to have to keep up with the whole risk concept."

I shook my head and slipped off him, looking down as my feet sunk slightly in the puffy clouds. "Okay, what's the plan? We need to figure out what we're going to do."

He sighed and sat up, scrubbing his hands down his face. "Eager to leave so soon?"

"It's not that. I'd stay in here forever with you if I could...and if the others were safe with me. Tomb, Crow, Cheryl, my aunt, Stiles..."

"Who the fuck is Stiles?" he suddenly asked, looking pissed.

I gaped at the sparks snapping off his knuckles. "Umm, my half-brother."

The sparks were quenched in an instant. "Ah."

With a snap of his fingers, we were both fully clothed again, in the same outfits as before. "Thank you," I said.

He stood up, buttoning his suit jacket and looking just as perfect as before. "You're welcome. Now hold your breath."

"For wh—"

Before I could finish the words, his arm was wrapped around my waist, and that same vacuum-packed sensation of being sucked through eternity wrenched over my body. I was squeezed and pulled, nearly bursting from the inside out, and then it was over, and I was slumped against the elevator wall once again.

I reared up and smacked him on the arm. "You bastard. A little warning would've been nice!" I hissed.

Risk chuckled before leaning in and placing a smoldering kiss on my lips that made me forget that I'd been pissed at him.

"Better?" he murmured against my lips.

"No," I grumbled.

He reached around and pinched me on the ass. "Liar. You owe me another gamble."

I rolled my eyes before reaching up and straightening his tie where it had gotten wind-whipped from teleporting. "Fine. What gamble am I taking this time?" I asked snarkily.

"This one."

Without any other warning, Risk took my wrist from where I was still fixing his tie, and before I realized what he was doing, his thumb was pressing over the charm on Spector's bracelet.

My blue eyes flew wide. "No! We aren't ready! We don't even have a plan!" I hissed.

The fucking insane risk demon just grinned as the elevator jolted up, careening all the way to the top floor.

"I know," he said with a wink, as if this was another rush that he couldn't wait to dive headfirst into. I wasn't sure if he was really this driven by his need to gamble or if he just genuinely was so cocky he didn't worry. Either way, I was certain that he didn't understand the mess he had just walked us right into.

I watched in horror as the elevator came to a stop, and

when the doors slid open, a wall of Spector guards swarmed us. One of them lunged for me, grabbing my wrists and yanking me out of the way.

Risk didn't like that.

He didn't like that one bit.

All amusement fled his face. "I suggest you release my mate before I burn all of you in hellfire. I'll come willingly, but I don't think hurting her is a risk you want to take," he growled while shoving aside the supes trying to restrain him and positioning himself at my side. He did it as easily as someone flicking off a bug. The man holding me seemed to battle with his sense of self-preservation but ultimately decided to let me go.

"I don't want any funny business," one of the gruff guards said while holding up his relic.

Risk laughed at the meager threat before plucking the relic from his fingers and swallowing it whole. My gut twisted with anxiety. *Was he insane?* That relic was going to burn a hole in his stomach.

Everyone's eyes widened as Risk patted his stomach. "It's like fine whiskey," he began while leaning closer to the guard. "Burns good on the way down."

The guards gasped and gaped, looking back and forth at one another, as if debating on what to do. "Relics only have power if you believe in the god they represent. I only believe in myself." At that, he turned and winked at me, proving just how cocky he was.

I shook my head. Risk was fucking with them and getting off on it.

It seemed like everyone realized at the same time that they couldn't actually restrain Risk. They started to step back, the fear they felt evident on their faces.

"Now. I hear someone would like to speak with me?" Risk

said amicably. "I suggest you hurry and fetch them before I change my mind and leave with my mate."

His arm wrapped around my waist possessively. He really *was* staking his claim, and very publicly too. I wasn't sure if his territorial behavior was necessarily a good thing. Spector had already proven that they were willing to use those close to me to get me to cooperate. I feared adding to the list of people I cared about.

The Spector guards exchanged looks.

"I'm getting impatient," Risk warned as smoke escaped his mouth in an intimidating fashion. The small space started to reek of hellfire and brimstone, an evident threat hanging in tangible strands of smoldering fumes between us.

The guards jumped to action, guiding us out of the elevator, down the hall, and toward a side room. Their shoulders were pulled back, and they eyed us warily, likely not sure what to make of this situation. They'd originally swarmed our elevator, intending to drag us back kicking and screaming, but now it was Risk calling the shots and demanding an audience with Belvini.

As we moved, I hissed at Risk. "Can you lay off of the *mate* talk? I'm not sure it's a good idea to tell them."

Risk chuckled and replied, not bothering to lower his voice, "Are you embarrassed of me, Wicked Love? I'm wounded."

I squeezed my eyes shut. He really didn't understand, and I wished that I had more time to explain what sort of mess we were walking into. We should've spent less time rolling in the orgasms and more time plotting. "I'm not embarrassed. I just think we should keep this quiet," I whispered in response while eyeing a particularly gruff guard on my left.

"I think that ship sailed when you moaned on my cock and branded me with your mark, darling," he replied evenly. A few of the men stumbled on their feet. Someone coughed awkwardly. I groaned. This new mate was proving to be difficult.

"The portal is just this way," one of the guards mumbled. His voice was conflicted. It was like the Spector guards couldn't decide if they wanted to be polite to appease the deadly demon, or if they wanted to run the other way. In our short time together, I'd learned that Risk was the sort to demand respect and fear, so I understood their dilemma.

Risk was cocky, but he was determined. I could see it in the setting of his jaw and the precision of his gaze. I just hoped that his power and determination would survive Spector's evil agenda.

I hoped *he* survived Spector.

Chapter 18

I WASN'T PLANNING on attending this meeting with Risk, but he refused to let me out of his sight. The second we stepped through the portal and arrived back at the Spector compound, he gripped me tightly and refused to let go, and everyone was too scared to defy him.

We were guided to Belvini's office, and each step closer made my chest constrict with anxiety. Belvini made my skin *crawl*. There was something so intrinsically sinister about him that even my spider wanted to creep out of my skin and escape his presence.

"Brother," Risk greeted in a disarmingly cheery tone as we walked inside Belvini's office.

Brother? *Brother?* Risk saw me bristle at that label and smirked over at me. Unease slipped down my spine.

"Hmm. Brother is a loose term, don't you think?" Belvini replied dryly. He was sitting at his desk, fingers threaded together and resting on the glass top in front of him. He looked unimpressed and irritated. It was obvious in the way he seethed that he didn't like that Risk took control of his own capture. "Our mother had entire legions of spawn. You were just another egg in the nest."

Hysterical visions of a naked Risk emerging from a giant egg made me want to snort, but I reined in the impulse. The corner of my new mate's mouth ticked just a fraction of an inch, as if he could predict what I was imagining.

"Oh, so your reason for this meeting wasn't to organize a family reunion?" Risk bantered with a sly grin. My hand was clasped in his, a detail that hadn't escaped Belvini's hard stare. I was uncomfortable at the blatant display, but Risk wouldn't let me shake him off. "Shame. I already invited Lust and Greed. The RSVPs were sent and *everything*."

I squeezed Risk's hand, silently pleading with him to stop goading Belvini. My own brush with demons taught me that they were always looking to flex their dominance and assert themselves as the biggest, baddest one in the room. But now was not the time to challenge Belvini.

"You know I don't associate with them," the annoyed Spector president said with a sneer. It looked like he was sucking on a lemon, as if the idea of spending time with other demons made him sick. If that was the case, then why was he building an entire army of us?

"You don't associate with a lot of us or our ways anymore, do you? You even changed your name, *Collector*."

Collector? Risk's name seemed appropriate for his own particular tastes, and I was now looking at Belvini with newfound understanding. He *was* a collector—a hoarder of objects, people, and power.

"Don't call me that," Belvini snapped.

My eyes travelled between the two of them. It was like watching a very intense ping pong match and trying to count the score. So far, I had a feeling that Risk was winning.

Risk's eyes flicked to the amber amulet on Belvini's neck. "Using little rocks to subdue your powers?" He tsked with a shake of his head. "I suppose I shouldn't be surprised you can't control your hunger to hoard."

Belvini glowered. The furious tension between them was palpable. I wanted to crawl out of there and get away from their crossfire, but my spider stood her ground. She wanted to support our new mate, even if he was impulsive and probably a touch insane. It would take some getting used to his impulsive nature and his addiction to adrenaline and chance.

"I've heard about this latest venture of yours. Collecting hybrids is your newest way to get off, yes? And now you need me. To be honest, I'm offended that you thought I'd be taken so easily. Do you not remember Prague?" Risk asked, while taking a step closer toward Belvini's desk. Though his tone was playful, his eyes bled with threatening char. "Although, I suppose I should thank you. I'm very pleased with my new pet, and I have you to thank for sending her." At that, Risk pulled me closer and rubbed his lips against the edge of my ear, growling with suggestive possessiveness.

I frowned over at him. His new *pet*?

Belvini cast a cool look in my direction. "When I implied that you should lure him, I didn't mean for you to go so far as to fuck him, Miss Coven." He shook his head, like I'd gravely disappointed him. "At least your spider didn't manage to kill him."

I stiffened my spine like a block of wood, but Risk simply sat down in the chair on the other side of the desk and pulled me onto his lap with him. I tried to get up, but he wasn't having it and locked his hand around my waist dominatingly.

"You know better than that," Risk replied to him. "A lowly creature demon can't kill me."

Warning bells screeched in my ears. *What the fuck was happening?* I wanted out of this office. I wanted away from these men. My spider was growing anxious, pacing around inside of me, and I felt like I was about to miss a step and go tumbling down.

"Good to know. She may serve other purposes for me then," Belvini replied, his eyes skating over me, still dressed up in my seductive clothes, with tousled just-fucked hair.

I went frozen. Completely still. I wasn't even able to take in a breath.

"I don't think my new pet likes you very much, Collector," Risk replied with amusement.

He began to stroke me, like he was doing it simply because he could. I cringed from his touch. This was all wrong. Inside, my stomach was twisted like a towel being wrung out, dripping with edginess and making a puddle of fear. I suddenly felt off-balance, like everyone in the room was three steps ahead of me.

My mind raced backwards, going over my time with Risk in The Between. It had all moved so fast. We latched onto each other in a whirlwind, caught up in the storm. It had felt so right. Relying on instincts and impulses, following my demon's lead. And yet now, nothing had ever felt so wrong. I didn't know the man I was currently perched on, nor did I understand what the fuck his angle was.

"You're always so impulsive, Risk," Belvini chided. "Unlike me, you don't know how to play the long game. You never have." He pulled out his BlackBerry, his demeanor changing when he looked at the screen. Once he put the phone back in his pocket, he looked back up at Risk with a smirk. A smirking Belvini was even more terrifying than a pissed off one.

Risk started playing with my hair, his fingers brushing it over my shoulder so he could run his nose over the skin of my neck. My body wanted to melt against him, but my mind was screaming. "You're boring me. Get to the point. I want to play with my new pet again."

Oh gods. How could I be so fucking stupid? My lip trembled, and I was forced to catch it between my teeth to keep it from moving. Risk wasn't who I thought he was. I'd been so drunk on his risk power, too naive to realize.

Belvini shook his head, annoyed. "Always thinking with your cock. Tell me, how many sexual partners do you think you've had over the years?"

Risk rolled his eyes. "If you're trying to make my new pet jealous, you're being laughably juvenile," he replied before running his hand up my thigh. My core instantly began to pulse, like a beacon trying to beckon him closer. I snapped my knees together, horrified at my body's response, but he wasn't deterred. His hot, sinful hand just kept trailing higher.

Belvini chuckled and shook his head. "No, nothing as crass as that," he assured him. "I don't particularly care for jealousy or other mundane emotions, especially from lowly supes and hybrids. But I wonder, do you even remember your last indiscretion with a certain elemental?"

"Mmm, perhaps." Risk reached the hem of my black dress, and his fingers stopped to toy with it, while I struggled to become numb to his touch and focus on what Belvini was getting at.

"Allow me to refresh your memory," he continued while standing up. He walked around his desk with slow deliverance. "She works on the council, yes?"

"I never understood your obsession with the supernatural government," Risk put in boredly.

"It seems I'm not the only one with an obsession," he said pointedly, watching Risk's hand where he played with my dress. "Though I'm surprised. The councilwoman was not your usual type, but you did what you always do—you took a risk." Belvini then motioned toward the door with a sly smile. "Miss Cainson, would you mind joining us, please?"

My stomach dropped. Risk's wandering hand stilled.

A pretty woman with blonde hair coiled up in a stiff bun walked through the door with her head held high and a snarl on her face. She was wearing wobbly heels and a business suit—a suit that barely covered her large and very pregnant belly.

"Hello, Risk," she greeted before positioning herself at Belvini's side.

My gaze hitched on the woman's stomach, dread collecting in the pit of mine.

"Up, pet," Risk said tapping me on the thigh in a clear signal. I practically bolted out of his lap, backing up as much as I dared to put distance between myself and everyone else in the room. Risk was on his feet in an instant, his eyes flashing. "What the fuck is this?"

The woman laughed, but it wasn't a nice sound. "I should think it's obvious, Risk. Can't you sense it? I'm carrying *your* child." She pressed a hand to her belly, looking smug.

Risk scowled. "The fuck you are. I believe I recall you saying you couldn't have children."

She lifted a shoulder in a lazy shrug. "Seems I misspoke."

Smoke started to gather at the ends of Risk's sleeves, the billowing black falling down his arms and coiling around his wrists. He looked furious. Scary. Like the high level demon from hell that he was. My heart started beating wildly.

"So you understand now?" Belvini asked, moving to stand next to the woman. "I have your child. Which means that unless you want to *risk* his or her life, then you'll do what I require of you. Because as uncaring as you try to appear, we both know you have a soft spot for women and children."

Risk's face was an emotionless mask, but everyone in the room could feel the heat of his fury. "And what is it you *require* of me, Collector?" he asked, not denying Belvini's claim.

"Simple," Belvini answered immediately. "You'll agree to

let me use your blood for the demon rituals. My current supply is running dry. It's so tedious to find high level demon participants, you know. The ritual is quite costly, and the demons get drained so easily. But I have a feeling you won't get as...depleted. Not now, at least." Belvini looked pointedly at me as he spoke, making me squirm.

More and more sulfuric smoke swirled around us, filling the entire office into swirling bouts of embittered gray. "You weren't up for donating to your own cause?" Risk asked dryly.

Belvini chuckled. "I'm not particularly fond of dying. You might be drawn to the risk associated with testing mortality, but I personally prefer to live. I also prefer to be efficient. Unfortunately, I've had to replace too many demons too many times. I needed a more permanent solution, understand? I have big plans for this company, and you'll be a part of it, whether you like it or not."

Risk watched him, his face expressionless. "You know that these rituals don't take just blood, brother. Every possession takes a higher level demon's essence. Are you even capable of something like that? A ritual of that nature will require a lot of power, and we both know how pathetically weak you are."

The vein in Belvini's temple pumped with anger, and I was afraid that he'd bring the fire of hells and destroy us all. I itched to flash away, but Spector was locked down, and I wasn't ignorant enough to think that I'd actually make it out of here. Besides, I couldn't leave Crow and Tomb.

"I know my limitations, *brother*. I also know that you'll have plenty of power to go around," Belvini replied. "I plan to mass produce the hybridization of supes. There are a lot of power hungry men and women out there. A friend of mine has just the sorts of connections I need to truly make this a profitable endeavor. My clinical trials have been a success. All we need is *you*."

Risk rolled his eyes. "How predictable. You've always been a greedy fucker. You're a collector of all things—money, power, and people. Seems you've found the trifecta with Spector."

That thought was horrifying. I didn't want Belvini to have more power than he already did.

"You have no right to judge. You're as much a slave to your nature as the rest of us."

Risk turned his attention to the woman. She didn't seem bothered by the threat to her unborn child's life. She simply shifted impatiently on her heels, like she wanted to get this interrogation over with. "And you'd let him threaten our child, Martha? You'd actually let him kill an innocent?" Risk asked.

"I never wanted this, Risk. I don't want your spawn," she said with contempt. "I'm on the council. I'm expected to uphold a certain elemental standard, and that doesn't include interspecies breeding. This solution is a win-win for me. If you cooperate, Spector has promised me a lot of influence over the council. Their contract would be financially beneficial, and then no one would dare say a word about our offspring. If you *don't* agree to help, I'll be rid of this *thing* growing inside of me and Belvini can do what he wants with it. A demon's spawn. Can you imagine the embarrassment? If my parents were alive, they would disown me."

I found myself baring my fangs in a quiet growl. My spider and I *really* didn't like her. What kind of heartless bitch was okay with giving up their child to a monster like Belvini?

Maybe it was because my own parents rejected me when I was just an infant, but something about her carelessness for the life growing inside of her made me rage. I didn't want Belvini or her to have anything to do with this child.

I wasn't the only one burning with rage over her words. One second, Risk was standing on the other side of the desk. The next, he was in front of her, his hand wrapped around her throat. Her eyes went wide with fear at his sudden intrusion, and though she tried to jerk away, she couldn't get out of his grip.

"You don't deserve to carry *any* child, let alone mine," he growled, squeezing her throat one more time before dropping his hand to her rounded belly. The smoke still spilling out of his sleeves coiled around it like a caress. "If you harm her, I will end you," he said, his tone so chilling that even the hairs on *my* neck rose up to attention. "Do you hear me? She's *mine*."

I didn't know how Risk knew that she was carrying a girl, but I did know that his promise was genuine. I had zero doubt that he would fulfill his word and kill the councilwoman.

When he dropped his hand from her belly and stepped away, the woman finally snapped out of her frozen shock and backed up, anger trying to cover up her fear. "Y-You don't have the right to touch me," she stammered, clutching the reddened part of her throat where his fingers had dug in. "And you're not calling the shots. Belvini is."

"Indeed I am," Belvini said, beaming. He pressed a button on his phone, and a team of Spector guards came in, guns cocked and at the ready, and they didn't hesitate to surround Risk and me. "We are hosting a demonstration for the council in a few days. There, you'll get more of an inside look at how our business works. This doesn't have to be an unfriendly deal, Risk. I think you might actually like the arrangement—and benefits—I have planned. My guards will show you to your rooms now."

I recoiled as two of the guards grabbed hold of my arms.

"Your blood will no doubt summon very powerful demons

for my new customers. I'm looking forward to it," Belvini said with uncontained glee.

Risk didn't even spare the guards a look as they lined up at his back. Fear was dripping out of me in steady streams of webs that fell at my feet.

But then, a wide, cocky smirk suddenly spread across Risk's face. It chilled me all the way down to my bones. "You sent her on purpose, didn't you?"

Belvini grinned maniacally. "What ever do you mean?"

Risk cocked his head in my direction. "My new pet you sent to retrieve me. Black Widow. Curious abilities, that one. Strength, webs, lure, sexual cannibalism…" he purred, making it sound like a delicacy. "It's rotten luck for the ones she feeds from…unless she takes them as a mate."

As Risk's words sunk in, hot tears collected in my eyes. Certainly Belvini didn't *intend* for me to mate Risk? That would mean all of this was a sham.

"I'm very aware of my hybrid's abilities, Risk. I created her, after all. We'd been studying how her mating works, even tested it on a hybrid to see how she chose. I figured her spider wanted an organic mating, which is why I sent her to collect you. She performed exactly the way I'd hoped she would."

The blood drained from my face. Risk's grin widened, and he pulled down the collar of his dress shirt, revealing the red hourglass mark right there on his skin. "Hmm, it does appear that way," Risk replied, looking like the cat that just ate the canary. "Such a pleasant welcome basket from Spector, brother. I knew the moment she stepped foot in that casino what you had planned. I'd been hearing whispers, you know." Releasing his collar, he started walking toward the door unassisted, while the wary guards followed after him. "I think this could be a fun arrangement. The risk appeals to me. I'm glad you reached out, and even more glad for the delicious taste of invincibility you've gifted me with."

Belvini nodded. "I'm a good man to be in business with, Risk. I'm glad you recognize it."

Risk paused at the door to speak once more. "I'll supply whatever you need. There was no need to threaten my child. But I want a cut of the profits. Wealth, power, status, and all that. Plus, my child's safety, of course," he added.

Risk looked at me, and my stomach dropped.

"Oh, and make sure that my new mate gets a nice room to stay in, yes?" Risk said offhandedly over his shoulder. "I might want to enjoy her specific...talents while I'm here."

Without waiting for a reply, Risk strode out of the room, with eight wary Spector guards trailing after him.

My mind exploded with spitting sparks of betrayal.

It had all been an elaborate ploy. Belvini *wanted* me to mate Risk. Risk *wanted* to work for Belvini.

I'd just given them an indestructible high level demon and an endless amount of blood to supply more possession rituals. I'd played right into their hands and made Spector even more powerful than they already were.

Chapter 19

I DIDN'T PAY attention to anything as I was escorted out of Belvini's office. *Escorted* was a loose term. I was basically dragged down the hall. Not because Spector was using overt force, but because my body forgot how to move.

I was spinning.

Round and round my mind went, replaying everything that had happened since I stepped foot in the casino. My head was stuck in a tailspin, screeching tires on pavement like the sound of my screams, repercussions spiraling out of control and landing me in the shattered remains of my own choices.

Risk tricked me.

That term was like a physical blow. Like someone had shoved a spiked spoon into my gut and emptied me out like a pumpkin on Halloween. I was hollow. Scraped raw. Lit up from inside my abraded heart with the realization of how thoroughly stupid I'd been.

I'd played right into his and Belvini's hands. It was so reckless. So...*risky*. I was disgusted with myself for thinking that Risk actually cared, when all along, he'd simply outsmarted me. I guess that was bound to happen with a gods-knows-how-old high level demon.

As the guards roughly led me down the labyrinth of hallways, I barely had the wherewithal to place one foot in front of the other. I was a mess of thoughts and a jumble of emotions, and every second I replayed how Risk had called me *pet* or how he'd told Belvini he wanted in on the operation, the knife of betrayal in my gut sunk in deeper.

I scratched at the blood-red hourglass on my throat as if I could skin it off Risk's neck.

He *used* me. Used my spider for the sole purpose of becoming indestructible. And now he was my eternal mate. He carried *my* mark. The mark that was also on Crow and Tomb. It was supposed to be something meaningful. Something that showed our everlasting bond to one another. But now it felt tainted.

I didn't even realize that tears were spilling down my cheeks until I tasted salt on my lips. My spider was in an agonized ball curled up inside me, refusing to come out. I was still floored that he managed to trick her too. My hands curled into fists in devastated anger, my sharp nails cutting into the skin of my palm, the pain just a fraction of what I was feeling inside. Spiderwebs immediately pushed out of my fingertips and wrapped around the wounds, fitting my hands with silk wrappings. My spider's way of trying to protect me from our shared heartache.

I hadn't been paying attention to where the guards were leading me, so when they suddenly stopped, I looked up, surprised to see I was at the cafeteria doors. "You're not taking me to my cell?"

The one to my right shifted on his booted feet. "Your, uhh, new room isn't ready. You're to come here first."

The fact that I was getting a newer, nicer room because Risk demanded it didn't do anything to help my mood. I'd rather stay in my cell with what dignity I had left. The guards wouldn't listen to my requests though, so I didn't even bother to waste my breath.

Walking past them, I pushed open the cafeteria doors and walked inside, finding only a trickle of Thibault hybrids here and there. Everyone looked over at me as I came in, and I realized belatedly that it was probably because I was still wearing a fuck me dress and boots.

"Oh. My. Gods."

Cheryl's voice was like whiplash snapping me to attention.

There was a rush of air that blew back my hair as she suddenly flashed in front of me. She grabbed me by the shoulders, staring me up and down with wide eyes. "You had a makeover *without me?*" she screeched.

I winced at the sound, fairly certain that some of her siren power had slipped through. "Umm, yeah," I said uncomfortably as the other people in the room continued to stare.

Cheryl's lips formed a thin line. "That is, like, *totally* rude, Motley! I would've invited you."

I sighed and knocked her hands off my shoulders before picking a table and slumping down onto the bench. Cheryl followed hot on my heels, staring at me pointedly from across the table until I gave in. "It wasn't like I was watching romcoms and having a spa day, Cheryl. They dressed me like this for a mission."

She crossed her arms over her chest, making the buttons on her pink blouse strain. "So you're saying you didn't even like it?"

"I'm saying I was forced."

Her eyes dropped down to my hands. "Is that—" She gasped and snatched up my hand. "You got a *manicure* too?"

I pulled my hand back and hid it on my lap. Her eyes narrowed. "Let me see your toes."

"What? No."

"I knew it!" she exclaimed, pointing at me with accusation. "You got a pedicure too, didn't you?"

I pinched the bridge of my nose. I wasn't in the mood for this. I was too raw from what had happened with Risk.

"If you tell me you got a facial, I might never speak to you again," she said while staring me down.

"I got a facial, Cheryl," I replied dryly before rolling my eyes. Part of me hoped that there was merit to her threat, and the other half was thankful for this brief moment of normalcy. Cheryl would always be Cheryl.

She opened and closed her mouth, assessing me with her selfish gaze while debating on whether or not she was actually going to go through with her no speaking promise.

"Motley?" a rigid voice called at my back. I turned around to see my brother, noting that he'd at least made an effort to clean up since I'd seen him last, though the bruises were still there.

"What happened? Is it true that you mated a high level demon that's agreed to help Belvini?" he asked, his expression stormy.

I felt eyes immediately come over to us, perked up ears trying to listen to our conversation. Stiles straightened and looked around the room, realizing that others were looking on with curiosity. Shame-filled tears swarmed my eyes and trailed down my face before I could stop them, and I shuddered with fresh, cutting pain.

"I-I didn't mean..." Short breaths escaped me, cutting off my words.

I was so fucked. I should have seen this coming. My body had become a vessel for powerful men's whims, and yet I'd foolishly allowed myself to think that I could win against them.

Everything crashed into me at once. Risk's betrayal. Spector's plans. The threat on my family. The bullying. My abandonment. There was an ache like a cavern in my chest. I held the power of two devastated souls in one body, and it was turning me into a panicked, distraught mess.

"Stiles, back off," I heard Cheryl say before I felt her wrapping her slender arms around me in a grounding hug. I never expected comfort to come from her, but I sunk into her arms and let myself fall apart.

"It's okay that you got a manicure without me. I'm not that mad," she cooed while awkwardly patting my back. I wiped the snot dripping from my nose on her blouse just because I could.

While clutching her tightly, I replied to Stiles, too ashamed to meet his gaze. "He tricked me. And I don't know how to help you if you don't explain to me what's going on," I said, punctuating my words with a sniffle while pulling away from Cheryl. I was so embarrassed for breaking down in front of everyone. My whole life, I survived on strength and a hardened exterior, but this was all too much.

Stiles looked around the room with a huff. He was always fucking huffing. "They're trying to market us," he explained in a whisper. "Belvini has perfected the ritual as best he can. The next phase in his plan is for Spector to bring in the council. In exchange for a cut of the profits, my father is helping with that, since he has connections to the council members."

"But the council will shut Spector down once they realize what's going on," I said hopefully. "They have to uphold the laws, and this breaks dozens."

Stiles shot me a look that said I should know better. "The council is power hungry, Motley. If they like what Belvini shows them, they'll sign on. They've already got one council person on their side."

My mind flashed to Mrs. Cainson—the pregnant woman

in Belvini's office. Hadn't Belvini said she was a council member?

"The council will privately finance Spector," Stiles went on. "Most of them will probably want to become hybrids themselves for the extra power. And then they'll force more possessions. On our enforcers, our supe armies...who knows who else? Belvini already realized with the last trial run at Thibault that the success rate for possessions is best with younger, more impressionable supes. The council could approve to do it to more students under the guise of protecting ourselves and evolving our species."

Horror washed over me. "But you have a plan?" I asked.

He nodded. "I take this info public."

"What do you mean?"

"I'm trying to come up with a way to show what Spector is doing. If I can leak it to the supe communities, the public outcry will be huge. The council is blinded by power, and controlling information is what they do best. But if the public finds out what's going on, the council will be forced to act against Spector in order to save face. The public won't want our leaders holding that much power or bringing demonic hybrids to the world. Demons are already feared and even hated in some circles. They won't stand for this, and hopefully, we can get Spector shut down."

It all seemed to click into place. "Can you really make that happen?"

"I'm trying," he said impatiently. "It's not easy. They watch our every move in here. And the timeline just got moved way up since you brought in that demon."

"I'm sorry," I said, my words quiet.

Stiles seemed stressed and tormented, and to my surprise, Cheryl left my side to give him a hug. He tucked her under his chin like he'd done it a thousand times, and my brows rose in surprise. "We'll figure it out, sugarplum," she cooed. "You're my big strong man."

Okay. That gross little sentiment yanked me out of my pity party like a rotten tooth.

"I know, princess. I'll get us out of here," my brother replied while stroking her hair.

Gross.

Ignoring them, I looked around the room, searching for Crow and Tomb. I needed to speak to them and figure this out. Maybe we could come up with a plan to help Stiles. Not to mention I needed to be held and comforted by people that understood the intensity of our bond and the betrayal I felt over Risk's trick. Plain and simple, I just wanted my mates—my *real* mates. I needed them.

"Do you know where Tomb and Crow are?" I asked.

Cheryl stilled.

Stiles looked guilty.

I felt like someone had stabbed me in the chest. "What happened?" I asked in a rush. "Where are they?"

"Oz was pretty pissed when Belvini took you away. He…" Stiles's voice trailed off, making me want to shake the words out of him.

"Where are they, Stiles?" I asked again, but this time it was Cheryl who answered me.

"They've been in the training room since you left. It was…loud. I heard screams."

I didn't waste a single second. My heels were marching over to the first guard I could find, protective need spilling out of me in a trail of thick webs as I went. I wasn't about to lose the two mates I cared about. Risk might have ruined me, but I still had *them*, and they still had me. I would protect them with every fiber of my webbed being.

I stopped in front of one of the guards that had dragged

me here, staring him down with a deadly look as my spider rushed forward to intimidate her prey.

It only took four simple words spoken aloud to get what I wanted:

"Bring me to Oz."

Chapter 20

"I WAS WONDERING how long it would be before you showed up." Oz greeted me the moment I entered the training room. I barely heard his cocky words. I was too busy staring, horrified at the scene in front of me:

Tomb and Crow standing in a capsule of hellfire.

The clear, vertical coffin was ignited with deep blue flames, burning away their skin and flesh, leaving nothing but pearl white bone. But I knew it was them. My mate bond gnashed and roiled inside of me. Tears immediately swarmed into my eyes and started spilling over my cheeks as I watched their bodies burn. They couldn't even scream because their throats were coated with the flames that consumed them whole. Curling cells, ashy organs, charred existences all contained in a glass cage.

"Stop it!" I screamed, sprinting toward the enclosed case. I pounded on the glass as my entire being shattered. Up close, I could see their bubbling bodies decomposing in the ravenous flames. I sobbed uncontrollably, my chest constricted with a devastating pain that was indescribable.

Oz simply laughed.

There was so much blood. It pooled at the bottom of their cage, mixing with devious destruction. It couldn't tell which skeleton was which. The air was singed with the smell of burnt skin and agony.

"Your gargoyle is stubborn. He could shift at any moment. His loyalty is pathetic," Oz explained at my back. I turned to face him, murderous determination sending sharp webs through my fingers and tumbling to the floor.

I was going to kill him.

"Stop it! Just fucking STOP IT!" I screamed, the words scraping my throat raw.

Oz looked amused by my rage, his eyes glittering with dark excitement. He was getting off on hurting my mates. I had no idea how long this had been going on. While I was fucking Risk, they were being burned alive. Bile coated my throat.

Oz lazily pulled his tablet out and clicked a button on it, turning off the steady stream of hellfire.

"I don't know why you're so upset. It's not like they can die," he said as I turned back to face my mates. It was torturous, waiting for their bodies to regenerate. Molten, steaming tendons, muscles, and fat covered their skeletal forms collapsed on the ground. Blood appeared, a heart began to pump with vigorous intent. Lungs expanded and filled with air. Eyeballs burst from their sockets, and screams escaped their scorched mouths the moment the breath of life filled their chests.

Sobs racked my body as I fell to my knees and caressed the glass separating us.

It took so long. So long for their bodies to heal and regenerate. Bones, muscles, organs, skin, hair. It was like a macabre puzzle being put back together.

When their skin knitted back together, the blackened char receded completely, leaving healthy and blemish-free skin behind. Their eyes opened as if they'd been asleep, and then widened in confusion at their surroundings, as if they couldn't remember where they were or why they were stark naked in a glass cage that smelled like burning death.

"I'm so sorry," I cried out, pressing my head against the hot glass. Their heads swiveled over to me at the same time. "I'm sorry, I'm sorry, I'm sorry," I repeated over and over again. I was in too much shock to get any other words out.

Tomb seemed to realize what was happening first. He got to his feet and stormed up against the container with protective fury, punching in a sad attempt to get to me, but it was no use. The glass was too strong—probably reinforced by some magical elements I couldn't see.

Crow started yelling so loudly that the veins in his neck bulged with pressure. "Get out of here, Motley!"

I shook my head. I wasn't going anywhere.

Oz was going to die for hurting them.

My decision was swift and definite. I turned around, straightening up to my full height, and stared at Oz with the smug, satisfied look on his face. Tomb was right. Power didn't make a monster. A monster made itself.

I might be the one with the demon inside of me, but he was the one who was evil.

I shot my webs out with quick precision, sending Oz flying backwards. He tried to bring up some pathetic air elemental power, but all he managed to do was whip my hair around my face. I had him pinned against the wall in an instant, my webs relentless as they covered him, keeping his body plastered there. He tried to reach for his gun, but that was yanked away from him with more webs, and I sent it flying across the room.

He let out a short, frustrated scream, but I simply shoved more of my webs into his mouth, blocking the sound. I knew that the guards watching the security cameras would quickly send out reinforcements. I shot more webs at the training room doors, piling layer upon layer of impenetrable protection to buy me some time. I didn't care about the consequences. I just wanted him to be punished.

I was tired of Spector holding all the cards. I wasn't a meek little puppet anymore, scared of my own shadow. I wasn't going to let them use my aunt against me. I wasn't going to let them torture my mates. I was going to make them all pay. Starting with Oz.

Once the wall of web was sufficiently thick enough, I flashed to Oz and sunk my hands through the webs to where I knew his holster was. The silky strands parted for me immediately, and as soon as my fingers closed around the tablet and yanked it out, they knit back together again. It didn't take me long to figure it out, and when I found the control center to the burn cage, I pressed the button and opened the door.

Oz screamed against his webbed gag, choking on the strings as I cocked my head and looked up at him. My spider and I were one—a united, vengeful front.

This man was going to die.

Crow and Tomb were weak, shuffling toward me with slow exhaustion. The sound of their struggle in their labored breaths and shuffled steps only made me even more enraged.

Oz tried to send more of his unimpressive air element toward me again, but his hands were strained against the bindings, limiting his movements.

I took a step closer, my hair blowing around my face. "Need your hands free, Oz?" I asked him with a malicious undertone in my voice. "Here, let me help with that."

With a flick of my wrist, I directed the webs near his hands to start coiling around his wrists. Layer upon layer, it entwined. At first, he just watched warily, his neck straining to look down as far as the webs allowed. Then he began to grunt at the first signs of pain. When he started to scream around his muzzle, my eyes glittered. He thrashed and yowled, like a dying animal trying to get away from a predator's teeth. But my webs kept wrapping. They cinched tighter and tighter and tighter. Until finally, his hands *popped* right the fuck off.

Agonized screams filled the room as blood seeped into the webs and pooled onto the floor on either side of him, dripping from his stumps in gruesome synchronicity.

Crow and Tomb reached me, flanking me on either side, and they said nothing as they watched me enact my vengeance. They didn't judge me or expect me to walk away. They just let me have my wrath.

Pounding fists suddenly sounded against the training room doors, shouts from Spector guards muffled behind the webbed wall that held them back. I knew I had only minutes—seconds—before they would burst through and take me.

"Motley..." Crow murmured in warning.

"I know."

I focused back on the prey I'd caught in my web. Oz's head was hanging down, sweat soaking his hair and running down his face in rivulets as he stared at the floor where his severed hands lay.

There were so many ways I wanted to kill him. Rip out his jugular and let him slowly bleed out. Constrict his entire body with webs until he popped. Rip out his heart, since he obviously didn't use it. But really, there was only one way that gave my mates the justice they deserved.

Tomb read my mind, because he looked over at me, his stony gaze holding my eyes. "You sure?"

I nodded, and then I pulled at my webs until I was yanking Oz away from the wall. His body fell to the floor with a smack, and then my webs were slinking across the room, dragging him over the floor. A pair of bloody lines trailed after him.

As soon as he realized that he was being dragged into the fire cage, he started to scream and thrash, his legs desperate to kick out of the webs binding him. His body was pulled inside, and with his tablet in my hand, I closed the chamber door, trapping him.

Flicking my wrist, I let the webs drop away from him, including the ones around his mouth. I wanted to hear his screams. I wanted to give them as a gift to my mates.

Oz scrambled to his knees, two bloodied stumps of arms pounding against the glass wall. Our eyes locked. His body trembled with his inevitable death. And then I hit the button.

My face was lit up with the glow of flames. My ears were filled with Oz's harrowing wails. Spector was pounding against the entrance, but their efforts were drowned out by the sound of the guard's burning death.

I watched as he turned red and bubbled, his skin coiling up and then turning to ash. I stared in rapt attention as his body melted before me, turning his tissue and organs into a pasty puddle on the floor. His eyes rolled back. His screams went silent. He died long before the flames fully consumed him, but I didn't tear my eyes away until he was nothing.

"Shit," Crow murmured while pulling at my arm. "We have to get out of here."

There was no way out. Let them come with their relics. Let them beat and abuse. I was fucking done with Spector and their games. My men were indestructible. No relic or threats could scare me away.

I burned Oz, but next, I'd burn this building until it was nothing but steaming rubble.

My spider hummed with appreciation as my men circled the training room, looking for a way out. Tomb tried to pull me out of my trance. "Motley. Wid! Come on," he urged. "They're smashing through the doors."

My spider rose up on her haunches, breaking past my empty lips to scream her indifference and lack of fear.

"Let them, Tomb. I'll ruin them all."

The doors opened with a blast of sudden force, and guards swarmed the room with weapons raised. Wind blistered my cheeks as an elemental sent a gust of air at me, trying to barrel me toward the wall. Tomb grabbed my wrist and turned to stone, weighing us down.

Crow called on his legions of birds, and soon, flapping wings and sharp beaks circled us, waiting to attack.

I didn't feel fear. I felt strong and secure with my mates at my side. This was what my spider wanted. She wanted to save her males, stand beside them with honor, and face the evil organization trying to hurt them.

"Stand down!" one of the guards screamed over the screeching caws of Crow's demonic birds. Fuck Spector. I wouldn't stand down. I'd never be a prisoner again.

One of the guards surged forward, and Crow weakly lifted his arm, sending his birds into a flurry of attacking chaos at the man. They picked at his skin and gouged his eyes. My spider laughed within me.

More guards filtered into the room. We were outnumbered. "Stand down right now!" another screamed.

"No."

Pushing power, I threw my arm up, and webs braided together faster than I could watch. By the time I closed my fingers around the corded webs, I'd created a whip that was at least twenty feet long. I forced my hand with a powerful sweep, sending the whip across the room and catching several guards in its wake. A crack rent the air, and the impact of the whip left bloodied slashes across every inch of skin that it touched.

Gunfire sounded, and burning pain tore through my right shoulder, and I dropped hold of my whip. I cried out and stumbled to the ground, trying to keep my head down away from the flying bullets.

But then Tomb was there, his body of stone blocking the assault from hitting me again. I tried to lift my right hand to direct my webs again, but I hissed in pain at the effort as blood oozed from my wound. Using my left hand to press against it, I forced myself back to my feet and focused on the rest of the guns still firing at us.

I was slower, but I managed to send a net flying, knocking a gun out of a guard's hands. With another, I shot a string out like a slingshot, knocking it away from his hold. To a third one, I managed to wrap his chest in a spool of strings, trapping the gun so the muzzle was jammed beneath his jaw. One pull of the trigger, and a bullet would be kissing his brain.

But Tomb was still getting littered with more gunfire, and a bullet managed to graze off him and hit me, this time into my left thigh. I fell to the floor, a gasp of pain tearing past my lips as more blood pumped out of me.

Guards closed in around us. My pulse pounded in my ears as a furious scream wrenched from my throat. I sent a stream of webs in front of us, trying to catch anyone I could, but I was sloppy. Slow. The guards managed to jump out of the way. There were just too many of them. My mates may be indestructible, but I hadn't tested if *I* was. And right now, I was losing way too much blood and had expended too much power.

"Enough!" A familiar, dominant voice broke through the mayhem, making everyone pause.

Risk strolled through in his chariot of Armani, sending guns flying out of the guard's hands with effortless blasts of hellfire.

Tomb and Crow went rigid when he broke through the line of birds and stopped in front of us to look down his nose at me. "I leave you alone for one hour, and look at the scene you caused, little pet," he said through clenched teeth. I bet he was furious with me for compromising his cushy *business opportunity*.

"Don't call me that," I snapped.

His dark eyes flickered with fire as he looked down, catching sight of the drops of red that surrounded me. "I do hope that's not *your* blood littering the floor. I take care of my possessions, and I need you in pristine condition for what I have planned," he said, his tone casual but his expression hard.

I struggled to my feet, holding Tomb's bulky body as I stood, keeping all my weight on my right foot. I refused to cower in Risk's presence or show him how much he'd hurt me.

"I don't belong to you," I told him, looking him straight in the eye.

Risk looked over his shoulder at the guards and chuckled, like my act of defiance amused him. "Actually, according to the contract I just signed with Spector, you do. So I suggest you rein in your little spider webs and follow me to our room. We need to discuss your disobedience."

My jaw clenched as a new rush of hate filled me.

When I heard Crow hiss, my eyes clashed with his. He was hurt, bullets pushing out of his body and falling to the floor as his body healed. But his pallor was gray, and he was swaying on his feet. He was too weak from his earlier torture and controlling his birds. He needed to rest, and I was certain that Tomb was in the same condition, despite his stony determination to protect me.

"Fine, but my mates come with me," I bartered, though I didn't really have any authority to make demands.

Risk simply sighed. "If they must," he huffed, like I was just a huge inconvenience.

He turned on his heels and started to stride away, but I looked around with residual fury at Spector, and it was obvious by the expressions on the guards' faces that they wanted to collect on the debt of Oz's life. They didn't seem too happy with the way Risk stepped in and took me from them.

When Risk noticed I wasn't following, he turned around, his eyes taking in the hostile stances of the guards. "If you have a problem, I suggest you speak with Mr. Belvini," he said. "The Black Widow is mine to do with as I wish, and I am the only one allowed to punish my pets." He paused for a moment while scanning the room again, his eyes landing on where my fingers were pressing into the wound on my shoulder. After staring down the men wielding guns, he spoke again.

"Who shot her?" he asked.

The room went completely silent; the only sound you could hear was my labored breathing.

"Who *shot* what's mine?" he asked again while circling the room. He stopped at a trembling guard with a rifle hanging loosely at his side. "Was it you?"

"N-no, sir," the man stammered in response.

He leaned forward and stared the man down, as if daring the man to lie to him. Neither of them moved for a moment. The silent standoff was filled with toxic tension, and I waited with bated breath to see what the crazy demon would do.

Risk rolled his eyes, then turned his attention to the next gun-wielding gun.

"Was it you?"

This guard didn't seem as terrified. His spine straightened as he looked ahead, fixing his lips in a firm line before responding. "I was just doing my job, sir."

Risk grinned maniacally. "Just doing your job?"

"Yes, sir," the man replied stiffly.

Risk lifted his hand up and capriciously removed a gold ring from his finger and placed it in his pocket. He then stared at his fist for a moment, as if debating what to do with it. No one said a single word. No one moved an inch.

The protectiveness was catching me off guard. Was he asking because he actually cared about me? Or was he just possessive? I got the impression that he would have easily been just as wrathful over a cracked teacup.

Within an instant, Risk shot his fist out and lodged it in the chest of the guard that shot me. His knuckles dug past the chest bone, deeper and deeper until his hand was able to wrap around the guard's pounding heart. Blood poured from the wound, creating a slick mess on the floor as Risk laughed. "I'm just doing *my* job," he said in a deadly calm voice. Then, in one swoop, he ripped the organ from his chest and tossed it on the floor.

The man went wide-eyed and groaned as he dropped to the floor.

Risk wiped the blood from his hands on another guard's jacket before speaking again. "If anyone touches her again, I will be inclined to burn your spinal cord with hellfire," he said nonchalantly. "Come along, pet," he said, addressing me.

My pride wanted me to plant my feet and not move a muscle. But my mates and I were hurt, and I had no doubt that as soon as he left the room, Spector guards would be all over us.

Limping forward, I gritted my teeth as I followed in his wake. Before I could even take three full steps, Tomb was there, his hard, strong body sweeping me up into his arms. The movement jostled the wound in both my leg and my shoulder, making me grimace.

"I got you."

I rested my head against his obsidian chest, and as soon as I made contact, his body rippled and turned back to skin. I sighed at the warmth and softness of his flesh. "I'm sorry," I whispered, my words meant for both of them.

Tomb's finger tipped up my chin. "I don't ever want to hear you say that again, Wid."

"But he was torturing you. Both of you," I argued, turning my head to look over at Crow where he walked beside us. "All because I mated you. Because I pissed him off in the training room."

"You don't get to feel guilty for something that was out of your control," Tomb said, his tone holding no room for argument.

"Tomb—"

"No, Little Spider," Crow said, cutting me off. "He's right. And you won't win this one. We outnumber you," he teased.

A shaky smile came over my lips as I rested back against Tomb. I could've fallen asleep from the swaying of his movements as he walked, but I was all too aware that we were being led into the lion's den.

Chapter 21

RISK LED us to another part of Spector I'd never seen before. Rows of apartments lined the halls where, apparently, the guards lived. I felt eyes on us as we traveled, and when we stopped in front of a door at the end of the long hallway, Risk opened it with a carefree whistle and then motioned for us to go inside.

It was a small apartment, similar to my dorm room at Thibault. There was a small kitchenette in the corner, a sitting area, and a large king-sized bed in the very middle. I wasn't impressed with the nice living quarters. Crow once said that all of Spector was a cage, and now more than ever, I believed him.

The moment the door shut behind us, Risk ripped me from Tomb's strong hold and crushed me to his own chest. "You stupid woman, what the fuck were you thinking?" he scolded while carrying me to a nearby couch. The emotional whiplash was almost as bad as the jerking pain my body felt with every jostle.

"Are you kidding me right now?" I hissed in response as

Crow and Tomb stalked after him, their muscles rippling with the urge to fight.

"Who the fuck are you?" Tomb growled, clenching his fists and looking like he was about to go full statue again.

Risk ignored both of us though and placed me on the couch, staring me down with obvious displeasure. "Take your clothes off, Motley. I need to look at your wounds."

"Like hell you are," Crow replied, though his voice was worn and ragged with exhaustion.

Risk rolled his eyes and started removing his tie. Once it was discarded on the floor, he unbuttoned his collar and flashed the scarlet mark of my shame for my mates to see. The pain in my shoulder and leg were forgotten. I was too busy writhing in the excruciating reality that I'd been used by this demon and cheapened the mating mark by bestowing one on him.

Crow's and Tomb's eyes widened, and they exchanged a look. My cheeks burned in shame.

"Why does he have a mark, Motley?" Tomb asked patiently. His faith in me made the pain even worse. Even though the answer was obvious, he wanted to hear it from my lips. He was giving me the benefit of the doubt even though I didn't deserve it.

"My spider made him her mate," I choked out, like the words had turned to burning cinders in my throat. "He tricked me. I thought he wanted me too, but he just wanted immortality so he could work with Spector," I replied while slumping my shoulders. Saying the reality of what Risk had done made me sick to my stomach. I was so tired of being used and so overwhelmed by his motivations. I felt jaded in the worst possible way.

"He did *what*?" Tomb asked before slapping down a rock hard hand on Risk's shoulder. Ever the careless demon, Risk simply rolled his eyes at the threat and spun around to face my gargoyle mate. Tomb was vibrating with rage. His protectiveness made every muscle in his body flex in anticipation.

If I weren't bleeding out and in burning pain, I would've wanted to jump his bones.

"You going to punch me? Let's get this territorial shit show over with so I can help *our* mate," Risk huffed out while unclasping the buttons on each wrist of his dress shirt and rolling them up.

Our mate? *Our mate?* What the fuck was that supposed to mean? He couldn't just play both sides of the relic coin whenever it suited him.

Tomb didn't respond with a witty retort, nor did he wait for Risk to finish undressing. He reared his onyx fist back and landed a harsh punch on the traitor's jaw. Risk's head whipped backwards at the sheer force of Tomb's hit, and his eyes widened at the shock of it.

Crow sighed, like he was too exhausted to actually deal with this, but he walked up to Tomb's side and held his fists up, prepared to join in and support his friend anyway.

Risk rubbed his jaw, and I probably enjoyed the blooming bruise on his face a little more than I should've. "Happy now?" he asked boredly. "Got that out of your system?"

"Not until you're dead, motherfucker," Tomb growled.

"Good thing I can't die then, hmm?" Risk replied, making a fresh wave of pain radiate across my chest.

Tomb was not amused by Risk's careless attitude. My gargoyle sent another fist flying, this time with one made of solid stone, hitting Risk directly in the gut. The blow had him bent over with a wheeze, but when he straightened back up, Risk was smirking. "Fuck, you can pack a punch, gargoyle. I'll give you one more because I'm feeling generous."

The risk demon's eyes glittered with excitement. He looked like he was enjoying this far too much, but Tomb was panting, his body blinking back and forth from black stone to sweat-coated skin. Crow's shoulders were steaming with sputters of shadows, tired feathers drifting onto the floor. They were too worn out for this shit, and I hadn't attacked a regiment of Spector guards just to let one fake mate taunt them into exhausting themselves even more.

"Stop. Don't antagonize them," I said, forcing myself to sit up with a grimace. "What do you want, Risk? You used me. You got to become indestructible like you wanted. Can't we just call this what it is and be done?" I asked as fresh tears filled my eyes.

It was all too much. Watching my mates being tortured. The deception. Spector's plans. I just wanted to rest and hold my mates—my *real* mates.

Risk looked over at me, his black brows arching up. "For hell's sake, are you *crying*?" he asked, looking surprised. "Who the fuck made you cry?"

I glared at him. "Don't mock me," I croaked.

"Tell me who made you cry and I'll *destroy* him. No one fucks with what's mine," Risk barked out with anger.

"She's *not* yours," Tomb growled quietly.

I shook my head, looking at Risk incredulously. "*You* made me cry, you asshole!" I screeched. "You tricked me into mating you so you could be in business with *Collector*," I spat.

"Who the fuck is Collector?" Crow asked.

"No idea," Tomb murmured, eyes flicking between Risk and me.

I stared Risk down. "You took something that was special to me—to my spider—and tainted it. I'm not disillusioned enough to think that we had some bullshit love at first sight moment. But I did think we were compatible. Mating is special, or at least it should be. My spider picked you, and you stomped all over her."

Risk sighed and tugged at the collar of his dress shirt. I

was trying *really* hard not to notice how sexy he looked with the sleeves rolled up on his forearms. "Hmm. It seems I need to explain myself," he said, sinking to his knees on the floor so that he could look me in the eye.

"There's nothing to explain," I griped, smacking his hand when he tried to lift the hem of my dress.

His dark eyes snapped to my face. "Once I get these bullets out of you, I'm going to explain everything, and then I'm going to make you cream my dick while these two dumbasses watch," he grumbled as his hands gripped just above the bullet hole in my thigh. My face heated at his words, but before I could argue, he pushed my dress up, exposing my bloodied legs in the process.

All three of the males hissed when they saw the amount of blood still pumping from my leg, the wound looking gruesome and deep. "Fuck, Wid," Tomb said, a flash of guilt covering his face. "It's my fault the bullet got past me and hit you."

"Remember our talk about not being allowed to feel guilty?" I said to him. "This applies to you now."

He shot me an unconvinced look, his lips thinning into a line, but he didn't argue further.

The sound of tearing jerked my attention back to the demon in front of me, who'd just ripped the fabric of my dress at my shoulder. My hands automatically flew up to hold my dress to my chest, not allowing it to slip down. But Risk's full attention was on the wound. "This one went clean through, so at least there's that," he said, gently checking the exit wound on my back.

I tried to swat him away again but was unsuccessful. I didn't want his hands on me. I certainly didn't want the thrill I got when his touch roved through my system. My body responded to him in earnest even though I tried to hold those feelings at bay. I felt comforted by his tenderness, and I hated myself for that instinctual response. Would this be how it was from now on? Would I always crave him? Would there always be an invisible chain keeping us together? More tears burned my eyes.

"This is going to hurt, okay?" he said before digging his fingers into the plush skin of my thigh. It felt unsanitary and gory, but he was rooting around the wound, burrowing deeper and deeper until he was tugging at the bullet lodged in the tissue of my muscles.

"Motherfucker!" I screamed, my body nearly launching off the couch.

"Hold her down," Risk snapped.

Tomb and Crow glowered at him, obviously not liking that he was causing me pain, but Crow was the first to realize that it needed to be done. He sat beside me on the couch and gathered me against him, my body slumping over his chest as his arms banded around my middle.

"Try to stay still," Risk told me before I felt his fingers begin to ferret around again, making another scream rip from my throat.

"Hurry up!" Tomb demanded. "You're hurting her."

"I wasn't the one that allowed our mate to get *shot*," Risk fired back accusingly.

Tomb's fists clenched, but I reached up and grabbed his hand before it could turn to stone and smash into Risk's face again. "Hey," I said, hating the shame that coated his eyes. "It's not your fault. I'll be okay as soon as he gets the fucking thing out."

Tomb knelt down and brought my hand to his lips, skimming a kiss over my knuckles. I tried to latch onto that feeling, even as Risk's fingers swiped around, making more blood ooze out. Sweat coated my skin, and a cry of pain slipped out of me as the demon's blood-soaked fingers finally grasped the bullet and plucked it out.

"There," he said, holding it in all its bloody glory. It was strange how something so small could cause so much pain.

Tomb's fist shot out, and he grabbed the bullet, crushing it in his stone fist. We all watched as metal flakes drifted to the floor.

"I'm sorry I did not protect you better," Tomb said, his head bowed.

I couldn't believe what I was hearing. If anyone should still be apologizing, it was me. I opened my mouth to talk some sense into him, but Risk stood up and said, "Time to heal, Wicked Love."

I glanced up at him warily. "I'll heal just fine now that the bullet is out."

He gestured to the wounds that were still weeping blood. "You aren't a simple vampire anymore, Motley."

"What does that mean? I won't heal?" I asked, frowning.

"Oh, you'll heal," Risk assured me. "But not the same way. Your spider makes her mates indestructible for a reason. You are now sustained through your bond to *us*," he explained.

My eyes widened. "Are you saying that every time I'm hurt, I need to fuck one of you so I can feed and heal?"

Risk grinned. "That's exactly what I'm saying. Rather pleasant way to heal, wouldn't you say?"

"Then Tomb and I will take care of her. She doesn't want anything to do with you," Crow said at my back, his arms tightening around me.

Risk cast a bored look to him. "Whether you want to admit it or not, she's my mate as well."

My head was growing dizzy, the sensation made worse when I started shaking my head. "You're not my real mate," I argued. "I'm just your *pet* you like to mock in front of Belvini."

Risk rolled his eyes. "Clearly, we were not on the same page."

"What?"

"It was an *act*," he explained slowly. "I was merely playing the hand that had the best odds in our favor. I know how to take risks and how to win. But just because I'm using it to our advantage does not mean I used *you*. You are my mate. I don't take that lightly. I needed Belvini to think that I didn't care for you more than a pet. I thought you understood, so I apologize for causing you pain."

I stared at him in disbelief and doubt, trying not to let the flare of hope catch fire. I was terrified that this was just another trick. "Belvini orchestrated our mating. How can we know if it's sincere? It just feels so tainted now."

"I chose you, not Belvini, Wicked Love"

His tone was serious and decisive. The barb of betrayal lifted off my heart, and I shuddered out another tear, this one of relief. Crow's thumb came up to swipe the tear away. "Don't cry, Little Spider," he whispered in my ear.

"Next time, tell me the plan *before* you act it out," I reprimanded Risk.

"Next time, have a little trust in your mate, hmm?" he countered.

"I've only known you for a few hours," I pointed out.

He blinked at me. "So?"

I rolled my eyes, then hissed when another wave of dizziness and pain tore through me, and I grimaced.

"Right. Time to heal, Wicked Love."

"We'll take care of her," Crow insisted.

"You two are barely strong enough to stand right now, let alone feed her. She'll drain you in an instant, and who knows how long it'll take for you to come back to life," Risk told him. "*I* will feed her. If you two can share nicely and be good mistermates, then I'll let you make her come."

My eyes widened, even as heat bloomed over my cheeks. I was surprised I even had enough blood in me to blush still, let alone feel the trail of heat start to build in my core that somehow dulled the pain I was feeling.

Crow looked over at Tomb, as if deferring to him, letting him make the call. Tomb stared hard at Risk, and I was certain that they were about to come to blows again, but to my surprise, Tomb nodded and held out a hand. "I don't like you. I don't trust you, either. If I think even for a second that you're fucking us over, I'll kill you slowly," Tomb promised in a steely voice before sighing. "But Motley chose you, and you're here now to help keep her safe, which means we share a duty."

Risk shook his hand. "Indeed. Let's see to our duty, shall we?" he said with a wicked glint in his eye that made my heart trip.

I felt Crow's hold loosen around me right before Risk scooped me up and carried me across the room, pushing the door open to the bathroom. He set me inside the shower, letting me sit on the bench, as Tomb and Crow followed him in.

"Let's get rid of this dress, hmm?" Risk pulled the strap of my dress down and pushed the blood-stained fabric to my waist. I wasn't completely convinced that he was on my side or that he was taking our mate bond seriously, but I was willing to use him up, like he used me. I just hoped over time we'd find normalcy in the bond we'd recklessly created.

"This is definitely in the way," Risk said while brushing a hand over my bustier. Heated goosebumps pebbled over my skin as he trailed a finger along the beaded curve of my lingerie, never touching my skin.

A whimper escaped my throat, making the devious demon smirk. "Tell me you understand I'm committed to this risky bond, and I'll kiss your perfect tits," Risk bargained in a raspy whisper.

I didn't want to lie, so I kept my lips closed and used my uninjured arm to undo the ties, letting the top fall from my shoulders and slip off my body. Risk's eyes flamed with heated desire and frustration.

"Crow," I began, turning my attention to him. "Kiss me."

My malphas demon didn't wait a single second. He surged forward and licked my salty skin with a long stroke of his hot tongue, landing right on my beaded nipple. My back arched, and my lips parted. He sucked on my breasts while cupping my neck, the slight squeeze of his fingers adding a sense of danger to his touch.

My body was charging up, lure seeping from my skin in uncontrollable waves. It was strange to be so turned on when I was so injured, but it was like my survival instincts were kicking in. I needed to feed in order to heal, so my body was getting me ready for pleasure, drawing in my mates and making them ready for it too. I could scent the desire in the air even more than I could smell my blood.

"Motley," Risk warned while unbuttoning his pants. "Tell me you know I was trying to protect you." I didn't respond. I couldn't. Maybe it was immature of me to make him sweat, but I couldn't even speak if I wanted to. My moans had grown needier, as Crow had migrated to my neck and was sucking on the sensitive skin there, pulling me through his teeth as he groaned.

"Tell me. Or I'll have to show you, Wicked Love."

I wanted Risk to show me. I wanted all of them to show me. I knew that we were physically compatible, but we had a long way to go before trust could be built. We had a lot to learn about one another before I could truly feel the connection I craved.

I opened my mouth to defy him, longing for the consequences of my disobedience like it was an addictive drug. Tomb interrupted me before I could speak though, stealing my mouth for his own with a cold, hardened kiss. His hand threaded through my hair, and he angled my face just so, delving his tongue deeper into my mouth. I kissed Tomb back with vigor, partly to make the demon jealous, and partly because my gargoyle was a damn good kisser.

The shower spray suddenly turned on, dousing me in cold water and making me pull back with a surprised yelp. Risk looked down at me, now shirtless and pantless, lifting a finger up in admonition. "Don't try to tease me. It won't end well for you." Fuck, his body was cut. Each muscle rippled with masculinity, and my eyes trailed the delicious lines that led to his hard cock.

I stood up, holding all my weight on my good leg as I kept an arm on Crow's shoulder to help me. Feeling defiant, I slipped down my panties, letting them hit the tile with a wet smack, and then I kicked away all the ruined clothes with my foot, letting the drain carry away the streaks of my blood.

"Oh, I think it'll end just fine for me," I said with a smirk before turning to Crow and kissing him this time. I felt Tomb's body come around behind me, his strong grip holding me up as my tongue tangled with Crow's.

I'd never been with more than one person before, but I didn't feel awkward when Tomb's hands came up to knead my breasts while Crow groaned into my mouth. I didn't even feel embarrassed knowing that Risk's hot, hungry eyes were on me. I *liked* it. I was building up to what I wanted most, my body pumping me full of pheromones to distract from the pain.

I thought my little teasing display of insolence would piss Risk off. I wanted that little piece of satisfaction. But I should've known better.

My eyes popped open in surprise when I suddenly felt his

hand cupping me, the heel of his palm grinding against my clit in rough, demanding strokes. My head fell back against Tomb's shoulder, and I started gasping for breath.

"Do you like that?" Risk asked, stepping up to me so that I could feel his cock press against my stomach. With Tomb at my back and Crow to my side, I was trapped between them, caught between three powerful, dynamic personalities and hot as hell bodies. My pulse was racing, my spider was salivating, and I had to bite my lip to keep from coming so fast, simply because I didn't want to give Risk the satisfaction.

"No," I answered breathlessly.

His lips tipped up. "A demon hybrid shouldn't be such a terrible liar. You're going to have to work on that."

His fingers came up to my clit, toying with and rubbing it with expert precision, and a whimper escaped out of me. *Don't come, don't come, don't—*

"You're close," Risk purred. "Your body wants to give in, doesn't it?"

"No," I repeated.

He tsked. "Remember what I said about lies and gambles?"

I was right there. So close. My resolve was shoved aside with the purely selfish need to come. I clamped my lips together, determined to hide it from him, to pretend that I wasn't riding my peak, but *just* before I hit it, Risk dropped his hand.

My mouth opened in irritated confusion. "What are you doing?"

He stepped under the shower spray, brushing his hair away from his face. "I told you not to tease me," he said with a shrug. "And I also still need to hear you say it."

My lips pressed together, and frustration blossomed in my eyes. I knew what he wanted, but I couldn't lie. "I don't know, okay?" I snapped, suddenly feeling very vulnerable standing here, naked and hurt. "I don't know if I believe you. I want to, I—"

My words choked off, and I hated myself for it. I hated him for having such a huge impact on my emotions. It had to be the mating bond. The force of it was more than I'd anticipated, and I was way more attached to him than I wanted to be.

Risk's eyes suddenly softened, and then he was pulling my head to his lips and placing a gentle kiss on my forehead. "Ah, Wicked Love. I forget how young you are," he said quietly against my brow. His thumb tipped up my face so he could look me in the eye. "I'm sorry for making you think I didn't care for you. I didn't realize what was going on in your pretty head. But I swear on my honor as a demon, I'm not deceiving you now."

I heard Tomb snort. "Does a demon have honor?"

Risk tilted his head in thought. "Depends on the demon, I suppose."

A stilted laugh came out of me. I was a jumble of emotions, and yet my hunger was growing, making me insistently needy.

"I want to believe you, and I guess I do. Just give me some time, okay? This is all really new."

"Fair enough," Risk replied before cupping me once more. "Let's just focus on making you feel good then." He started teasing me once more, coaxing my cunt with grounding pleasure. I rode his palm as Crow began to nip my ear and Tomb kneaded every inch of skin he could get his hands on.

"Are you close? Don't lie to me this time," Risk said as I grinded against his strong hand.

"Y-yes," I whimpered. "So close." I couldn't lie again even if I wanted to. I was hungry for my orgasm. Hungry for that full feeling of being thoroughly fucked. I needed to heal, and I needed them to make that happen.

Like he was reading my mind, Risk casually slipped two fingers inside of me, joining that hungry connection between us so I could finally feed. My spider went haywire. She started sucking the dark demon's life essence, and I immediately broke apart in his hand. He continued to work my clit as a scream broke past my lips. I was so slick, so wet with the satisfying orgasm and the thrill of my feeding.

"Our mate is so beautiful when she creams my fingers. I wonder if she tastes as good as she looks right now," Risk said while turning to Crow. "Would you like a taste?"

Risk pulled his fingers from my pussy and held them up to my malphas demon. "Suck her cum from my fingers."

I thought for sure Crow would shove his hand away, but instead, his violet eyes flared, and he latched on, sucking my wetness from Risk's fingers in one aggressive swipe, his fingers clenched around Risk's wrist. When he let go, Crow's gleaming eyes roved down to the spot between my thighs. "You taste like our own personal brand of syrup. So fucking sweet."

I whimpered, feeling my body slowly starting to heal as my spider continued to pull on Risk's thread. It was satisfying my hunger, but the rest of me still needed to be filled too.

"Please," I began. "I need more."

My men didn't waste a single second. Tomb picked me up and cradled me to his chest, leading me back into the bedroom and gently laying me down on the bed. "You need more, Wid?" he asked, a wicked gleam in his eyes as he rubbed his hard hands along my slit.

"Yes," I whimpered, writhing on the bed.

"Like this?" he asked while lining his dick up with my pussy. He didn't fill me up though, he merely teased me with the head of his cock, pressing on my sensitive entrance with a subtle, teasing force.

"Please?" I asked as Crow got on his knees on the bed. I turned my head to greet his hard cock, licking my lips at the sight of him.

"You want this, Little Spider?" Crow asked while rubbing droplets of precum against my lips.

"I *need* it," I begged.

Risk settled beside me, his bulky frame pressing into the mattress as his hand reached around to tease my ass, kneading, rubbing, taunting. His long fingers stroked and baited, positioning themselves at my puckered hole. Fuck. It felt dangerous and wrong to have him there, but so fucking *right*. Each of my mates were waiting to be devoured.

"I can't wait to fill you up," Risk sighed. "But I'm going to ease you into that."

They all floated along my barriers, waiting for my plea, waiting for my scream.

"Feed me," my spider begged.

Crow slid his cock past my lips, dragging his piercing along the roof of my mouth as I gagged on the sweet and salty taste of him. I didn't even have time to fully appreciate the feeding connection between us, because Tomb slammed into my pussy without warning, stretching me and stuffing me with his giant cock.

My spider latched on to him too, blissful delirium guiding my shaking and trembling body. A euphoria like I'd never felt before made every ounce of my existence plume and settle into satisfaction. I'd never felt so full, never felt so cherished or worshipped. Feeding from all three of them at the same time was like nothing I'd ever imagined. Crow tasted like cool shadows, Tomb was a savory comfort, and Risk was like pure, unadulterated spice and heat. It was bliss.

And then Risk eased his finger inside of my ass, bringing my rapture to an all new high. My spider relished in consuming her mates. I felt myself grow stronger with each pull of their combined essences, with each thrust, with each hard rock against my body.

"Fuck, Little Spider. Your mouth fits so perfectly around my cock," Crow groaned.

I sucked him vigorously and watched as his head tipped back, those gleaming white teeth of his sinking through his plush bottom lip in delight. He looked so beautiful as I siphoned carnal ecstasy from his cock and devoured his life core. He started to look exhausted, though. I could see the tiredness in his hooded eyes, could see the way his body swayed on the mattress.

I pulled his cock out of my mouth, his metal piercing scraping against the roof of my mouth. He collapsed on the bed beside me and lazily stroked his dick with easy strides, running his thumb over the head of his piercing with an easy-going smile on his face.

Tomb started pounding me harder, stealing my attention for his with hard, thumping strokes as he tipped up my hips to drive deeper into me. I shuddered at the invasion, little gasps escaping my lips at the fullness of his racing movements. I unfurled, my back arching as zings of pleasure shot through me.

The air was perfumed with our slick sex. I breathed in the smell of arousal, letting my spider get off on how turned on her mates were. I reveled in the power I had over their pleasure. I felt their bonds as surely as I felt my own heartbeat thudding wildly in my chest.

The four of us were latched together in sensuous exhilaration and merged needs. In that moment, there was zero doubt that they all wanted me. With us like this, being driven by our basic instincts and carnal desires, I could read the bond clearly, and I knew that they couldn't fake this. They couldn't trick the bond—not even Risk. So when I reached over and grasped the demon in my palm, I did it because I wanted to. Because I wanted to show him that I felt the truth of his intentions in the cord that linked us.

Risk sucked in a breath between clenched teeth as I swept my thumb over the head of his cock, coating him in his own cum. My shoulder had already healed, and it didn't hurt at all when I reached up to cup his balls and roll them through my fingers. Looking down at where Tomb was moving in and out of me, I could see his hand squeezing protectively over my thigh where the bullet had once been, my skin unmarred.

They'd healed me already, and my spider released them, humming in gluttony at how well they'd fed us. All that was driving me now was my own lust, and it was amplified by their own hardened desires.

Risk's hand came down to curl around mine. "Squeeze my cock harder," he said, so I gave him what he wanted, my hand closing tighter around his hard, thick cock as I stroked up and down.

"Fuck, just like that. Squeeze my dick *just* like that while your gargoyle fucks you and your other mate watches."

My gaze locked on Crow, my tongue wetting my lip as I watched him stroke himself, his movement matching the movements of my own hand. "Do you want to hold his dick too?" Risk asked.

"Yes," I whimpered.

Risk chuckled. "You heard her."

Crow leaned forward so I could reach him, and then I had both of their lengths in my palms. The velvety feel of their skin combined with their hardness was a delicious combination. I squeezed Risk even harder, and he let out a hiss.

"Fucking *hellfire*," he gritted. "Squeeze that cock, Wicked Love. Squeeze it so I can cum all over your pretty tits."

I did. I pumped them faster and faster, never letting up on the force of my fist, and watched in awe as they came nearly at the same time. Streaks of cum shot from their dicks, painting a criss cross pattern over my chest and belly.

"Fuck, that's dirty," Tomb murmured, right as he brought his thumb down and pressed it to my clit.

I came with a scream, and Tomb roared out his own release above me. My back arched, my limbs shook. My orgasm was a rolling, never-ending rope of pleasure, tugging at my core, releasing the pain from my muscles, and calming my spider with the confident connections between us.

I started to come down, feeling invigorated. Tomb pulled out with a hiss, leaving me feeling sated but empty. We all lay in heady silence for a moment, listening to the slowing of our breaths, the steady sighs of our contentment.

My spider was curled up within me, licking her fangs and relishing in her feast.

And I was happy.

I was really, really fucking happy.

Chapter 22

"AND YOU DO THAT FOR *FUN?*"

I looked at Tomb with an eyebrow arched as I rested against Crow's chest in bed. The four of us had spent the last who knows how many hours doing nothing but getting to know each other better. That included talk...and a lot of sex.

I hadn't killed anyone once. I was feeling smug as shit.

I was also feeling a bit tender down there. My mates had very impressive dicks, and they knew how to use them.

But now, we were taking a sex hiatus, and they were showing me things they liked to do for fun...and Tomb's answer apparently included cage fighting.

Tomb chuckled, and I ran my fingers over his knuckles where there were some old scars. "It's an adrenaline rush," he replied. "I used to do it for money on the side. Lost a lot. But I won a lot too."

"You'd kick some serious ass now since you're half gargoyle demon," Crow put in.

"Indeed. No wonder you had such an impressive right hook," Risk commented where he was sprawled out on the bed beside me.

Unlike my other two mates, he was still stark naked, hands behind his head and not giving a single fuck that his dick was out for all to see.

"Impressive enough to let me punch you in the face again?" Tomb asked with a smirk.

"I'm always up for a wager," the demon drawled, his eyes glittering with excitement. I swear, the male had a serious addiction to risks.

"No," I quickly intervened. "No wagers or risk-taking between the three of you," I told him. "You *always* win."

He let out a disappointed sigh. "Life is boring if there isn't a little risk, Wicked Love."

"We take risks *together*," I said sternly.

He grinned. "I can work with that."

"Mm-hmm, I'm sure. So what about you?" I asked. "What do you like to do for fun?"

"I enjoy a good hellfire fight now and then," he answered before looking over at Tomb as my gargoyle moved down the bed to rub my feet. His strong fingers dug into the arch of my foot, and it felt *divine*. "Probably not too different from your cage fighting, in fact. Except it's in hell. And usually ends with someone burning in hellfire," he mused.

The three of us just stared at him in dismay before Crow shook his head. "Man, can you put your cock away already?" Crow griped at him. "Unless it's buried in our mate, I don't want to see it."

I laughed. "I need clothes too."

"No one said anything about *you* covering up," Crow replied, his hands coming around me to play with my breasts. My nipples were still pink and slightly sore from their earlier attentions when he and Tomb had each claimed a nipple and teased me with their mouths until I came.

I moaned slightly, my head lolling back against his chest

as his hands continued to grip me. "I've already had way too many orgasms, Crow. I don't think I could come again even with a vibrator stuck to my clit."

"Hmm, want to make a wager?" Risk purred.

"No," I said, laughing as I looked over at him. "We *just* talked about this."

"You'll come to realize I don't give up so easily," he said with a wink before getting up from the bed and striding toward the dresser. He frowned at the contents when he opened the drawers. "All that's in here is Spector-issued sweatpants," he said with utter disdain.

"What did you expect, a row of Armanis?" I joked.

He looked back at me with an expression that said yes, he *had* expected exactly that.

I rolled my eyes with a chuckle. "Just toss me a shirt and shorts please."

He acquiesced, and I got up from the bed to pull on the overly large black t-shirt and shorts. I had to roll the shorts a few times at the waist to get them to fit, and the shirt hung down so far it looked like I wasn't wearing any pants, but at least I was dressed. Risk opted to put on his suit from earlier, which somehow still looked pristine.

"We should probably discuss the ritual," Risk said as he buttoned up his shirt.

At hearing that word, all the earlier relaxation and feel-good endorphins drained out of me. I wanted to keep pretending that we were here in this bubble. I didn't want to leave it, but I knew time was running out. "Belvini probably has other schemes up his sleeves" I pointed out. "We need to plan for him to turn on us."

"Let him try. Besides, I can flash us all out of here with a snap of my fingers, even save your aunt, too. I'm not too worried about Belvini. The moment I heard demons were being possessed against their will, I decided to shut them down."

"I want them shut down, too. But I want us to be smart about this. If at any moment we don't feel in control of the situation, I want to back out, okay? I never want to experience what happened yesterday again."

"I can assure you, Wicked Love, I'm always in control," Risk replied with a wink.

I appreciated Risk's confidence, but unease settled through me. This wasn't a simple gamble or game. If Risk overplayed his hand, it could mean disaster of epic proportions.

I still hadn't told them about Stiles, either. I just didn't know where to begin. But if he was trying to get the council to shut Spector down, that was a factor we needed to consider.

"Listen—"

My words were cut off when a horrible, deafening screech sounded through the air. Everyone's hands clapped over their ears in unison.

"What the fuck *is* that?" Tomb bellowed.

I was too busy trying to stuff my fingers into my eardrums to answer him. When the noise suddenly cut off, my brain caught up with me, and my blue eyes widened. "Cheryl."

I was on my feet and running out of the room in a second. Racing down the hall, I tried to pinpoint where I thought the noise had come from, and then followed her sugary sweet perfume in the air. My mates were racing after me, hollering at me to slow down, but I kept flashing forward, trying to follow her scent. It sounded like she was hurt, or maybe Spector was forcing *her* to hurt someone else, or maybe—

I burst into a room where her scent lingered and shoved the door open, my mates hot at my back. "Cheryl!" I screamed while rushing in. She was standing next to Stiles with tears running down her cheeks, fanning herself in a flurry of emotions.

"Cheryl? Are you okay?" I asked as I ran over to her. Stiles was staring up at the ceiling and rubbing his temples.

"Stiles proposed!" she cried out before wrapping her arms around my neck and squeezing me tightly. I gaped at her, patting her back as I processed her words.

"Proposed?" I asked. "Proposed what?"

She broke our hug to swat at the tears streaming down her cheeks and giggled at me. "To be married, silly," she replied before waving her hand in front of my face. Sure enough, I was nearly smacked in the nose with a ring that had a rock the size of Tomb's cock. It glistened under the fluorescents and created a light show between us.

"Congratulations. I love weddings. Did you know that fifty percent of all marriages end in divorce? Those odds are delicious," Risk said while grinning ear to ear. I would have swatted him if Cheryl wasn't blocking me.

Stiles finally looked at me and grimaced. "For the tenth time, Cheryl, it's not real," he said painfully slow, like he was talking to someone that didn't comprehend English. "When shit hits the fan, I want to make sure I can get you out of here safely. This isn't *actually* happening."

"Right," Cheryl replied absentmindedly, though she was staring at the ring with admiration. "Damn, I need a manicure."

"Cheryl," Stiles pleaded while inching closer. She spun around to face him with a mischievous smile. "Please tell me you understand that this isn't real."

"We should get married in spring," she replied.

"We're not getting married in spring. We're not getting married *at all*," Stiles countered.

"I'm going to wear Valentino. It's so classy and timeless; it'll look great in the photographs."

"I admire her persistence," Risk said under his breath, making Crow and Tomb chuckle.

Stiles grabbed her shoulders and lightly shook her before peering deeply into her eyes. "Cheryl, we are not getting married."

From my vantage point, I could see the dreamy look on Cheryl's face. Nothing he said was breaking past her determination. Something told me she'd have my brother tied up to the altar if she had to. Instead of replying, she cupped his cheeks and kissed him in a way that made me slightly nauseous.

Stiles melted at her touch, all frustration fading away into the passion of their kiss. It got heated *fast*.

"Uh, I'm standing right here," I protested while covering my eyes. I was worried they'd start going at it regardless of whether or not they had an unwilling audience.

"Oh, Motley!" Cheryl exclaimed when she pulled away. "Don't worry, I will find a dress that compliments your washed out skin tone and obnoxiously red hair. I won't let my Maid of Honor look bad, I promise."

Once again, Cheryl had rendered me speechless. "Maid of Honor? Cheryl, there's no way in hell—"

Her pout stopped me in my tracks, and I glanced over her head to peer at Stiles, who was pressing at his lips with the tips of his fingers. For some reason, I didn't want to upset her, so instead I decided to fuck with my brother.

"I think a spring wedding will be lovely," I finally replied, though it pained me to say.

"Godsdammit!" Stiles muttered. "I'm going to tell my father we're engaged. The faster we get out of here, the faster we can be done with this, and I can get that ring off your finger."

He stormed out of the room, shoulder checking a growling Tomb in the process. Once he was gone, I grabbed

Cheryl's wrist and led her to the bed. "Can we have a minute?" I asked my guys with a small smile.

Crow grabbed Risk's and Tomb's arms, pulling them out of the room. "Sure thing, Little Spider. We'll wait in the hallway."

"But I wanted to hear more about this wedding," Risk teased. I glared at him until the door slammed shut.

Turning my attention back to my daydreaming roommate, I nearly laughed out loud when I saw her admiring her ring. "Cheryl, you do realize you aren't marrying Stiles, right?" I asked tenderly, scared to spook another deadly scream out of her.

"Well, of course I know that. But a girl can dream, can't she?" she replied calmly before lacing her fingers through mine and giving my hand a friendly squeeze.

"So why are you fake engaged? I don't fully understand what's happening here," I replied.

"My family is rich, as you know. Mr. Trant is lobbying to get contracts for Belvini and needs connections in the community. Stiles thought it would be a good idea to pretend to align ourselves with him for now. It'll keep me safe until we get out of here, and even if it's not real, it means that Stiles actually cares about someone other than himself for once."

I nodded in understanding. The Trants definitely liked to *align* themselves with powerful people. It's how we ended up in Spector's clutches in the first place.

"Also," Cheryl began with a wince. "You should definitely keep your head down for a while. I heard that Mr. Trant doesn't like what happened with Oz. Risk is smoothing things over, but he was pretty pissed that you weren't punished for killing one of his guards."

My back snapped up straighter, and my fangs punched

down. "Well, I'm not too happy that his guards were torturing my mates," I curtly replied.

She nodded. "I get it. I really do. But it's not just that. Since you killed Oz, there has been more...defiance. The other hybrids like that you stood up to Oz. There are whispers, and it's making Spector anxious. Just be careful, okay?"

She looked around the room, as if looking for Spector spies to be eavesdropping. "People are acting out. Lavinda Carre threw a hellfire ball at one of her trainers, and Moses Greene let out his hellhound demon, and it gnawed on a lab tech's leg. People are acting up, and Spector is taking notice."

Dread gathered inside of me like ice forming. Even if I hated my peers, I didn't want them punished for acting out. "Are they still making you use your siren ability to kill people?" I asked her.

"Not so much now that I'm with Stiles. Though I heard they've started to send out our former classmates to do jobs."

"What kind of jobs?"

She lifted a shoulder. "I don't know. Maybe something like the job you were sent out on?"

That was not a good thought. If Belvini was looking for more high level demons, then that meant he could churn out more hybrids.

"Okay, thank you for telling me, Cheryl," I finally replied.

Risk might feel in control of the situation, but there were too many variables. It was time the guys and I made a plan to get out of here before it was too late.

"Of course. What are friends for?" Cheryl beamed. She really was proving to be a good ally here. "Oh! And when you have time, I'd like to discuss your duties as Maid of Honor. I'm just not sure you're experienced enough to throw the kind of high-caliber bachelorette party someone like me will need, but don't worry, I'll be holding your hand through the entire planning process."

"Oh boy." I stood up and headed for the door.

"Motley, I'm serious! Don't make any plans without me!" she called out as I shut the door behind me.

I smirked to myself. Stiles was going to have to cut her hand off if he ever wanted that ring back.

Chapter 23

"WAKE UP, LITTLE SPIDER," Crow's voice whispered in my ear.

I rolled over in my bed, not wanting to wake up. Today was demonstration day. Council members and influential supes from all over the world would be in attendance. Spector called us to the training room last night and announced that there would be a *show and tell* about our gifts. They weren't clear on what exactly would be expected of us, but I was anxious they'd make me drain a victim dry with everyone watching.

"I don't want to go," I pleaded before snuggling deeper into the mattress.

Risk had already left earlier that morning to coordinate plans with *Collector*. Now that I knew his true name and that he didn't like it, I found myself calling him that regularly. I didn't like that Risk was working with him, but my demon reveled in taking chances.

"You have to go, Little Spider," Crow cooed while stroking my cheek.

I knew he was right. Since the incident with Oz, the guards had become more brutal, using whatever power they had to crush the hybrids under their boots. I didn't want to openly defy them again, not until I had a plan for getting out of here and ensuring my aunt's safety.

"Come on, Wid," Tomb said from where he was standing at the foot of the bed. "You can do this, and we'll be right there with you."

"Actually, you won't."

We all turned to look at Risk striding into the room, the door slamming shut behind him. He eyed my bare thighs where they were peeking out from under the sheets. "Why are you still lying prostrate and naked? We have to leave in five minutes."

I groaned and sat up, placing my feet over the side of the bed before hurrying to the dresser where I pulled on a new Spector uniform. I felt all three pairs of eyes watching me as I pulled on the tee and black legging pants. "What did you mean that they wouldn't be right there with me?" I asked before turning around to face them and pulling my hair out of its messy bun to comb it through with my fingers.

"Exactly as I said," Risk answered where he leaned against the wall. "Collector handpicked which hybrids would be in attendance today, and neither Tomb nor Crow are on that list."

I exchanged a worried look with them and bit my lip. "I don't like being separated."

"I don't either," Tomb agreed. "You couldn't pull your weight and get us in there?"

Risk shrugged a shoulder. "Haven't you ever heard the term pick your battles? I can't request your presence without it looking suspicious. Motley as my pet? Yes. Her other two mates? No."

Tomb sighed and ran a hand over his bare scalp. "I don't like the idea of her being there."

"I'll take care of her," Risk said with all the confidence in the world. "Collector would be stupid to try anything today. The demonstration is all about showing off. He doesn't want to make waves. He wants Spector to look good so the council will want to support him."

I quickly pulled on a pair of black training boots, tucking my pants inside of them before straightening up. "Okay, I'm ready," I said, even though I didn't feel ready at all.

Risk cast a look my way from head to toe. "Hmm," he said, coming forward. He tugged on a strand of my wavy hair before trailing a single finger down the curve of my neck and resting it against my hourglass mark. "You have just-fucked hair and swollen lips," he mused. "You look like you've just spent all night ravished in my bed."

My face heated. "Umm, I *was* ravished all night in your bed. By all three of you. At the same time," I reminded him.

He grinned. "Exactly. You look the perfect part as my pet."

"I really don't like that nickname," I grumbled. "Couldn't you call me something less degrading?"

"What?" he asked while leaning even closer. He cupped his hand around my neck and brushed his lips over mine. "Like Mate? Wicked Love? Baby? Sweetheart? *Mine?*"

"Kitten," Tomb offered offhandedly.

"Snookums," Crow added.

"Little pet doesn't have to mean something derogatory, Motley. I treasure you. I *own* you. You're mine to do with as I please," Risk rasped while squeezing even tighter. Our colliding chests created delicious friction, making my nipples pebble.

"We so do not have the time for this," Crow mumbled, though he sounded as heady as I felt.

"Are you sure? She could be fashionably late," Tomb added.

Risk lavished me with a brief, soul-crushing kiss. I could

taste the coffee on his breath and the sulfur in his soul. It was devastatingly quick, leaving me wanting more of his decadent tongue sweeping across mine. "We don't have time, my pet," he said, though his face was filled with regret. "We have to go."

Crow whistled, and one of his birds animated to life, fluttering toward me before landing on my shoulder. "Russell is going with you. If I can't go, then I at least want my eyes on you," he said as the bird nuzzled my cheek.

"Russell the crow? That's his name?" I deadpanned. The bird cawed happily at me, as if pleased.

"All my birds have names. Magnus. Bernadette. Gigi. Fabia. Aerin is a pain in the ass and eats all my chocolates."

"Can we please discuss how you name your crows another time? I'd like to get there on time," Risk interrupted with a roll of his eyes.

"Shit. I don't have something to send her off with," Tomb said while frantically looking around the room.

"Chisel off one of your appendages. She could beat her enemies to death with your cock rock," Risk teased.

Tomb's eyes brightened for a moment, as if considering it, then shook his head. "It's too big. She'd never be able to carry it all that way."

I rolled my eyes. "Okay, we're going now," I said, slipping by Risk to land a kiss on both Tomb's and Crow's lips.

My mates shared a serious glance as I made my way to the door. "Take care of her, demon."

"On my honor," Risk said with a hand to his heart.

"He keeps saying that word, but I'm not comforted," Tomb mumbled to himself.

Risk and I walked out into the hall, and I gave them one last wave before the door closed behind us. Turning around, my brow shot up in surprise when I saw the heavy presence of Spector guards. There were way more than usual. Some were posted at the end of the hallways, while others were marching back and forth doing rounds.

"What's with the extra security?" I whispered to Risk, hurrying my steps to keep up with him.

He reached down and grabbed my hand, tucking it in the crook of his arm. His hand lingered over mine, his hot fingers dancing over my knuckles in a light caress.

"Oh, them? They're here for you. Your stunt with burning that guard alive made them a bit more fearful of you than they were before," he answered with a smirk, as if he were thrilled by that. "Such risky behavior, Wicked Love," he taunted. "Though the webs you spun at the front of the door? Brilliant. I particularly liked you constricting the male's hands until they popped right off. It's sexy to see you get so bloodthirsty."

"Only you would get turned on by that," I murmured as we passed another pair of guards. I didn't miss the way they eyed me, as if they wanted to litter my body with bullets and punish me for taking one of their own.

Russell kept close, staring down the guards with his beady red eyes as we navigated the hallways. Although I'd been much more comfortable since Risk showed up, I wasn't disillusioned enough to think that I was suddenly free. I was just an accessory to the demon they wanted to keep happy.

The demonstration was held in the training room, and the moment we walked through the doors, a shiver of fear traveled up my spine. I hadn't been there since I'd killed Oz, but the blood was mopped up and my webs whisked away. There was no evidence of what I'd done, and I wasn't sure how I felt about that. Chairs, set up like an arena, lined the floor, and chatty supes had already found their seats. They looked around excitedly, like the presentation was more of a movie premier instead of a sinister presentation.

"We need to stand with the other hybrids," Risk murmured in my ear while directing me toward the side wall.

"Why didn't they want Crow and Tomb participating in the demonstration?" I whispered as the lights dimmed. "They're strong."

"They're also unpredictable," he countered.

"So am I."

"Yes, but I'm trying to convince them that you're my little pet, so you're going to rein in the murderous tendencies and let me do my thing. Okay?"

Risk and I were definitely going to have a conversation about who wore the pants in this mate bond.

Risk led me to the other side of the training room, where all the hybrids were gathered together. "Stay here a moment while I look for Belvini."

I nodded before he walked off, but as soon as he was gone, I found a dozen pair of hybrid eyes looking at me. About half of them were Thibault students, and the other half I only recognized from brief sightings in the cafeteria or training room. Uneasy under their stares, I turned away, choosing instead to face the supes watching us with open curiosity.

Potential investors for Spector's scheme. I recognized some of them, and my eyes landed on the council members—particularly the pregnant female who was staring daggers at me.

Okay, so facing that direction wasn't much better.

I was ready to just opt for a staring contest with the floor when I felt a tap on my shoulder. I turned around and saw one of the shifter students standing in front of me. "I wanted to introduce myself to you, Black Widow," she said quietly. "We all heard about what you did with that guard."

"Yeah," another hybrid said, pushing forward. He was a

necro with jet black hair and gangly limbs. "Finally someone fucking stands up to these sadistic pricks."

"Shh, not so loud!" a girl to his left hissed at him. He just shrugged.

The shifter girl nodded. "We just wanted you to know, we want to fight back too."

Shock made my eyes widen. These were people who had once taunted me in the halls of Thibault. The people who had looked at me with fear and revulsion after I'd killed Byron. Now they were...aligning with me?

"Listen, I don't want anyone to get punished because of me," I insisted quietly.

"We *already* get punished," the necro said. "This whole place is one big fucking punishment. We want to get back at them."

The conversation in the room was growing steadily louder as more people filtered in, but Risk and Belvini were still nowhere in sight. My surprise at their demeanor toward me was quickly turning to dismay. I knew we were powerful, but most of us were young, and we were also vastly outnumbered.

"Yeah, let's fucking attack them all right now," a male vampire said, pushing forward. I caught his eye. One of Byron's friends.

"No," I said quickly. "Did you not notice all the guards around? They're everywhere. If we fight back, we have to be smart about it."

The shifter girl nodded. "We will listen to the Black Widow," she told the others, her stern expression brooking no argument.

I wasn't so sure that I was up to the task. We had to get organized—and fast. But first, we needed to learn everything we could about Spector, which meant we needed to pay attention to this demonstration and hope like hell the council didn't agree to buy their contract.

"Right now, we watch. We learn. When we're ready to do something about Spector, I'll let you know," I finally said before fixing my face forward on the makeshift stage.

Everything was just about to get started, when I saw Cheryl and Stiles enter the room. She was waving her hand and pressing it against Stile's chest, making sure everyone in the room saw the gigantic rock on her hand.

"Oh, Motley!" she screeched from across the room. "Did you see that Laverne Bromine is here?" She was trying to whisper-scream at me and was drawing the attention of all the spectators. I slunk backwards toward the wall with a shaky nod and a forced smile.

Stiles led her away with his hand clamped over her mouth and found them both seats in the front row. Risk appeared from the side and was heading toward me with a determined scowl.

It was time to see what Spector was made of.

Chapter 24

BELVINI LIKED the sound of his own voice.

He'd been speaking at his glossy black podium for nearly an hour, while a projector showed video clips and statistics on the wall behind him. Everyone in the audience was held in rapt attention, hanging on his every word.

Meanwhile, the other hybrids and I were standing like cattle in a herd, waiting to be shown off. We couldn't see very much, since there was a wall of Spector guards standing in front of us, but I caught enough of the information displayed to realize just how many rituals Belvini had to have implemented in order to get the numbers he boasted. Five years. This program had been going on for five years while Belvini tweaked and perfected the possession rituals. When he showed a graph boasting his higher success ratio, my stomach churned. So many deaths. So many lives altered forever.

No one in the audience asked anything about where he found his "volunteers." All they seemed to care about was one thing—power.

Risk was leaning up against the wall to my left, hands

stuffed into the pockets of his black dress pants as he watched with a bored look on his face. But every time Belvini stated the name of a demon whose blood he'd used to perform the ritual, I saw Risk's jaw tighten.

The crow at my shoulder stayed watchful, never once leaving from its perch beside my head. Every once in a while, when my anxiety spiked, I felt a little beak burying itself in my hair and nipping lightly at my neck, like it was trying to comfort me.

Finally, the lights brightened, and that part of the presentation ended, and then it was time for the main event.

Us.

"Now, you all were invited here for an exclusive demonstration. We'll show you exactly the level of power Spector can bring," Belvini announced, waving his hand in a flourish to point to us.

As one, the guards moved aside, parting like curtains to show actors on a stage.

Belvini called the male necro up first. He stood ramrod straight on the stage, staring out at the crowd with a blank look as the demon went over his file. "One of our Thibault graduates who decided to volunteer," Belvini said by way of introduction. The fact that he made it seem like we willingly joined Spector made me sick.

"Necro. Nineteen years of age. His demon gave him the ability to take any physical injury that others sustain onto himself and then heal at an accelerated rate."

Damn. No wonder he hated Spector so much. I didn't even want to imagine all the trials and tests they'd put him through.

One after another, Belvini called up the hybrids, showing their stats and video clips of their powers in action. Some of them—like the shifter girl who could duplicate objects—were made to use their power on stage.

"This is worse than the time my mother made me do that beauty pageant in Belize, and those presenters were super skeezy," she said under her breath with a shudder.

"Now I'll bring up Black Widow, one of Spector's most promising hybrids," Collector said while gesturing toward me.

My eyes snapped over to him, my heart rate picking up in speed. Cheryl nudged me forward when I still hadn't moved, and I reluctantly made my way up the steps to the makeshift stage, my legs trembling in trepidation. I obviously wasn't moving fast enough for them though, because one of the guards pressed his gun at my back, pushing me toward the podium.

"The Black Widow is a vampire hybrid and was successfully possessed two months ago. She has unique abilities. She can lure her prey, spin webs from her fingers, and is significantly stronger after she feeds," Belvini continued while nodding at the screen projector behind him.

As the screen loaded, he addressed the crowd again, that sly smile of his firmly in place as he adjusted his tie. "I felt that for her particular demonstration, a video would be more appropriate." Some of the guards chuckled at that, and I felt my stomach drop. *No.* I couldn't do this. I couldn't just stand here while all these people watched me fuck and feed.

My eyes reluctantly snapped to the screen, and sure enough, I was front and center, teasing my meal with my demonic grin. The man was naked and barely lucid, drunk off my lure.

"The Black Widow feeds off the essence of others through sexual contact. Once penetration is achieved, she feeds from their life force, making her stronger than any of the other hybrids we have in our arsenal."

I glanced at the shadowed crowd. Some of them looked horrified. Some looked intrigued. Risk looked *murderous*.

It was an intimate video, showing my arching back and the sweat dripping down my spine. It showed the human's flinching body growing gradually still, until there was nothing left but vacant eyes and my demon's satisfied grin.

"But this isn't her only ability. We're still working out how to mass produce her talents, but she does have the ability to form mate bonds, and her partners become invincible," Belvini began. The screen then flipped to a shot of the tank. I was sobbing in a web of grief, and Tomb's lifeless body was lying on the ground in front of me.

"Here, one of her mates died during a feeding, but as you can see..." Belvini said while fast forwarding the tape. "He emerged with a mate mark on his neck that matches her own, and he is now indestructible."

The screen then changed again, showing the very training room we were standing in. Clip after video clip, Tomb was murdered. Tortured. Suffocated. Burned alive. I watched the entire scene with anger in my blood and revenge dripping from my fangs. They fast forwarded through most of it, but the message was clear.

Tomb was everlasting, and I'd made him that way.

At the end of the clip, dozens of hands shot up. "Is she for sale?" a man greedily asked while eyeing me. He was a shifter male that reeked of alpha authority.

"Not at this time, no. We're hoping to research her abilities more and somehow reproduce her bonding effects once we can control the outcome. Mate bonds can be fickle, but we think we've found a way to streamline the process," Collector replied.

A few hands went down at his answer. Sick bastards. I'd burn this place to the ground before I let them commercialize my mate bond. Supes were always looking to level up. It wasn't enough that they didn't age, they wanted the guarantee that nothing could ever kill them either.

"So she kills anyone she sleeps with unless they become a mate? How can you guarantee that we won't get possessed with something like that?" a man asked. "I don't know about you, but I value my sex life, and my husband would probably kill me if my dick turned murderous." The room chuckled at the male's words, like it was one big joke—like what I'd done was a joke. They didn't care that they'd watched me murder humans. All they cared about was the potential for themselves.

Once the laughter died down, Collector continued. "I can assure you that her demon is very rare. The results of her possession are an anomaly." Collector turned his gaze to me with pride and wonder, though I felt the annoyance beneath his façade. He didn't like me one bit, but that didn't matter. He would happily use me up and bleed me dry. "Spector will hold your hand through the entire process. Our scientists are well equipped to help you learn and wield your new abilities. We understand how important it is to feel in control, and our services include making sure you have a successful hybridization by overseeing your transition and helping you through the process."

"But you can't guarantee what demon we get, right?" another person asked.

"No, but if you feel incompatible with your new abilities, we have procedures to reverse the possession. We're contracted with a priest who can conduct exorcisms, and we have the tools to help suppress your demon desires if they become too much."

One woman stood and faced me. She had a notepad in hand and was ready to scribble down my answer. "Are you happy with your demon ritual? Do you feel like it was a good decision?"

I scoffed, which made Collector stiffen. I could feel the

threatening warning rolling off of him and see the forbidding caution in his stare.

I didn't care.

"No. I do not like being the Black Widow. Would you?" I asked. I kept it short and bitter. I didn't want to piss off Collector too much, but also wanted to make my stance known.

"I-I guess not. That would really put a damper on my sex life," the woman replied cheekily, making the room chuckle.

Collector slid into the conversation with grace and efficiency. "I'd like to remind everyone that the Widow's possession was rare. We do not anticipate this happening to everyone. Please remember that we included her in this demonstration to illustrate future possibilities, like the mate bond. These projects require donations, and we are excited to explore the endless opportunities associated with that—with the proper funding, of course."

Spoken like a true politician.

Another hand went up. "How does the ritual work, exactly?" a man asked. Of all of them, he looked the wariest. His face was twisted up in a frown, and from the looks of it, he wasn't completely sold on what Spector was offering.

Collector gnawed at his lip in annoyance before responding. "I'm so glad you asked, my friend. Allow me to show you."

The black curtains that had served as a backdrop drifted open, and my eyes widened when I saw what was behind them.

A male, bound in chains with an ethereal glow to them, was sitting on a metal chair. His head was hanging low, and there were a few scientists in white lab coats around him, gathering his blood that dripped slowly from an IV attached to both arms.

He had shaggy blond hair and a full beard that looked like

it was there out of neglect rather than choice. He wore faded Spector sweats, and the ragged breaths he took at unnatural intervals let me know how bad off he was. I couldn't even sense his power the way I could sense Collector and Risk. All that was coming off of the gaunt male was a faint trail of fading life.

My eyes immediately shot over to Risk, who had straightened up from his spot at the wall. His dark eyes were locked onto the captive demon, and flickers of flames were peeking out from his sleeves.

Belvini cut through the murmurs in the room. "As you can see, the ritual requires the blood of a high level demon such as myself. This particular demon has donated his blood twelve times. The average duration for a single demon's life-span usually ends around the tenth donation," he explained, making it sound utterly clinical. "Luckily, thanks to our Black Widow, we now have a donor with an unlimited blood supply. We will never run out. As long as demons are spawned in hell, we will have hybrids in our realm."

I took backward steps off the stage, getting out of the way. Cheryl waved me over, and I quickly took the seat beside hers while listening to Belvini's speech.

"The ritual requires the blood of a high level demon, an ancient rune circle, and some ceremonial chants. I've heard jokes about a virgin sacrifice, but I can assure you we aren't *that* uncivilized."

Some of the crowd laughed at that, but I couldn't find it within myself to find his words humorous. I was too busy feeling trapped in my memories, sucked into the blinding pain and the terror of hearing the chants during my ritual. What they did was menacing and wrong.

Cheryl snorted. "They'd be hard pressed to find a virgin at Thibault anyways, am I right?" she said while holding up her hand for a high-five. I didn't return the gesture, making her pout.

"It's a fairly painless ritual that has a high success rate. We've polished our process to ensure a safe, beneficial hybridization for all our participants. We hope that you see the value in Spector and the value in our program."

Collector flashed an award-winning smile to the crowd, and all around us, supes erupted in applause. I looked at Risk, but he was still staring at the tied up man on stage, his eyes filled with anger. With fists clenched at his sides, he bore a hole in the stage with his gaze.

"We have sign-ups and investment paperwork stationed at tables around the room. Once you've made your decision for participation and have transferred your fee, we will get you set up with an information packet and will schedule you for a consultation prior to your possession. The first round will be in three days, and I highly recommend reserving your spot, as placement is limited."

At that, Mr. Trant stood up from his spot in the front row and proudly made his way over to the nearest table, making a big show of pulling a pen from his jacket pocket and writing a check. Everyone watched in rapt attention, and the moment he collected his spot, many others followed.

One by one, each chair emptied.

One by one, everyone signed their name.

One by one, I lost hope that people would see reason—that they would see that what Spector was doing was wrong.

Realization settled in my bones, and I shared a look with the other grim-faced hybrids. If we wanted to take Spector down, we were on our own.

After everyone had signed up and Belvini worked the room for higher checks, we hybrids were forced to stand on the stage while lingering patrons eyed us like prized ponies. The business attire clad supes walked around us, talking about us as if we weren't standing right there. Russell kept ruffling his black wings as if he were annoyed on my behalf. I reached up and pet him to calm him down, which seemed to help.

"What did this one do again?" a female vampire asked the person next to her.

The male regarded Cheryl boredly before flipping through a brochure that I realized had our pictures on it. "Ah, a siren."

The female made a noise of disappointment. "Hmm. That's rather dull."

Cheryl frowned in offense, but at least she had the sense to keep her mouth shut for once.

"Ah, Black Widow. I'd like one of her."

My eyes snapped forward, greeted with an overweight shifter wearing a suit and a smug grin. He and his companion —another shifter, based on the scent of him—looked me up and down.

"Fascinating merging," the portly male said. "Tell me, how many times do you have to fuck to sustain yourself?"

My mouth popped open at the bluntness of his words. "That's none of your business," I snapped.

The shifters exchanged a look, as if they were surprised by my unwillingness to discuss how often I had sex.

"How many mates did the brochure say she had? Ten? Twelve? She's probably riding a cock every hour," the younger shifter chuckled as he eyed my breasts.

Webs started to coil around my fingers as anger sparked through me, but before I could do anything, Risk was there, stepping in front of me. "Gentleman, I've taken Black Widow here as my pet. The only cock she's riding is mine for the foreseeable future," he said with a charming grin.

The shifters chuckled. "Ah, I don't blame you there."

I knew what Risk was doing—protecting me the only way

he could—but I hated the act that I was nothing but a sex pet.

"In fact," Risk began before shifting his body and wrapping his arm around my waist. "I think she and I will be leaving now. All this talk of fucking has left me feeling *famished*."

Risk started pulling me out of the room, not caring that there was a line of influential people staring us down, eager to pick and prod at me like I was a prized possession to be owned. Russell flapped overhead, following us out the doors and into the hallway.

"That was awful," I croaked.

"I know," Risk replied in a whisper while petting my head. He was staring down a pair of guards blocking off the hallway in the distance. "And you put on quite the show. Collector is pissed."

"I can handle the Collector," I gritted.

"I'm sure you can, Wicked Love," Risk replied tenderly as we came to a complete stop in front of the guards.

The two men were holding rifles and staring down at me with looks of vile disapproval, but as soon as Risk and I approached, they moved out of the way. The moment I was out of that room, I was able to take the first full breath after what had felt like hours.

Risk led us toward the elevators, but I nearly slammed into his back when he stopped suddenly. Looking around him, I saw what had halted his steps. The chained demon was being escorted down the hall, and Risk's entire body tensed.

"You know him," I said in a murmur. "Who is he?"

"A very old friend," Risk replied, his tone like steel.

Risk's eyes followed the demon's back as the guards led him away.

"Come. I'll take you to your room," he said, hurrying into

action. "Then I want to see if I can get to where they're taking him."

"Go," I urged him as I pushed him toward the hallway they disappeared down. "I'll take the elevator to your room. You'll miss where they're taking him if you don't hurry." Risk hesitated, but I shooed him with my hands. "Go."

He pointed a finger at me. "Go straight to my room. Understood?"

"Yeah, yeah, now go!"

He pressed the button of the elevator for me before turning and striding away, following the trail of the demon.

The elevator dinged, and I went inside, pressing the number for Risk's floor. Russell flew around in the enclosed space as it moved up, and when it dinged and the doors slid open, I started to step out, only to realize that it was the wrong floor. I pressed the correct floor again, but the doors wouldn't shut. Frowning, I peeked my head out of the hallway, trying to see where I was, when a pair of arms suddenly grabbed me and shoved me face-first into the wall.

My head exploded with pain, and I struggled to call my webs, but I felt something tie around my wrists, wrapping so tight that it cut into my skin. I looked down, noting the amulet I once saw Collector wearing in his office was now binding me with a thick leather strap, the amber gemstone hanging off of it.

"What the fuck?" I yelled before trying once again to access my powers.

But nothing came, no webs, no dark energy from my spider. There was just...nothing. Like my demon had been sucked into a void.

Guards started dragging me down the hall as I kicked and screamed, and I could hear Russell cawing out in frantic cries above me.

"Shut her up!" one of the guard's demanded.

Hands covered my mouth, but I sunk my teeth into my attacker's rancid flesh. Twisting and turning, fighting, clawing, screaming, I tried everything to get away. None of it worked.

And then sharp pain struck across my temple.

And the world went black.

Chapter 25

MY EYES CRACKED open with exhaustion. I could smell the rusty scent of blood in the air. It coated my tongue, covered my face. A steady flowing wound fell from my temples, and my wrists burned where they were bound.

I looked down, noting the relics tied to my skin and burning away the flesh there. My feet were chained to concrete cinder blocks on the ground.

"Motley? Wh-where am I?"

I snapped my attention up and forced my blurry vision to settle. I was in a dark room, and ten feet away, my aunt was sitting on the floor beside a pile of empty blood bags.

"D-did I have another frenzy? I don't remember," she said while scratching her long black nails down her face. She was in a Spector hospital gown, and her normally groomed red hair was tangled and frayed, spilling out of her head in electric waves. Her eyes were locked on the bags of empty bags, her nostrils flaring as her pupils began to dilate.

"Aunt Marie? How did you get here?" I asked, though emotion clogged my throat. This wasn't what I wanted. If she was here, then that meant…

"I don't know. I don't know where I am," she began while standing up. Her thin legs looked so frail. She shook with each step, circling the room in wide-eyed terror. "Do you smell that?" she asked. Her button nose tipped up and sniffed at the air, like she could pinpoint the scent. I recognized each body movement for what it was.

She was falling into a daze of bloodlust.

"Aunt Marie, you have to get out of here, okay? Can you unchain me?" I asked, though I knew she wasn't paying attention. She padded around barefoot, her toes dragging on the concrete with each shuffled step.

"Yes, yes," she began. "But do you smell that?" she asked again before turning her body to me. "I'm so hungry."

I winced the moment her eyes landed on my bleeding wounds. She transitioned between taking in the pity on my expression and licking her lips at the holes in my arms. She was at war with her nature, fighting to make sense of what was happening while desiring the dripping crimson substance I was coated in.

"Aunt Marie, listen to my voice," I coaxed as she slipped closer.

She tripped on a groove in the concrete, landing with a painful jolt, and then started crawling on her hands and knees, scraping up her porcelain skin with each staggering movement.

"You're bleeding, Motley," she said in awe, though she sounded far away.

"Aunt Marie, we have to get out of here," I pleaded. It was a special kind of cruelty, using the person I loved most in this world to torture me. Though my head pounded with anxiety, I knew that Spector put us together as punishment.

"We have to get out of here," she repeated robotically.

Once at my feet, she licked her lips before reaching out with her index finger and pressing on the relic burning into my skin. Hot blood bubbled up and oozed out of the wound. Her eyes widened.

"Aunt Marie, it's me. It's me," I pleaded.

She leaned closer, pressing her cold cheek against my skin. "Blood," she croaked.

Slowly, Aunt Marie got to her feet. I watched in horror as the woman that raised me, the woman that rocked me to sleep and sang me lullabies cocked her head and stared at me with predatory intent. I closed my eyes and imagined us in her kitchen, baking blood cookies and dancing to music. I imagined her braiding my hair and cussing out my no-good father.

I refused to see her like this. I refused to let Spector warp my perception of the woman that gave up her life to raise me. Her head came down to my arm, and I felt her teeth scrape against my skin.

"I love you, Aunt Marie," I whispered.

Fangs punched through my skin, and I let out a little stuttered cry as I felt her hands latch around my arm to hold me in place as she drank.

I didn't fight her. I didn't try to pull away.

"I love you, Aunt Marie," I repeated, feeling her take another long pull from my veins.

She paused, and I cracked my eyes open. *Were my words helping?* I spoke my affections even louder. "I love you, Aunt Marie."

She unlatched from my aching arm and looked at me with blood trickling down her chin. She blinked. Once. Twice. The third time, she let my arm drop and took a step back.

"I love you, Aunt Marie," I practically yelled, hoping that I could break through the haze of her addictions and bring her back to me—to us.

"M-Motley?" she croaked, her eyes holding a newfound clarity that wasn't there before.

A wrecked sob escaped me. "Yeah, Aunt Marie. It's me."

She looked around, frowning at the dark cell and the mess of blood all over the floor. "Where am I?"

Gods, I didn't want to lose her to the bloodlust again, and I wasn't sure how much longer we had. I knew exactly what Belvini's intentions were. I'd acted out of line when I told the truth at the demonstration. I'd made him look bad, and now he was punishing me for it by using her against me.

"Aunt Marie, listen to me—" I said as calmly as I could.

"You have puncture wounds on you," she interrupted, looking at my arm with worry.

"That's not important right now," I said, moving my arm to block the wound from her view. "Try to focus, Aunt Marie. I need you to try to get me out of these bindings."

She took a step but noticed all the blood bags on the floor. "Did I..." Her eyes drifted back up to my arm, and she covered her mouth with a trembling hand. "Oh, gods, Motley, I...I hurt you. Attacked you."

"No, it's okay. It wasn't your fault," I said, hating the way her eyes filled with tears and how her frail body began to shake.

"I don't know where I am!" she cried, digging her hands through her scalp and tugging on her hair.

"Aunt Mar—"

My words were cut off when the solid metal door suddenly banged open, and three guards stormed inside. My aunt tried to flash toward me, but one of the guards was a vamp too, and he overtook her in a second. Holding her arms behind her back, he made her face forward, the other two guards flanking her.

"Let her go!" I demanded, trying to escape the binds, but the relics just burned deeper inside of me, making me scream.

Belvini strolled in, along with a scientist trailing after

him, and he took in the scene with mock surprise. "Oh, dear. What seems to have happened here?"

"You son of a bitch! Let her go!" I screamed at him, letting all the hate I felt for him show on my face.

He tsked and shook his head, placing his hands in his pockets like he was meandering around a museum and taking in the sights.

"The vampire bit the hybrid, President Belvini," one of the guards reported.

I glanced down at the puncture mark oozing blood and then glared at them. "It's not her fault," I insisted. "You fucking set her up. You knew all of those blood bag scents would put her into overdrive, and then you wounded me and left me in here to set her off with my blood."

"Motley, I'm s-so sorry." My aunt's crumpled face and sagging body nearly undid me.

"It's not your fault," I repeated. "Do you hear me? It's *not*."

"You know the punishment for harming one of Spector's hybrids," Belvini said, nodding to the guards.

"Yes, sir."

"What—"

I didn't get to finish my sentence. I didn't even get to breathe.

The vampire at my aunt's back dropped her arms, making her stagger forward, and then his hands were around her neck.

My eyes widened. A word tried to form on my tongue.

But he twisted. He snapped. And then he tore her head right off her body and tossed it on the floor.

And the word died.

Right there, landing with the weight of my only real family, I became incoherent, my soul ripped out. My eyes latched onto her severed head, the look of shock frozen on her face forever. Blood pooled beneath her jagged neck.

And I split.

A scream that was not from this world tore from my chest and detonated through the air. Agony. It was agony I felt. The wounds on my body were *nothing*. I didn't feel the burns of the relics or the bump on my temple or the puncture in my arm. I felt the all-consuming torment of my aunt's death in an unbearable explosion.

I was cleaved right out of my own self. Too destroyed, too hurt, too full of violent rage to exist as Motley.

My spider extended. Like skeletal tree limbs stretching out and taking over the tree. She surged out in a shock of energy, breaking the bindings in one fell swoop and letting them fall to the ground like they were nothing. Not even the amulet could contain her.

Black light poured out of my body, lifting me off the ground as my guttural screams of rage continued to rip out of my throat. My spider pushed and pushed and pushed, her body taking over my own.

The guards looked on in horror. Belvini backed up as black appendages pushed from my form. My sight sharpened. Scents intensified. My body cracked and twisted, grew and spread, that black light continuing to pour out of me like my unequivocal anguish.

Spider legs ruptured from my blackened skin. Fangs as big as rifles punched from my mouth. And then I was standing ten feet tall in the crowded room, my colossal body thirsty for revenge.

"Back up!" one of the guards screamed while aiming a gun at me.

Silly prey.

Venom spewed from my lips, dousing him in eternal flames that hissed with black sparks. I watched for a moment, enjoying the way his limbs flailed and his body dissolved into a bubbling pile of carnage.

Once the guard was gone and his screams had been silenced, I swung my gaze on Collector, observing him through eyes that weren't my own and senses that expanded past the abilities of my vampire. I saw him for the evil he was. I saw the consuming energy of his nature and the selfish desires of his soul.

He was *nothing*. A weak demon hiding behind the things he collected.

Collector backed away slowly and tried to make it out the door, but I lunged for his feeble body. He wouldn't be getting away. He was trapped in my web. I released silken ropes at his heels, latching onto him with a simple flick. Swooping him up, I dangled him over the concrete, enjoying the sight of his body jerking at my demand.

Fight, little fly.

Run away, little fly.

Die, die, die, little fly.

He burned away my webs with hellfire and went crashing to the ground below, landing on his back with a wheeze. I watched in amusement as he scrambled to his feet, rushing toward the steel door to get away from me.

You can try, little fly.

Run as you might, little fly.

You will die, little fly.

My demon had taken over my entire being, lashing out with more venom and webs, tangling her attackers in strands of poetic justice.

I moved to shoot out more webs when the sound of a gun went off, echoing around the room. Sharp pain hit my chest and bloomed with bloody betrayal throughout my body. I staggered before I could straighten up on all eight legs, towering over my prey. It hurt, but it was a dull sort of pain.

It was nothing compared to the roaring in my soul or the all-consuming grief in my heart.

Twisting my massive body and temporarily forgetting Collector, I approached my new attacker with glee. His shaky hands were covered in blood. My aunt's murderer.

I whipped my webs around his neck, squeezing, squeezing, squeezing.

His eyes bulged from the pressure. His back arched from the way I picked his body up by his neck. I tortured and played with my prey until blood dripped from the pressure of my webs and his head rolled back. And then, with a snap, his neck crumbled under the pressure of my wrath.

A fitting death.

The door slammed shut, drawing my attention back to the man that started it all. But when I spun back around, Belvini was gone. He'd disappeared like the coward he was while I was distracted killing the guard.

But oh, I'd wait for him.

I'd spin my web.

I'd lure him in.

I'd kill him with glee.

Monsters weren't born, they were made.

I found solace in the dark destruction of my demon. I allowed her to calm my mind with her potent brand of rage. She stalked the concrete room and wrapped up her kills with thick webs like silken trophies. All the while, I sunk deeper and deeper into her existence. It was easier to be the avenging monster than to be the girl who would grieve.

It was easier to accept my demon than to accept a world where Aunt Marie didn't exist.

It was easier.

Chapter 26

TIME DIDN'T EXIST in grief.

There was no passing by. There was no dusk on pain. The world didn't light you up with a new beginning of dawn. It just highlighted what you'd lost in the dark.

So I stayed burrowed.

Consciousness was a strange thing when your soul was severed. I saw snippets of the world through my spider's eyes. I watched her take vengeance. I watched her kill. Destroy. Lash out with venom and webs in a flurry of rabid ire.

She was vicious. She was malicious. She was beautiful.

The sway of her body as she splintered concrete and battered guards nearly rocked me to sleep. The roars and hisses from her mouth were like lullabies. Our realities had flipped, and I was now the one buried inside, like she was cradling me and keeping me safe while she faced the world and let it suffer her wrath.

Death followed her wherever she crawled. Every time she caught another fly, elation soared through her. I could feel her pride as if each kill was a present she was gifting to me.

For you, she whispered to me. *For her*.

No. I didn't want to think about *her*. The tears that welled in familiar eyes. The head that landed at my feet. I couldn't. Overwhelming despair crippled me.

So my spider went on.

Pain flared when they hurt us. Her rage boiled over when we were surrounded. *Kill them all*, she rasped. *Kill, kill, kill,* she chanted as more power besieged us.

I tunneled deeper.

Dark and nothingness were such cool, comforting balms. I wanted to stay here forever, I wanted to drift away and not have to feel.

But then...

A voice. Insistent. Loud. Demanding. What was it saying? *Motley, Motley, Motley*.

No, not *a* voice, I realized belatedly. *Three*.

I sat up from the blackness that shrouded me. I blinked through her eyes so I could see. I observed like I was detached, watching things play out like a movie on a screen.

So much death.

Bodies were everywhere. They littered the ground like blood red rose petals down a morbid aisle. I took it all in—the ruined room I was in resembled some sort of massive storage area. It was large enough to hold my spider's body, and there was a regiment of Spector guards surrounding my spider, guns all trained on us.

"Stop!" a voice yelled. It sounded like crackling fire.

I blinked down at the body standing before me. His back faced my spider, his hands filled with an orange blaze.

"The next person that shoots her will die by my hand," he said.

My spider trilled. *Mate*.

But then a guard—one off to the side—moved to aim at my mate and shoot him. My spider hissed and lashed out, sending a long limb crashing into the one who dared harm my demon.

Guns fired. Popping bubbles of pain skidded off my body. My spider roared, ready to wipe them all out.

"Motley! Motley!"

My spider faltered. I paused to look. Two more faces came into view. One made of black stone and the other with hair as blue as the sea.

Mates.

A feeling of comfort washed over me.

Hands touched my spider. She was so tall that we towered over the males. I looked down, intrigued.

"Motley. You need to come back out now. Come on, Little Spider."

I frowned. I didn't want to come back out. My spider shook her head, backing up, but then the other one was there next. "Wid. You gotta come back, baby," the gargoyle begged. "You gotta come back so we can take care of you."

Didn't they see? My spider *was* taking care of me. This was easier. I didn't have to think, didn't have to feel…I should go further back, burrow in deeper…

"Motley!"

My attention snapped to the demon who now had his full attention on me. His eyes smoldered as smoke dusted past his lips. "You need to come back out now, Wicked Love."

A whine escaped my spider's lips, and her fangs bared, but my mates weren't deterred. They just came closer.

"You did beautifully, Black Widow," Risk cooed. "You took care of her. But we need her to come back out now so that *we* can take care of *both of you.*"

My spider and I paused. Our eyes started to sweep the threat in the room again, but shadows and crows blocked our view. "Down here, Little Spider," Crow muttered. "Just focus on us."

"We'll protect you now," Tomb put in.

"We've got you," Risk added.

And just like that, my spider started to shrink.

"That's it. Good girl," the demon purred.

I tried to hold onto her. Tried to burrow in, but she was too strong. She was pushing me forward, and only then did I feel how badly injured we really were. Slowly, black light eked out of our body and sunk into the recesses of our soul. Legs dissolved, fangs deflated, our body compressed until I was just a naked, shivering girl with tangled red hair on her shoulders and a blanket of tears in her eyes.

Strong arms lifted me up. Gentle birds settled on my limbs. Warmth brushed across my cheeks, making the wetness from my grief turn to steam.

"We've got you," they said again.

And they did.

The darkness of sleep claimed us.

PAIN SWEPT over me like the sharp, brittle ends of a broom. It raked over me, scraping me into consciousness.

"Easy, baby," a voice said as my eyes opened.

I blinked around at Risk's bedroom before my eyes trailed to my body. I was naked and sore, but fully healed. My mates hadn't pressured me at all, just let me be in my grief, but at some point during the night, the bullet wounds and other injuries I'd sustained had become too much. I slipped between the three of my mates on the bed and pleaded with them to help me forget and to heal.

They were tender. Slow. They gave me soft kisses and reverent touches and gentle love. Every time a tear would trail down my cheek, Crow's lips were there to kiss it away. Each knotted muscle was massaged by Tomb's sure hands until my body uncoiled and relaxed. And every sorrowful shiver that threatened to rack my body was pushed away with the warmth of Risk's body pressed against mine.

They took care of me in every possible way, slowly bringing my body to pleasure again and again, until every physical wound was healed and my mind was able to sleep.

It was nice to forget for a little while.

But now I was awake, wholly consumed with my mourning, wishing that they could heal my emotional wounds too.

Aunt Marie was dead.

The agony of that fact was stuck in my mind on repeat. I couldn't stop seeing every memory of what had happened—of the moment when her life was ripped away from her in careless violence.

"They killed her," I whispered, like the realization was still sinking into my brain.

I'd always tried to take care of her. But it was her connection to me that had gotten her killed. I hated Spector, but most of all, I felt a distant hate with myself. I had wanted a steady job so desperately that I willingly signed my life away, which led to a chain of events that killed the one person I treasured most in this world.

"We won't let them get away with this," Tomb growled while stroking my tear-stained cheek.

"How? How are we going to do that? How am I still alive? My spider… She killed…"

I refused to feel guilty about what I'd done. The guards earned every bit of wrath they'd gotten. I could still hear their screams, their pleas for help. I could still taste their blood.

"You're too valuable to Spector," Risk answered. He was sitting at the edge of the bed, his dark hair a delicious mess, like he'd been anxiously running his hand through it all night. The dark circles under his eyes seemed out of place for his usually carefree and handsome face, and his tie was gone, leaving just his dress shirt which was unbuttoned at the top. "They sent us in to calm you down. Fucking Collector. Every time you killed a guard, he grinned, like it thrilled him. I think he was intrigued at your ability to fully manifest into your demon's body. That took an incredible amount of power. He'll be interested in that. Will probably want to determine if he can get you to do it again so he can learn how to control it."

Tomb and Crow stiffened at that, and I grimaced. *No, no, no.* I couldn't even think about Belvini trying to control us like that.

"What are we going to do? How are we going to fix this?" I knew in my gut that there was no fixing this. I couldn't bring Aunt Marie back to life, I could only resurrect the pain. Over and over and over again.

"We don't have to talk about that right now, Little Spider. You need to rest," Crow replied tenderly. He reached out and placed a hand on mine, rubbing my cold skin with his thumb.

"We don't have time to rest. We don't have time to cope," I croaked. "What they did was wrong, and they're about to have more power. We need to get them shut down."

"We've got it handled. Stiles is working with his contact to go public. Right now, *you* are our priority, Motley. What happened yesterday…we almost lost you. It was like you weren't going to come back," Crow said, his violet eyes intent.

The three of them went silent, and I felt a twinge of guilt for giving in to the emptiness my spider offered. It was so easy to hide behind her and escape my sadness. "I'm sorry," I whispered.

"Don't you fucking say it," Risk gritted while standing up. He started stomping across the floor of our small safe haven, muttering to himself and clenching his fists. "None of this would have happened if I had stayed with you." He paused and turned to look at me, regret written all over his face. "I'm sorry. It was my responsibility to see you safely back in our room, and I didn't do it."

"Risk—" I began, but he cut me off.

"No. Don't," he warned, anger flashing in his eyes. "Crow's right. We almost fucking lost you, and if that had happened…" He whirled around. "Fuck!" he yelled through clenched teeth before throwing a blast of fire crumbling into the drywall.

Flames flared up, and smoke filled the room, but it was Risk's guilt that permeated through the air. I stood up, clutching the sheets to my chest as I padded over to him. I didn't want Risk to take the blame for this. He wasn't the one that locked me in a room with Aunt Marie. He wasn't the one that squeezed her skull with his hands or tore her head from her body. He wasn't the one that broke my spirit.

I moved with slow sadness, watching my mate's beautiful presence twisted up with torment. "Spector is to blame for this. Not you, not me. *Them*. I need time to grieve, but that's going to have to wait, and you're going to have to let go of your guilt, too. We have to work fast to bring Spector down, and that means we need to focus. So what are we going to do?"

My men went quiet. Tomb got up and wrapped his arms around me, pinning me in his stone comfort. "You're right," he said in his gravelly tone. "We need a plan. And I'm so damn proud of how strong you are, Motley. But just know that we're here with you, and we have your back."

Slowly turning, I faced him and cupped his cheek. Tomb looked worried yet determined. Of all of us, he knew the horrors of Spector best. He understood their toxic methods and deadly games. He had the scars and trauma to prove it.

I remembered our time in the tank together—his plea to

escape Spector, his desire to leave it all behind for good. At the time, I didn't get it. But now I did. It was easier to bury yourself in the darkness sometimes. It had been easier for me to hide behind my monster. Easier to slip away and fade into nothing rather than face reality. But Tomb found a reason to live *with me*—because of our mate bond. And I didn't take that lightly. I wasn't going to give in to the numb darkness again. I was going to find a reason to fight for them *and* Aunt Marie.

And that meant figuring a way to get the fuck out of here.

An idea suddenly struck me, and I turned back to my demon. "We need to go to the Between."

He tilted his head to the side and scratched at the dark scruff on his strong jaw. "It's risky for supes. I wasn't even completely sure *you'd* survive it. It's a place for demons," Risk answered.

"Since when are you afraid to take a risk?" I asked with a small smile. It was the most amusement I was capable of.

He didn't smile back. "Since I almost lost you."

I swallowed hard at his reply. I broke away from Tomb and wrapped my arms around his neck, pulling him close with a sigh. "I'm here. I'm not going anywhere," I promised in a raspy whisper. He breathed in my smell, burrowing his nose in my neck with a steady inhale.

"We need to get all the hybrids to the Between for a meeting without Spector's prying eyes," I said, pulling back to look at him. "Time doesn't work the same there, right? We could go, rally the troops, and figure out how to bring Spector down."

"Are you even sure they want to fight? Spector is holding everyone hostage with punishments and threats. You aren't the first to have a loved one killed. They aren't afraid to use brute force to keep everyone in line," Tomb explained.

"They'll help," I replied. "They were ready to fight at the demonstration. They just need some organization."

Risk pondered my statement for a moment, his hand cupping the back of my neck and fingers brushing over my skin as he thought. "The more people in the Between, the more temperamental it is. There's hundreds of hybrids here. It would take a lot of power to maintain, and I'm not completely confident I can keep it running for too long," he mused.

"We won't need more than that. Spector's been training us for months. We just need a lot of planning and a little time," Crow interjected.

"I'm still not sure they'd survive the trip," Risk replied, his fingers now lightly massaging my scalp. "Supes get ripped to shreds while transporting there. It's a demon safe haven."

"But we're demon hybrids," Tomb replied.

Risk nodded. "You're right. That's why Motley survived it. It was why I attempted it in the first place."

Tomb bristled and stared Risk down with brutal intensity. "I'm going to ignore the fact that you risked our mate's life," he deadpanned. "But we *will* be discussing your recklessness later."

Risk tugged on my hair playfully as he looked back at my fiercely protective gargoyle. "I look forward to the fist fest, Rocky Balboa."

I rolled my eyes at their banter. They'd bonded so quickly, it almost seemed seamless, like we'd all known each other for years. And what had happened yesterday seemed to solidify us more. We were in this together.

"Are we doing this?" I asked them all, making sure to look each of my mates in the eye. Risk with his sly grin, Tomb with his protective gaze, and Crow with his unfailing devotion.

"It'll take some time to bring them all and take them back. We'd have to be careful," Risk pointed out.

I shrugged. "Just wing it. You'll figure it out."

"Sounds risky," he replied with a slow grin. "I like it."

Crow stood and joined me at my side. Tomb positioned himself at my back, grasping my waist, and Risk faced me, holding my cheeks in the palm of his hands.

"Let's build an army, Wicked Love," he whispered.

"Let's ruin Spector," I replied.

Chapter 27

RISK WORKED EFFICIENTLY to get everyone to the Between. Some got vertigo. Some started vomiting on the sheer vast nothingness. Some screamed.

Cheryl complained.

"All this white is washing me out," she whined as she looked around the white nothingness that surrounded us. "I look terrible. And who even designed this place? I'm all for clean, modern spaces, but would a sitting area be too much to ask?"

I rubbed my temples. She was clinging to me like a spider monkey, though her annoying comments provided a good distraction. I embraced the predictable nature of her complaints to keep sane. I couldn't grieve right now. Right now I had to fight.

Risk rolled his eyes at her comment. He was definitely not a fan of Cheryl's. With a snap of his fingers, he made a chair appear for her to sit on and shut up.

Cheryl wrinkled her nose. "Mm, it's nice...I guess," she murmured before sitting down and crossing her legs.

"*Nice?*" Risk sighed while shaking his head. "What in the hellfire is wrong with it?"

"It's just...black leather? That is so dated."

I grabbed Risk's arm to stop him from throwing a fireball at her head. He sighed like he was disappointed, and shook out his smoking hands.

I looked over at Russell who was currently perched on my shoulder again. Ever since he'd gotten separated from me when I was taken by the guards, he'd been particularly clingy. Crow said the bird evaporated and appeared at his side the moment I was taken. It was how the guys knew something was wrong. And although his beady red eyes were a bit unnerving, and his claws dug into my skin somewhat painfully at times, he had grown on me.

When I reached up to pet him, he nipped my finger playfully, and a small smile slipped over my lips. Across the room, I saw that Crow was watching the exchange with a sexy smirk on his face. He liked that his bird and I had gotten close. It felt like our own special thing. And when Crow looked at me the way he was now, it filled me with warmth.

"I miss Stiles," Cheryl sniffed, bringing my attention back to her. Worry clung to her eyes. "He said he would be back right after the demonstration, but I haven't seen or heard from him."

I gently rubbed her shoulder in comfort while sucking in a steadying breath. "He'll be okay. He has to be careful, but I'm sure you'll hear from him soon."

I didn't let my own worry show, but I was *really* hoping we'd hear from him. Stiles was an intricate part of our plan. It wasn't enough to fight Spector and their guards. We had to show the world what hybrids were capable of and what Spector planned to do with us.

Once Risk transported most of the hybrids, I took in my peers with trepidation. He'd managed to bring in about a hundred of us, and he'd already explained what we were doing and how time worked in the Between. And although time wouldn't pass, having this many people in the emptiness was making the edges of this space vibrate with energy. It was like ripping fabric that couldn't hold onto reality. We needed to work fast.

"So why are we here?" a shifter girl asked. "Is this another Spector test?" she was rocking back and forth on her feet and pinching her flesh with dull nails.

"No, we're—"

My words were cut off as an unhinged elemental hybrid with wild eyes started backing up from the group. "No! I'm not doing any more tests!" he yelled. "You can't make me!"

The mental health of everyone had been deeply warped with all of Spector's tests and trainings. I was lucky enough to have my mates teach me to accept the two warring sides of myself, but I wasn't sure everyone else was gifted with the same relief. One necromancer was breaking his finger over and over and over, just to watch the bone mend. I could hear the continuous crunch of his skeleton echo in the empty air.

"We're here to bring down Spector," I announced loudly, hoping to cut through everyone's questioning worry.

Some stared at me with hopeful eyes, some scoffed. A few of them looked distrustful of me, like they couldn't believe that this wasn't a trick.

The worst ones, though, were the ones that had vacant stares. They were too lost in their own minds to comprehend what was going on around them. I realized that it was unfair to expect everyone to participate, but we needed all the help we could get.

"Spector has gone too far," I began. I wasn't one for making speeches; I'd spent so long in the shadows at Thibault that having everyone's eyes glued to me made me nervous. But, just like at the demonstration, they were all looking to me for direction. "They want to commercialize these demon possessions. Make more of us and force more demons out of hell. You *know* where that will lead. They'll use us for whatever schemes they come up with. I know none of us are naive enough to think that Spector will ever let us go. And I for one don't want to be a Spector pawn for the rest of my life. I don't want to be a member in their hybrid army," I said, holding more conviction with each word I spoke. "They use our loved ones against us, lock us in cells, force us to train, and study us like animals."

A shifter huffed, likely offended by my metaphor.

"Which is why we need to fight back."

"Fuck yes!" the shifter girl from the demonstration called out, fist raised in the air. I'd learned her name was Tara. "That's what I'm talking about!"

An elemental cleared her throat. "I don't know…I tried to leave, but they threatened my baby sister," she said. "I hate them, but how can we fight back? They have too much power, and I don't want them to hurt my family."

A few voices murmured in agreement.

My chest constricted with pain, and my spider surged forward to protect me from the onslaught of emotions coursing through me. Aunt Marie. "They killed my aunt," I admitted out loud with a shaky voice. Russell ruffled his feathers and tipped his beak into my neck. Webs began to pool from my fingers and wrap around my trembling body, like my spider wanted to safely cocoon me, keeping me away from the fresh waves of pain. Wide, wary eyes watched me.

"I defied them, and they killed my aunt right in front of me."

My words were greeted with gasps and pitying looks. It nearly undid me. But warmth at my back made me pause. My men were behind me, offering me their support.

I cleared my throat. "You might follow their rules, play

their games, and deal with their shit. But a day from now, a month from now, or even a year from now, you could slip up. Get tired. Hell, get mad. And Spector could decide to flex their muscles. No one can keep up with their demands forever. We can't live like this. We can't bow down and submit, or accept that they're holding our loved ones over our heads. We have to stop them. As long as Spector exists, our entire community is at risk. But I won't force anyone," I told them honestly. "It's your choice—something that Spector also likes to take from us. I choose to fight them. And I hope you choose to fight with me."

Everyone was silent, and I glanced around, my anxiety spiking. I meant what I said. Everyone had a choice to join us. It was a huge risk bringing them here and telling them this information. Any one of them could rat us out to Spector. But I had hope that we could band together.

"Spector outnumbers us," a male said from the back. I recognized him as a Thibault graduate.

"They do," I conceded with a nod. "But we're hybrids. I haven't seen what everyone can do, but I've caught glimpses in the training room. We're strong. And we have the element of surprise."

"I thought the demon was working with President Belvini?" a pixie-like female asked, her eyes watching Risk with apparent nervousness.

"I enjoy playing the double agent," Risk replied with a grin. "It raises the stakes nicely."

I suppressed the urge to roll my eyes at him. "It's time to decide. If anyone wants out, now's your chance to speak up. My mate will return you back to Spector."

"And just so we're clear," Risk cut in, "if any of you whisper a word of this to anyone at Spector, I'll know. And I'll personally tear the eyeballs from your sockets and shove you into hell where you can stumble around blindly for all eternity, trapped in darkness and fire."

Crow sighed and shook his head. "Too harsh," he mumbled.

"Eh, I think it was a good touch," Tomb shrugged.

The hybrids looked like they were ready to pee in their Spector-issued pants.

"Okay," I said, clapping my hands once to break up the tension. "On that happy note, who'd like to join us?"

Oddly enough, all of them did.

"YOU DON'T NEED to rehearse, Cheryl," I groaned out for what must have been the thousandth time.

She ran a hand through her blonde bob in annoyance. "Look, you asked me to put on this concert, Motley. You can't just expect me to sing without any sort of preparation or warm up. I'm not fucking Beyoncé, okay?"

"It's not a concert. It's not even a middle school talent show!" I yelled back. "All I need is for you to scream and knock out as many guards as you can while we stand behind Johnny's force field bubble."

Johnny was a necromancer with quite the handy skill. It wasn't overly impressive, but he could create force fields that blocked light and sound. He had a silencing demon, giving him the ability to trap his prey in a secluded, dark bubble, and block all sound from the outside until his prey went insane. It couldn't stop bullets or knives, but he could stop Cheryl's screeches. Though I wasn't sure if I preferred insanity to her singing.

Cheryl huffed and scowled, and I stopped myself from snapping. She was an integral part of our plan, but if she asked Risk for one more sequined dress, I was going to lose my shit.

We had a plan. Everyone had a purpose and a part to play. It was shaky and probably wouldn't work, but we'd at least slow Spector down until Stiles could get the word out.

"Little Spider, come here," Crow called over his shoulder.

He was standing off to the side with my mates, all three of them huddled over something. I slowly sauntered toward them, dodging fireballs and acid mucus from the training hybrids. It was fucking mayhem in here.

"What's going on?" I asked while peering over their shoulders. Russell happily flapped around above me.

"We're thinking about building a house in the Between. Just in case we need to hide out for a while after this. But Tomb here seems to think you need some goddamn gothic cathedral."

"It's timeless architecture, Crow," my gargoyle frowned. The two of them stared each other down for a moment, making me bloom with amusement.

"I like more modern buildings, myself. Sleek lines, an infinity pool, that sort of thing," Risk interrupted with a wink.

Crow wrinkled his nose. "What's wrong with something traditional? Why can't we have a simple A-frame with a wrap-around porch? And a kitchen, we need a big kitchen, of course."

I watched them argue for a moment and let out a shaky sigh. If I were being honest, I didn't think we'd get the chance to come back here. I didn't want to get my hopes up with a house if we didn't make it out of Spector alive. But I'd appease them. If they wanted to pretend that we could live happily ever after in the Between, I'd play along.

"I always wanted a big shower," I mused.

"How big?" Tomb asked curiously.

I shrugged. "I don't know. I've just always had tiny showers."

"Would you like a shower big enough for company, Wicked Love?" Risk asked teasingly, dark eyes glittering.

Butterflies danced in my stomach at the suggestive look he was giving me, and I felt a blush appear on my cheeks when I remembered the sexy shower times I'd spent first with Crow and then all three of them.

"Maybe," I hedged.

"She does," Crow said, his violet eyes trailing over my body as if he could see right through my clothes. "Her moans echo beautifully in the shower."

"I do like seeing her skin flushed and dripping wet," Tomb added as he drew a hand over his jaw.

Fire sparked to life in my core. I loved this. The normalcy of sexual banter. Of sexy flirtation. Of thinking that we were actually going to be able to enjoy a shower together and live safely away from Spector. They were distracting me from the danger and my grief, and I loved them for it.

"If our mate wants a big shower, then that's what she'll get," Risk said with a decisive nod.

"A big bed too," I put in. "You guys take up too much room."

Crow and Risk chuckled, but Tomb shook his head. "I like you sleeping on top of us."

I jabbed him playfully in his hard, muscular chest. "Well, you're terrible pillows. You especially because you actually turn into solid stone sometimes in your sleep."

He captured my hand and placed a kiss on the inside of my wrist. The sweetness of the gesture made me sigh in contentment. "I like feeling your body on mine. Hearing your breaths. Smelling your skin," he murmured.

"Grinding your dick into her ass," Risk supplied, making me choke out a laugh.

Tomb didn't miss a beat. "Yeah, that too."

I smiled, shaking my head. "You guys are insatiable."

Crow leaned forward and nipped at my lip, sucking it in his mouth for a moment. "You like it."

I did. I really, really did.

"I—"

A horrible noise sprung through the air, and I cringed. I swear to gods, Cheryl was going to be the death of me. I turned so I could find her and tell her to shut the hell up, but Risk grabbed my arm and placed his mouth against my ear. "It's not the siren. It's the Between. It's grown too unstable from so many of us in here. I need to get everyone out."

I nodded, and just as he pulled away, the whole place began to shake slightly, a bare tremor that moved with subtle vibrations beneath our feet.

Risk went to grab me, but I stepped away. "No, everyone else first."

He scowled. "Absolutely not."

"You have to!" I argued. "We're leading them, Risk. How do you think it would look if you took me out of here first?" I challenged. "Besides, it's the right thing to do. And I'd just be worried that everyone didn't get out. Go. Just hurry."

I pushed him away slightly, and he clenched his jaw, clearly pissed. He cast a look to Tomb and Crow. "Watch her. And don't let anyone leave this spot. I haven't formed anything else besides this space in the Between. If anyone panics and tries to run, they could get lost in the unformed abyss, and I won't be able to bring them out."

"Don't let anyone sprint into the abyss. Got it," Crow said.

"Hurry," I told Risk again.

With a terse nod, he turned and dashed away, grabbing the first group of hybrids he approached before disappearing in a swathe of smoke as he transported them out.

I rushed over to the rest of the cowering hybrids and found them looking at Cheryl accusingly. "It's not me! I don't sound *that* bad," she huffed, crossing her arms in front of her chest.

Everyone looked at her dubiously.

"Who's gonna tell her?" Tara asked with a smirk.

"Okay, everyone," I cut in before Cheryl could really lose her shit, and then we'd *never* hear the end of it. "I need you all to just stay right here," I said, while Tomb and Crow walked around the outskirts, directing everyone closer together.

Risk popped up, gave me another glare, and then stalked toward another group. He barked directions at them until their hands were linked, and then he disappeared with them.

"What's going on? And why is this place shaking?" someone asked.

"We have to get you out now. We stayed as long as we could, but the Between is too temperamental to hold so many of us. Risk is bringing us back to Spector."

My demon reappeared again and took more hybrids out.

The vibrations steadily grew stronger, and the awful noise in the air became louder. I gave a worried look to Crow and Tomb. Risk transported in and started taking larger groups, but by the seventh time, I saw that it was taking its toll on him. His suit jacket was long gone, his shirt disheveled, and sweat coated his handsome face.

When there were only a dozen hybrids left, the ground—for lack of a better word—was shaking so hard that it tossed us all on our asses. It felt like an earthquake that was gearing up to rip the space apart. And the sound...I realized belatedly that it resembled something ripping apart. Like the fabric of existence was tearing in two.

Risk appeared just as colorless pieces of the Between began crumbling down around us. Hybrids screamed, and one girl tried to run off, but Crow exploded into action, sending his birds to surround her and cut her off, herding her back to us.

"Stay calm!" I yelled, but they couldn't hear me over the sound.

Risk took one look at the pieces falling around us and grabbed hold of me. "No, Risk, not y—"

But my words were torn from my throat and my body was squeezed through time. One second I was standing in the shaking space as the Between collapsed around me, and the next, I was back in Risk's bedroom alone.

"No!" I yelled at the empty room.

But no one heard me.

Seconds passed. Then minutes. I was biting at my nails, pacing around the room, tearing at my hair. What if it totally caved in and the bubble of the Between burst from existence? Would they all be stuck in the abyss forever? What if—

Risk suddenly popped into the room with Tomb and Crow in tow.

Relief washed over me for a split second before anger overruled it. I stalked over to him. "You son of a bitch! How dare you? I told you to take me last! The other hybrids—"

He grabbed me roughly by the arms. "I don't give a *fuck* about the other hybrids," he growled, his face so full of fury that my voice cut out. "*You* are my mate. I already left you behind in danger once. I was not going to fail you again. So go ahead and be fucking pissed, Motley. I don't give a shit. That place was minutes from falling apart."

My eyes widened. "The others?"

"I got them out," he said through gritted teeth. "But it was close. Too fucking close."

I let out a shaky breath, but it seemed Risk wasn't done. "Don't ask me to do that *ever* again," he ordered, his tone low and chilling. "I won't fucking put you last, and I won't let you be in danger."

Defiance warred in me, but Crow cut in. "Little Spider, he's right," he said gently. "You're our mate. Our priority is always going to be keeping you safe."

"It would go against the bond otherwise," Tomb added.

My anger deflated out of me at their words, and my eyes softened. "I'm sorry," I said quietly. "I was just trying to do the right thing."

Risk sighed and tugged me forward to press his forehead against mine. "I was fucking terrified that I'd try to transport back and it would be gone. That *you* would be gone."

"I'm sorry," I said again, realizing that his own anger stemmed from fear of losing me. It stunned me how intensely he worried for me—how connected we were.

Risk placed a short, heated kiss against my lips before pulling away again. "Good. Because I finally found it," he said.

"Found what?"

He looked me steadily in the eye. "The one thing I'm not willing to risk."

Chapter 28

"AGAIN," the trainer spat at me.

Since my spider's murderous spree, the trainers had been doubling down on me, using even more aggression in an attempt to get my demon to manifest again. But no matter what they did, she stayed happily burrowed inside, while I gritted my teeth and took whatever they threw at me. I was biding my time.

Half of the hybrids were in the training room with me, while the other half were either in the cafeteria or locked up in their cells, waiting for our signal.

We were all just waiting, casually going through the motions of Spector's demands while watching and waiting anxiously. Risk found out that the ritual was going down tonight. He was gone, trying to find info on where the ritual was going to be held, while also trying to find out where Stiles was.

I was worried that something had happened to my brother—on a personal level *and* a strategic one. We needed the entire supernatural community to see what Spector was doing. We wanted to broadcast the madness to the masses.

And even though Stiles and I had never really had a relationship before, things had changed between us. I still thought he was an entitled ass, but he was trying to do the right thing, so we were allies in this.

When a blast of freezing water whizzed by my head, I lazily shot my webs out at the trainer who'd tossed it at me. But I wasn't really putting any effort in my moves. I wanted to conserve energy. We were all just waiting on the signal—waiting for battle, and I had to be ready.

We were heavily guarded today. They wanted to protect their investments, no doubt, and had been steadily bringing in more and more reinforcements as the day went on.

"You're not even trying," the trainer snapped at me.

Since Oz's death, Dave had taken over my training. The water elemental was just as insane as his predecessor and twice as careless. I didn't know if he had a death wish or if he genuinely didn't fear me—though he should.

He was testing my boundaries, trying to crack open my mind and entice my demon out. But my spider was resilient, refusing to surface until the time was right. Dave could fucking try whatever he wanted. I wasn't going to break. When he whipped water at my feet to make me fall on my ass, I took it. When he shot frozen bits of it at my face to cut into my skin, I put up the thin webs to block most of them. He came at me again and again and again, and I took it all without a word. It was pissing him off.

He looked me up and down and stalked closer, his eyes hungry with seedy intent. Nearby, I saw Tomb bristle at the way Dave assessed me. They'd kept Tomb and Crow separated from me, but I tossed my mate a brief look, letting him know I had it under control. Tomb wouldn't be much help if he was in the tank during our attack. Besides, I wasn't afraid. I didn't fear much of anything these days. By taking my aunt from me, they didn't bring me to heel like they'd hoped. If anything, they strengthened my resolve.

Dave began circling me like a predator. "Belvini wants your spider to come out. He wants to show it to the military, perhaps sell your services to the highest bidder. There's a bonus awarded to the trainer that can make it happen," he told me, scratching at the bushy blond beard at his chin.

That news had me curling my hands into fists, but I kept my face impassive. "Oh, yeah? How predictable," I said in a bored tone.

"You won't be such a cocky bitch when you get sold off like cattle. I heard the people looking to buy you want to use you for *all kinds* of things," he said with a lascivious sneer.

Somewhere flying above me, I heard a crow make a displeased noise.

"You know what I did to my last trainer that pissed me off, right?" I asked pointedly. "If I were you, I'd back the fuck up and keep shooting your pathetic little rain drops at me as we train."

His fair face mottled with anger.

"If you had any sense of self preservation, you wouldn't taunt me or my spider."

The other hybrids had stopped training to watch. We were already anxious as we waited for a signal—any signal—from Risk. And that apprehension was making us all a bit jumpy. But for once in my life, I felt like my peers had my back. Instead of looking at me like they were glad it was me and not them, or watching me be bullied and want to join in, they looked pissed on my behalf. A sense of loyalty washed over me.

We were in this together.

"Your spider broke out when your aunt died, right?" Dave callously asked, like we were discussing the weather over breakfast, or stock patterns in the human world. Not like

Spector had taken my beating heart out of my chest and stomped on it. "I heard it was a brutal murder. Took her head off with their bare hands. Must have been a lot of blood."

I lifted my hand up and inspected my fist, trying my best to keep my emotions under control, even though my spider was itching to play, itching to torment. "I'd be happy to demonstrate it on you," I said in a falsely polite voice. Cheryl had been filing her nails in the corner all morning, but I saw her walking closer to me out of my peripheral. I gave a subtle shake of my head, warning her away. I could handle this.

"That won't be necessary," he began. "I watched the footage. Over and over *and over*," Dave replied while stalking closer to me. My spider rose even further to the surface, making my hourglass mark burn with vengeance. "So maybe we just need to kill someone you care about, hmm? Your mates are indestructible, but I'm sure we could find someone else. Or maybe torturing your mates is enough?" He was still circling me, still stalking in that predatory way all Spector idiots did. "You were already on edge when Oz did it. I bet a few more minutes of torturing them, and you would have gone full spider."

The guards that lined the walls were chuckling amongst themselves, as if the idea of burning people alive was amusing to them.

Soon. Soon they'd all pay.

My eyes flickered to the door once more. *Where was Risk? Where was Stiles?*

"I can see her, you know," Dave whispered in my ear. He was too close now. His chest was touching my arm, his body flush against mine. His whiskey breath coated my skin with its fumes. "I can see your demon wants to come out to play. She's just itching to feed from me," he said suggestively low, and when I felt his erection grind into my hip, my fangs grew and I envisioned ripping out his throat.

"I wouldn't feed from you if you were the last cock on the planet," I gritted before spitting on the floor to accentuate my point.

Dave didn't seem fussed by my comment; he simply tipped his head back and chuckled, making the other guards laugh too. Once his amusement tapered off, his green eyes bore into mine, an intimidating stare down that made me want to shove my thumbs into his eye sockets and make those leering organs *bleed*.

"I can't *wait* to break you. You know what happens to spiders in my training room, Black Widow?" he asked while grabbing my wrist and spinning me around, crashing me to his chest. His greasy lips found purchase on the ridge of my ear. "They get squished under my boot."

I felt frozen with anger, ready to snap, but then the training room door opened.

Stiles.

My breath puffed out in relief, and my focus was redirected. Stiles gave me a single nod.

My eyes found Dave again, and I let out a slow grin. "You know what happens to flies that pester the spider, Dave?" I asked while taking a step back. "They get eaten."

I whipped a web out and wrapped it around his throat before the last syllable even left my lips. My spider wanted to draw out his death, punish him for his words, but I knew we didn't have time. I squeezed swiftly, removing his head in one simple move that had blood splattering across my cheeks, and his head rolling on the hard tile.

Everyone was spurred into action. Guards lifted their weapons. "Now!" I screamed.

All of the vampires flashed our fellow hybrids into the center of the room. Johnny was there first, holding up his hands and creating his sensory bubble for us to stay in. I flashed inside of it with the others, standing shoulder-to-shoulder with the other elemental hybrids like we planned. Gunshots were ringing out, and alarms were going off, but we ignored it all. As one, we started making a shield of webs, rocks, vines, ice, and fire. It might not be enough to keep all the bullets from hitting us, but it would help buy us time. Johnny's hands shook as the bubble built up around us slowly, dropping down over our heads in an iridescent dome.

In another blink, Cheryl flashed over, standing right outside our line. "How much longer?" she yelled, ducking down in a squat as another barrage of bullets came our way.

"Sixty seconds," Johnny shouted back, shaking from exertion as he struggled to drop the bubble around us completely.

We were running out of time. Our layers of defense were being littered with bullets, and then waves of offensive power were being thrown at us, trying to break down the circular wall we'd surrounded ourselves in. But the guards were strong, and more reinforcements were coming.

"Johnny!" I shouted, feeling as my webs were blasted apart and smoke erupted in the air.

"Almost...there..." Sweat dripped down his face as he struggled to complete it. It was to our torsos now, covering all hundred or so of us.

Hurry, hurry, hurry, I silently pleaded.

Cheryl screamed when a ball of ice tore through our wall, hitting her squarely in the arm like a massive frozen bullet.

"Fuck."

We couldn't let her get hurt. I rushed forward, my body passing through the dropping bubble, and I hauled her to her feet, holding up her weight. I sent webs to wrap around her wound and staunch the bleeding.

Our walls were breaking down. The elemental hybrids couldn't keep up with the onslaught, and my webs were frantically trying to shield Cheryl.

"Now, Johnny!" I screamed. We were surrounded. I could

see hundreds of Spector guards on the other side. Tomb was fighting them off, his gargoyle form blasting through them, but he was going to be overtaken. Hundreds of crows were attacking too, but elementals were holding them at bay.

Johnny let out a frustrated scream, and then *finally*, the bubble dropped, encasing the others.

"Now, Cheryl!"

She opened her mouth and let it all out. Screeching like a nineties cover band, she shook the room with her rattling song. Her siren call blasted the room with wails and vibrato, making the guards drop like flies. But I couldn't even enjoy the victory, because my own ears burned from the assault. Blood dripped down my neck, and I quickly spun webs to shove them in my ears, lightly blocking the sound.

I forced a hole in part of my web wall and staggered over to Tomb and Crow. They were both writhing on the floor, crying out in agony alongside the Spector guards. I created the same ear plugs for both of them, but it was no use. The screeches were too much. I was getting weak too. My head felt like it was going to explode, like a baseball bat striking glass until it shattered.

We just had to outlast the guards for a minute. Just one more minute.

One by one, the guards stopped moving. One by one, power petered out. Tomb's stone body turned to flesh. Crow's birds dropped from the air, landing on the concrete with a crack. It was a never-ending torturous song, but I didn't want Cheryl to stop until the room was dead.

My sanity split in half.

My spider shriveled up and begged for relief.

My mates flickered in and out of awareness until finally they died.

At least they wouldn't suffer anymore.

Seconds felt like an eternity. I couldn't die, not yet.

Breaking, cracking, shattering, blistering.

Agony. Pure agony.

My mind was a severed jumble of thoughts. Short hisses of reality and fizzing neurons shriveling up and expanding into more budding torment.

Then finally, Cheryl stopped, relieving me from the devastating pain in my skull.

"That was fun, can I sing again?" Cheryl's voice broke out as she walked over to me.

I was still reverberating with pain, my eyes filled with bloodied tears that echoed her torture. With a moan, I crawled over to my mates to check them over. Cold bodies greeted me, but I stared at the marks on their necks, waiting for them to reanimate.

"Come on, guys," I pleaded.

Crow's finger twitched. Tomb let out a muffled groan. Their lungs expanded with a gasp, and I finally allowed myself to breathe a sigh of relief.

"Fucking hell, Cheryl," Crow said while rolling over on his stomach and curling up. "Your voice was like a hacksaw to my brain."

"I know, right? I'm a pretty powerful demon, huh?" she preened while brushing her hands together with a satisfied smirk.

We looked around the room, searching for even the slightest movement. I stared at the broad chests of some of the Spector guards. I sniffed the rancid blood in the air, breathed in the tantric smell of death.

No one survived.

So how the hell did I?

The black bubble Johnny erected popped, and out spilled the other hybrids. Some of them were trembling, some of them were injured from the fight. "We did it!" one of them yelled while fist pumping the air. Others cheered, but I knew this was just one battle in the war.

"Uh, *I* did it. You all just took a cozy break in Johnny's black hole," Cheryl scoffed.

Crow snickered inappropriately. "You familiar with Johnny's black hole?" he muttered with a smirk. I elbowed him lightly, and he gave me a contrite shrug.

Cheryl went on, totally oblivious. "Also, do any of you assholes have a healing power? My arm is killing me."

"Are you okay, baby?" Stiles asked while hurrying toward her. He had been in Johnny's bubble during the singing. My brother inspected her arm for a moment, noting the webs I'd wrapped tightly around her to stop the bleeding. "I hate that you got hurt."

"I'm fine," she assured him. "But a kiss would make it better."

Her eyelashes fluttered flirtatiously as he wrapped her up in a warm hug. Stiles whispered, "You did amazing," before kissing her passionately on the lips. She squealed against him for a moment, and when they pulled apart, she stared at him in wonder.

"The whole world got to hear your performance," Stiles said with a sly smile.

"What do you mean?" I asked as Crow and Tomb got up to stand by my side.

"I was finally able to hack their security feeds. Every supe in America just watched what happened. The ritual feeds are being leaked, too. Soon everyone will know what's happening here."

Excited, I wrapped my brother in a hug. "You did it."

A crackle from the speakers overhead drew our attention away from the short-lived celebration. It was a fuzzy sound that lacked depth. A dead, monotoned song suddenly cut through their cheers, chilling me to the bone.

Belvini.

His voice was in taunting amusement as he spoke in echoing sing-song over the speakers.

The itsy bitsy spider
Went up the water spout.
Down came the rain and
Washed the spider out.

"It's a beautiful day for an exorcism, don't you think, Black Widow?" he finished.

Goosebumps littered my arms at his chilling voice. Foreboding crashed over me. "Where's Risk?" He should've been here by now.

Tomb and Crow shook their heads, their worried expressions matching my own.

"What's that?" the shifter Tara asked from behind me. She lifted her nose and sniffed, and that's when I saw the orange smoke filtering through the air vents. I snapped my eyes to the door, wincing when the emergency locks closed us in. We'd anticipated this, but we were hoping to be out of here before Belvini realized what had happened.

Some of the hybrids started tossing powers at the door, but it was no use.

"Shit," I hissed. "Don't breathe it!" I shouted at everyone. "It's gonna knock us out!"

Looks of panic rippled over the hybrids.

"I can get them out of here," Stiles said, coming up to my side.

"How?" Everyone was holding their hands or arms over their faces, trying to block out the poison filtering in.

Stiles wriggled his hands. "My demon feeds off electricity. If I don't control it, I can electrocute people with a single touch," he said, and my mind flashed back to the Thibault ritual, when he'd sent Crow's birds to the floor in lifeless heaps. "Maybe it's not too impressive to my father, but I've also learned how to manipulate the signals," he said with grim satisfaction.

"That's how you're sending everything to a live feed," I breathed, the pieces falling together.

He nodded. "I can get the doors opened to get us out too. I've been mapping the place, learning how to unlock their electronic doors. I can do it," he said decisively.

Someone gasped behind me, and the first hybrids dropped. We were out of time.

"Go!" I urged.

"Come with us," he urged.

I shook my head. "I'm not leaving Risk behind. Go," I said.

Stiles hesitated, but Cheryl staggered on her feet beside him, and he swooped her up in his arms.

"Now, Stiles!" I urged, shoving him away.

He turned to the others. "Hybrids, follow me, and let's get the fuck out of here!"

"I'm staying to fight," Tara said, her face determined.

"Help Stiles fight off the guards you meet along the way," I told her, my voice muffled from the sleeve I held against my mouth. She looked like she wanted to argue, but I shook my head. "I have to get my mate. I need you and Stiles to get the hybrids out. Please."

After another moment, she nodded tersely. "Fine."

"Hybrids, hurry your asses!" she shouted before she and another male picked up one of the passed out hybrids on the floor and took off.

The air was slowly turning orange from the fumes, and my head was growing dizzy. Tomb and Crow were at my side in a moment, as the rest of the hybrids rushed after Stiles, sprinting toward the exit.

"What's the plan, Wid?" Tomb asked anxiously.

More and more orange fumes engulfed us. The massive

size of the room was our only saving grace, but soon, the toxic air would be all over us. More hybrids were dropping like flies, while others struggled to drag them out.

Black dots littered my vision. "We gotta get to Risk."

Birds started dropping all around us, and my eyes flew to my other mate. "Crow!"

His eyes rolled to the back of his head, and he fell, Tomb catching him and hoisting him over his stone shoulder before he could hit the ground.

"Come on!"

We ran as fast as we could for the door, just as the last of the hybrids made it out.

My steps faltered when were five feet away, the black dots of my vision blocking out everything else. "Tomb," I croaked, but I stumbled to the ground and couldn't get back up again.

Chapter 29

I WOKE up in a dark auditorium of some sort, strapped to a wooden board at my back and dangling above the ground. I had to blink away the exhaustion and force myself to stay alert. My eyes were still coated with burning, toxic sleep.

"Hello, Black Widow," Collector said in a deep voice that was laced with cynicism. He was shadowed in a red glow, standing off to the side with a manic grin.

I struggled against my restraints, bucking my body in short bursts of weakness, but it wouldn't budge. "Stay calm, Wid," a gravelly voice said to my left. My eyes widened when I slowly twisted my neck as far as the restraints would allow. Beside me was Tomb shackled with steel chains, his hands forced into a prayer pose at his broad, chiseled chest.

"Tomb?" I whimpered. "Are you okay?"

"Yeah, Wid. I'm okay," he replied, but I knew he was lying.

I swiveled my head again, this time turning my attention to my right. Crow was still passed out from the sleep toxins Spector had baptized us in at the training room. My mate's head hung loosely, like his neck had been snapped in half. Drips of sleepy drool coated his lips as he lightly snored.

"Crow?" I called out. "Crow, wake up!"

He still didn't move. My heart began to race. Why were we here? What was happening?

"Black Widow," Collector began, drawing my attention back to him. "You've been nothing but trouble since the moment you arrived here. I can appreciate your defiance. Rebellion is in a demon's nature, after all." Collector talked down to me with cocky superiority, all while walking toward a switch on the wall. "But rebellion has consequences, Black Widow." With a simple flick of his wrist and a turn of the switch, a spotlight kicked on, drowning the center of the room in harsh, unforgiving light. I gasped.

Risk was directly under the bright beam. He looked almost angelic, chained to the center of the floor with a halo of glowing light covering his sweaty skin. He was in his dress pants and white dress shirt, but they were disheveled and appeared singed in some places with defined wrinkles in the fabric, which was off for his normally polished appearance. He was gagged with something that was tied around his head and shoved between his teeth, but muffled groans still rumbled from his chest.

"Risk?" I choked out, barely believing the scene before me.

My eyes took everything in with caution, not really sure I was ready to see more. I quickly realized that he was in the center of a demon ritual circle drawn with white chalk on the floor. Looking down, I then realized those same circles were drawn below me, Tomb, and Crow as well.

Panicked, I tried to bring my webs out to attack and save my mates, but nothing happened. There was no power at the answering end of my desperate call for protection. I could feel my spider, but it was like she was bound as much as I was, unable to come out from an invisible cage within myself. Whatever these demon circles were, they were keeping my spider locked up, and I couldn't access her powers.

What the fuck was happening?

Squeezing more heavy exhaustion from my eyes, I looked around the room and saw supes sitting in chairs on the other side of Risk. They were dressed nicely and staring in rapt attention at Collector, but their features were shadowed by the harsh spotlight on Risk, making it impossible to recognize anyone. Was my father there? Had Stiles gotten out?

"Ladies and gentlemen, I have a wonderful opportunity for you all this evening," Belvini began, addressing the onlooking crowd while looking totally cool and collected in his black suit and red tie. He would've been handsome if it weren't for the sneering set of his mouth and greedy glitter in his eyes. "You've all signed up for a normal possession, but I wanted to show you another service that Spector offers."

"Let us go!" I screamed as loud as I could. My hoarse voice scratched and clawed against my vocal cords as I struggled against the bindings. Tomb's head tipped up, and his dark eyes locked on me, his own muscles bulging against his restraints. No matter how hard he tried, he couldn't turn to stone, and he couldn't break free.

"Someone silence her, please," Collector said evenly, sounding bored at my outburst. "Sometimes you have to muzzle the dogs," he joked to the audience, making several of the patrons chuckle.

A hooded man carrying a large gun stalked over to me. I struggled and screamed, waking Crow up in the process as leather was shoved between my teeth, and the strap was secured tightly at the back of my head. Crow started struggling too, but he couldn't even call out a single bird to help us.

"As I was saying," he went on, "we've taken your

comments about our procedures seriously here at Spector. Many of you have expressed concerns about the randomness of our possessions, so our talented team of experts has perfected exorcisms so that we can transfer a demon from one supe to another."

My eyes widened. Dread pooled in my gut. *No. No. No.*

I fought against my chains, shaking the metal with loud rage as I moaned against my gag. Drool collected in my mouth against the leather strap that my vampire fangs were trying to rip apart. Sweat made my red hair cling to my salty skin. People watched me with wary curiosity, like I was a feral beast they wanted to look at from a safe distance away.

"As a new service, Spector has started a catalogue of our current hybrids that will soon be made available to you. If you find a demon that you desire for yourself, we will hold an auction. The highest bidder will then be possessed by the demon of your choosing. No more risk. No random, unplanned demon to merge with. With this service, you'll know exactly what you're getting. You'll have total control."

Murmured whispers of excitement broke out through the crowd, but my own body trembled, and tears pricked my eyes. A totally new kind of fear struck me. Would they take my spider?

I pondered over the implications of Spector's new *program* and then felt an immediate sense of guilt. In the beginning, I would've *wanted* an exorcism. When I first arrived at Spector, I'd hated my demon, resented her for what she turned me into and the people she made me kill. But things had changed. She brought me my mates, she defended me, and now, she *was* me. I'd accepted her fully, and there was no way in hell that I would let anyone take her away. And if they tried to exorcise our mates too, I'd kill them all.

But I needed help. I couldn't reach my spider. Even my vampiric strength wasn't working right. I couldn't break free of the chains no matter what I did. I didn't know how much time had passed since I'd gone unconscious either. Had Stiles gotten the hybrids out? Was this being broadcasted now?

Collector went on with his speech. "Many of you have expressed interest in Black Widow. Due to recent developments, Spector believes she would be far more valuable if she were in a more viable host, since the one she's currently inhabiting is not...agreeable to Spector's vision. As you can see, she's a bit rabid."

Everyone chuckled at my expense again, as if I was melodramatic and ridiculous. I bared my fangs at them as the last of the leather strap fell from my mouth in tatters, letting them see just how feral I was.

Of course Collector would want to capitalize on my spider's strength and cunning. But she wasn't just some sex-crazed killer. I didn't want to imagine her being forced to possess someone else or being used to kill. Collector wanted to weaponize Black Widow, but she was so much more than that. She was a protector, a lover. She defended fiercely and loved her mates with everything she had. And my spider was an extension of me. If they took her from me now...it would be like severing my soul in half. I could feel her in every particle of my being. We'd merged in every sense of the word, and I needed her.

"We want to assure you that this ritual has the same success rate as our other model, and it is perfectly safe," Collector was saying.

Safe? He was lying through his teeth. Nothing about this was safe.

"In fact, we've decided to perform yet another demonstration. Miss Cainson, if you would?"

My head turned in the direction he indicated, and I watched as Risk's ex-lover stood up from her seat and walked forward. Her eyes were bright, and her steps were light, despite her large, round belly. "It's so safe that, today, we will be performing the ritual on councilwoman Cainson, who just so happens to be pregnant."

No. What if this hurt Risk's child?

My eyes burned as fear and disgust rolled around in my gut. How could they do this? How could they perform such a dangerous ritual when there was a baby involved? Risk's eyes were locked on the woman, his gaze so cold and soulless that it gave me the chills. I could feel his fury like it was a palpable thing.

Ignoring Risk completely, Miss Cainson went up beside Collector at the podium and smiled at everyone, like she was a politician's wife, winning votes with lies and a flirtatious grin. On the ground, Risk pulled and fought against his restraints. Smoke and ash burned through the chains, making them burn red, but they didn't break. The circle was restraining his powers too.

"We will now be exorcising some of the high level demon's essence and putting it into Miss Cainson," Collector explained. Risk looked like he wanted to rip him apart.

The hooded man came forward again, this time walking into Risk's circle. With deft movements, he ran a blade against Risk's forearm. His blood spilled onto the floor in an erratic spray, but my demon didn't even flinch. His eyes held the fires of hell as he watched Collector. There was no doubt in my mind that if Risk could get free, he would annihilate the entire room in a heartbeat.

Collector cleared his throat, keeping his eyes averted from the fuming demon. "Have a seat, darling," he said to Miss Cainson, indicating a cushioned chair just on the edge of Risk's demon circle. The woman stepped inside and sat down primly, folding her hands in her lap patiently like she was in a doctor's office waiting for her name to be called.

"You've all signed the disclosure agreements that prohibit you from speaking about Spector's rituals and functions, but I think you'll understand the importance of our discretion once you see this. After all, this kind of power is not for the masses. This is for you. The *elite*," Collector said, his pompous ass stroking the egos in the room. "The elite that will now have the opportunity to become more powerful than ever. We can take new territories, win wars, rise above humans or even our fellow supes. With this, we will attain a new level of influence."

His words were like a drug to the room, making council members and prominent supes nod their heads with new urgency, the promise of power sinking into their pores and getting them high off the rush. They would use these demons so that they could hold the rest of the supernatural and human communities under their thumbs. It was a grim future of disputes and wars and maybe even genocide.

"Let's begin."

Those two words were like a gavel striking down, calling forth dread to rule my body.

"Stay in your seats, please," Collector said. "And be advised, this will be...violent."

Eerie chants began to sound in the room as a group of twelve shadowed figures surrounded Risk's circle. I watched helplessly as he struggled against the bindings once more, but the strange chanting grew louder, and the chalked demon circle began to sizzle and spit with acrid smoke. I half expected the world to open up and for evil to spill through the floorboards, coating us all in vengeful hellfire.

Risk's body began to jerk unnaturally. The haunting chanting drowned out all other sounds. I couldn't even hear my own breath. My demon let out a raspy, agonized scream that seemed to shoot straight to my heart. Tears dripped out of my eyes as his body was pulled taut against the chains, as if an invisible force was trying to yank him in all different directions at once.

"Stop, stop, stop, STOP!" I screamed, but no one listened. No one could even hear me over the chants or the unnatural wind that had come up or the smoke that still crackled or the blistering yells that were now tearing from Risk's throat in endless streams. My throat was raw. My soul was chained. My heart thudded with pain for my mate.

The whole room started to shake. Sharp, piercing cries littered the audience, but no one dared move. They were like statues in their seats, looking on with wide eyes as hell rose up to meet them.

Miss Cainson seemed wary, but her mask of confidence was still capriciously fixed on her face. The only slip in her façade was the way her bony fingers gripped the armrests.

Then all hell broke loose.

Literally.

A surge of power unlike anything I'd ever felt before came up from the ground. My face was blasted with sweltering heat as unnaturally red flames erupted along the lines of the circle surrounding Risk and Miss Cainson. They were five feet tall, ten, twenty, fifty. They licked the ceiling in the auditorium, running into some sort of invisible barrier that the elementals must have put up. I searched the dancing, roaring flames with intensity, seeking between the gaps in the menacing fire for glimpses of my mate, but I could barely see him.

Thick black smoke clogged the room, but it wasn't natural smoke. This smoke moved with faces of the damned, skeletal beings with eyeless sockets and mouths open in a scream. It was like the ground birthed unnatural beings. Neither dead nor demon, supe nor human. These were otherworldly, terrifying souls scraping the corners of existence.

And then Risk's body began to glow.

Like metal being heated over a fire, his skin lit up in reds and oranges that gave off even more light than the fiery flames. And then his demon's essence started to yank out of his body.

Collector was right. It *was* violent.

His body thrashed against the chains as an incorporeal form began to pour from Risk's chest and race around the barrier of the ritual circle. It hissed against the flames, as if it was pissed off to be contained. But then it saw its intended target.

Miss Cainson screamed shrilly as Risk's demonic essence raced toward her body and started pouring into her mouth. Her head tipped back, and the veins in her neck throbbed as her body was consumed. My eyes stayed on her stomach as I prayed Risk's child would be okay.

But then...it just *stopped*.

Everything froze for a single second.

The chanting, the screams, the ghoulish smoke, the licking red flames. The essence pulling out of Risk and pushing into Miss Cainson...it all got suspended in time. It couldn't have been more than a few seconds, but a terrorizing eternity passed between us.

And then, it was like there was a *snap*. A vacuum suddenly started pulling in every single source of power in the room. *Everything* rushed at Miss Cainson in a violent sweep, and I knew something had gone terribly wrong.

Risk's essence was no longer being forced into her mouth. Instead, it was like she was sucking it in. The essence, the fire, the smoke, even the elemental's barrier. It all started pulling to her like a magnet, while black, depthless smoke billowed around her, like she was a black hole sucking everything in and devouring it whole.

Collector shouted orders, sending a violent gust of his own demonic power straight at the demon ritual circle. The chanting stopped under his command, forcing the fires to recede in steady waves, like all oxygen had been starved from the burning hellfire and suffocated the evil ritual in steady waves. As soon as he broke the circle, the strange hold from Miss Cainson stopped, and Risk's essence cut away from her and flew back into Risk.

Risk slumped against the chair, and Miss Cainson fell onto the floor, both she and Risk unconscious.

"Risk!" I screamed, but he didn't rouse. "Risk! Wake up!" My words were a garbled mess. Cries and pleas shaken with terror. "Risk!" I yelled again, my voice a booming outcry that echoed against the stunned silence in the room.

"He'll be okay, Little Spider," Crow said, trying to comfort me.

"You're hurting yourself," Tomb pointed out, staring at my arms where I'd struggled so much against the chains that my skin had been scraped raw, and blood dribbled down like crimson tears.

"What the hell just happened, Belvini?" someone from the audience demanded, snagging my attention. I scanned the room and noticed that everyone watching looked obviously shaken.

Collector spouted off rushed instructions for the hooded figures, and they quickly picked up Miss Cainson and took her away as he addressed the crowd. "It seems that Miss Cainson was unable to hold the demon's amount of power," he said, though his eyes shifted nervously.

A lie. He was lying. I knew that for a fact, but the truth wasn't as clear.

"Have no fear, she will be perfectly fine. We prepared for that scenario, however unlikely we thought it to be. We'd hoped because of her level of elemental power that she was strong enough, but it appears not."

He was blaming it on her now. His PC excuses were

almost laughable. *Something* had happened, that was certain, but he was lying about this and saving face by claiming she hadn't been strong enough.

"If this ritual didn't work, how do we know the other exorcisms will?" someone else in the audience demanded.

"People, people, calm down." My eyes tracked the familiar voice, and I recognized my father standing up from his seat, his expression smoothed to boost morale to the dwindling confidence of the crowd. "That was unfortunate, but it just shows you the level of preparedness Spector has. That was an attempted exorcism on a *high level* demon. No one else has ever been able to do that before. Councilwoman Cainson will be fine, and there's no harm done. But the other rituals will go off without a hitch, I can assure you. So long as you're strong enough and don't fight the merging, the demon will possess you without issue."

"How do we know that's true?" the person demanded.

They were losing the audience. Ripples of doubt and unease were taking over, and my father could sense it. "I'm sure President Belvini can put on another demonstration right now." He turned to Collector expectantly.

Collector's jaw ticked, but he forced an easygoing smile on his face. "Of course. Let me put your minds at ease," he said smoothly before gesturing to me. "The auction for the black widow demon starts now. Let's start the bidding."

Chapter 30

I NEVER MUCH thought about what I was worth.

As a poor kid growing up, worth was always determined for me. People would see me in thrift store clothing, living at my rural address and drinking stale human blood bags, and they'd put a label on me. Poor. Underprivileged. Inferior. Unimpressive. Unimportant.

If anyone would've asked to buy me then, I wonder if I could've even inspired two pennies to rub together.

It was strange to have an exact price put on my head simply because of the demon that was inhabiting my body. They were buying *her*, my spider, trying to take away the thing that had made me whole—the thing that had made my life have worth and value and purpose. Not because I was suddenly worth seven figures to these people, but because she was my soul's partner, and with her presence, I'd found myself.

Numbers were shouted with enthusiasm. People were clawing at the chance to claim power, bidding their fortunes like there was nothing to it.

"Sold! To Mrs. Glenda Wind, Councilman Wind's wife." Collector's voice boomed throughout the room.

There was murmuring, ranging from the disgruntled disappointment of those who didn't win the bidding war, to the enthusiastic talk about seeing her inhabiting the black widow demon.

I took in the shifter woman. She was ardent in desire, her wide eyes filled to the brim with the promise of taking what was mine.

Everything started happening so fast—too fast. I didn't even have time to process that these people were stealing my demon and, in addition, my mates.

I was terrified. Shaking so hard that the metal chains bound around my hanging body were echoing with morbid rattles around the room.

"Don't fucking touch her!" Crow yelled as five hooded figures came forward to stand around my own ritual circle.

Tomb was grunting and straining, his neck muscles popping as he tried with all his might to break free of his bindings. But it was no use. "Risk! Wake the fuck up!" he shouted hoarsely, but my demon was still passed out cold.

The figures started to chant.

"Oh gods," I whimpered, tears blurring my vision.

This was it.

They were going to take her from me.

"Please don't," I begged, my blue eyes pleading as I stared at Belvini. "Please don't do this. I need her, and she needs me."

He walked forward until the tips of his shiny dress shoes touched the outside of the chalked lines. "Begging now?" He tutted his tongue. "It's a bit late for that, Miss Coven. I'd hoped that your punishment with your aunt would force you to behave and submit, but you didn't. You brought this on yourself."

"She's *my* spider!"

He shook his head slowly, making his dark hair glint in the dim light. "No, Miss Coven. Spector gives, and we can take away," he said evenly. "As of this moment, you are no longer eligible for an internship. You don't deserve the demon we bestowed on you."

The chanting from the five started getting louder. Latin words long forgotten that I had no knowledge of sunk into my skull. It was a taunting sort of chant, coaxing out parts of my soul with devastating yanks. Belvini watched with morbid fascination as my body began to steam. Slowly, single rays of black light began to erupt out of my skin in dancing tendrils. Two beams on my right arm. Three on my left. One through my hand, and another at my chest. More and more and more, they shot out of me, like splinters of light trying to be plucked from my body.

And that's when the pain came.

It tore through me like an electric pulse. Like something in my soul had been electrocuted with a lightning bolt. Screams gutted my chest and lacerated my throat. My tongue burned with blood that filled my mouth as my fangs punched through my lip. My fingertips bulged, like webs were trying to come out but couldn't, the ends of them filling like helium in a balloon, the pressure so painful that bile rushed up my gut and spewed through my lips.

It hurt. Gods, everything fucking *hurt*.

"Let her go!" Crow sounded anguished, his supplication heart-wrenching to my ears. I didn't want him to see this. I didn't want any of my mates to see this.

Tears ran down my face like a dam breaking free. I was going to lose them. Spector was taking *everyone* that I cared about away from me. First my aunt. Now my spider. And once they did this, my mate bonds would sever. I would lose the connection to my men forever. I would have nothing. No one. Crushing sadness and agonizing loneliness spun out of me even as more beams of black light stabbed through my form.

My mind spun, my body trying to push me into unconsciousness so that I wouldn't have to feel such agony anymore. But I held on. I couldn't hide from my grief behind the strength of my spider like before. I was left empty and shaking, forced to fight for myself all alone.

"I'll fucking kill you for this," I heard Tomb say.

Collector chuckled. "You won't get the chance, Gargoyle. You're next."

No.

Another sob tried to pass through my lips, but it was cut off with a terrible scream. My body jerked forward, like someone was picking me up and trying to throw me across the room. The chains groaned and snapped as my body jerked free of the bindings, and I hung suspended in the air in paralyzing stillness.

And then there was fire. Not around me, but *inside* of me, and I heard my spider scream. The shocking sound lacked humanity. It was otherworldly and hellish. It was hisses and roars and clicking all rolled into one. My spider sounded feral and furious and made the hair on my skin stand up at attention.

Pain. We felt unbearable, scorching, tearing pain.

The chants pulled at her, like phantom hands from hell latching onto her body and ripping her away. We screamed together. We held on. We held on *so fucking hard*.

But the forces that pulled her were too strong. And at the middle where our souls had merged, we ripped apart.

I felt her yanked out of me like someone had stabbed my heart and ripped it from my chest. Hanging strings of bloodied webs were all that was left in the gaping hole where she once was.

The force that had held me was suddenly gone, and I slammed to the ground in a painful heap. With my cheek and chest plastered against the floor, I watched as my spider's demon form was dragged toward the awaiting woman who'd bought her. My spider hissed and clawed, her form only about three feet tall of writhing black light and smoke.

She fought against the pull toward her new host, and that fact alone made me both filled with pride and unfathomably sad. They were forcing this on her, but no matter how hard she tried to stop it, she couldn't.

Glenda Wind gasped, wide-eyed and fearful, and then my spider was forced down her throat.

The woman writhed and gurgled, her body being surrounded with the same black light that I'd had. The transition lasted seconds, yet it felt like hours.

And then...it was over.

The hooded people were done chanting. The light and smoke were gone. Glenda Wind had gone still, her breathing slow and even as she and my spider began to merge.

And I was empty.

A husk. A crumpled form on the ground with bile on my tongue, tears on my cheeks, and smoke in my nose. Everything was gone. *Everything*.

I didn't have the strength to move, but I knew my fingertips were barren of webs. My soul felt like it had been cleaved in half and then ripped into shreds. She was gone. The other half to my soul was just...*gone*. And my mate bonds, the strings that I hadn't even realized were tied to my heart...they'd all been severed.

I felt nothing. I was numb. Hollow. Utterly desolate.

"Motley? Motley, baby, are you okay? Talk to us," Crow pleaded, but I didn't have the strength.

When Glenda Wind woke up and the audience clapped, I heard nothing, saw nothing. When Belvini droned on about the next auction, I felt lost. He seemed giddy about the new bidding war beginning, but my mind couldn't even keep up. I felt like a ghost, haunted by my own loss.

"How do you feel, Glenda?" Councilman Wind asked.

The blonde shifter turned to her husband, getting up on shaky feet as Spector guards helped her. She touched the spot on her throat where a red hourglass now marked her. The spot on my own throat felt cold and wiped clean.

"I feel...strange, but..." the woman's voice trailed off.

"But what?" her shifter husband asked, crossing his bulky arms in front of him.

"But *strong*," she said with a thrill in her voice, her eyes glittering.

Without warning, she lifted a hand and webs shot out, hitting the wall with a splat. She made a noise of surprise, before she started to laugh with excitement. "Oh my gods, this is amazing! Look! I'm Black Widow!"

Those shattered pieces of my heart stabbed deeper into my chest.

"Yes, dear," the councilman said placatingly. "And it's a good thing, too, for all the money you just spent." He then chuckled in dry amusement, making the people in the audience laugh along with him.

"Don't worry, I'll use my new *lure power* on you later after you get one of the demon mates in you," she said with a wink. "I can't wait to test out feeding. I bet it's positively *feral*."

Her husband's eyes widened with lusty greed. "Yes, I think I'll go for the gargoyle one, President Belvini. My wife is particularly interested in that one," the shifter councilman said.

"It's because you'll have a solid stone cock," someone joked crassly.

The shifter barked out laughter. "Indeed."

I wanted to vomit. They just...joked about it all. As if they weren't talking about ripping half our souls out and taking our mate bonds from us. I lay prostrate on the ground, forgotten and discarded, as tears pooled beneath my cheek.

"Alright, let's get the gargoyle ritual started," Collector said amicably. "Councilman Wind, if you'd be so kind as to take your seat inside the gargoyle's circle?"

I watched through wet, heavy lashes as the shifter's feet scuffled by. I could hear the chains around Tomb's body jingle and creak. They were going to do to him what they'd done to me. That thought...triggered something inside of me. To imagine my strong, protective gargoyle mate reduced to this hollow shell? It sparked a fire of black rage from spitting flint in the dark. I guess when you're empty inside, there's plenty of room for rage to catch fire.

I wasn't going to lie down and die. All my life, I'd been the kicked dog, taking everything the world threw at me. But I wasn't going to just *take it* anymore. I was done being the lonely, bullied girl who rolled over with every kick. I may not have my spider anymore, but she taught me that I didn't have to take it. She taught me to fight back.

It was a mistake to leave me on the ground, forgotten and overlooked. With my ritual circle now broken, I could tap into my vampiric abilities again. I was dizzy, in pain, with soul-deep vertigo and a feeling of wrong emptiness, but I pushed past it all.

As the Spector figures came around to take their places around Tomb's circle, I forced my fingers to move. *Twitch, twitch, twitch.* Each miniscule movement took considerable effort, but I was determined.

Once I was able to flex both of my hands, I did the same to my toes. Then my legs, my arms, my shoulders. Like a ripple moving up me, my brain reconnected to my body, and my fangs dipped out of my gums in greeting.

The room was still dim, and everyone's attention was on Tomb and the figures who'd begun to chant around him. I couldn't see him or Risk at this angle, but when I moved my chin up a tiny fraction, I saw Crow looking right at me. His violet eyes were locked on me, his normally bright blue hair looking like dusky shadows. I didn't know how he knew what I had planned, maybe it was the resolve in my eyes, but he gave the smallest shake of his head, his eyes begging me. But I looked steadily back at him, letting him know with my expression what I couldn't say to him with words. *You're all mine, and I'll protect you until the end.*

Crow's face screwed up in anguish, but then his spine straightened, and he gave me a resolved nod, telling me what I needed to know. He was with me. Always.

My heart squeezed. I wished I'd told my mates I love them when I had the chance. I wished I'd done things differently. But all I could do now was protect them until my last dying breath. So I would. My spider had protected me from the beginning. She'd protected *them*.

It was my turn now.

I had *one* shot at this. One weakened vampire girl against a room of the most powerful supes in existence. I had to be smart. Driven. Resourceful. I nearly smiled. I was Motley fucking Coven. Those words were my middle name.

I plastered a look of confusion on my face and sat up, looking around the room in dismay. The chanting faltered, and Collector's eyes swivelled toward me as I staggered to my feet. "Wh-where am I?" I stuttered, my voice wobbly and frightened, and I used the opportunity to look around worriedly as if taking in my surroundings, while noting every guard in the room.

Collector walked over to me, signalling three guards to accompany him. They stepped around me, and I used my vampire scent to pick out each power. Shifter. Water elemental. Vampire.

Collector approached me with interest as his gaze swept over my trembling form. I didn't have to fake that. My body was still in shock.

"Miss Coven?"

I frowned. "Who are you? Where am I?" I asked him.

His eyes practically smiled as the wheels turned in his head, and he regarded me with opportunistic intent. Me, an empty, weak girl with no memories. He could use me all over again.

Fuck. That.

High level demons like Collector were hard to kill. There was only one way that I knew of, and it was nearly impossible if the demon expected a fight.

But he didn't.

With all the stealth and deadly grace I'd learned from my spider, I locked eyes with Collector.

A single second. That's all I gave him to see the truth behind my damsel in distress façade.

His eyes widened for a moment, but I already had my hands wrapped around his thick neck. One twist, a single monumental crack, and then with all the vampiric strength and speed I possessed, I pulled and yanked the motherfucker's head off, enjoying the sound of his tendons ripping, his skin tearing open as I pulled. Then tossed his head at his own feet.

For you, Aunt Marie.

His body hit the floor a second later, and then his entire form burst into ashes.

I wanted to spit on the pile, but I didn't have time. I was

already flashing toward Crow, using the last seconds of shock that I had left to gain the upper hand. I dragged my bare feet across Crow's circle on the floor, breaking the chalky lines of the ritual. I flashed in front of him and yanked on the weakened chains with all my might. Now that the ritual circle was ruined, and the restraints had lost their power, he'd be able to tap into his powers.

"Get Tomb!" I yelled, already racing away, because I knew he had my back.

The second his feet hit the floor, shadows burst from his outstretched arms and shoulders, and a cacophony of furious crows burst into existence. They crowded the room in an instant, hundreds and hundreds of them taking form. I heard their shrill cries, and then I felt the ground shake when a roar sounded behind me, and my lips split into a grin. My gargoyle was free.

The room had erupted into chaos. Supes started to use their powers, and birds converged to attack. My mates were fighting off guards, but I ducked and dodged it all as I ran for Risk.

"Stop her!" my father's voice boomed through the pandemonium, his finger raised to point me out.

I hissed in pain as a shot of fire lobbed and managed to hit me on the leg. It knocked me down, but I scrambled forward on hands and knees, hurrying to Risk's side.

I ripped the remaining chains from him, and his body slumped to the floor. My hands came to his cheeks, but his skin that was normally always hot felt cold to the touch. "Come on, Risk. Wake up. I need you," I told him, but he didn't wake. I shook him, pleading with him to wake up, but he stayed locked in his unconscious form.

Hands suddenly locked around my middle, and I was hauled up, the breath knocked out of me as the person's grip locked around my ribs.

"You'll be punished for this," my father spat in my ear. "You just ruined *everything*! Belvini was my fucking chance!"

Furious spittle hit my ear as he hissed against me, his arms squeezing so tight that I felt one of my ribs snap. I screamed, black dots littering my vision.

"You're really going to hurt your own daughter?" I choked out.

"I don't claim you," he hissed.

Fucking bastard. He never did, though, did he? I guess now wasn't any different.

I raised my hands out of instinct to shoot him with silky strands, only to remember that I didn't have any webs anymore. People from the audience were scattering, leaving the room as fast as they could go, as Spector guards struggled to take down my mates.

Tomb was in his gargoyle form, blasting through people left and right, their bullets merely nicking off his skin. Crow was hidden in a cyclone of shadows and feathers, as more birds than I'd ever seen flew around the massive room, causing mayhem and violence in their wake, making it difficult to see.

I suddenly felt my father's hands grip my neck. "Stop, or I'll kill her!" my father's voice shouted behind me.

I watched Tomb falter. The birds in the air paused, their beady eyes focusing on me. "No! Don't listen to him! Get yourselves out of here!" I screamed.

But my stubborn mates didn't listen. They immediately stopped fighting, and a sob tore from my throat as Spector guards converged around them. "No! Go! You have to go!" I cried.

"We won't leave you. *Ever*," Tomb growled, sweat tracking down his obsidian body.

"You're our mate," Crow said as he rushed forward, his

body bruised and battered. My heart squeezed. They were still mine. Still my mates, even if the bonds were gone.

"Now you get to watch her die, and then I'll kill you both," my father's icy voice cried out.

I heard my mates scream my name just as my father's hands tightened around my throat.

And then he snapped my neck.

Chapter 31

TOMB

I FELT the mate bond sever when the black widow demon was ripped from Motley's soul. Like a limb suddenly being torn from my body, it was cleaved away from me in one fatal swoop.

I watched her scream and writhe. I watched her crumple to the floor in a motionless heap. And I couldn't do anything. I couldn't protect her. I wanted to throw my fist into the wall and make the whole roof cave in with my wrath.

I didn't give a shit that the mate bond was gone. Motley was mine. Just like the black widow belonged to my gargoyle, Motley belonged to *me*. And we wanted them both back—we desperately wanted to feel whole again.

I felt my gargoyle roaring and rippling beneath my skin, but he couldn't come out, no matter how hard we tried. He was budding with unbridled fury, angry at the people that had hurt us, angry that the one person who'd given me a reason to live had half of her soul taken away from her.

When the Spector fuckers started chanting again, I grappled with panic and rage.

And then...she got up. I ignored the fuckers as they stumbled through the ritual, because my eyes were locked on her form as she struggled to stand. She was confused, scared. I wanted to hold her, but she looked past me as if she didn't recognize me at all.

Looking utterly lost, she stammered to Belvini, and a razor sliced through the center of my heart. She didn't remember me. She didn't remember *anything*. My heart. My will to live. She didn't remember.

Crow caught my eyes just as I was ready to slump against my restraints and give in. The blue-haired fucker *winked* at me, and I frowned. What the fu—

My eyes flew wide when Motley suddenly moved faster than I'd ever seen her move before. She was a blur. One second cowering and shaking in front of Belvini, and the next, she'd yanked off the asshole's head like she'd just plucked an apple off a tree.

She tossed the rotten head on the ground, and I smiled like the sick bastard I was. *That's my girl.*

I was free within seconds by Crow's hands, and then we were attacking. My gargoyle burst out of my body, and I let my demon take over on a full-blown rampage. We crushed skulls with single fisted hits. We broke bodies as we flung them aside with easy swipes. Our stone body repelled bullets and hits, unfeeling of everything except the fury.

We were going to destroy everyone in this godsdamned room. We were going to make them pay for what they did to our mate. I wouldn't stop until every last Spector guard was a motionless form at our feet. I would make the room run with blood. I would—

"Stop, or I'll kill her!"

My head snapped over to see Belvini's favorite lap dog—Trant—holding Motley in front of him, his arm banded around her middle and his other hand gripping her neck.

There was no choice. I immediately stopped fighting, even

as she argued and begged for us to leave. My dark eyes bore into hers. Did she really think we would just leave her here? I was somewhere between wanting to lecture her or spanking her ass and fuck her hard until she realized how much she meant to us.

"Get yourselves out of here!"

Tears filled her blue eyes as she pleaded with Crow and me, but I shook my head. "We won't leave you. Ever."

The sob that tore from her throat nearly undid me. I watched Trant, noticing how hard he was gripping her, trying to determine if I could get to him before he hurt her.

But I didn't get a chance to decide. Because before I could work out a way to free her, the bastard snapped her neck right in front of us.

No.

No, no, no.

My heart. My light at the end of the tunnel. The one who made me want to live again. After all the torture Spector had put me through, *nothing* was as painful as watching her small body drop to the floor, her neck at an odd angle, her heart no longer beating. I would've rather endured every test and punishment Spector had ever given me. Suffocation. Drowning. Severed limbs. Stabbing. Being shot. Burnt alive. Because none of those carried the agony I was feeling right now at seeing her lifeless body.

He killed her.

He fucking *killed her.*

A roar filled the room and rang through my ears. A part of me realized belatedly that the noise was coming from me.

"Kill them and burn the room," Trant ordered, already turning to leave with a contingent of guards.

I couldn't move. Shock had crippled me. Crow was on his knees at my side, his fists slamming into the floor and cracking open his knuckles as he yelled out incomprehensible words of violence and loss.

I didn't care when I felt the guards surround us. My reason to live had just been killed in front of my eyes.

All of the fight left me like a plug being pulled on my will. I joined Crow on my knees, my head hanging down in despair, because it was over.

When our mate bond severed, I still had hope. Despite the intricate magic binding us together, I knew that wasn't the only thing that connected us. Motley was for me, plain and simple. I fell in love with her strength, her will to survive, her tenacity in the face of cruelty. I fell in love with the way she encouraged me to live.

Life was a dull nothingness before her. I'd lost my sense of self, but I'd found purpose again in her. I didn't think I was capable of love until I met her, and then it had been all too easy. I fell into her web willingly, and I'd do it all over again. Because I fucking loved her.

I'll find you in the wandering afterlife, I promised. I may have failed her in life, but I wouldn't fail her in death. I'd follow her there.

Chapter 32

CROW

GONE. She was just...*gone*.

One second, her scared blue eyes were locked on me, and the next, the direction of her glance had been forced away as Trant snapped her neck.

Did she say something about being his *daughter*?

Red rage and black despair clouded my vision as the bastard tossed her to the ground like a discarded toy he was done playing with. My crows descended on her body, their cries of sorrow filling the room with vociferous mourning. Hundreds of them gathered around her still form, like a grim veil draped around her, their black heads bowing down in respect.

My eyes fucking burned with grief as I fell to my knees. We didn't save her. We *failed* her.

I didn't even feel it as I started punching the hard stone floor. Again and again my knuckles connected, until blood was splattering and bone was showing through. I heard Tomb's bellow of rage before he dropped beside me, merged in our grief.

The guards surrounded us, but we didn't move because

we had no reason to fight. We were done. Without her, nothing mattered.

"Wait...I..."

I looked over at the unfamiliar voice and saw the woman—Glenda Wind—stumbling forward to Trant. "I feel ssssss—I ffffeeeel straaaaa—strange," she stuttered. Her skin was grey, her eyes white with shock and pulsing power.

"Mrs. Wind?" Trant and the guards reached for her, but she folded over and started vomiting. Everyone backed up, including her husband who'd been trying to tug her back toward the exit.

"What's happening to her?" Councilman Wind demanded.

"I..." Trant shook his head, at a loss.

The woman continued to retch until she was making horrible choking sounds.

"She's suffocating on it!" Her husband rushed forward, trying to smack her on the back to dislodge whatever it was, but she just kept choking, her hands clawing at her throat and her eyes wide with terror.

She fell to her hands and knees, more vomit spilling from her lips. But I realized that it wasn't just vomit coming out. It was black light.

"Tomb," I murmured, my mouth dropping open as I watched.

I had no idea if he heard me or not. I was too engrossed in the scene unfolding. I watched the prim woman suddenly open her mouth wide in a gaping, soundless scream. Blue veins strained against her skin. Dark smoke pooled from her terrified eyes, and her hair unraveled from the tight bun on her head. Her body vibrated and shook. The vision of her was so fucking creepy that it brought chills to my arms.

And then the black light from her mouth *exploded*. Her jaw broke open, hanging down with dangling tendons and muscles. Her body was thrown backwards by an invisible force, and then I was staring at a writhing black mass of light and shadows that slowly stepped out of her and expanded into Black Widow.

"Holy shit."

Just like when I'd seen her before, I was in awe of her. Eight long legs, massive fangs, cunning eyes and a sleek body. She was deadly. Wicked. Frightening. *Beautiful.*

And she was fucking pissed.

She moved with such grace I could do nothing but watch in awe. A blast of dark, fiery power shot out from each of her limbs, taking everyone in the room down. If I hadn't already been on my knees, I would've been face down on the ground, my teeth digging into the hard floors. Smoke filled my vision, but I kept my eyes open, watching the tragically beautiful way she rained hell down on Spector. And then webs descended from her spitting mouth.

A hundred Spector guards were obliterated with venom and webs, left trussed up and dying as they hung from the ceiling like corpses of stalactites.

"Fuck," I breathed, looking around at the destruction around us. Limp bodies surrounded us. The room had gone completely silent from the sudden rush of death. Seconds. That was all it had taken for her to kill them all.

I looked back just as she encased Trant in a full body cocoon of webs, wrapping him up with tight vines of silk until you couldn't see an inch of his skin. She suffocated him with her webs, and then she ate the fucker whole.

I heard bones cracking and gurgled screams of pain right before all noise cut off and she swallowed him down with gnashing fangs and venomous intent. His screams turned silent, and his body was gone in an instant.

Tomb whistled beside me. "Damn."

Her head turned toward us, and my heart sped up as

inklings of fear washed over me. I had no idea if she still felt the mate bond, but I hoped to fuck she did, because I really didn't want to be eaten alive or be wrapped in poisonous webs like these sorry fuckers.

But she simply walked over to us, brushing a fuzzy leg against Tomb and I almost affectionately.

"Is she purring?" Tomb whispered.

I nodded with a hard swallow. "Yep. I'm pretty sure."

He frowned, watching her. "What's she doing now?"

"I don't know..." I watched as she walked over to Motley. My crows parted with mournful squawks to let her by. Then she stood over her, and the spider stared down, a keening noise leaving her raspy throat.

"She's gone," Tomb said quietly. His voice was broken and full of raw emotion, but the spider just hissed in reply.

She's gone. That phrase made me crumble. *She's gone. She's gone. She's gone.* I watched the spider jerk, and I frowned. Then she jerked again. And again. And again.

"Wait. She's...*shrinking*," I murmured.

Within moments, Black Widow's body narrowed and compressed until she was so small that I'd be able to carry her in the palm of my hand.

"Is she..." Tomb's breathless words cut off.

The black spider crawled up Motley's arm and chest, webs spreading over her as she passed. Her ribs, her chest, collarbone, jaw, cheek. And then the spider crawled into Motley's mouth and disappeared with a flare of black light.

"Holy fuck."

Tomb and I were back on our feet in an instant, running past the flapping crows as we skidded to her side. Motley was pale, with a nasty burn on her leg and scrapes all over her arms. Seeing her crooked neck made my eyes sting with grief all over again. Was this how she felt when she saw us die?

"Look," Tomb breathed. Every muscle in his body was tense with anticipation.

My eyes locked onto the mark that slowly appeared onto her neck. The hourglass stood out against her pale flesh, matching her bright red hair and searing hope into my soul.

Right in front of our eyes, her scrapes healed. Her burn faded. Her ribs straightened. And her neck snapped back into place. The invisible cord in my gut pulled tight, the mate bond tying back in place.

And then the most beautiful blazing blue eyes snapped open.

She was *alive*.

Tomb and I wrapped her up in our shaky, bloodied limbs, and I knew that we wouldn't be letting her go anytime soon.

Chapter 33

"I CAN DO IT," I said with a not so subtle roll of my eyes.

Furious dark eyes locked on me. "You fucking died."

I was getting really tired of their overprotectiveness. "Yes, Tomb. As you've pointed out many, *many* times over the last week, I died. But I still don't need help opening the door to the bathroom," I said dryly.

My stubborn gargoyle looked me dead in the eye...and opened the godsdamned bathroom door before I could get there. I sighed and walked inside, issuing him a thank you as I closed the door after me. At least I'd finally convinced him not to follow me inside. Having an audience while I was in the bathroom was not the sort of bonding experience I wanted with my mates. That had been a fight for a good forty-eight hours after my death. He and Crow had been extra protective of me ever since I, well...died. Luckily for me, my crazy spider basically ate her way out of poor Glenda Wind and burrowed back inside me. What can I say? We belong together. We were a match made in hell.

I finished my business in the bathroom and then headed for the door, only for it to sweep open before I could even touch the knob. I scowled at my mate. "You know, you were dead for *hours* after the first time I fucked you."

Tomb just crossed his muscled biceps in front of his chest and stared down at me. "And?"

"And...we've all died here. Let's be adults about it," I said reasonably.

Crow snorted behind me, and I turned to look at him where he was resting in the blue armchair near the window. Russell was perched on the sill, eyeing me just as closely as my mates.

"Give it up, Little Spider. Rock Cock over there won't be letting up on you anytime soon. His demon's protective instincts basically went into overdrive when you died."

Softening, I turned and wrapped my arms around Tomb. His tense body instantly softened, his arms coming around to hold me, and he buried his face into my hair. It was annoying, but I understood why they were acting this way. I felt the same crushing fear whenever they were in danger. It was natural to care. "I'm sorry. I know how that must've felt. But I'm right here. I'm okay."

"Are you?" Tomb asked, tipping my head back to look at him. He was so gorgeous. His chiseled features and intense eyes, dark skin and bright teeth.

It had been a week since the bloodbath at Spector. Stiles had stayed true to his word, and everything was broadcasted to every supe community in the country. The outcry had been instantaneous. But it had come at a price. Even now, in this spacious room with nice furnishings and sunlight streaming in through the windows...it was a farce. We were being held in a room in vamp city's council headquarters, waiting for ongoing deliberations to hear what would happen to Spector and everyone involved. Stiles was testifying on trial and giving explanations, but I wasn't sure what was going to happen.

Even so, that wasn't what worried me.

Crow stood up and walked over, pressing against my back so I was being comforted by both of them. "I'm scared for him," I admitted softly.

Tomb nodded. "We know."

Risk still hadn't woken up.

A week, and nothing. He was being seen by healers and human doctors alike, and nobody could say a damn thing except he was in something like a coma. Whatever had happened to him during the ritual had affected him gravely.

As if on cue, a knock sounded on our door. Tomb went into protective mode instantly, his body turning to stone as he went to the door. Russell landed on my shoulder with a caw, while Crow stayed at my side.

Tomb opened the door, his body tensing. "Who are you?"

"Hmm. A gargoyle demon? The ladies must *love* that," an English voice drawled.

I moved beside Tomb to see the male standing in our doorway, and my skin instantly prickled. "You're a high-level demon," I said, looking him over. He had deep red hair and bright green eyes. A green so vivid and pure that it was almost hard to stare into his jade gaze. He was wearing a plain black t-shirt and jeans, his stance relaxed and his expression easygoing. But I could sense an incredible amount of power wafting off of him.

He grinned at me, showing off a set of perfect teeth and dazzling dimples. "I am, love. And *you* must be the notorious Black Widow." His gaze swept up my body as if I were wearing lingerie instead of jeans and a shirt. "Mmm. You're positively *decadent*. I can see why Risk mated you. I might even be tempted to tumble with a known sexual cannibal."

My mouth dropped open in shock at his forward words.

Tomb moved, blocking me, and his muscles rippled.

"Don't fucking talk to my mate like that," he roared. "She's *mine*. And you better back the fuck off."

My eyes widened at Tomb's outburst. He was protective and possessive, sure, but this was extreme. My eyes narrowed on the demon. "What kind of demon are you?"

His grin widened. "You can call me Envy, love."

"Stop calling her love!" Tomb snapped, looking like he was ready to snap the demon like a twig.

I crossed my arms and glared at the demon. "Stop provoking him."

Envy shrugged. "Jealousy is easy to bring out with this one. He's quite greedy where you're concerned. It makes an excellent meal."

I sighed. "Why are you here?"

The man clicked his tongue. "Care to invite me in? It's rude to keep guests in the hall."

Tomb growled, and I was sure he was about to punch the demon in the face, but Crow intervened. "Sure, come in," he said, giving Tomb a clap on the back. He wanted to know what this demon wanted, and so did I.

Tomb reluctantly moved away, and the red-haired demon strode inside and circled the room. "Nice. But the council gave me a *much* nicer room. I have a king-sized bed. And a jacuzzi tub. Also a balcony."

Jealousy flared in me. "A jacuzzi tub? How did—" With a scowl, I clamped my mouth shut. "Stop doing that."

He simply laughed and sat down on the chair that Crow had been sitting in earlier, before kicking his feet up onto the black table.

"The council invited you here?" Crow asked him curiously.

Envy nodded. "I'm their demon consultant."

I frowned. "I didn't know there was such a thing."

"There wasn't. Until now," he said, flashing another grin.

I walked over until Tomb's fingers pinched the back of my shirt, keeping me from getting any closer. I guess the jealousy that Envy spurred in him was still a little heightened. "What are they consulting with you about?" I asked nervously. I thought about Risk, currently upstairs in the medical ward, being watched over by healers and enforcers.

"Mmm, a little bit of this, a little bit of that," Envy answered vaguely. "But I'm more interested in Risky Business upstairs."

My nerves twisted. "What about him?"

The demon watched me carefully for a few moments before blowing out a breath and setting his feet back on the floor. He leaned forward, elbows braced against his thighs. "He's not gonna heal, love."

His words caught the breath in my chest and shoved it back in. "What do you mean he won't heal? Of course he will. He just needs time or—"

"No, love," he said, surprisingly gently. "Risky won't be healing. At least not here."

Tears burned in my eyes. "What are you saying? That he's dying?" I couldn't take it. My spider let out a sad keening noise in my ears, and I rubbed my thumb against my hourglass mark as an ache sprouted in my chest.

Envy stood up. He moved to come closer to me, stopping a foot away when Tomb growled. "He needs to go back to hell."

I stared at him, the words refusing to settle in my brain.

"Hell? But I thought your kind of high demons ascended here because of your high level of power?" Crow asked.

"Very true. But when we're mortally injured, like Risk is, there's only one place we can heal, and it isn't topside."

"But he can come back right?" I asked. "If we send him to hell, he can come back once he's healed?"

Envy gave me a pitying look. "Our source of power stems

from hell. If you want him to heal, he's got to go back. But I'll tell it to you straight, love. When a demon is *that* damaged, it can take years for us to heal and regain the power necessary to ascend back to topside."

I shook my head in denial. "No. No, he'll wake up," I insisted.

But Envy just looked at me with more pity, and I wanted to smack it off his face. "No!" I was suddenly turned around, my face buried against Tomb's chest as hot tears spilled from my eyes. I'd just gotten my spider and my mates back, and now Risk was going to go back to hell? It wasn't fair. Tomb ran a hand up and down my spine, trying to soothe me, but I was gripped in a fist of distress.

"How do we send him back to heal?" Crow asked somberly.

"Just say the word, and I can do it for you. I figured I'd leave it up to his mate," Envy said.

I felt everyone's eyes on me, and I knew that they really would leave it up to me. Even if I decided to be selfish and keep him here, not healing, stuck in a never ending unconscious limbo.

"But he's my mate," I began, searching for another solution. "Why isn't he regenerating?"

Envy brushed his thumb along his jaw, contemplating my question. "I don't know how to explain it. I'm not even convinced it was the ritual that caused this. That baby mama drama was like some sort of void, sucking his power away—including the ability to heal. Think of your mate bond as like a regenerative power that manifests after mating. Whatever happened sucked it all up or nulled it. Hell is the only way."

I didn't want to send Risk away, but I couldn't do that to him. I wiped my wet face against Tomb's shirt before turning back around and raising miserable eyes to Envy. "I want you to send him back so he can be healed," I said quietly, my voice cracking.

The demon nodded, his eyes scanning my mates where they flanked me, both of them running soft touches and reassuring caresses over me. "I'll go straight up to do it as soon as I leave here."

"I want to come."

Envy shook his head. "The council has you all watched like hawks and him as well. You won't be allowed in the room."

My fangs dropped in anger. "I'll convince them," I growled.

"I wouldn't," he warned. "Listen, the council is embarrassed. People are calling for their heads after what happened. They've got to appease the public. That probably means nothing good for you lot. You need to be prepared for them to make an example out of you, even though it wasn't your fault. Risk is in danger up there, unable to defend himself. Let me take care of your mate and send him back where he can heal. He'll be out of their clutches, at least."

I probably shouldn't trust a high level demon I just met who fed off the jealousy of others, but for some reason, I did. I breathed out in defeat. "Okay."

Envy gave me a single nod. "I'll go now." He stopped short, fishing for something in his pocket before holding out a necklace. "Almost forgot. I found this in the exorcism room when I did a sweep," he explained. "Collector had a hard-on for magical rocks."

I took it, studying the amber amulet. "He used this on me so my powers wouldn't work," I said grimly, remembering how it had been wrapped around my wrists while I was in the cell with Aunt Marie.

Envy nodded. "He was able to wield it to absorb power."

I held it in my hand, curling my fingers around it before stuffing it in my pocket.

The jealousy demon gave us one last parting look and then walked out of the room, greeting the enforcers in the hall as he left.

I buried my face in my hands and sobbed profusely, and Crow immediately moved forward and held me close, while Tomb continued to stroke my back. "Am I doing the right thing?" I asked.

"You know the answer to that, Little Spider," Crow murmured against my forehead before placing a kiss there.

"I didn't even get to see him. I won't get to say goodbye," I choked out. All I wanted was a sense of normalcy. We kept getting shoved from one place to the next, leaving one prison to the next, mourning one loss to the next.

I just wanted all of my mates together. I wanted to relish in our bond, make a life for ourselves and figure out what we were going to do. I wanted to go to Aunt Marie's home and pack up some of her belongings, flip through photographs and breathe in her scent. Every passing moment faded into the next as I was stuck in limbo and couldn't find my footing.

"He'll heal, and maybe one day, he can come back."

"He will," Tomb cut in.

I lifted my head to look over at him. "How do you know?" I sniffed.

Tomb's fingers came up to brush away my tears. "Because he has *you* for a mate. He'll do whatever he can to get back to you, for as long as it takes."

Chapter 34

RISK'S newborn daughter looked like him. She had his playful smile and hopeful eyes.

My eyes were riveted on Ms. Cainson. She was seated in the courtroom at council headquarters. The stadium seating was packed shoulder to shoulder and was noisy from the constant murmuring in the audience. The proceedings for the Spector trial were all over supe news. It was the biggest story in our communities, and everyone was watching the council's every move.

I was sitting on the council's side, along with Tomb, Crow, and Stiles, as well as several Spector employees, including the exuberant Vick. Judge Braxton resided over everything at the center podium while sitting in his golden chair, where he was currently listening to more testimonies from a Spector guard. But my attention was solely on the baby currently being held by Ms. Cainson.

I knew it was part of a ploy to give her more sympathy from the public. She hadn't been painted in a good light, since she was on the council and had attempted to get a high level demon's essence put into her. But a woman holding a newborn baby was hard to incriminate. Based on the glances she was getting from the audience, her manipulation was working.

But with every muffled coo and soft cry that came from the bundle held in her lap, my heart clenched for an entirely different reason. The baby was beautiful. And despite the fact that she had wispy blonde hair and feminine features, she had dark, glittering brown eyes that were the exact same shade as her father's.

My heart gave another squeeze. I missed him. I missed him so damn much. And now he had a daughter that he hadn't even been able to meet. My eyes swelled with heartache.

The council had been up in arms when Risk disappeared. They had no idea where he went, until their very helpful demon consultant told them that hell had simply zapped him back below, and nothing could be done about it. Envy was currently sitting on the other side of the council's seating box, his feet kicked up on the railing in front of his seat. When he saw me looking, he tossed me a wink. Tomb must've seen because he clamped a hand onto my thigh and squeezed.

It took hours to listen to the testimonies. Some of them were horrible. Spector guards would spew off awful things about me or my mates and what we'd done, and the audience ate it up, becoming more and more hostile toward us—me especially. And I just had to sit there and take it, because...well, it was true. I *had* done those things they were saying. But I didn't get to say my side or explain *why*. Judge Braxton wasn't interested in allowing the hybrids to have much of a voice.

The only person who was permitted to speak on our behalf had been Stiles, and only because our father held some sway. But even my brother hadn't been given much time to speak, and based on his tense expression, I knew the truth as much as he did—we were fucked.

I gave Tomb and Crow a worried look. This was going all wrong. We hadn't even been given a chance. I shared a look with Stiles, but his mouth was pressed into a thin line. He'd shown the truth of what Spector was doing to the public so that it would get shut down, and he succeeded in that. But in doing so, we'd doomed ourselves, because now we were painted as monsters who killed without conscience.

I looked at my mates, ready to tell them that we needed to do something. Intuition was pulsing dread through me. "Guys…" We needed to run, we needed to—

Judge Braxton's gavel slammed down. My stomach clenched in fear.

"After taking testimonies and public votes into account, I hereby rule that Spector Incorporated and all their unlawful practices of demon rituals and possessions be hereby terminated indefinitely," he declared, his voice ringing out through the crowd. He gave a hard stare over the entire auditorium. "It is also my decree that all Spector hybrids be destroyed immediately. These abnormal supernatural amalgams are too volatile and powerful to be allowed to exist. Therefore, under the jurisdiction of the council, it has been decided that all hybrids are to be arrested immediately, and executions will be set for public viewing. If any hybrid should attempt to flee or become violent, enforcers are permitted to kill on sight. Stiles Trant will step down as Paragon, as punishment for his involvement with Spector. I will pardon the other council members, as they were coerced by demon influence to participate. That is my ruling."

The gavel snapped.

The audience exploded with voices.

My fingers laced through Tomb's and Crow's, my hands holding on tight right up until the moment the enforcers wrenched us apart. They snapped handcuffs on our wrists and led us away, while the crowd booed and spat obscenities at me. Shock kept my lips locked with silence, as I followed the enforcer's directions numbly.

Was this really happening? Did I go through all of that just to be "destroyed" by the council?

"It's not fucking right!" Stiles shouted and struggled beside me. "We showed you the truth, and we fucking saved you!" he yelled, but no one cared to listen. "We saved you all, and she did what she had to do! You should be fucking *thanking her*!"

He looked livid, ready to launch himself at the crowd, but I shook my head. "Don't," I pleaded. "It won't help, and it'll only get you killed faster. You heard Judge Braxton."

We were all pulled through the courtroom and led through the doors in the back, leaving the cheering and leering mob behind. The enforcers roughly directed us down a long hallway, guns pressed to our backs. Stiles was still yelling and cursing everyone for Judge Braxton's ruling, and the guards slammed him to the ground.

They weren't fucking around. Even though my mates and I could regenerate, it would take time, and I had no doubt that they would gladly shoot us in the skulls before ripping our heads off our bodies and burning us to ash. And if that didn't keep us dead forever, I was willing to bet that the council would keep us imprisoned for the rest of our immortal, indestructible lives.

―――

"HOW MUCH LONGER DO YOU think it'll be?" I asked while I paced our cell.

Before the hearing, they'd at least pretended to care about us, putting my mates and I in rooms that had a bed and bathroom. Now, we were in a cell no better than the ones we had at Spector, left with nothing to do but pace the floors and wait for an execution date.

The other hybrids who hadn't made it out of Spector were taken into custody by the council. And as soon as the ruling came to have us destroyed, their executions were ordered. It was swift and broadcasted to the masses. It was a way to appease the pissed off supes angry at what Spector and the council had been involved in.

But it was also a warning. In case anyone else thought to recreate the ritual and steal some power. The council wasn't fucking around. A new law was passed stating that anyone who performed a demonic ritual would be sentenced to death immediately.

They made us watch the executions. We stood in the blistering cold, the harsh wind whipping against our cheeks as each of their heads was severed. The crowd cheered. Some hissed. Ms. Cainson stood by Judge Braxton, smiling broadly at the spectacle and clapping when the hybrids' heads rolled along the concrete.

My mates and I were still alive for the sole reason that they couldn't figure out how to kill us. At first, we wondered if they would torture us until we stopped regenerating, but then we realized that they didn't want to look like failures. If we kept coming back to life, the public would lose faith in the council's ability to take care of the *hybrid problem*.

So we waited. And waited. And waited some more. We heard whispers of exorcisms and beheadings, but nothing was set yet. The Spector scientists had surrendered all of their studies to the council, which meant they got to see just how indestructible we were.

Every day that went on, the waiting was like an added barb to my gut. I hated waking up every morning and not knowing. Not knowing if today would be the day that the council would decide to try to kill us. I feared a life separated from my mates. I feared watching them suffer needlessly. I feared our end.

"Stop pacing, Motley," Crow whispered while patting the cold concrete beside him in our cell.

At least they let us stay together. Honestly, I think Tomb would've gone berserk and smashed his way over to me if they'd separated us, power blockades be damned. I wasn't sure what kind of magic they used to keep our abilities at bay in this prison, but it was different than the demon ritual circles. Instead of my powers and my spider feeling bound, this just made us tired and our powers weak.

"I just hate that we're locked up here waiting. My spider feels anxious," I replied with a sigh before shooting webs onto the floor and creating a pillowed cushion of silk. The effort of that small use of power left me feeling dizzy with exhaustion. Fucking magical power block.

The moment I sat down, Crow pulled my legs over his lap and started rubbing my legs, massaging the sore muscles with skilled, precise fingers. Tomb was asleep—finally. He went two days of just staring at the door in his stone form, daring anyone to try and steal me away. I was thankful that he'd finally gotten some rest.

"Any secret messages from Cheryl in your blood bag today?" Crow asked, though he already knew the answer. He just liked to keep up conversation. I think it worried him when I got too quiet and withdrawn.

Three days ago, I'd gotten a hidden note inside a blood bag from my eccentric, self-centered friend. I was certain that Stiles arranged it. The guard that delivered it wasn't our usual, and I'd been keeping an eye out for him ever since, but I hadn't spotted him.

"No," I replied with a slump of my shoulders.

"It's probably for the best," Crow replied. "I'm really not

in the mood for another monologue about how angry she is at us for being on television for the trial and not bothering to put makeup on."

I snorted before reading the letter again.

DEAR MOTLEY, Stiles says I need to keep this short, but there's way too much to say. I saw you on the news, and I have to be honest, it wasn't your best day. The TV didn't just add ten pounds, hun, it added pasty skin and under eye circles too. I won't get started on your hair. I don't have the room on this paper. You should've really asked Vick to get you and your mates some makeup for the event. At least try to get the public to like you, you know? All they've seen otherwise is you going all murder-y and killing, like, a hundred people. Concealer would've been a big plus.

Anyway, Stiles got us out. I'm not allowed to say where, just in case this note gets confiscated, but right now, I'm drinking a mai tai, and I'm working on my tan. Some of the others are here, but most of them split up and went their own ways. Stiles was really strict about them lying low for awhile though, which is awful because I was really hoping to invite everyone over for an engagement party once Stiles and I get settled. A winter wedding would just be divine, don't you think? And—

Hey, Motley. Stiles here. Sorry about...all of the above writing. When I told Cheryl we could smuggle in a letter, I didn't think she'd start blabbering, but I should've known better. I've been pardoned for my superior blood line. It's a bunch of fucking shit. I signed a contract to never use my powers and to work for the council. A few other paragons and influential members of society were privately given the same deal. Cheryl also was pardoned because of our engagement and her family's standing in the community. She bragged about her family until she was blue in the face, but what else is new? I guess they didn't want to publicly show preference for the elite. Twenty-three of us made it out. We lost...a lot. But twenty-three lives counts for something.

I tried to break you and your mates out, but I couldn't get to you. They want to make an example of you. We all know the real enemy, Motley, and I won't rest until they're punished. I'm so sorry I know I've been a shit brother all your life, and our father was even shittier. By the way, if you're worried that I'm angry with you about our father's death, I'm not. He had it coming.

Hang in there, okay? I need a week, and then I can get you guys out. I have a plan.

—Stiles

I LOOKED OVER AT CROW. "I don't want him getting caught trying to break us out of here. That could go really badly for him."

Crow just shrugged and pushed his blue hair out of his face, clearly not as concerned with Stiles's safety as I was. "He's an adult, and he's on the outside. If he thinks there's a way to get to us, then he can have at it. There's no use worrying over something you have no control over."

I knew Crow was right, but I still didn't like the idea that Stiles would get caught and then killed because of me. I also wasn't a martyr. I didn't *want* to be left behind, but I knew that enforcers were crawling all over this place. Security was even tighter than Spector.

Crow's thumb came up, dragging my bottom lip out from between my gnawing teeth. "Don't bite that lip of yours off. I like it too much," he said quietly before leaning in and placing a soft kiss on my mouth.

Pulling back, he moved his thumb up between my brows. "And this frown. I don't like seeing this frown on my mate," he murmured, smoothing the pad of his thumb over the spot until the tension left my brows.

"That's better," he said before placing a kiss there.

His hands went back to kneading my feet and warming

my toes until I was practically melted against him. "Why are you so good to me?" I asked, placing my hand against his chest as I rested my head on his shoulder.

"You're my mate," he said simply.

My heart swelled at those simple words, and I traced the lines of his muscled chest, thinking about everything we'd been through. "Crow, when you escaped Spector the first time, how did you do it?" I asked curiously.

He tensed beneath me, and I looked up at him curiously. "It's not a nice story, Little Spider."

"Please tell me?" I asked.

He let out a sigh, and his hands went back to his ministrations on my feet. "I can't help but think what would have happened if I'd been able to save you that night during Thibault's ritual," he said. "My demon knew that his mate was there. Even if I didn't understand it yet, my birds knew."

"You tried. That's what matters. And besides, if I hadn't been taken to Spector, I never would have met Tomb or Risk. Without the ritual, I never would've had my spider in the first place. I don't regret it."

He nodded slowly in understanding. "There was a woman guard," he said suddenly, his eyes focused on my feet. "She...uh, was known to give hybrids some leniency if we…"

I nodded. "Gotcha. What happened?"

Crow scratched the back of his head, and there was a faint blush on his cheeks. "She'd had her sights set on me for awhile, but I always shrugged her off. Tomb too," he said, tilting his head at my sleeping gargoyle. "But one night, when she came to my cell, I could tell she'd been drinking. She was a necro, but not very powerful. I think that was why she liked fucking hybrids. She got off on us using her powers. Anyway, I let her in. My birds *hated* her. As soon as she was...distracted, I let them attack. They killed her pretty brutally, but no one was around. I stole her keycard and broke into the kitchens of the cafeteria. I killed one of the cooks, but a few of the guards shot me before I made it into the air shaft. It took about an hour to climb all the way up, and I kept getting stuck and getting dizzy from the blood loss, but I made it."

"Gods, that must've been awful."

"It wasn't my best day," he agreed. "After that, I passed out in some random alleyway and waited to heal. And then I just ran. But then there was this tugging that I couldn't ignore. And when I saw that my crows had led me right back to another Spector ritual, I laughed. I thought it was some big fucking cosmic joke." His violet eyes finally looked up at me. "Turns out, I was just supposed to find you."

I reached down and laced my fingers through his. "I'm glad."

"Me too, Little Spider," he said, placing a kiss on the crown of my head.

Tomb suddenly shot up into a sitting position, his skin threatening to turn stone as a yell erupted from him.

Shit.

I was on my feet in a second, rushing over to Tomb's side. His eyes were wild, and the moment I reached to put my hand out to comfort him, he snarled and reared back like he was going to attack. I flinched, but before Tomb's massive fist could come hurtling my way, Crow was there, shoving me back and taking the punch in his own arm. "Shit," he hissed in pain. At least he hadn't been in his stone form. "Tomb, it's us!" Crow shouted.

My heart pounded in my chest as I watched Tomb snarl and jump to his feet, looking like a rabid animal trying to find a way out of his cage. His fists were up, ready to keep attacking, and sadness gripped me. Was this why he'd fought sleep so much? Did nightmares of what he'd endured plague him?

"Tomb," I said, trying to step around Crow.

My mate stopped me. "He's not himself yet," he warned.

"Tomb," I repeated determinedly. "It's me. Motley."

This time, when I touched his arm, he flinched, but stopped himself before moving onto the offensive. Feeling bold, I let my hand gently run up his bicep to comfort him. "It's just us," I cooed. "You're okay."

He shivered, and I watched as recognition slowly came over his face, and the tension in his body drained out. The glaze of fury left his eyes, and he blinked several times, taking in his surroundings.

"Wid?" he asked tentatively.

When he realized Crow's protective stance, Tomb let out a breath. "Did I hurt you? Fuck!" He turned and threw a fist into the wall, making the concrete crack.

"Hey, it's okay. I'm okay," I assured him. "Really."

"I could've fucking hurt you," he snapped. "Both of you."

"We're fine," I insisted.

"Yeah, that punch you laid on me was pathetic. More like a tap, really," Crow joked, even as he touched the spot on his arm and winced.

I smiled, thankful for Crow lightening the mood. I pressed a hand against Tomb's cheek. "Bad dream?"

He nodded slowly, placing his hand over mine to hold it there. He didn't elaborate, and I didn't push him to say more.

"Want to come lie down again?" I asked him, but he shook his head.

"No. I think that was enough for me."

I wished he'd been able to get more sleep, but I understood. "I can make some web baseballs again, and we can toss them around like old times," I joked.

He smiled and placed a tender kiss on my lips, in such contrast to his hard body. "That—"

Tomb's words were cut short when our cell door was opened with an electronic beep, and it slid open to reveal none other than Judge Braxton and a team of enforcers standing behind him.

When Tomb growled, I looked down and noticed that there were red lasers tagged on each of our chests, the enforcers ready to fire if we made a single move at the judge.

The man was arrogant, but not stupid. He didn't pass over the threshold. He just stood in the doorway, staring at us. Crow and Tomb stayed at my side, and the tension grew thick as the four of us stared at each other.

The judge had sleek black hair that was so shiny it was reflecting the lights off of it. He wore his black judge robe with its high collar done up at his throat, telling me that he'd just come from the courtroom. Which meant...

"You've declared a ruling on our lives," I stated as understanding came over me.

The man nodded. "Indeed. You three have been deemed too dangerous to live and are an unlawful abomination to our kind."

Tomb growled at the word *abomination*. I reached down and squeezed his hand in comfort. It wouldn't be a good idea to attack the leader of the country's entire supernatural community.

"Your execution date has been set. In exactly twenty hours, you will be beheaded, burned, your ashes contained in magically-reinforced boxes, and the boxes dumped into the ocean at an undisclosed location. All in the hopes that, should you regenerate through all of that, you will still be contained."

My mouth went dry, and my breathing picked up the pace as the blood drained from my face.

Judge Braxton gave no emotional response whatsoever. "That is the ruling of the council, hereby decreed by myself." He gave us all another long look. "I suggest you prepare yourselves for the end."

He turned and walked out, the gang of enforcers following him out until the last laser disappeared. Our cell door closed behind them, slamming shut any hope that had been left.

We were going to die in twenty hours.

Stiles couldn't get to us that soon, even if he managed to be successful. This was happening. We were an abomination to the public, and they wanted us dead.

Even if we regenerated, we would never be found. We'd be lost at sea, forever trapped, with all hope gone.

I buried my face against my mates, and I cried.

Chapter 35

OUR EXECUTION DAY was fucking sunny.

Mother Nature probably liked being ironic.

Beams of light beat down on our shackled bodies as we looked around. There was a pleasant breeze, carrying the scent of spring flowers and hope. It was bright—too bright. I wanted rain clouds and storms. I craved an icy chill to match the desolation in my soul. I wanted to hear thunder and lightning. I wanted the air to crack with the sound of my breaking heart.

Just like all the other hybrid executions, it was very public. We were standing in the middle of an outdoor arena that was usually used for vampire professional sports games. The entire place was *packed*. I guess the three of us had become celebrities in the supe world. Just not the kind of celebrity you wanted to be.

I heard one of the guards bragging that he bought his entire family tickets to the spectacle. Young children with eager eyes stared at us from their seats in the crowd. Grandmothers. Kids skipping school. Public figures. Collector would have loved to see everyone gathered for his creations.

My spider could smell the bloodlust in the air. Everyone was getting off on our impending suffering. Lusty venom dripped from the vampires' fangs. Shifters could barely control their rabid animals. Elementals were tossing fire into the air, littering the sky with magic fireworks in celebration of their conquering.

The boos and hisses and hate were palpable throughout the arena. Our faces were shown on the massive screens and broadcasted to every other supe in the world who wanted to watch. They branded us as the enemy, marketing our deaths to hide the fact that most of the council wanted our gifts. I guess if they couldn't have the unlimited power of our demons, no one could.

I was put in a black dress that wasn't mine and didn't fit right, while my mates stood at my sides, also dressed in black clothes that swallowed them. My red hair had been braided back by some mute shifter woman before we were herded outside, because I guess they didn't want it in the way when they chopped my head off my body.

The three of us stood on a wooden stage that looked like it had just been built for this purpose alone. Our hands were shackled with steel chains. Sweat dripped down my spine from the anxiety and heat. I knew that this would be painful. I prayed that what the council did stayed, because I couldn't imagine an eternity of suffering for my mates.

Judge Braxton was droning on into the microphone, listing our crimes. We'd been standing there for a while listening to them because there were *a lot*. Murder. Misuse of power. Conspiracy. Demon ritual involvement.

But when he got to the part about me using my lure to purposely make Oz aroused so that I could stop doing the rope climb in the training room, I don't know what came over me. I just started laughing. Laughing so hard I couldn't stop. I knew I was hysterical. I was terrified out of my mind. I was shaking harder than a leaf in autumn. I hadn't slept, and I'd cried so much that my eyes were swollen nearly twice their normal size.

And now? I was finally snapping.

Everyone looked at me with wide eyes. I felt like a self-fulfilling prophecy, cackling on stage as tears of disappointment streamed down my blotted cheeks. They wanted a terrifying, manic hybrid, and I'd become that. I was at the point where I wasn't sure who the fuck I was angry at anymore. Spector. The guards. The council. Myself. I was just *angry*.

There was so much going on in my mind. The loss of Risk, knowing my mates would be tortured, Aunt Marie... I was just devastated. I'd finally gotten to the point where the list of injustices was piled so high that it blocked the sun. All I could see was darkness.

All I could feel was the soul-crushing realization that it was always meant to lead to this. I was always meant to die. I was always meant to lose the people I cared about. I was always meant to be alone.

I drank in the look of my mates and reached out for my spider. I wanted to fight, I wanted to pull her from my chest and burn the world down with her protective fury. She couldn't take on an arena of supes, but I wanted to go down fighting. I wanted to make them bleed.

But she had been noticeably complacent throughout the entire ordeal. Webs didn't spill from my fingers, anger didn't burn across the mark on my throat. I'd expected her to take over like she'd always done. I wanted to become the thing of nightmares, but she was nothing but a whisper in my soul. Waiting. Waiting. Maybe she had given up. Maybe death didn't scare her.

The judge continued to drone on and on and on. Each accusation became more and more redundant. At this point, I just wanted to get on with the process. I couldn't handle the limbo any more. I closed my eyes and reached out to my spider for the last time, seeking comfort in her presence while I still could. I sought to mirror her emotions, sinking into how she felt about this deadly sentence to make sense of my own debilitating grief.

And she seemed content. Bored. She was...excited?

What the fuck?

My brow dipped in confusion, shocking me out of my pity party. What did my spider know that I didn't?

"I would like to thank the supernatural community for banding together to take down these abominations with my guidance," Judge Braxton boomed with pride from his spot on a nearby podium. Enforcers flanked him on both sides, looking at me with disgust. I glared back at them, imagined wrapping them in webs and consuming them whole. "I look forward to moving forward past Spector's indiscretions. I look forward to living as the gods intended us to." Cheers and yells littered the crowd. My spider laughed within me, amusement filling every cell of our shared souls.

We knew the truth. They just wanted to save face.

Judge Braxton then went on to describe in graphic detail how the council would ensure that we would stay dead. He described the beheading, the burning, the ocean's depths that would consume our ashes.

"Motley, I love you," Crow said beside me as a hooded figure carrying an axe started ascending the stairs toward us.

My breath stuttered in my throat and got caught on my panicked fangs. My only consolation was that Risk was safe.

This was really it. After days and days of waiting, we were about to feel a blade at our necks. The wait was over. It felt surreal almost. But this was happening. I was facing it whether I was ready or not.

I didn't know what was worse—staying dead or regenerating inside a steel box that we'd never escape from. My entire body trembled.

"Hey." Crow's soft voice halted my panic, and I turned to look at his steady violet eyes. "I love you so much, Little Spider," he said, hooking his pinky finger around mine since that was as far as we were able to reach with the magical bindings around our wrists. "My birds won't ever stop looking for you—either in this world or the afterlife. We'll find you, okay?"

I gave him a sad smile, wishing his reassurance held merit. I wanted to kiss his lips. Aside from the sadness in his gaze, he was calm. Crow was my sliver of peace. He was my support. My home. My eyes glazed over with tears. "Okay."

I turned to look at Tomb next, and his eyes were already on me. He didn't offer words of love or reassurance, but that was because Tomb didn't need words. He bled love through his adoring gaze, instilling promises in my soul with a deep, penetrating look. His face was pure stone, not letting any emotions slip for the crowd to see, but I felt his love. I felt his adoration.

I realized in that moment how short our time had been. We didn't have the eternity I craved, but it felt like I knew them better than anyone. Our relationship matured with damage, not with time. We grew together. We loved together. We suffered together. And now we'd die together.

I claimed every second of our bond and felt thankful for it in the end.

"Let the executions proceed," Judge Braxton boomed while gesturing toward the hooded man holding an axe.

Enforcers stood at our backs, and they pressed us down to our knees with brute strength. Tomb struggled against them, refusing to bow in submission. Crow cursed and kept his eyes on me as he shrugged them off and knelt on his own terms. I dropped with grace, landing on my knees while looking up at the sunlight, letting the bright rays fill my blue eyes. I wasn't sure when I'd see the sun again, or if I ever would.

The executioner walked up to us, and I looked at the hooded man. The axe he wielded looked big and imposing, and I kept wondering how my head would roll, how the splatters of blood would look against the clean blade. Would everyone laugh when we died? Would they cheer with triumph? Would Cheryl and Stiles be watching from afar? I saw my reflection in the shiny blade as blood pulsed in my ears.

My spider stretched out suddenly, filling my belly with giddy anticipation. A gasp escaped my lips as a deep tether within me snapped into place. Relief, happiness, and shining light bloomed inside of me, and beautiful lace-like webs descend from my fingertips that fell in intricate designs on the ground. I guess my spider was welcoming death with open arms.

The hooded man stood in front of me, his shadowed face hidden from view, but a sense of nostalgia and love overwhelmed me. The axe he wielded glittered in the sunlight, casting glares across my vision. He said two words I could barely hear over the cheering crowd.

"So risky."

Shock shoved at my pulse. My mouth dropped open, and my eyes widened despite the glaring sun.

And then, all hell broke loose.

The stage burst into flames as he lifted the axe high over his head. But instead of the blade coming toward me, he turned at the last second and sliced behind me. I turned just as a rain of hot, sticky blood fell over the side of my face.

A heavy, wet noise dropped beside me, and I looked down to see a head rolling to my left, landing at Crow's thigh.

Screams. So many screams as the crowd went fucking *berserk*.

Enforcers attacked the stage, only to be blanketed in furious flames the moment they got to the hellfire that circled us. The hooded man swiped the bloodied blade of his axe across the enforcer's chest behind Tomb. Elementals were trying to put the flames out with their powers as water doused the arena, but it wasn't working. This fire wasn't from topside. It was from the pits of hell. Ash singed my cheeks, and a smile broke out across my face.

Tomb quickly stood up and headbutted the enforcer behind Crow, instantly cracking his skull and exposing brain matter through his concave head.

"You assholes ready to get out of here?" the executioner asked. Wind whipped at his hood, revealing the sly smile of my mate but still concealing his identity from others.

"Risk," I said in crashing relief as Tomb and Crow hauled me to my feet.

He grinned. "This is fun. Want to kill a few more of these assholes or get out of here?" he asked, looking around. "Damn, it's like a feast of risk here!" He snapped his fingers, making the flames around us rise even higher and wider, killing more people and bringing more screams. It went up ten feet. Twenty. Fifty. We were in an impenetrable wall of flames. Power laced the air with thick smoke.

I didn't even care about his cocky words. Risk was here. He was safe and awake and he was fucking *here.*

"You came back," I said, a sob choking out of me as I stared at him. I was afraid to blink. I didn't want this to be a hallucination that would go away.

"Took you long enough, asshole," Crow yelled.

Risk laughed, showing off his stark white teeth. "I leave for a little bit, and you almost get our mate killed. We really need to talk about your escape skills," he said before sending another flame toward a group of shielded enforcers that were getting Judge Braxton out of the arena. The boiling heat rolled off of them, but the scrawny judge still escaped through a side tunnel. "Damn. I really wanted to kill that fucker."

"Get us the fuck out of here, you crazy ass demon," Tomb growled before wrapping his stone arms around my shoulders and pulling me closer to him.

Crow and Risk bunched together near us as bullets flew past. The crowd was revolting, rushing out of the auditorium while enforcers were coming at us in droves.

"Aw, but I thought they were bringing more enforcers. Five more minutes?" Risk asked with a teasing glint in his eye.

A gust of wind nearly knocked me back, but Tomb's grip kept me in place. "I swear to gods, if you don't get us out of here, I'll send you back to hell," my gargoyle yelled at him.

Risk breathed in a slow inhale, as if feasting on the risk in the air one last time before leaning forward to kiss me on the cheek and whisper in my ear, "Let's go home, Wicked Love."

"*Finally*," Crow gritted before sending a few of his birds at an elemental that managed to break through the flames. The birds immediately pecked at his eyes, bloody splatters and screams making me look away from the gruesome sight.

"Hold on," Risk told us as I clasped my mates' hands. I felt a charge in the air, and then it felt like we were sucked through a thin straw, yanking us out of this reality and into the next.

I didn't even mind the painful jarring of traveling through time to get to the Between.

I had my mates. We were okay.

We were okay.

I smiled.

Chapter 36

HE BUILT ME A HOUSE.

It was a beautiful place that somehow seemed to combine all of our personalities into one beautiful home. It stood tall with sharp angles on the roof, mimicking a gothic cathedral, and a wraparound porch with recliners surrounded it. Large, modern windows filled every wall, letting the white light of the Between stream inside. The backyard was a mass of bird houses and trees as far as the eye could see.

"Look at this kitchen!" Crow yelled while opening and closing cabinets, going through it like a kid looking over presents on Christmas morning. I noted that it was stocked with every food imaginable, and my malphas demon was drooling at the sight. The months of prison food and Spector cafeteria lunches had left him salivating for a home cooked meal.

Risk looked on with pride. "How?" I asked him as he wrapped me in a hug and kissed the top of my head. He smelled like smoke and felt like safety.

"I woke up in hell about three weeks ago. Envy was there and told me what was happening. Once I was able to go topside again, I found Stiles, and he helped me slip in as the executioner. It was a little too easy for my tastes," he said with a tinge of disappointment. "You'd think an arena full of those pretentious assholes would fight a bit harder. I wanted to make them suffer more."

I shook my head with a smile, still shocked at everything that had just happened. Tomb was silent, sitting at the wood-grained kitchen table and staring at the ground in stoic contemplation. "Are we really safe? Is this real?" he rumbled while rubbing his thighs. My heart sank at his disbelief. Tomb had suffered more than the rest of us. He lived in captivity for so long that I wasn't sure he could comprehend his freedom yet.

I crouched down to look him in the eye, using my fingers to lift his chin and meet my stare. "We're free, Tomb. No one will hurt you ever again. No one will hurt me, ever again," I promised him.

His eyes shone with relieved, unshed tears, but he gave me a single nod.

Risk moved to stand at my back. "We will have to stay here for a while. At least until Judge Braxton is taken care of. We just need to stay low, let some time pass until people forget Spector and the hybrids."

"You'll stay with us, though, right? What about your daughter, can you bring her here?" I asked while looking over my shoulder at him. I didn't like the idea of Ms. Cainson raising Risk's daughter. She was cold and heartless. "I still don't know how you did all this."

Risk sighed and held his hand out to me. I felt uncertainty in his grip, but I followed him as he led us into our large blue and gray living room and sat on the plush suede couch.

"Once I was in hell, my healing sped up, and I was able to come back."

I shook my head in disbelief. He had to be even more powerful than I realized. "And we'll be safe here?"

Risk shook his head, but I could tell he was struggling with words to say. "Envy helped—he owed me a favor. I once saved his mate, and he's been pissy ever since that I could do what he couldn't," he began with a sigh. "His damn ego wanted to even the playing field, so he offered to take the fall for saving you. As we speak, he's probably causing chaos at the stadium, taking credit for my risk," my demon huffed under his breath as he shook his head.

"Why?" I asked.

"We decided it's best if they think you're in hell. Only very powerful demons can ascend topside, so Envy is telling them that he banished you there. I needed to appear innocent so that I can walk topside. Right now, everyone thinks I'm off healing in hell still. When the time is right, I'm going to go back and help my daughter. She can't come here," Risk said with a frown.

My heart squeezed. "Why not?" I asked. I didn't want him to doubt my involvement or dedication. "Risk, I'm in this. I'm all in," I affirmed. "I know we haven't had *the talk*, but your daughter is a part of you. I'd love her like my own, you know that, right? Her mother doesn't deserve her," I said, my voice trembling. I was young and wildly unprepared to raise a child, but she looked like Risk. She had his smile, his bright eyes. Aunt Marie taught me that motherhood wasn't always determined by who birthed the child, but by who *loved* them. And I would love her unconditionally.

"We could make her a nursery!" Crow interjected. "Let's paint birds on the wall. We'd need a rocker too. And a crib. What else do babies need?" he mused.

"I'll protect her like my own," Tomb said while putting his fist to his chest in a solemn promise.

I was so proud of my mates in that moment. We were all in this. Together.

Risk smiled but shook his head. "I would be proud to share my daughter with all of you, but Devicka is special. She has a lot of powers within her. I can sense it. They haven't fully awakened yet, but I feel its allure." His gaze went to me, and he chewed on his next words. "She's a Void, Motley."

My mouth dropped open in shock. I'd studied Voids in school, but only briefly. I couldn't imagine that perfect baby living such a hard life. Voids were ostracized and feared. They always battled their gift, often times being wholly consumed by it. "The ritual," I said, as the pieces of the puzzle clicked into place. I remembered Ms. Cainson seeming to absorb all the power in the room during the exorcism. That hadn't been her, it was Risk's *daughter*.

Risk nodded. "She can't come here because she would absorb the Between. This place is just a giant orb of power," he commented while rubbing his jaw. "That reminds me..." He dug into his pocket and pulled out the amulet that Envy had found after the exorcism. "Envy gave me this. Said he was wounded that you lost his gift."

I smiled with a roll of my eyes. "It wasn't like the enforcers were going to let me wear magical jewelry to my own execution."

Risk's jaw tensed at that last word, but he nodded. "It's out of juice now, but I'm going to try to get it to work again. Granted, I'm not gifted with this particular magic like Collector was, but I'm sure I can figure it out."

"Why?" I asked curiously.

Risk pocketed the amulet again. "Right now, Devicka has to stay with her mother. We can't go back, since everyone still wants the hybrids dead, and my daughter can't come here, since the Between would be destroyed. As much as it kills me to be separated, it's the only way to keep us safe. But councilwoman Cainson won't hurt our daughter. She's under a microscope right now. And later, when it becomes public that I'm back from hell, I'll pay her a visit," he said with a dark look on his face. "Eventually, when Devicka's power forms, she'll need something to help her keep the Void at bay."

Realization lit up my face. "The amulet."

Risk nodded. "Exactly."

We looked at each other, and I recognized his conflict. He'd either have to be here in the Between with us, or topside watching over his daughter.

"I'm sorry, Risk," I said somberly before stepping into his chest and giving him a hug. My heart broke for him. I knew he loved his child. Being apart from her would be difficult, and watching that evil woman care for her would make it that much worse.

"I'll have to do what I can. I'll be here with you and go back regularly to watch over her," Risk said while pulling away. I watched my cocky demon run his hand down his face in worry.

Crow snapped his fingers. "I'll send Russell to watch her too. He has a direct link to me, and he's good at being incognito. If anything happens, we'll be the first to know."

"We'll make it work. And once the council is purged, we'll go back to her. I promise," Tomb added with a firm look on his face.

Once again, I appreciated the unity my mates were showing. Even so, I had doubts that we would ever go back to the real world. The ringing of the angry crowd was still fresh in my ears. We were hated and feared, a deadly combination that might forever make the Between our home. In that way, I could commiserate with how Devicka's life would be as a Void. My short time in the public as a demon hybrid hadn't been welcoming to say the least. I could only hope that her reception would be much better.

But I knew that even if we never met Devicka, we would know her. We would *love* her. She'd have an unseen family, watching her back and supporting her every step of the way.

TIME PASSED DIFFERENTLY in the Between.

We took time to mourn and cope, settling into our new home with gratitude and slow acceptance. Risk split time between here and topside, updating us on Devicka and the council. Envy's plan had worked. Everyone blamed him for banishing us to hell without bloodshed, but the public was thankful that we were gone.

Occasionally, Risk would bring letters from Cheryl and Stiles. We'd become pen pals of sorts, updating each other on our lives. I wished they could visit, but the Between was fickle. Risk could only maintain it for the four of us due to our mating bond. One letter even contained a photo of them getting married on a secluded beach. I guess Stiles never got his ring back.

Years topside went by in a matter of months here. Risk had made time in the Between move faster than the rest of the world. My mates and I cocooned ourselves in waiting anticipation while the supernatural community forgot all about Spector and the hybrids.

We loved fiercely. We danced in our seclusion, creating entire worlds in the Between while watching over our daughter from afar. I considered her *mine*. My spider claimed her without question. We sent gifts with Risk, and we hung her photos on the wall. We helped Risk pick out her first bike and then her first motorcycle. She grew up so fast. Every day, she hit a new milestone. Every second, she grew up. Every breath, I craved to have our family together topside.

Being in the Between was an awesome seclusion at first, but as more time passed, I missed being in the real world. I wanted to see everyone. Walk to a store. See a movie. Be around people and visit my old childhood home. I wanted to meet Devicka and see Stiles. Hell, I even missed hearing Cheryl's voice.

Risk didn't tell Devicka about us. He said it was safer for her if she didn't know. Judge Braxton was still in charge, ruling the world with his power hungry and prejudice fist. But I knew her despite not being able to meet her. I knew her affinity for risk. I knew her best friend, Reed. I knew that she had a fierce heart and fiery nature.

I was spinning webs idly in our bedroom one day, since it was one of my favorite pastimes. When I was feeling frisky, I liked to write raunchy messages in them. I'd gotten so good at it that I could even create some raunchy pictures. Tomb was a big fan.

I was busy making a particularly explicit one of all four of us that had me smirking to myself when Tomb, Crow, and Risk appeared in the doorway. They were all wearing broad smiles and taking in the sight before them.

"Hey," I greeted, spinning around in my web seat.

Last time Risk was here, he mentioned Devicka was in trouble with the council. I looked at him with a question in my eyes. "The council has been dissolved," he said as he walked up to me. He wrapped me up in a gigantic hug and pulled me up. He spun me around and around, making me dizzy before sitting me back down.

"What do you mean?" I asked, my cheeks flushed.

"We can go back, Motley. We can be with my daughter. We can be with *everyone*."

Excitement lit up my eyes. "We can go back?" I asked in disbelief.

"We can go back," Tomb promised with a nod.

"Thank fuck," Crow added.

I wrapped my mates up in a group hug, squealing with excitement at the idea of seeing everyone again. It didn't feel real. We were finally free, *really free*.

"I see you've been busy," Risk said as we pulled away.

I simultaneously blushed and smirked as my mates looked at my creation. Tomb tilted his head at the inventive pose.

"Hmm, I think a celebration is in order," Risk said, pushing a strand of my hair away from my face as he looked at me with that heated look in his eyes that I loved. He was right. My spider and I were *definitely* feeling celebratory. "And our mate obviously has cocks on the brain," he added with a smirk.

I shrugged. "My spider is hungry."

"Don't go blaming it on your spider, Wid," Tomb replied with a chuckle. "We all know that you're insatiable."

My cheeks heated again, and then Risk reached over to grasp the front of my white dress. It already dipped low in the front to reveal my cleavage since my mates liked the view, but he tugged it even lower.

"Mmm." He leaned forward and nipped at the swell of my breasts. Then he tugged at it until it tore down the middle, making me gasp. The fabric fell off of me in shreds, and goosebumps pebbled over my skin. I was completely naked beneath my clothes.

Crow made a hungry noise. "You know I love it when you don't wear panties. Makes touching that perfect pussy of yours very easy," he said while tracing his eyes up and down my body.

I sighed in mock annoyance. "I've learned not to bother

with it. You all just like to rip my clothes." I stared pointedly at the ground where my dress lay in shreds. "Case in point."

"I prefer you naked," Tomb rasped.

I preferred them naked, too. In fact, they were currently wearing far too much clothing for my tastes.

With a smile, my spider shot webs from my fingers and pinned all three mates to the wall, side by side, with a single flick of my wrist. I watched in amusement as their expressions went from surprise to heated craving. They liked when my spider took charge. They enjoyed the feel of her silk restraining them and how I took control of their pleasure.

Risk grinned while he pretended to struggle against his restraints. I knew that if any of them really wanted to, they could tear out of my webs and snatch me up. But it was all for fun, and they liked to see my predator come out to play.

"Wicked Love, are we going to have some fun?" Risk asked as I slowly lowered the zipper on his pants, freeing his cock with certain fingers and a sly smile.

I wanted to show him the sort of *fun* we were going to have by slowly easing his pants and underwear down his muscular thighs and tossing them to the ground. "Guess that depends on your definition of fun," my dark voice replied as I stared at his hardening cock. It grew and grew, steel flesh greeting me with greedy desire. I loved seeing that it was already slick with precum.

I turned to look at Crow in the middle, and his chest expanded with each sultry inhale. Tomb was looking at me in that stoic way of his while he kept impossibly still, drinking in my appearance with his heavy eyes.

I tossed more webs toward the ceiling and then grabbed hold of the strands to pull myself up to sit on the thin threads like it was a swing. "My spider has been busy spinning," I noted while pitching my legs back and forth so that I swung closer and then further away from them. "She's feeling adventurous."

"I like it," Risk replied.

With a smile, I stopped my momentum, braving both feet on either side of Risk, before shifting forward to hover over his cock. Our noses brushed, and he snapped for my lips, but I moved away before his hungry mouth could crash to mine. I swung back, pushing with my legs while shooting another web toward Crow and spinning toward him.

My malphas demon was already writhing with desire, and I hadn't even touched him yet. "Little Spider, you look so gorgeous dancing around your webs."

"I like to play with my prey," I rasped as I leaned in closer. I crawled up his body, trailing my tongue across his neck and nipping at his ear before pulling myself up and tilting backwards until I was hanging upside down and my glistening cunt was at his mouth.

"Want a taste?" I teased.

Crow didn't even reply, he just leaned forward and let a long lick swipe up my wet slit. The sensation of that, along with the fact that I was hanging upside down, was such a rush that my entire body quivered.

"Mmm. You taste sweet, Little Spider."

"Mmm," I mimicked him. "Less talking, more licking."

He chuckled, the noise vibrating up from his chest and sinking into me as his tongue reconnected to my pussy.

"Aren't you gonna let us free, Wid?" Tomb asked. I looked over, noticing his dark eyes latched onto my cunt where Crow was licking me.

"She likes to tease us," Risk answered, his fists curling and releasing in anticipation as he watched me. He looked like he was desperately trying to restrain himself from tearing through my webs and shoving his cock into me. Tomb was rippling from stone to skin, his arousal so apparent that his erection was clearly outlined through his pants.

I loved seeing them like this. Trapped in my webs. Hanging at my mercy. Their hands restrained, and their hungry gazes consuming my naked curves. With every second that they were forced to watch but not touch, they became more and more aroused. My lure power pulsed out of me in gentle waves, making their nostrils flare and their pupils dilate.

"You like to be teased," I replied, right before Crow shoved his face against me and started fucking me with his tongue. I sucked in a breath, my hair swinging down around my head as I moved.

He was relentless, showing me exactly how he wanted his cock to slide in and out of me, and that visual alone had me growing wetter. But I wanted more. I reached over and tried to pull his head up, but he just chuckled again and continued his tongue thrusts.

I looked over at Risk and reached my hand up to fist his cock through my webs, making him hiss out a breath. "Such a good girl stroking my cock," he hummed, staring down at my hand as I moved it up and down. When more precum dripped out of him, I swiped a finger over it and then stuck it in my mouth, letting my tongue swirl around it.

He watched me with hooded eyes. "You're going to do that to my cock," he said.

I pulled the finger out of my mouth with a smile. "Am I?" I taunted.

His eyes narrowed. "You are."

"So *cocky*," I said, emphasizing the word and making an impish grin appear on his face.

Quick as a whip, I struck fang-first, sinking my teeth into his inner thigh. He let out a groan as my vampire venom hit his system, and I groaned as his delicious, smoky blood rushed down my throat. I took a few hearty gulps before pulling away.

"So tasty," I said, licking his blood from my lips.

"My cum tastes even better," he said with a wag of his eyebrows.

"Mm-hmm."

I turned to Tomb and unzipped his pants, stroking him up and down just the way I'd done to Risk. But unlike Risk, my gargoyle's cock shifted back and forth from hot velvety skin to smooth black stone. I was making him lose control, and it was so damn sexy.

Crow continued to eat me out while I switched back and forth between teasing Tomb and Risk with my hands, but he was focusing entirely on my slit and tongue-fucking me, and I wanted more.

"My clit," I said insistently, a demand that was nearly a plea. He was ignoring it on purpose, teasing me as much as I was teasing them.

"If you want your clit played with, then you have to let us free," Risk replied.

"It's not polite to gang up on me," I said breathlessly. I should've kept tormenting them to prove a point, but I was so damn needy that I couldn't wait.

With a small wrist movement, I loosened the bindings around Risk's and Tomb's arms, and they immediately broke out of the hold. Tomb reached out, grabbing hold of the webbed rope, and flipped me right side up, making me giggle as I spun.

The blood from my head must've all rushed down to my pussy, because I started throbbing there as moisture gathered between my thighs. In front of me, Crow licked his lips, my arousal shiny on his scruffy jaw. The obvious sight of my juices on his face made heat rise to my cheeks.

"Look at that," Tomb said, reaching out a hand to skim his knuckle against my cheek. "Our mate is blushing."

Risk smirked. "If *that's* making her blush, we clearly haven't been doing our job lately," he said wickedly. "I think she needs to be reminded of the many, *many* other filthy things we like to do to her."

Oh gods. I bit my lip, his words making me blush even harder.

My three mates shared a look. Fuck, I loved that. I loved when they spoke to each other without words, and I could practically *hear* the dirty things they had planned for me.

"Sit back on your swing, Wid," Tomb instructed with that deep, gravelly tone of his that I adored.

Swallowing hard, I gripped the ropes on either side of me and thickened the portion I was sitting on while letting the rest of my webs loosen around my men so they could slowly undress in front of me. It was one of my favorite views.

Risk stepped forward with some of my webs looped around his arm, but when I opened my mouth to ask him what he was doing, Crow sealed his mouth to mine, swallowing my words. My eyes closed in bliss as his tongue stroked against mine. "Can you taste yourself on me?" he asked against my lips. "I fucking love how you taste. I could lick you all day."

He wasn't exaggerating either. The Between gave us plenty of opportunities for my mates to spoil me with every kind of sexual thrill they could offer.

He deepened the kiss, turning my head so that he could get me right where he wanted me. I was so into it that I didn't even feel Risk loop webs around each of my ankles and stick the ends to the wall until my legs were suddenly pried open, leaving my pussy open wide as I hung in the air.

My eyes flew open, and Crow stepped back, and I looked at all three of my mates as they circled around me. Gods, the view of their muscled bodies was enough to make me bite back a whimper.

"Mmm, that's better," Risk purred as he looked at me, spread before them.

I felt Tomb's hands slide down my shoulders to my waist as he stepped up behind me, his big hands clutching the globes of my ass as he squeezed. "*Much* better," he said huskily, his lips pressing against the top of my ear.

"Please," I said before I could stop myself.

"I do love to hear her beg," Risk mused.

"What do you want, Motley?" Crow asked, his hand stroking up and down his impressive length.

"All of you," I answered honestly.

He and Tomb circled around me again, until it was Tomb standing in front of me and Crow's hands were running up and down my spine. Crow's hands came to my hips, and he nipped my ear. "Lean back," he said, and I did, letting my back rest against his chest.

Tomb made a rumble of appreciation as he stared in rapt attention at me spread before him. "Like a feast laid out," he murmured.

"Please, Tomb," I said, feeling needier and needier by the second.

My gargoyle stepped forward and dragged his cock up and down my slit a few times before finally lining up with my entrance. He was big, and even after all this time and all the times we'd had sex, I still tensed as he entered me because of his size. He was thick and long and so fucking hard. With every inch, he sunk into me, his cock vacillating from skin to stone, back and forth until I was writhing and whimpering.

When he was finally all the way in, he let out a ragged breath. "Fuck, baby. You're clenching on my cock already."

I was. I couldn't help it. My entire body was squeezing him from the inside out.

"Well, that won't do," Risk tsked. "She's going to be much fuller than that in a second, so we'd better loosen her up a bit."

I looked over with heavy lidded eyes as Risk stepped forward, his proud cock jutting up, and he pressed a thumb against my aching clit.

"Yes," I breathed, so relieved and excited to finally be touched there that I nearly wept.

"Give me your touch, and I'll give you mine," he said with a devious gleam in his eye.

I didn't waste any time. Tomb had started to rock into me, and I wanted to come so badly. I reached down and gripped Risk's cock, and he rewarded me by using his expert touch to circle my clit, his thumb and fingers feeling hot as fire where they brushed against me.

I struggled to keep my eyes open as I watched Tomb's dark length move in and out of me while Risk strummed the point of my pleasure. It was sexy and stimulating, but then I felt a slick finger probing me from behind.

I bit my lip hard, my fangs dying to come out as I looked over my shoulder at Crow. "Ready to be filled even more?" he asked.

I nodded, but a quick pinch to my clit had me looking back at Risk. "Use your words, Motley," he reprimanded. He loved to hear me say dirty things—they all did.

"I'm ready," I said breathlessly.

"Ready for what exactly?" he questioned, his thumb pressing against my clit in rough strokes.

Gods, it felt fucking *fantastic*.

"Umm..." I lost my train of thought for a moment when I felt Crow add a second finger to my ass, and my body clenched again, making Tomb hiss out a curse.

Risk pinched my clit to regain my attention, making me

cry out in delicious pain and ecstatic pleasure. "Answer me," he demanded. A thrill shot through me.

"I'm ready for Crow's cock in my ass," I admitted, feeling my cheeks heat all over again.

"Hmm, there's that blush again," Risk said quietly.

I was shifted slightly on my web swing, my upper body gently pushed forward as Crow's cock started to enter me from behind.

"Fuck, fuck, fuck," I chanted, feeling the sting of his entry as his slick head pushed into me. We'd done this many times before, but it still burned with pleasure. I loved the fullness of their cocks inside of me.

"Relax," Risk whispered, drawing my attention back to his perfect attentions to my clit as Crow continued to work into me. Tomb struggled to stay still, his cock jerking inside of me at the effort not to thrust. "Feel how we fill you up, Wicked Love? You like having us all at your mercy, pumping into you, don't you?"

"Yes," I whimpered. "I want all of you."

Risk gleamed. There was nothing like feeding from all of them at once. Their essence was a feast for my spider, and our bond felt tangible when all four of us were writhing with lightning hot pleasure. My body contracted when Tomb started to move in and out as Crow's cock pushed in the last inch. They all stroked my body, teasing my nipples, working my clit, kissing my neck, until I was loose and languid and ready for more. They were so in tune with my body that they knew just the right moment to start moving. They timed their thrusts in perfect synchronicity. There was a frenzy of energy surrounding us, building up, and I fed in slow sips, relishing in their beautiful essences. It just needed Risk's cock to be complete.

I shot more webs out, coiling them around Crow and Tomb. I twisted my webs, lifting us until my gargoyle was parallel with the ground and I was riding him. I draped my body over Tomb's chest so that Crow could continue to pump into my ass from behind, his hands wrapped around my neck. The light squeeze of his palm made my mouth part open in bliss. I could feel my pulse against the padding of his fingers, roaring on that edge of control and release.

"You want to suck my cock, Wicked Love?" Risk asked as more webs slipped from me. I wrapped them around his body, using them to hoist my demon mate up until his silky cock was brushing against my lips. "Open for me."

"No," I replied cheekily while clamping my lips closed.

I spun more webs, wrapping them around Risk's wrists and yanking his hands behind his head. I spread his legs and designed cutting threads across his chest. I had him pinned again, constricted by my interlacing fabric with his dick poised at my mouth. Risk smirked, loving my challenging move of dominance. He led our family so often that nothing got him off more than surrendering to me.

"Wicked Love, open that pretty mouth for me," he said, and still I shook my head. Crow came in for the assist though, and started diving into my ass with a grunt, making my body buck forward and my lips part open for a scream laced with lust.

My scream was muffled as Risk's dick stuffed my mouth. I moaned as the taste of him hit my tongue and I licked the head of it up and down with my tongue. I devoured his molten heat, whimpering at the dual taste of control and cock.

I loved having all three of them inside of me. I was riding Tomb's concrete cock beneath me as Crow thrust into me from behind. Risk was suspended above me, his hard dick sliding up and down my tongue. It was erotic and exciting and so fucking perfect. I had never felt more full—more content. My spider clamped down on more of their sexual essence, feeding from each of them as we rocked in her web.

"I'm so close," Crow cursed before biting my shoulder.

Tomb lifted his cool hands up to knead my breasts. Risk fought against his restraints to touch me, but I didn't let him go. I wanted him to surrender to bliss as I choked and drooled on his cock.

"Fuck, Wid," Tomb grunted as his body jolted.

Crow gripped me harder, pounding into my ass without restraint. I coveted the burn of their bodies stretching me, filling me. "You feel so fucking good," Crow hissed. Each rise of their bodies against mine created filthy, slick, slapping sounds. I was fizzing with an impending orgasm, ready to burst. Risk groaned when the head of his cock bumped the back of my throat.

Faster.

Harder.

The four of us finally came together in a hard and unrelenting detonation. Tomb gave one last squeeze to the heavy flesh of my breasts as his body contracted and released. Crow held onto my hips, his nails digging into my body with greed. Risk ferociously tore free from his restraints with a moan and grabbed the back of my head, holding me down as he shot hot cum down my throat.

I fed and fed on their desire until breaking apart on the three of them. My back arched, my body convulsed. Thrilling bliss burned every cell in my body as I flexed and gushed out an orgasm.

We slowly came down from the high of being together. My webs lowered us to the ground with reverent grace, gently placing our heaving bodies like an offering on the floor.

I shifted positions and rested my head on Tomb's chest, wrapping my legs around Crow's body while my hand clasped Risk's. Our breathing slowed. Our bodies smelled like sex and sweat. We drifted into that safe space of comfort where we knew this was it, this was where we belonged.

My spider purred in my chest as I traced the web of events that led me right here, to this moment. The pain and suffering. The sadness and loss. The exquisite change. All of it brought me this.

I was blessed with a beautifully fatal demon that broke me down and built me back up. She made me stronger. She took the worst things about myself and polished them with blood and silk. I gave in to the monster, fostered her taste for darkness and death. And in the end, she rewarded me with what I wanted most of all—family and love.

Epilogue
RISK

I tapped my foot anxiously while scenarios played in my mind. I was wearing a tux and sitting in the auditorium at Thibault Academy, waiting for my daughter to cross the stage and accept her diploma.

I was so fucking proud of my little girl. I'd had other dalliances over the many years of my existence, and some of those resulted in children, but I didn't have a connection with any of them like I did with Devicka. Hell, before Motley, I never even had a *desire* to settle down. My demonic nature was a wanderer, always seeking the next thrill.

But not anymore.

I sensed something special about my daughter from the very beginning. I'd evolved and settled into a sense of contentment I didn't even know I was missing out on. I'd watched over her from afar, but now that I could finally be more present in her life, I was ecstatic, yet uncertain. I wasn't sure how she would feel about being introduced to Motley, Crow, and Tomb. I wasn't sure how she would react to the truth.

Motley squeezed my hand reassuringly while wiping

proud tears from her eyes. She'd been emotional all day, pacing the floors and dropping trails of webs everywhere she went. I wasn't sure what she was more nervous about, leaving the Between to go topside for the first time since the council was overhauled, or meeting Devicka.

I tugged her close to my side. "She's going to love you," I whispered in my mate's ear as she stared at the stage. My Wicked Love was so strong. Her heart was open and ready. Devicka might be too old now for the mother she deserved, but I knew Motley would be whatever my daughter needed. A friend, a protector, a confidant.

The hardest part of this would be convincing my daughter that I'd been settled down this entire time. She had perceptions about me that I encouraged to keep us all safe. If the council knew I was mated to Motley and was hiding her in a world of my creation, they'd demand I bring her forward. I'm no fucking saint, but my life changed the moment I met Motley. I just had to bide my time before showing the rest of the world the new and improved me—the committed bastard hopelessly in love with his mate and determined to protect his daughter.

"Are you sure? Maybe we should do this another day," Motley asked, and it wasn't the first time.

Crow chuckled beside me. "Little Spider, it's kind of cute seeing you so scared. I thought you were the big bad Black Widow," he teased with a wink.

Tomb growled and punched his shoulder, punishing him for making fun of our mate.

"She's going to love you. I promise," I reassured her once again before lacing my fingers through hers.

"I hope so," she whispered back just as the headmaster—a newly hired vamp with long, blond hair and a flair for the dramatics—called Devicka's name. Much to my pleasure, Torne had been fired recently. I was happy to know he wasn't allowed to work at the school anymore. Every single one of the assholes that used my mate as a scapegoat got theirs in the end.

I watched my daughter cross the stage with her head held high and a smile on her face. Her mates were there, standing under the spotlights and waiting for her. As council members, they had particularly handy perks and were allowed to assist in handing out her diploma. They were a bunch of cocky assholes, but they loved my daughter and treated her right. And now that they were in charge of the council, Motley, Crow, and Tomb were finally able to live topside without fear. I couldn't help but feel grateful as fuck for that.

She stopped at Hyde first, and he bowed before her. I'd never admit it to any of them, but I actually liked that crazy fucker the most. He was odd—most necros were—but good. He'd go to hell and back for my daughter, and that was all I really cared about.

Devicka stopped at Gritt next. Of all of them, he and I butted heads the most. I liked to leave photos of his pink dragon lying around just to fuck with him. The alpha was too brash, but he'd calmed down some since mating my daughter. I loved how Devicka didn't put up with any of his shit. She held her own with him, and it made me proud.

Render then flashed up to her and wrapped her in a big hug, kissing her on the mouth in front of everyone. I rolled my eyes and sighed. Fucking cocky vampire. He was way too affectionate for my tastes. I wasn't stupid, I was a fucking demon, for gods' sakes, but that didn't mean I wanted to see him mauling my daughter every five seconds.

Beside me, Crow and Tomb bristled at the scene, and I loved them for it. I had a feeling I would enjoy ganging up on my daughter's mates with our combined over-protectiveness.

Lastly, Quade handed her the diploma with his usual

pious bullshit nod, like he was the gods' gift to the supernatural community. I didn't know what my daughter saw in that uptight rule-abiding citizen, but I supposed opposites attracted or some shit. There was still hope we could corrupt him and possibly add a little risk to his routine. I grinned at the thought.

Motley was shaking with nerves when Devicka exited the stage and her mates followed after her. My own questions continued to plague my mind, though I kept a calm expression so that I wouldn't worry my mate.

I didn't know if Devicka would resent me for keeping such a large part of my life a secret. I hated how quickly she grew up and how little I got to see of her. But damn, my kid was awesome. Strong. Resilient. Risky, but smart.

And loved. Gods, my daughter was loved. I wished that Motley could have raised her. Many nights, I imagined them cooking in our kitchen in the Between or snuggling on the couch. Motley was furiously protective of her and would have killed anyone that dared to treat Devicka poorly for being the Void. My mate knew firsthand what it felt like to be feared and hated for the power inside of you.

"You ready?" I asked my mate.

She let out a shaky exhale before responding. "I think so," she began, extending up on her tiptoes to kiss me on the cheek. "There's just one more thing."

"Oh?" I prodded. "And what's that?"

"Should we tell her now or later that she's going to be a big sister?"

My mouth dropped open in pure shock, and I staggered back a step, but Motley didn't even give me an opportunity to formulate a response. She was already out of her seat and scurrying toward the reception area. I turned to Crow and Tomb, who were both wearing identical looks of confusion and dumbfounded surprise on their faces.

Epilogue

I watched her retreating figure. "Did she just..."

"What did she mean?" Tomb asked.

"Holy shit, we're having a baby," Crow choked out before breaking out into a broad grin.

Motley paused at the door, patting her stomach while giving us a playful wink. I wanted to haul her out of here and show her just what I thought of her little surprise. *A baby?*

For the first time in a long time, I didn't calculate the chances associated with growing our family. I didn't feel for the risk. I just felt *right*. Before, I'd always been so caught up in filling life with empty pleasures and thrills. But with Motley, I was a better man. The first time I saw her, I was drawn to her like sparks to a flint. I knew she was mine the moment I touched her neck. She was a fighter. A lover. My equal in all ways. And I fucking loved her.

"You think it'll be a boy or a girl?" Tomb mused.

"Maybe one of each," Crow replied with a smirk. The gargoyle blinked, he was already trying to mentally prepare for two crying newborns at once.

I laughed and clapped him on the back before we all got to our feet. "There's four of us. I think we can handle it."

Famous last words.

We got into the reception area and then paused, leaning against the wall at the sight before us. My red-haired mate and my dewy-eyed daughter were embraced in a hug. And just like that, all my worries emptied out of me as my heart swelled in my chest.

This moment right here? This was worth all the fucking risks in the world.

About the Author
RAVEN KENNEDY

Raven Kennedy is a bestselling international author and a voracious reader. She enjoys writing all kinds of genres, because each one brings a different experience. Whether it be romantic comedies or romances on the darker spectrum, she hopes her words connect with people. She lives with her husband and daughter in California.

Raven's website: ravenkennedybooks.com

About the Author
CORALEE JUNE

Coralee June is an international bestselling romance writer who enjoys engaging projects and developing real, raw, and relatable characters. She is an English major from Texas State University and has had an intense interest in literature since her youth. She currently resides with her husband and two daughters in Dallas, Texas, where she enjoys long walks through the ice-cream aisle at her local grocery store.

For more information about her and her upcoming releases, please visit her website at:

www.authorcoraleejune.com

Also by CoraLee June and Raven Kennedy

Cruel

Tame

Wild

Void

Printed by Amazon Italia Logistica S.r.l.
Torrazza Piemonte (TO), Italy

54129196R00256